Without Sin

Born in Gainsborough, Lincolnshire, Margaret Dickinson moved to the coast at the age of seven and so began her love for the sea and the Lincolnshire landscape. Her ambition to be a writer began early and she had her first novel published at the age of twenty-five. This was followed by twenty-five further titles including *Plough the Furrow*, *Sow the Seed* and *Reap the Harvest*, which make up her Lincolnshire Fleethaven trilogy. Many of her novels are set in the heart of her home county but in *Tangled Threads* and *Twisted Strands*, the stories include not only Lincolnshire but also the framework knitting and lace industries of Nottingham. Her 2012 novel, *Jenny's War*, was a top twenty best seller.

www.margaret-dickinson.co.uk

ALSO BY MARGARET DICKINSON

Plough the Furrow

Sow the Seed

Reap the Harvest

The Miller's Daughter

Chaff upon the Wind

The Fisher Lass

The Tulip Girl

The River Folk

Tangled Threads

Twisted Strands

Red Sky in the Morning

Pauper's Gold

Wish Me Luck

Sing As We Go

Suffragette Girl

Sons and Daughters

Forgive and Forget

Jenny's War

The Clippie Girls

Fairfield Hall

Margaret Dickinson

Without Sin

PAN BOOKS

First published 2005 by Macmillan

This edition published 2014 by Pan Books
an imprint of Pan Macmillan
20 New Wharf Road, London N1 9RR
Associated companies throughout the world
www.panmacmillan.com

ISBN 978-1-5098-9558-8

1 3 5 7 9 8 6 4 2

A CIP catalogue record for this book is available from the British Library.

Typeset by SetSystems Ltd, Cambridge CB22 3GN
Printed and bound by CPI Group (UK) Ltd, Croydon, CR0 4YY

For Robena and Fred Hill,

my sister and brother-in-law

Acknowledgements

The Workhouse at Southwell, Nottinghamshire, which has been magnificently restored by the National Trust, is the inspiration for the setting of this novel. However, the characters and story are entirely fictitious and have no relation whatsoever to any inmates or staff, past or present.

My love and thanks, as always, to my family and friends for their constant support, help and encouragement.

One

June 1910

'You're not going to leave us here? Not in this place?' Meg turned her wide green eyes accusingly on her father. 'You can't.'

Beyond the black wrought-iron gates, the three-storey, red-brick building surrounded by high walls was an ominous threat. Its regimented rows of windows were like watching eyes. The young girl, face like a thunderstorm, wild long red hair, glanced at her mother, willing her to say something. But Sarah's pale face was expressionless, her eyes dull with defeat. Her thin frame drooped with weariness, yet she held one arm protectively around the mound of her belly. Sarah's time was near and she was anxious to have a decent place for her confinement. Despite their dire circumstances, Sarah didn't want to lose this baby. She'd lost so many that even the humiliation of the workhouse was better than giving birth in a ditch. Beside her, five-year-old Bobbie sucked his thumb and said nothing. He gripped his mother's hand tightly, his huge brown eyes glancing nervously between his sister and father.

Reuben Kirkland passed his hand wearily across his brow. 'I've no choice, Meggie. I'm sorry, we've nowhere else to go and till I can find work again . . .' His voice trailed away and he avoided meeting his daughter's belligerent gaze.

Reuben's sudden dismissal from his work as a waggoner at Middleditch Farm had come as a shock to all the family, but Meg was the only one who had dared to voice her indignation. Sarah had said nothing.

'Why, Dad?' Meg had challenged him the previous evening when, still in their cosy tied cottage, Reuben had brought home the devastating news. 'What's happened? And what about me?' Meg worked for the farmer's wife in the dairy, but she helped with outdoor work too, at haymaking and harvest and at potato-picking time. 'Am I to go an' all?'

Wordlessly, Reuben had nodded.

Meg bit her lip, casting about in her mind. Was it her fault? Had she done something wrong, something so dreadful that her whole family were being put out of their home? Eyes downcast, Reuben had muttered bitterly, 'It's the missis. Got her knife into me, she has. The mester'd've been all right, but her with her tittle-tattling.' He had spat the last words out with unusual viciousness.

Fresh hope had surged in Meg as she cried out eagerly, 'But what about Miss Alice? She's my friend. Her dad'd listen to her. She'll not let him turn us out.'

Her father had refused to listen. He'd turned away towards the back door, wrenched it open and disappeared through it. Meg had stared after him. Then she'd felt her mother's light touch on her arm. 'Leave it, love,' Sarah had said softly, speaking for the first time.

Why? Why? *Why?* Meg had wanted to scream. But her mother's pinched face and tear-filled eyes had stilled her angry outburst. Instead, she'd been sorely tempted to run to the farmhouse, to bang on the door and demand to be told the reason for her father's dismissal.

And, more importantly, her own. She was sure there had been nothing wrong when she'd left the dairy earlier that evening. The mistress – Mrs Mabel Smallwood – was a hard employer. She was strict and humourless, but she'd never been cruel or unjust.

Meg couldn't understand the sudden, soul-destroying change in their fortunes. How had they come to this? A sorry little group in the pale light of early summer, standing outside imposing gates. The workhouse lay on the outskirts of the small town of South Monkford, the nearest place to Middleditch Farm and the home they had been obliged to leave. They'd left at dawn, tramping the five miles here. As they walked, the rising sun heralded a warm day. Pale pink wild roses dappled the hedgerows and elderflower bushes were laden with their heavy cream blossom. Birds flew overhead in frantic frenzy to feed their young. But Meg saw none of it.

'Why can't we look for work?' the girl persisted, in no mood to 'leave it' as her mother suggested. 'You and me, Dad? There must be something. It's shearing time. There must be plenty of work—'

'I'm a wagoner, Meg. 'Osses is all I know about. What would I know about sheep?'

'But—'

'We've been sacked without a reference. Both of us.'

Meg gasped. That was the worst thing that could possibly happen. New employers always, but always, demanded a reference from the previous master or mistress. Without it, finding work was almost impossible except for the most menial, disgusting of jobs.

Like in the workhouse.

Standing at the gate, which seemed to the young girl like the bars of a prison, Meg shuddered. 'Why, Dad?' she whispered, once more searching her mind for something – anything – she might have done wrong. 'What's happened? It's not because of me, is it?'

She knew she was often pert and saucy, but the mistress wouldn't dismiss the whole family just because the dairymaid was a bit cheeky sometimes, would she? More than likely, Mabel Smallwood would have let Meg feel the back of her hand.

Then a far more worrying thought came into the girl's mind.

'You're a bad influence on my lass,' Mrs Smallwood had said more than once. 'She should be making friends of her own age. Nice girls who aren't fluttering their eyelashes at the farm lads half the time.'

'Alice talks to the farmhands, missis,' Meg would begin defiantly. Wasn't it from Alice that Meg had learned to laugh and flirt with the boys? 'So why can't I?'

'I'll hear no more of that sort of talk from you, miss. My Alice is different. She knows how to behave, knows where to draw the line. I can trust my Alice.' Her tone implied that she did not trust Meg. 'But how can you know at your age? Fifteen, indeed! Playing with fire, my girl, that's what you are. You'll come to a bad end, if you don't watch out. You mark my words.'

Remembering all this, Meg, suddenly afraid, asked her father, 'Is it to do with Alice? Is it because I'm friends with Alice and the missis doesn't like it?'

Beside her, Sarah gave a little sob and covered her mouth with her fingers. Reuben glared at Meg for an instant and then his gaze fell away. He turned towards his wife. 'I'm sorry, Sarah. Truly. I – I will come back for you. But I must get right away from here so – so that I can find work. You do understand, don't you?'

White-faced, Sarah lifted her head slowly and stared back at him. She bit her lip so hard that she drew blood, but she made no gesture of understanding. Her eyes held only suffering and silent reproach.

Meg gasped. Her mother's look was directed, not at her as she had feared, but at Reuben. Sarah held her husband entirely responsible for their predicament. Meg pressed her lips together, making her firm jawline even more pronounced with new determination. 'Well, you needn't think we're going in there, Dad, cos we're not. I'm going back to the farm. I'm going to see Miss Alice. She'll speak up for us. I know she will.'

She started to turn away but her father's hand shot out and gripped her arm. 'You'll do no such thing, girl. You'll go in there with your mam and your brother and you'll look after them. You hear me?'

Meg gaped at him and twisted her arm free. 'You're hurting me.'

Reuben was at once contrite. 'I'm sorry, love—' He rubbed his forehead distractedly. 'I just don't know which way to turn. Now, be a good girl, Meggie, and take care of your mam and Bobbie. Will you do that for me, eh?' His brown eyes were pleading with her. He touched her face gently and Meg was lost.

'Oh, Dad!' She flung herself against him, hugging him. Muffled against him she said, 'You will come back for us, won't you? Promise?'

For a brief moment, Reuben held her close whilst Meg clung to him. She felt his chest heave beneath her cheek, heard the gulping sound in his throat, but then, without warning, he tore himself from her, turned and stumbled away.

'Dad,' Meg cried, 'Dad, don't go. Don't leave us . . .' But Reuben hurried on and though the forlorn little family stood staring after him, not once did he look back.

Two

The small, whitewashed cottage on Middleditch Farm, owned by George Smallwood, had been home to the Kirkland family for the past three years. Meg's childhood had been punctuated by moves almost every year as her father shifted from farm to farm. With a new home in a strange place, a different school where she was cast adrift in a playground full of strangers with scarcely a friendly face amongst them, Meg had learned early to rely on no one but herself. Often she had been the butt of bullies, the object of ridicule for her bright red hair and her second-hand clothes.

'Look at carrot tops,' some boy would tease, pulling her red curls. The name would be taken up by them all – even the girls.

'A' them clothes your mam's hand-me-downs?' A jeering ring would form around her in the playground and the laughter and the pointing would begin. 'Look at 'er shoes. Reckon they're 'er dad's.'

'I've seen better shoes on 'osses.'

That most of the other children were similarly dressed to Meg didn't seem to matter. She was the new girl, the object of derision, fair game for the bullies.

As a little girl Meg had worked hard to become one of them, to earn friends, but as she grew older she learned not to care. She would stick her nose in the air and make some scathing retort. She became handy with her fists and many a time a harassed teacher had to prevent the red-haired she cat from pulling the hair of her opponent out by its roots. But at the age of ten Meg learned another way to deal with the taunts and jibes. She joined in the teasing directed at herself. She was the first to say, 'This is me mam's old skirt –' then she would pull a wry face and add – 'and you should see the bloomers I have to wear.' Instead of using her fists, Meg used her lively wit. She would laugh the loudest at herself, but behind the laughter in her green eyes, there was a hint of steel. Meg was learning fast how to stand on her own two feet in an unkind world.

There was only one reason why Meg was still goaded into using her fists now and then – if anyone dared to tease little Bobbie. Then his assailant would end up with a bloody nose and running to his mother.

'She hit me. That big girl hit me.'

Meg would clench her fists, narrow her eyes and, gritting her teeth, turn to face the irate mother.

'You're old enough to know better than to hit a little chap half your size.'

'Then your little chap shouldn't hit my brother.'

'My Arthur wouldn't do a thing like that.'

'Then why has Bobbie got a black eye?'

' 'Spect you did it and you're trying to put the blame on someone else.'

Meg would take a step closer and the older woman would back away, intimidated by the young firebrand. 'I *never* hit my brother.'

'All right, all right, but you leave my Arthur alone.'

'I will.' Then Meg would add ominously, 'As long as he leaves our Bobbie alone, an' all.'

When Meg was twelve, Reuben found work as head wagoner to George Smallwood and brought his family to the cottage that came with the job. Reuben was good with horses, loved them and understood them. Meg loved them too, the way the huge shires shook their great heads, snorted and stamped their heavy hooves. She loved their power, their might.

'You'd make a good wagoner, Meggie,' her father told her proudly and then spoilt it by adding, 'if only you were a lad.'

Meg did not go back to school. She was old enough now to be employed on the same farm and soon she was under Mrs Mabel Smallwood's eagle eye in the dairy. But Meg had never known such happiness and contentment. She worked hard, though she rarely earned even the most grudging praise from the farmer's wife.

And at last she found a real friend in the Smallwoods' daughter.

Although Alice – buxom, fair-haired, blue-eyed and pink-cheeked – was five years older than Meg, she was kind to the young girl. There were no girls of a similar age to Alice on the neighbouring farms, so the two were thrown together even in their spare time. Though there was not much of that for either of them, Meg thought wryly. Alice took Meg to the big church in South Monkford every Sunday morning. They knelt together demurely during the service, but on the walk home Meg watched as Alice smiled coyly at the youths gathered near the church wall, laughing and talking whilst they watched the girls parading in their Sunday best.

'Come for a walk with us, Alice.' One spotty-faced youth was a particular admirer, but Alice only tossed her hair and stuck her nose in the air. 'What? With you, Harry Warner?'

The young man grinned. 'I was all right to walk out with last Sunday.'

Alice laughed her tinkling laugh and dimpled her cheeks. 'That was last week.'

'Oho, someone else, is there?' He pressed his hand to his chest. 'My heart is broken.'

'I'm sure Lizzie Lucas will help it mend.'

'Lizzie Lucas means nothing to me.'

'That's not what I've heard.' Tossing her hair, Alice linked her arm through Meg's and, with a cheery wave to all the watching youths, walked down the lane, swinging her hips. Meg, too, turned, grinned saucily at the lads and then tried to copy Alice's provocative walk.

Middleditch Farm lay in the rolling countryside of east Nottinghamshire. The nearest town was South Monkford, with narrow streets of shops and a market held on Wednesdays and Saturdays. On the outskirts was a racecourse that was becoming quite famous and it was George Smallwood's ambition to own a racehorse one day.

'You'll look after it for me, Kirkland,' the farmer would say, clapping Reuben on the back. 'We'll rear a winner, eh?'

And several times a year, when there was a big meeting on, George and his wagoner would disappear for a day at the races. On those days Meg would lie in her bed at night under the eaves and listen to her father stumbling about in the room below when he arrived home late and much the worse for drink. Her mother would be tight-lipped for days afterwards, but there was little Sarah could do about it when it was their employer who was the ringleader in such escapades.

The family's three years at Middleditch Farm had been the longest they had stayed anywhere that Meg could remember. And they had certainly been the happiest years for her. But suddenly, disastrously, that had all changed. And Meg was very much afraid that somehow it was all her fault.

Had Mabel Smallwood found out about last Sunday's picnic, when she and Alice had taken sandwiches, cakes and beer into the recreation ground beyond the church? They had sat on the grass in the sunshine, talking dreamily about the kind of man they'd like to marry, when they'd been startled by two youths from the town whom Alice knew vaguely.

'Well, well, well, if it isn't the lovely Alice Smallwood. And who's this?' The taller of the two young men had turned his attention to Meg, but it had been Alice who had invited the lads to join their picnic. The four youngsters had had a merry afternoon. There'd been a little flirting, a little horseplay and when they parted in the early evening, a chaste kiss. Though it had all been innocent enough, Mrs Smallwood wouldn't think so. And, Meg thought fearfully, she would not blame her own daughter. In her eyes, Alice could do no wrong. No, the mistress would lay any blame squarely on Meg's head. But without going back to Middleditch Farm, there was little Meg could do to find out if this was the reason for their sudden dismissal.

One day, the young girl vowed, *I will find out. And I'll tell Mrs Mabel Smallwood exactly what I think of her – and her precious daughter*. For what hurt Meg more than anything was the growing realization that, whatever had happened to cause this catastrophe, Alice – her dear friend and confidante – had not spoken up for her.

That hurt the young girl much more than the fact that she and her mother and brother had now to enter the much-feared workhouse.

Lifting her head with a show of defiance, Meg said,

'Come on, Mam – Bobbie. We'd best go and knock at the door.'

She pushed open the heavy gate and marched up a long, straight path leading through an orchard and neatly cultivated vegetable gardens. Sarah, with Bobbie holding her hand, trailed listlessly behind her. They passed between high walls surrounding yards on either side of the main entrance at the front of the building and then climbed wide, stone steps to the white pillared door. Meg rang the bell. Somewhere deep inside they heard a faint clanging. It seemed an age until the door was thrown open and the biggest man whom Meg had ever seen stood there looking down on them.

Isaac Pendleton, master of South Monkford workhouse, was six feet tall with a girth that seemed almost the same measurement. A large, bulbous nose dominated his florid face. His lips were fleshy and wet and heavy jowls bulged out over the starched white collar. His dark hair, greying at the temples, was thinning and smoothed over his crown in a vain attempt to cover advancing baldness. Yet his eyes seemed kindly.

'What's this? What's this? Ragamuffins knocking at my front door?' His voice was as large as his frame, deep and resonant. He was dressed in a dark, sober suit, but a multi-coloured waistcoat, stretched tightly over his ample chest, lightened his otherwise sombre appearance. Looped across it was a gold watch chain. It was as if his position demanded that he dress with sobriety and authority, yet his waistcoat revealed a more flamboyant side to his nature.

Sarah quailed and Bobbie shrank against his mother's skirts, but Meg stood her ground and gazed boldly up at him. She opened her mouth, but before she could speak the master boomed, 'Round the back with you.

You'll find someone there to direct you.' He seemed about to shut the door in their faces, but then he hesitated. His gaze roamed over Meg's face and hair.

'By,' he murmured, 'but you'll be a beauty one day an' no mistake.' Then his glance went beyond Meg to Sarah's face.

Though at present she was pale with distress and heavy with child, Isaac Pendleton, who prided himself on being a veritable connoisseur of women, could see beyond Sarah's temporary weariness. She was undoubtedly feeling humiliated too, he thought, at having to present herself at his door, but she was a pretty, gentle-looking creature with lovely eyes.

Isaac smiled. 'My dear lady, pray come in.' He bent closer, as if sharing a confidence. 'We'll break the rules for once, shall we? This is the main door to the guardians' meeting room and to my apartments. It's not normally used by the – er – inmates. But come in – come in.' He extended a long arm and ushered the reluctant little family inside.

Isaac Pendleton was not at all what Meg had expected the workhouse master to be like. From the imposing look of the building's walls and windows from the outside, she'd expected the man in charge to be as threatening, treating people down on their luck as idle, good-for-nothings. Yet this man was leading them down a room, past the long, polished table to a door at the far end on the left-hand side. Reaching it, he paused and turned. Putting his finger to his lips, he chuckled, 'Now, not a word to the others, mind, else they'll all expect to use the front door. Go through here and out of the door on the right into the yard and then to the buildings on the far side. That's the way you should have come in.' He beamed benevolently down at them. 'The porter's lodge is at the end near the entrance gate. See old Albert Conroy. He'll admit you and then arrange for someone to take you to the bath room and fit you out with uniforms.' He took Sarah's hand and raised it to his lips. 'Don't fret, my dear lady. You'll be well looked after here. You and your little ones.'

For the first time since Reuben had brought home the dreadful news, Sarah managed a weak smile. 'You're very kind,' she murmured and a faint tinge of pink touched her pale cheeks.

Three

They crossed the yard towards a door in the high wall – the door by which they should have entered the workhouse. Near it, at the end of a row of buildings, was the porter's lodge. As they approached, an old man appeared. He was scowling at them, his bushy white eyebrows drawn together. Several days' growth of grizzled beard gave him the look of an unkempt tramp. His clothes, crumpled and threadbare, hung loosely on him.

'And where might you three 'ave come from? I didn't see you come in.' His voice was gruff and accusing. He walked with a limp that gave him a curious rolling gait, like a sailor who has just stepped ashore after weeks at sea.

Bobbie cowered behind Sarah, burying his face against her skirt. 'Mam,' he wailed. 'Mammy!'

Surprised, the old man looked down him. 'No need for that, little feller. I ain't gonna hurt yer.' His voice, though still growly, was now kindly.

Meg stepped forward, protective of her little brother as ever, protective now of her mother too. 'We came to the wrong door,' Meg explained and treated him to her most winning smile, 'but we've been told to report to you. Are you Mr Conroy?'

The old man stared at her for a minute. White-haired, wizened and crippled with arthritis, Albert Conroy lived out his existence in the lodge near the workhouse's back gate, by which the inmates entered and left. Each night it was Albert who admitted the vagrants and directed them to the bath room. From there they went to the casual ward, where they were allowed a meal and to stay overnight in return for several hours' work the following day. And it was Albert who saw other folks enter the building, never to leave again until they were carried out in a plain, rough pauper's coffin.

Few stayed to talk to old Albert and even fewer gave him the courtesy of addressing him by name. And now here was this pretty little thing calling him 'Mr Conroy' just as if he were some toff in fancy clothes. He rubbed the back of his hand across his nose and mouth and sniffed. He tried a toothless smile, but found he had almost forgotten how to summon one up.

'Aye, I am.' His voice quavered. 'Long time since anyone called me "Mr Conroy".' He paused and then added wistfully, 'Time was when I was "Albert" to mi friends, but now it's just "Conroy" or just "eh-up, you".'

Meg put her head on one side. 'Wouldn't it sound cheeky of someone like me to call you by your Christian name?'

Albert's eyes watered. 'Nah. Not a bit. I'd – I'd like to be called Albert by a pretty young wench like you.'

Meg held out her hand. 'Albert it is, then. I'm Meg Kirkland and this is my mam and my little brother, Bobbie.'

The smile, long unused, quivered on his mouth and his voice was unsteady as he said, 'Pleased to meet yer, mi duck, though I'm sorry to see you in a place like this.'

'We won't be here long,' Meg said, forcing a cheerfulness she didn't feel for the sake of her mother and

Bobbie. 'But as you can see –' she gestured towards her mother's obvious condition – 'mi mam needs somewhere to stay.' Then she added quickly, 'Mi dad's gone to look for work and then he'll be coming back to fetch us.'

For a moment the old man looked doubtful, but then he said, 'Aye, course he will, mi duck, course he will.' More briskly, he added, 'Now, let's get down to business . . .'

They followed Albert into the porter's lodge, a grand-sounding name for what turned out to be one small, square room where the old man obviously lived.

'They let me sleep here and eat here,' he said with a note of pride, as if to live in this cold, sparsely furnished room was a privilege. Perhaps it was, Meg thought, for him, though she couldn't imagine a harsher fate than to end her days in such a way.

Just inside the door of his lodge was a table and open upon it was a ledger. A list of names was neatly written in copperplate script on each page. Albert picked up a pen and, poised to write, looked up at Meg. 'Now, tell me your full names, starting with yer mam.'

He wrote down the information with painfully slow deliberation, yet he was justifiably proud of the finished result. He asked a few more questions and then stood back, looking down with satisfaction at the neat rows of writing.

'It's beautiful handwriting,' Meg said.

'I allus did have a good hand,' Albert murmured. 'And I like to keep mi book nice. The guardians always ask to see it when they 'ave one of their meetings here. I teks it across to the committee room and the master shows them it.'

'I wish I could write like that,' Meg said.

'Oh, it's just practice, that's all,' the old man said

modestly, but Meg could tell he was gratified by her praise. 'Right, now I'd better get her ladyship to tek you to the bath room and so on.'

'Who's "her ladyship"?'

Albert guffawed wheezily. 'Waters.'

'Is she in charge?'

'She'd like to think she is. Nah. She's an inmate – just like me. Mind you, the silly woman 'ad the chance to leave years ago, but wouldn't.'

'Wouldn't leave?' Meg was incredulous. 'Why ever not?'

'Ah, well now, it was like this—' He seemed about to launch into a long story, but one glance at Sarah's face, white with fatigue, changed his mind. 'Mebbe I'll tell you all about it one day, but now I reckon you'd best get yer mam settled. She looks fair done in. Ah, here comes Waters. How that woman knows when there's new folks arrived beats me, but she always does. Nowt seems to get past her beady eyes.'

The woman coming across the yard towards them was more what Meg had imagined those in authority in the workhouse might be. Thin-faced with a beak-like nose and small, ferret eyes, she snapped, 'How did you get in? I saw you coming across the yard.'

'We came in the other way. Sorry,' Meg smiled winningly, trying not to let slip that they'd come in by the front door. 'We saw a gentleman who told us where to come.'

Waters looked puzzled and Meg hurried on, explaining. 'He was very tall and – and big, but he was ever so nice and—'

The woman's eyes widened. 'Mr Pendleton? You saw Mr Pendleton?'

'I don't know his name, but he was very kind.'

'It must have been Mr Pendleton.' Then Waters gave a start, her mind obviously working fast. 'You – you don't mean you went to the front door?' she asked, appalled by the newcomers' audacity.

'Er – well,' Meg stammered.

'What Miss Pendleton'll say, I don't know,' Waters muttered, sniffing her disapproval.

'The man – Mr Pendleton – didn't seem to mind,' Meg insisted. 'He was very nice about it. Who is he?'

The woman's tone was suddenly reverential. 'Mr Pendleton is the master of the workhouse. He's a wonderful man.' For a brief moment her eyes softened. 'A wonderful man.' But the look was gone in an instant and her eyes hardened again. 'And you'd do well to remember it, girl.'

Waters moved into Albert's lodge and ran her finger down the list of names in his ledger, noting the new arrivals.

'So –' her disapproving glance raked them up and down, taking in the faded work clothes, the shabby, dusty boots – 'homeless, are you?'

Meg and her mother exchanged a glance and the girl's mouth tightened as she was obliged to say bitterly, 'Yes.' Then in a rush she gabbled, 'But mi dad's gone looking for work. We won't be here long. He'll soon be back for us.'

'That's what they all say, but they're still here years later.'

'Well, *we* won't be.' Meg was belligerent. 'He'll come back.' She turned towards her mother. 'Won't he, Mam?'

But Sarah only hung her head whilst the other woman sniffed yet again. 'How old are you, girl?'

'Fifteen.'

The woman grunted, dissatisfied with her answer. 'You look older,' she said, eyeing Meg suspiciously. 'Sure you're not trying to make out you're younger than you really are just to get out of a bit of work?'

Meg tossed her head. 'I'm not frightened of work. I've worked on a farm for three years. I'm sixteen next month.'

The woman's lips stretched in what passed for a smile, though it did not reach her eyes. They were steel grey, cold and hard. 'My name is Ursula Waters, but we're all called by our surnames in here. That is –' she paused and hesitated fractionally, before adding – 'unless the master decides to call you by your Christian name.'

Pertly, Meg asked, 'And do we call him by his Christian name then?'

Ursula Waters gasped. 'The very idea! You've a mite too much to say for yourself, child.'

'I'm not a child,' Meg retorted hotly.

'You're a child in here if you're only fifteen. It's the rules.' Ursula leant closer. 'Are you sure you're not older?'

For the first time, Sarah spoke. Haltingly, her voice husky with shame and despair, she said, 'She is only fifteen, ma'am. I assure you.'

Meg turned and stared at her. Why was Sarah kowtowing to this harridan? It was obvious the woman was only an inmate too – though probably an inmate who held some sort of position. No doubt the woman enjoyed special privileges because of it. But Waters was no better than they were, Meg thought. She opened her mouth to retort, but caught her mother's warning glance and closed it again, pressing her lips together.

Bobbie, sucking his thumb, began to whimper and tug at Sarah's skirt.

'I'd better fetch Miss Pendleton. She's the matron and Mr Pendleton's sister.' Unbending enough to impart a little information in which she seemed to take great pride, Ursula Waters said, 'Poor Mr Pendleton lost his wife some years ago and his sister came to take her place as matron. Of course, it's quite unusual for that to happen. The master and the matron are usually man and wife, but the guardians' committee gave special consent. They didn't want to lose Mr Pendleton as master, you see.'

Meg nodded, pretending to understand.

'Wait here whilst I fetch matron.' Waters glanced down at Bobbie with distaste, sniffed once more and left the room.

'What a dragon!' Meg burst out, almost before the woman was out of earshot.

'Hush, Meg,' Sarah whispered. 'Don't make things worse than they already are, there's a dear.'

Meg looked at her mother. 'Mam, was it my fault . . .?' she began, but Sarah was bending over Bobbie, trying to quieten his crying, and at that moment Miss Pendleton bustled in, followed closely by Ursula Walters.

Letitia Pendleton was younger than her brother. Meg guessed she was about forty, but Isaac Pendleton had looked over fifty. The matron was small and round, and dressed in an ankle-length, dark blue dress with broad, starched white cuffs. A white bib apron covered the dress and she wore thick dark stockings and lace-up shoes with small heels. Her hair was completely covered with a starched white square of cloth, which fell in a triangular shape at the back of her head. Her face was plump, her cheeks round and rosy, but it was not the rosiness of good health, rather of too much indulgence, especially from a bottle. Young as she was, Meg recognized the signs. Farmer Smallwood had just such a look. Like her brother, Letitia Pendleton had hazel eyes that twinkled merrily. Once again, Meg was surprised. To her, Ursula Waters was the epitome of workhouse authority – the type everyone on the outside dreaded – not this buxom, smiling woman, who reminded the girl more of a fat and jolly farmer's wife. Not that Mrs Smallwood had been like that; she had been thin and wiry and shrewish. Meg pushed away the painful memories that threatened to overwhelm her.

'Now then, who have we here?' the matron greeted them.

Her glance lingered a moment on Sarah's swollen stomach. Then her gaze fell upon Bobbie, whose cheeks were now stained with tears. He was hiccuping miserably and sucking his thumb hard.

Letitia Pendleton's eyes softened. 'Poor little chap,' she said, taking his hand. 'I bet you're hungry, aren't you? You come along with me.'

'Oh, I don't think—' Sarah began.

'I'm sorry, my dear,' the matron said, but there was understanding in her tone. 'It's the rule in here. You all have to be segregated. Women, men – and the children.'

'You'll do as you're told,' Ursula put in sharply. 'It's the master's rules.'

'I tell you what,' Miss Pendleton said kindly. 'Maybe he can stay with you until the medical officer has seen you tomorrow morning, but then I'm afraid he will have to go with the other children.'

Meg noticed that Ursula's lips pursed even more tightly and her eyes flashed with anger. But she said nothing.

Sarah was close to tears, desperation on her face, but

Bobbie, with his small hand in the matron's plump grasp, had stopped crying. He was looking up at Miss Pendleton and she was smiling down at him with such compassion in her eyes, such fondness, that, to Meg's surprise, a tremulous smile hovered on the child's mouth.

'Do you look after the little ones, Matron?' she asked.

Letitia looked up, reluctantly dragging her gaze away from the little boy, but before she could answer, Ursula snapped, 'Mind your tongue, girl. Just remember who you're talking to. It's not your place to be asking questions. Not in here.'

'It's all right, Waters. The girl is concerned for her brother. That's only natural and very commendable too.'

Again Ursula sniffed her disapproval but said no more. Letitia turned back to Meg. 'The schoolmistress and I have care of the children between us. She teaches the younger ones during the day, whilst the older ones go to the local school. Outside school hours we share the supervision of all the children.'

'The schoolmistress?' Meg asked. 'Is she –' she glanced meaningfully at Ursula – 'nice?'

Meg saw that the matron pursed her mouth to prevent a smile. 'Louisa Daley? Oh yes, she's nice. Only young and the little ones love her.' Letitia glanced at Ursula. There was something pointed in the look that Meg couldn't understand as the matron added, 'We *all* do.' And she noticed that an angry flush crept up Ursula's scrawny neck and into her face.

Meg felt herself relax. She turned and touched her mother's arm. 'That's all right then, isn't it, Mam? Bobbie will be all right.'

Sarah's eyes lingered on her small son. She touched

his hair and then, not trusting herself to speak, she nodded.

'Now,' the matron said briskly, 'Let's get you admitted to the receiving ward. Waters, have you got all their details from Conroy?'

'Of course I have.'

Meg was surprised at the insolence in Ursula's tone. It was almost as if she was in charge – not the matron – and yet Meg knew that this could not be the case.

'They were all born within the county.' She sniffed – a sound that Meg was already coming to know very well when the woman was expressing her disgust. 'Though they've moved about a lot. Like gypsies.' On Ursula's lips the word implied disgrace.

'Mi dad's a farm worker. A wagoner,' Meg retorted defiantly, lifting her chin higher. For a brief moment there was a note of pride in her tone as she spoke of her father, remembering the position he had held, the respect his skill with horses had commanded. But then the pride faded from her tone when she relived the moment he'd told them that he'd been dismissed. 'We – we moved about a bit with his job, but we've been at – at the last place –' she couldn't bring herself to say the name of Middleditch Farm – 'for the last three years.'

'Well,' Letitia said, 'that'll make it easier for the guardians to decide. In the meantime, we'll get you settled in. Come along.'

'Goodbye, Albert,' Meg said to the old man, who had remained silent ever since Ursula Waters had stepped into his room.

' 'Bye, mi duck. For now.'

They followed the matron and Ursula across the yard, which was enclosed on all sides either by the buildings or walls and solid gates.

Meg shivered as she looked about her and once again the feeling of guilt swept through her. Was it her impertinent tongue that had landed them here? Or had it been because of her friendship with Alice? The thought of the girl she had liked so much was like a knife in her heart. Alice had betrayed her. She had done nothing to help Meg and her family. Surely, Alice could have done something.

Oh, Dad, Meg begged silently, *come back for us. Don't leave us in this place. Please come back, Dad. Please.*

Four

'Take your clothes off.'

Appalled, Meg stared at Ursula. 'All of them?'

'Yes. You wear the workhouse uniform whilst you're in here.'

'But – but what happens to our own clothes?'

'We have them cleaned.' Ursula eyed the newcomers up and down, assessing them. 'Fumigated in some cases. Just in case you're riddled with lice and—'

'We most certainly are not,' Meg said, deeply insulted. She turned to her mother. 'Tell her, Mam.'

But Sarah only murmured, 'Do as Miss Waters tells you, love. Don't make a fuss.'

'I'm not making a fuss, I just want to know what happens to our clothes. Miss Alice gave me this dress and . . .'

At once her mother's face was bleak and Meg was sorry she'd brought back memories of the comfortable, happy life that had been so suddenly and brutally torn away from them. She bit her lip. She still couldn't believe that Miss Alice had been party to their dismissal.

'We label all your clothes,' Letitia said and Meg felt the matron was trying to lessen Ursula's harshness. 'You'll get them back when you leave.'

Meg heard Ursula mutter darkly, 'If you leave.'

'That's all right, then,' Meg said, addressing her remark to the matron and ignoring Ursula. 'We won't be without them very long. We'll soon be out of here.' She felt embarrassed as Ursula stood watching them undress, gaping at Sarah's swollen belly.

'When are you due, Kirkland?' Ursula asked, once more taking the lead. To Meg's surprise, it was the matron who was helping Bobbie out of his clothes, smiling down at him and talking to him in gentle, reassuring tones, whilst Ursula stood to one side as if to have to touch the newcomers offended her.

Quietly, Sarah said, 'Sometime this month, I think.'

'The medical officer will inspect you tomorrow morning and classify you.' Then Meg saw Ursula lean towards the matron. 'If you ask me that girl ought to be classed as an able-bodied woman. She's no child.'

Meg felt them gazing at her young breasts, slim waist and firm, rounded buttocks. She faced them boldly, but it was hard to do so. Being naked took away her last vestige of dignity, leaving her humiliated and vulnerable. 'I've told you, I am fifteen – nearly sixteen – and I'm not afraid of work. I don't want to be with the children.'

'We'll see what the medical officer thinks,' was all the matron would say. 'Now, let's get you bathed and don't forget to wash your hair.' She bundled up their clothes and the few possessions they had brought with them. 'Here you are, Waters. See these are washed and properly labelled.'

The look of distaste on Ursula's face as she was forced to take their clothing made Meg want to laugh out loud for the first time.

'Bet that's the last we see of them,' she muttered, though not loud enough for the matron to hear as Ursula disappeared through the door.

The matron was bending towards Bobbie. 'Come on, little man, you come with me.'

'I'll wash Bobbie,' Meg began, but Miss Pendleton said firmly, 'You help your mother and see to yourself. He'll be fine with me.'

She led Bobbie away. Sarah and Meg looked helplessly at each other as they listened for his protesting wails. But Bobbie made no sound and trotted off, his hand happily in the matron's plump grasp.

Sarah closed her eyes and swayed. She might have fallen if Meg hadn't been quick to steady her. 'Let's get ourselves bathed quick, Mam, and then perhaps we can go and find him.'

Sarah nodded weakly and allowed Meg to help her.

It was the first time that Meg had seen her mother's body. Standing naked in the lukewarm water, she tried to avert her gaze, tried to leave her mother some shred of dignity.

But what self-respect was there left for either of them in this place?

When they were bathed and their hair washed, but still wet and clinging, Ursula returned. She handed them coarse scratchy underwear and the grey dress and white apron that were the uniform of the workhouse, saying, 'You can keep your own boots.'

'Where's Bobbie? Where's she taken him?' Meg demanded when they were fully clothed once more.

'If by "she" you mean matron, then she'll have taken him to the children's dormitory, I expect.'

Meg glanced at her mother, willing her to stand up to these people, but Sarah seemed to have lost her spirit completely. Meg could hardly believe the change in her. Sarah had always been quiet, but content with her lot and happy with her husband and young family, despite the sadness of losing three babies. She'd always had a gentle smile on her face and, even when Meg had been her naughtiest, Sarah had never raised her voice. Her chastisement had been a disappointed admonishment that had always left Meg feeling guilty at having hurt her mother by her wilfulness. But now Sarah was defeated by the shame of entering a place which she'd been taught since childhood was the ultimate in degradation.

So it was the young girl who turned back to face Ursula. *She's like a jailer*, Meg thought. 'Matron said he could stay with us. At least until tomorrow.'

'It's the rules,' Ursula snapped. 'Everyone's classified and segregated in here. Until the medical officer's seen you, you'll be in the receiving ward.' She pointed upwards, indicating the room on the next floor up, directly above their heads. 'He classifies you and then you go into the dormitories in the main building.' With a sideways flick of her head, she gestured towards the long, three-storey building across the yard. She ticked off the categories of inmates on her fingers. 'At the far end there's the able-bodied men's day room on the ground floor with their dormitories above on the first and second floors. Next to that are the old and infirm men. Then on the ground floor there's the clerk's office and the master's room. Right in the centre of the building is the guardians' committee room with the school room behind it and above them are the master's bedroom and the children's dormitory. Still on the ground floor is the kitchen, then the old women and then right at this end there's the able-bodied women.'

'Where are the children? Where will Bobbie be?' Meg demanded.

'He'll spend most of the time in the school room or the dormitory, but they're allowed into the women's exercise yards.'

'Are those at the front of the building, behind those walls?'

'Yes. That's where the privies are too. And there's a privy in this back courtyard too. Here, next to the bath room.'

For the first time Sarah spoke. 'Will I be allowed to put Bobbie to bed?'

Ursula shook her head and Sarah's shoulders drooped even more.

'I'll show you upstairs. You're going to be a bit crowded in the receiving ward. It's the casual ward where the vagrants stay overnight, as well as people like you waiting to be admitted. Come along.'

The small dormitory was jammed with beds – if they could be called beds, for they were nothing more than rough hessian bags filled with straw, grubby grey blankets and a lumpy pillow on the floor. Meg and her mother were obliged to share, and later on, through that first night they huddled together, hardly sleeping in their anxiety over Bobbie.

'He'll be all right, Mam. Miss Pendleton was kind to him. Much nicer than the dragon.'

In the darkness, Sarah buried her head against Meg's shoulder and wept. With her arms about her mother, Meg lay staring into the darkness, listening to the snuffling and snoring of the other women. Real sleep was impossible and she dozed fitfully, waking in the early light of the following morning still unable to accept what had happened to her family in the short space of the last thirty-six hours.

Was it really only the night before last that her father

had come home with the news that they had to leave their home?

I wish I could have seen Miss Alice. Perhaps her mam or her dad stopped her seeing me. I can't believe she wouldn't have tried to help us, Meg thought, trying to find excuses for the older girl. She still did not want to believe that Alice, her bright, vivacious friend, had really deserted her so cruelly. Perhaps it hadn't been Alice's fault. Perhaps . . .

Somewhere a loud bell was being rung, disturbing her thoughts. The other women in the room were stirring.

'Come on, Mam,' Meg said, gently shaking her mother awake. 'We have to get up.'

Meg and Sarah stood side by side, submitting to the medical officer's thorough examination. Once more they were obliged to be almost naked before a stranger, with Miss Pendleton standing in the background. And Ursula was there again, by the door, her beady eyes missing nothing.

'Now, Mrs Kirkland,' the doctor said, 'I think your baby will come very soon, so only light duties for you. But I shall put you with the able-bodied women. Matron –' he half turned towards the woman standing behind him – 'you'll see to it?'

'Of course, Doctor. She can help in the kitchen, preparing vegetables and such.'

'Excellent, excellent. She can be allowed to sit down to do that.' It was an order rather than a suggestion.

'Whatever you say, Doctor.'

'She could pick oakum,' Ursula put in, a malicious smile on her face. 'She can sit down to do that.'

The doctor frowned at Ursula. He could not interfere directly with the internal running of the workhouse, even if he wanted to. But unpicking lengths of old, tarred rope, though a sedentary occupation, was painful work resulting in raw and bleeding fingers.

He sighed as he beckoned Meg forward. 'Now then, young lady, let's have a look at you.'

Dr Collins was young, only in his early thirties, Meg guessed. He was very good-looking and, as he examined even her most secret places, Meg grew hotter and hotter with embarrassment. He was tall with fair curly hair and the brightest blue eyes that Meg had ever seen in a man.

Moments later he pronounced her, 'Fit as a flea and strong as an ox. Now –' he glanced down at his papers before adding – 'Meg, you're fifteen, but sixteen next month.'

'Yes, sir, and I don't want to be with the children. I can work. I—'

'Hold your tongue, girl,' Ursula snapped from her place by the door, but the doctor held up his hand, smiling at the girl standing before him.

'What I was going to suggest is that you should be with the children for the first month—'

'Oh, we won't be here as long as that. Mi dad will be back for us. I know he will.'

'I'm sure he will, but just in case he – er – encounters a few difficulties, we'll plan for a little longer, shall we?'

Meg stared into the man's blue eyes and saw sympathy there. A lump came into her throat and she nodded. 'All right,' she agreed huskily.

'What I suggest is that you should help the schoolmistress with the little ones. She is responsible not only for the teaching, but for the general care of the children too. I'm sure Miss Daley would be glad of some help and –' he leant towards Meg and lowered his voice – 'you'll be near your little brother for a while. Help him settle in. The little chap looked none too happy when I saw him earlier.'

Meg realized suddenly that the doctor was trying to do her a favour. She beamed at him, her whole demeanour changing in an instant. Her eyes shone and her cheeks dimpled prettily. It was like the sun appearing after a rain shower. 'Thank you, sir. Oh, thank you,' she breathed.

The doctor stared at her for a moment, then blinked, glanced down and shuffled his papers. Clearing his throat, he said, 'Don't mention it. I can see that you are a nice family, who've hit a bad patch in your lives.' He looked up again and smiled, once more in control of himself. 'I hope you're right and that your father returns for you very soon.' He glanced towards Sarah. 'Perhaps by then he'll have become a father again. In the meantime, we'll take good care of you all.'

Outside the infirmary, where they had been summoned for the medical officer's examination, Meg helped her mother down the stone steps.

'I don't believe this place, Mam.'

Sarah drew in a deep breath. 'Why? What do you mean?'

'Most of them are so nice, Mr Pendleton, the doctor, even Miss Pendleton isn't a bad old stick. But that Waters is a dragon. I thought they'd all be like that. I mean, everyone's always so frightened of the workhouse. It's like a terrible shadow hanging over anyone who can't work or falls sick.'

'It's the shame, Meg. That's the worst thing. And you're right. A lot of places are dreadful, with awful people running them. When I was a girl, we heard terrible stories about this place. It was our worst nightmare that we'd end up in here. And now –' tears threatened – 'here I am.'

Meg put her arm around her mother and hugged her close. 'Don't worry, Mam. Dad'll soon be back. He'll find work and come back for us.'

Sarah's only answer was a sob and a slight shake of her head.

Reaching the foot of the stairs, they stepped out into the men's backyard and Meg glanced about her. There was a pump in the centre of the wide open space and three or four men were queuing at it, bending their heads down and opening their mouths to drink. Others strolled around the yard in twos and threes, hands in their pockets and chatting together, but their shoulders were hunched, their heads bent forward. One or two walked alone, a defeated look on their faces. To one side older men, bent and crippled with age, shuffled along. But in the middle of the yard, youths, who must have been sixteen or more to be classed along with the men, played a rowdy game of football with a stone.

Meg looked about her, half-hoping to see someone she knew, but at the same time hoping no one would recognize her. One of the young lads glanced across at her and, giving the stone a last kick, left the game and swaggered towards her, grinning cheekily. 'By heck, it's nice to see a pretty girl in here. Where've you come from?'

Meg put her nose in the air and said loftily, 'What's that to do with you?'

The lad laughed, showing surprisingly even white teeth. His face creased and his brown eyes twinkled. He was thin, but wiry and energetic with thick brown curly hair cut short. He shrugged his shoulders. 'Nowt, just interested that's all. No offence meant.'

Meg capitulated and grinned back at him. 'None taken. Just that we've done nothing but answer questions since we got here.'

The youth nodded. 'I guess it's like that, but I wouldn't know.'

Now Meg was intrigued. 'Why? Didn't you have to answer a lot of questions when you came in?'

He laughed again. 'Nope. I was born in here. Me mam died having me, so they tell me. I've been here all me life.'

'Oh, how terrible!' The words escaped from Meg's mouth before she could stop them.

'Is it?' he asked solemnly, the laughter dying on his face. 'I've never known owt else.'

'No,' Meg said slowly, beginning to understand. 'I see that now.'

'Meg,' Sarah began, 'we ought to go. I – I need to sit down.'

At once Meg was contrite. 'I'm sorry, Mam.' With Sarah leaning heavily against her, they began to move back towards the gate in the wall, which led from the men's courtyard into the women's.

Meg glanced back over her shoulder towards the youth. 'What's your name?'

'Jake. What's yours?'

'Meg. I'll see you again.'

He pulled a face and lifted his shoulders. 'Not much chance. *They'll* see to that. But I'll watch out for you.' He winked at her. 'There are ways – if you know 'em.'

Meg nodded, wondering who 'they' were, but she could stay no longer. Sarah was looking pale and had deep purple shadows beneath her eyes. 'Come on, Mam. We'll find the dormitory and you can lie down.'

'But she needs to rest. Look at her.' Meg flung out her arm towards her mother as she stood facing Ursula Waters. 'She's done in.'

'She can't lie down in the dormitory during the daytime. If she's ill, she should report to the infirmary. And she's not, else the doctor would have said.'

'She's not ill, just exhausted.'

The woman pursed her thin mouth. 'I'm sorry. There's nothing I can do about it.'

'You don't want to, you mean,' Meg muttered.

'What did you say?' Ursula snapped.

'Nothing,' Meg answered morosely. How she would like to give this woman a mouthful, but she realized her runaway tongue would only make matters worse, especially for her poor mother.

Ursula sniffed. 'She's supposed to start work in the kitchens.' She glanced at Sarah, who was sitting on the chair and looking as if she was about to fall off it at any moment. Sarah's pallor must have touched even Ursula's hard heart, for she relented enough to say, 'I'll see what matron says.'

'Thank you,' Meg said, with more than a hint of sarcasm.

Ursula glared at her for a moment, before turning and leaving the room.

'Never mind what that dragon says, Mam. Come and lie down. Here, these are our beds next to each other.'

In the able women's dormitory the beds were still straw palliasses with rough grey blankets and one pillow, but the mattresses were now sitting on a four-legged wooden frame.

Sarah allowed Meg to help her to one, where she lay back and gave a weary sigh.

Meg sat beside her holding her hand, concerned by its feeling of limp clamminess. Letitia appeared beside them and stood for a moment, looking down at Sarah. Then she gave a brief nod.

'We'll let her rest today, but tomorrow she must try to do a little work. And the following day you'll have to be interviewed by the board of guardians. That's when their next meeting is.'

Sarah lay quite still, her eyes closed, and made no sign that she had even heard the matron. Letitia Pendleton glanced at Meg. 'But you go with Waters, Kirkland. She'll introduce you to Miss Daley, the schoolmistress. I'm sure she'll be glad of your help. She's run ragged by the little tykes.' But the matron spoke the last few words with a fond smile.

Meg rose, bent and kissed her mother's damp forehead and followed Ursula out of the room. 'Where's Bobbie? Is he all right?' she asked.

'Of course he's all right,' Ursula snapped. 'Why shouldn't he be?'

'No reason,' Meg said swiftly. 'I just thought – I just thought he might be missing Mam.'

'Well, he isn't. He stayed with matron last night. She keeps a truckle bed in her room in case any of the little ones are fretful the first night in a strange place.' She sniffed. 'Though goodness knows why. It's spoiling the little brats, to my mind.'

Meg bit her lip. She wasn't sure of the matron's motives. It sounded, on the surface, as if the woman was kindness itself, but surely, she thought, if Miss

Pendleton had really had Bobbie's best interests at heart, she would have let him stay with his mother and sister.

Keeping her tone polite and deferential, Meg asked, 'Couldn't he have stayed with us? Like she promised?'

'It was better to make the break straight away. We must stick to the rules. The master's rules.' Ursula's words were a pious chant. 'The place would soon be in an uproar if we didn't.

Meg said nothing, but she wondered if it had been the matron or Ursula Waters who had enforced a rule that was harsh enough to keep a lost, lonely, little five-year-old boy from his mother.

Ursula led the way along passages and through doors until they came to a large room which Meg recognized. This was the guardians' meeting room – the room through which they had passed when they had arrived. There was a large door at the end, opposite the entrance door through which Meg and her family had first come in. Behind it, Meg could already hear the noise of children.

Ursula opened the door and stepped inside. Meg was close on her heels, anxious to see Bobbie.

'Quiet!' Ursula bellowed, making Meg and everyone in the room jump. Twenty pairs of eyes turned to look at her, including those of the harassed young schoolmistress.

Suddenly there was the scrape of a stool being pushed back and a little figure hurtled towards them, flinging himself against Meg.

'Bobbie, oh, Bobbie,' she cried, hugging him.

'Stop that this instant.' Ursula grabbed the child's arm and pulled him away. 'If you're to help Miss Daley, Kirkland, you must treat your brother just like all the other children. Do you understand?'

Giving Bobbie a quick smile, Meg said, 'Go back to your place.' She bent close and whispered in his ear. 'I'm to help the teacher, so I'll be with you every day. But we'll have to behave.'

Understanding quickly, the little boy nodded solemnly. He turned, glanced up at Ursula and mumbled, 'Sorry, miss.' Then he trotted back meekly to his seat next to a boy with a shaven head and scabs on his face.

To see her mischievous, sunny-natured little brother so docile and in such a place as this broke Meg's heart.

Five

Miss Daley didn't look much older than she was, Meg thought, though surely the schoolmistress must be in her mid-twenties at least. She was small and slim with gentle eyes. Her black hair was fastened up into a bun on the back of her head, though curly tendrils escaped onto her forehead. She wore a navy blue costume with a fitted jacket and beneath it a blue and white striped blouse. Her pretty face with a small nose and perfectly shaped mouth was marred by a perpetual worried frown that creased her forehead.

As soon as Ursula had left the room, closing the door behind her, Louisa reached out to Meg.

'I'm so pleased to see you. I've been asking for some help for ages, but the guardians won't approve the employment of another teacher. And they keep telling me there's no one suitable amongst the women here, which,' she added wryly, 'I don't believe. But, there you are.' Louisa smiled and the anxiety left her face for a brief moment.

Meg warmed to her at once. 'What am I to call you?'

'Miss Daley or just miss in front of the children.' Louisa leant closer and lowered her voice, 'But in private please call me Louisa. And you're Meg, aren't you?'

Meg nodded. 'Yes, but I thought we had to be called by our surnames?'

'Ah – well – yes. And in front of the class I'm afraid

that is the name I'll have to use. Kirkland, isn't it? You're Bobbie's sister?'

Meg nodded.

'Good, good. Now for today if you would just help in general, but this evening, when the children are in bed, I should like to give you a few tests and then I can assess what you will be able to do in the way of teaching.'

'Teaching? You're going to let me help with the teaching?' Meg's eyes were shining.

'It depends,' was all Louisa would say. 'I can't promise until I see what you can do.'

For the first time in her young life, Meg wished that she had not been so eager to leave school and start working. Perhaps she too could have had a career like this smart young woman.

In the middle of the morning the door to the school room was flung open and the huge figure of the master filled the doorway. With one accord the children scrambled to their feet and stood in silence, their heads bowed. One or two of the little ones trembled.

'Miss Daley,' Isaac's deep voice boomed. 'I see you have a new helper. What a pretty picture you both make.' He moved forward into the room towards them, totally ignoring the children. For him they did not exist.

He stood close to Miss Daley and took her hand. The young woman blushed and looked as if she would like to pull away, but did not dare.

'Bring your little friend to see me whilst the children take their exercise after lunch, my dear.'

He raised her hand to his lips and then, without waiting for any kind of reply so sure was he of her obedience, the master turned and walked back down the room. As the door closed behind him, Louisa closed her eyes and shivered. 'One of these days,' she murmured. 'One of these days.'

'What?' Meg said before she thought to stop herself. 'What do you mean?'

Startled, as if she had forgotten Meg's presence, Louisa's eyes flew open. 'What? Oh – oh, nothing.' She took a deep breath before she said briskly, 'Now, please see that each child has a slate and I'll write on the board what I want them to copy.'

The morning passed quickly and soon the children were being given their lunch and sent out into the women's back courtyard.

'Poor little mites,' Louisa murmured as she and Meg ushered them through the door and watched one or two rushing towards the women there. 'It's the only time they get to see their mothers.'

To Meg's surprise, most of the children stayed together and began to play a game. 'What about those? Don't they want to find their mams?'

Louisa glanced at her and then looked back at the group of children. The girls had found a long piece of old rope. Two of the girls, one at either end, turned the rope and the others queued up to take turns at skipping in and out. All of them took up the chant, 'One, two, buckle my shoe; three, four, knock at the door . . .'

At her side, Louisa said quietly, 'They're the ones who haven't got any mothers. They're the orphans.'

Horrified, Meg stared at her. 'You mean – you mean they've got no one? No father either?'

Louisa, her gaze still on the skipping children, shook her head. Then with a sigh she said, 'Come on. We'd better go and see Mr Pendleton.'

From the yard they went in through the back entrance, turned left along the passage past the kitchen and went into the committee room. Instead of turning left again back into the school room, Louisa led the way across the room to a door on the opposite side, along a short passageway and turned to the right. There were two doors close together, one to the left and one directly in front of them. Louisa gestured towards the one on the left. 'That one's the clerk's office. You won't see much of him. He comes in each weekday, but he – he doesn't live in.' There was a note of envy in the young woman's voice. Louisa raised her hand to knock on the door facing them. 'This one's the master's room.'

At the sound of Isaac's booming voice, the two young women glanced at each other and, taking a deep breath, Louisa opened the door.

'Ah, my dear, come in, come in,' the master welcomed as they sidled into the room. 'Come and sit down. You, too, my dear,' he held out his arm invitingly to Meg.

The room seemed to be used mainly as an office. A large leather-topped desk occupied the centre of the room and behind it was a swivel chair that looked battered and well worn. Meg smothered an impudent laugh as she imagined the poor chair suffering Mr Pendleton's bulk. No wonder it looked in such a sorry state.

The surface of the desk was littered with untidy heaps of papers, a silver inkstand, a glass tray for pens and a long, thin cane like the one the headmaster at Meg's last school had always kept near at hand.

At the far end of the room a fire burned in the grate and above it an ornate mantelpiece held ornaments and framed photographs of stiff-backed figures, self-conscious as they faced the camera. In front of the fireplace was a lumpy yet comfortable-looking sofa with battered easy chairs on either side. As Meg moved closer, she saw that one of the photographs was of the master. His round face was solemn as befitted the serious business of sitting for a photographer – yet it was unmistakably a much younger, fitter-looking Isaac Pendleton. There were two other photographs. One was of a thin-faced, shy-looking young woman with fluffy fair hair. But it was the other that caught and held Meg's attention. The girl in the picture was very pretty with a sweet face and beautiful dark hair cascading in curls and waves down to her waist. Meg stared in astonishment. The photograph, she was sure, was of Letitia Pendleton.

The master waved Louisa and Meg to the sofa, where they sat side by side as if seeking reassurance from each other. The big man took one of the easy chairs. He beamed at them. 'Well now, this is nice. Shall I ring for some tea?'

Louisa shook her head. 'That's very kind of you, sir, but we really only have a few minutes. The children—'

'Ah yes. Of course, the children,' he murmured. 'We mustn't forget the children, must we?' Then his smile widened as he glanced at Meg. 'But now that you have a helper, my dear, perhaps you will have a little more free time, eh?'

Without warning, he leant across and squeezed Louisa's knee. Meg almost gasped aloud as she saw Louisa flush. To Meg's amazement, the young woman made no attempt to move the master's hand.

I'd have slapped him, Meg thought disgustedly. *The dirty old man.*

'It – it's very kind of you to permit Kirkland to help in the classroom,' was all Louisa said.

'I've been thinking about it for a while, but we had to wait until someone suitable arrived, didn't we?' Now he looked directly at Meg. 'And how is your dear mother, my child?'

Meg ran her tongue nervously around her lips, forcing herself to be respectful. 'Matron has allowed her to rest today, sir.'

'Good, good. I'll try to visit her myself later.'

'I'm sorry, but we must go,' Louisa said, standing up. The master's hand was dislodged from her knee and he too rose.

'You must let me know how your little helper shapes up.'

Louisa inclined her head obediently and began to move towards the door. Meg sprang to her feet and followed close behind, anxious not to be left alone with Isaac Pendleton. The big man lumbered forward, opening the door for them with a great flourish. 'I'll see you again, my dears, very soon.'

As the door closed behind them and they hurried back along the passageway, through the committee room towards the school room, Louisa murmured, 'I'm sorry you had to see that, Meg. It – it's not what you think. At least – not on my part.'

'Then why don't you say something – tell him – slap his hand away? I would,' Meg declared.

Louisa gasped and stopped in her tracks. Shocked, she turned to stare at Meg. 'You don't know what you're saying.' She shook her head. 'What d'you think would happen if I did that? I'd be dismissed at once. And without a reference.'

Meg stared as the young schoolmistress went on, 'We all have to do just as we're told in here. The inmates, the staff, everyone.'

'Why?'

'Why do you think? We'll be turned out into the street if we don't.'

'Haven't you any family to go to?'

Louisa's face was downcast. 'I – I've a widowed mother,' she muttered, but the confidence was shared reluctantly. 'She's not well and can't work. It's only because I've got this job that she can stay in her own home. Otherwise . . .'

She said no more, but Meg understood the implication. Otherwise, Louisa's mother would be forced to end her days as an inmate of the infirm women's dormitory.

The children clattered back into the classroom and Bobbie ran straight to Meg to be picked up and hugged. Though Louisa glanced at them, she said nothing.

Meg soon realized that Louisa's time was totally taken up with caring for and teaching the children. The children's dormitory was on the first floor, just across the landing from the master's bedroom, and the young schoolmistress slept in a tiny room at the far end of the dormitory.

'Don't you get any time off?' Meg asked, finding that she too was expected to be with the children all day long.

'One day a month when I go to see my mother.'

'Does she live nearby?'

'Yes. In the town.'

'Don't you get any time to yourself in the evenings when they're in bed?'

'I . . .' Louisa began and then bit her lip. 'I – have to be with them. They're still my responsibility.' She bowed her head, avoiding Meg's questioning gaze.

'Well, it seems unfair to me. I'd've thought you could have had a bit of time off in the evenings.' Meg was beginning to see how easy her life on the farm had been in comparison with this young woman's existence. An existence that was perhaps now going to be hers too, she thought with dread.

Six

Sarah, Meg and Bobbie stood before the guardians' committee. A row of bewhiskered, rotund gentlemen sat on the other side of the long table. The only faces they knew were those of the master and the medical officer. Dr Collins was not officially a member of the board, but he was frequently asked to sit in on their meetings to give his opinion and the findings of his examinations of those applying for admission.

A portly, red-faced man with bushy grey sideburns, sitting in the centre of the row, took charge of the meeting. He tapped on the table to bring the guardians to order. Then, in a gravelly voice, he asked Sarah for their names and demanded that she explain how they had come to present themselves at the workhouse door.

Sarah's face was deathly white, her eyes huge pools of suffering and shame. Her head sank lower and she spoke in a whisper.

'Speak up, woman. I can scarcely hear you.'

Meg put her arm about her mother's shoulders and faced the row of disapproving faces. 'My father's employers turned us out of our home. They dismissed him and me too. But don't ask me why because no one will tell me.'

'Who were your employers, girl?'

'Mr and Mrs Smallwood at Middleditch Farm.'

'Smallwood? I know him,' the chairman said. 'Meet

him at the races now and then. He's a decent enough chap.' He turned towards his colleagues on the board, first one way and then the other. 'A good man. Yes, yes, a good man.' Frowning, he turned back to Meg. 'Your father – or you – must have seriously displeased him in some way for a man like Smallwood to dismiss you. Without a reference, I take it.'

Meg was forced to nod.

'Humph,' the man grunted. 'That says it all, in my opinion.'

Suddenly, Sarah gave a little cry and leant heavily against Meg. She clutched at her stomach and bent forward.

'Mam, what is it . . . ?' Meg began, but her mother's weight was too much for the girl to hold and Sarah slipped to the floor in a faint.

At once, Dr Collins rose and came round the end of the table. Isaac Pendleton, too, was instantly on his feet. He pointed at Bobbie. 'You, little boy. Run and find the matron.'

But Bobbie stood transfixed. He took no notice of the master and began to whimper, squatting down beside his mother and shaking her. 'Mam, Mam . . .'

'I'll go,' Meg muttered now that the doctor was bending down beside Sarah. Without waiting for permission, she whirled around and ran towards the door.

Dr Collins took Sarah's limp wrist in one hand and placed the palm of his other over the mound of her stomach. Several of the guardians shuffled their papers and looked away in embarrassment. They murmured amongst themselves and then the chairman said, 'Well, that seems to settle it. You'd better admit the family, Master. We'll review their situation once this woman has been delivered of her child.' He cleared his throat and stroked his right sideburn. 'Another mouth for the parish to feed, I'll be bound.' He went on muttering and grumbling under his breath. 'Something should be done about these people who have no more sense than to go on breeding even when they cannot support themselves.'

Isaac Pendleton cleared his throat. 'Mr Finch – I have checked our books and there is no record of this family having been in the workhouse in the last few years. Some misfortune has befallen them. I'm sure it's only temporary and—'

'That's as maybe,' Mr Finch interrupted gruffly, 'but they should make provision for misfortune.'

Isaac frowned, but bit back his words. Theobald Finch lived in the Hall, the largest house in South Monkford. He owned almost half the commercial properties along the High Street as well as cottages and houses in other parts of the town. He had considerable influence in the community, yet there was no love lost between the chairman of the board of guardians and the master of the workhouse. They had clashed on all sorts of matters on numerous occasions. Indeed, Isaac knew that Theobald Finch would have him removed from his post if he could, but there were reasons why Theobald would make no move against him. Isaac allowed himself a satisfied smirk. His position was safe. He knew that and – better still – he was aware that Theobald Finch knew it too. Besides, the rest of the board members liked Isaac Pendleton. The workhouse had never been run as efficiently or economically as it was under his authority. They would never agree to his dismissal without reason. Just because the two men disliked each other was not a good enough motive in their opinion. In fact, it amused the other members of the board to watch the two men needling each other whenever they got the chance. Theobald was glaring at Isaac now. He nodded towards the prone form on the floor. 'One of your lady friends, is she, Pendleton? I wouldn't put it past you . . .'

But at that moment Meg rushed back into the room, followed by Miss Pendleton and Waters, and in the general hubbub that followed whatever Theobald had been about to say was lost.

The matron bent down over Sarah and held a small bottle beneath her nose. In a moment Sarah began to splutter and revive. After a few minutes Meg and Waters were able to help her up.

'Take her to the infirmary, if you please, Matron,' Dr Collins said. 'She's going into labour. I'll come along in a few minutes when you've got her into bed.'

Although Miss Pendleton laughed and tapped the doctor playfully on his arm, there was an undercurrent of huffiness as she said, 'There's no need for that, Doctor. I'm sure me and Waters know what we're doing. We've delivered more babies into the world than you've got patients.'

'I'm sure you have, Miss Pendleton.' The young doctor smiled placatingly. 'I'm sure you have, but—'

'We'll send for you if we need you, Doctor,' the matron said and though she was still smiling there was a firmness to her tone that forbade him to overstep his authority. Within these walls her brother and she were in supreme charge.

'Quite so, Matron,' Mr Finch, who had been listening to the exchange, put in. 'We don't want the bill for your services here getting any longer than it has to be, Doctor.'

'I wouldn't dream of charging anything in this case,' Dr Collins said mildly. 'But as you wish, Matron, as you wish.' So saying, he walked back to his seat behind the table.

As the matron and Waters helped Sarah towards the door, Meg and Bobbie, holding hands, fell into step behind them.

'You, girl. Kirkland –' Meg turned to see the master pointing at her – 'take your brother and go back to the classroom.'

'Oh, but I want to go with Mam—' Meg began.

Dr Collins sprang to his feet again and beamed at Meg. 'Now, Meg, your mother is in good hands, so how about I come with you and say hello to all the children, eh?' He turned and smiled charmingly at the chairman. 'And no, Mr Finch, there will be no charge.'

He moved towards Meg and Bobbie and, stepping between them, put an arm around each of their shoulders. As he ushered them towards the double doors at the end of the room leading into the school room, he whispered in Meg's ear, 'Don't worry, my dear, I'll hang around here for a while and make sure your mother's all right before I leave. Now, here we are, I'm sure the lovely Miss Daley will be delighted to see you back.'

He removed his arms from around them and threw open the doors with a flourish. There was a scraping of stools as all the children stood up. Meg saw Louisa look up, dread on her face, but when the young schoolmistress saw who was standing there, a pretty, pink blush tinged her cheeks.

The doctor moved between the rows of desks, not even glancing down at the children as he passed between their ranks. His gaze was all for Louisa Daley.

*

Meg's mind was hardly on her job during the rest of the morning. She longed for lunchtime so that she could run across to the infirmary and see how her mother was. Dr Collins, after a long, whispered conversation with Louisa, still did not leave the classroom. He pretended to be interested in the children's work, but his glance strayed every few seconds back to the schoolmistress. The blush on Louisa's face deepened.

A few minutes before twelve, the door flew open and a flustered Waters, cap awry and hair falling from its prim bun, appeared.

'Doctor – thank goodness I've found you. Please come at once. The baby – it's not breathing. Matron's tried everything, but—'

He stayed to hear no more but was through the door and gone before anyone else could move. Meg dropped the slate she had been holding and, picking up her skirts, fled after him, almost knocking Waters over in her haste.

'Meg! Kirkland!' Louisa began, but the girl had no intention of heeding her. 'What is it?' Louisa asked Ursula. 'What's happening?'

'Kirkland's mother's had her baby.'

'And?'

Waters glanced round the room at the twenty pairs of staring eyes. Her gaze came back to meet Louisa's. She said no more but lifted her shoulders in a helpless shrug.

Louisa closed her eyes and gave a groan. She opened them to find Bobbie tugging at her skirt. 'Mammy? I want my mammy. Where's Meg gone?'

Louisa knelt on the rough wooden floor and drew the little boy into her arms.

*

Meg heard her mother's wailing as she raced up the stairs to the infirmary which was situated across the men's backyard and above the bake house.

How many times before had she heard that sobbing? Three, was it, or four? The young girl couldn't be sure. There had been a couple of times when she had been very little and had not understood what had happened. Then, when Bobbie had been three and she thirteen, Meg had understood only too well. Her mother's pregnancy had ended in a stillbirth and Sarah's raging tears.

And now, in this awful place, it had happened again.

Later, Meg was allowed to sit beside her mother's bed and hold her hand.

'Just a few moments,' Matron said gently. 'Then you must leave her to rest. She's had a bad time, poor thing.'

'Can Bobbie come and see her?'

'Best not. But don't you worry about him. I'll look after Bobbie. He can have his tea with me in my room.'

Meg smiled wanly, surprised at Miss Pendleton's kindness.

'I'll go and find him now and tell him what's happened. He's too young to understand. Good thing, really.'

Meg nodded, a huge lump in her throat and her eyes full of tears. As Miss Pendleton left the room, Meg leant towards her mother. 'Mam,' she whispered softly, 'Mam – how are you feeling?'

Sarah, her face flushed from the effort of giving birth and from her weeping when all her efforts had come to naught, lay still, her eyes closed.

'Do you – do you want me to go and find Dad?' Meg suggested. 'I could–'

Now Sarah roused herself. 'No!' Her voice was surprisingly strong. 'No,' she said again as she sank back. 'You look after Bobbie. There's a good girl. Ne'er mind about your dad.'

'But – but he'll want to know.'

Sarah was silent now, her eyes closed.

'He ought to know,' Meg insisted and when her mother did not answer, she pressed again, 'Mam?'

'Leave it, Meg. There's a good girl. Just leave it, will you?'

Meg sat beside her for a few moments more, chewing her little finger agitatedly. Her dad ought to be told. Whatever had happened, he would want to know. Perhaps he had already found work and, as soon as her mother was well, they could all leave here and be together again.

When she could see that Sarah was sleeping, Meg crept away. As she stepped out of the doorway at the bottom of the stairs and into the yard, a figure emerged out of the shadows.

'Hello, again. I thought it was you I saw running across the yard earlier.'

It was the boy who had spoken to her on the day they had arrived. Now, what was his name? Frowning, Meg tried to remember.

'It's Jake,' he said helpfully, grinning at her through the gloom. 'Don't tell me you've forgotten already.'

'Sorry,' Meg smiled faintly. 'I'm not thinking straight. It's me mam.'

At once the boy's face sobered. 'Is she poorly?'

'Well, sort of. She – she's just had a baby, only . . .' She bit her lip to stop it quivering, but failed. Tears spilled over and ran down her cheeks.

'Aw, don't cry. A babby's nice, even in here.' Awkward with embarrassment, the boy put his arm about her and she rested her face against his shoulder.

'I know, but – but it was born dead.'

Jake could think of nothing to say to comfort her, but his arm tightened about her.

They stood together in the empty yard in the growing dusk. Then suddenly, the silence was shattered as a window on the first floor was thrown up and the master leant out.

'Hey, you there. What do you think you're doing?'

Startled, the two youngsters looked up.

'Oh heck,' Jake said, his arm falling away from around Meg. 'Now we're in for it.'

Isaac's deep voice echoed across the yard. 'My office now. The pair of you.'

Then the window was slammed down with such a force that the small glass panes rattled.

Seven

They stood together outside the door of the master's office. Jake was trembling.

'What are you so frightened of?' Meg asked. 'What can he do to us?'

Jake glanced at her, then looked down at the floor. 'It'll be a beating for me. Or – or the punishment cell. He can't wait to send me there. Mind you – he should get the guardians' agreement before he does that.' Then he muttered beneath his breath, 'But usually he doesn't bother.'

'What – what'll he do to me?'

Again Jake glanced swiftly and then looked away again. Then he shrugged. 'Nothing, probably. If – if you're nice to him.'

'Nice to him? What do you mean?'

'I dunno really. I just know that he's not so strict on the girls. And you're new here, so if you smile prettily at him and say you're sorry, mebbe you'll get away with it.'

The door flew open and Isaac stood there. He looked nothing like the kindly, avuncular figure he had seemed before. Now he resembled a raging bull.

'You, boy, in here.'

As Jake stepped forward, Meg did so too, but the master said sharply, 'No, you stay there, girl. I'll see you in a moment.'

The second that Jake stepped into the room the door was slammed behind him, but because the master was shouting Meg could hear every word.

'How many beatings do I have to give you, boy, before you learn the rules? Eh? Eh? Answer me that. It's not as if you've any excuse. You've been here all your life. You were born here, yet you still flout the rules at every end and turn. And don't expect Miss Pendleton to come running to your aid. Not this time when I tell her what you've done. Such disgusting behaviour with a young and innocent wench. In broad daylight and in the middle of the yard too. Have you no shame, boy?'

Meg heard Jake's muttered response, but she could not make out the words. His voice was too low.

'Upset, you say? Of course the lass was upset. Her mother has just lost her baby. But that's no excuse for what you were trying to do.'

Again, a low reply from Jake.

'Comfort?' Isaac laughed cruelly. 'I know the kind of "comfort" you had in mind, you dirty little tyke. Taking advantage of the poor lass when she was upset. That's what you were doing.'

Another murmur from Jake and then the sound of a slap. 'Don't answer me back, boy. And like I say, it'll be no good running to matron. Not this time. You may have been her blue-eyed boy up to now, but when she hears you've been after a young girl, then she'll have no more sympathy for you. You mark my words. You'll have blotted your copybook with her good an' proper.'

Meg blinked. The master sounded gleeful, as if he had been waiting for just such an occasion.

'It's the cell for you, boy, for a couple of days and nothing to eat but bread and water. Let's see if that'll curb your beastly desires.'

This time, Meg heard Jake argue. 'You can't do that. Not without the guardians' say-so.'

Isaac's answering bellow seemed to shake the door. 'How dare you argue with me?'

Heavy footsteps moved across the room, then came the sound of something swishing through the air. Meg shuddered, knowing that the master had picked up the cane from his desk. 'Bend over, boy. We'll see what a good thrashing can do for you. I don't need to ask the guardians' permission for that!'

Meg was forced to stand listening to every swipe of the cane. They seemed to go on and on, yet Jake made no sound. Not a cry, not even a whimper.

When she could bear it no longer, she turned and ran out into the men's backyard, looking wildly to right and left. But the dusk had deepened. It was almost dark now and the yard was deserted. Then she heard a noise behind her in the building and turned to see a strange man just inside the entrance locking the door to the left of the master's room. He turned and came towards her, stepping out into the evening air. A tall, thin man dressed in a dark suit with a starched white collar. His face was pale and gaunt and he stooped slightly, as if he spent too much time indoors bending over his books and ledgers. He paused for a moment and straightened up, taking in a deep breath as if it were the first time he had breathed fresh air that day.

'Sir – oh, sir,' she cried. The man jumped and blinked. He took a step back, startled by the girl rushing towards him. 'Please help us. The master. He's thrashing a boy. Jake. Oh, please stop him. Please do something.'

The man's lips curled. 'Jake Bosley?'

'I – I don't know his second name. Only that he's called Jake.'

The man nodded and said curtly, 'That'll be him, all right. Trouble, he is, with a capital T. You'd do best to keep your distance from him.' He bent closer, squinting at her through the darkness. 'I haven't seen you before. Just come in, have you?'

Meg nodded. 'Three days ago.'

'So how do you know Jake?'

'I don't. At least, I mean, I met him in here. In the yard.'

'What's he done?' Again the man's lips were tight with anticipated disapproval.

'He was trying to comfort me. My mother's just – just lost her baby and I was upset. He only put his arm around me.'

'Put – his – arm – round – you!' The man was scandalized.

'Well, yes. I was crying and—'

'He's not even supposed to talk to you, let alone have physical contact. Where do you think it would lead if we allowed that sort of thing to go on? Why do you think we separate the men from the women? Oh no, I'm sorry, girl, but there's nothing I can do. And let me tell you, even if I could I wouldn't. Bosley deserves every bit of punishment he gets. And if you've any sense, you'll get back to the women's quarters pretty sharpish and stay there.'

Meg stared at him in disbelief for a moment, then her shoulders dropped with defeat. 'I – I can't. I was told to wait outside the master's room.'

'Then I suggest you get back there at once.'

Without another word the man stepped aside, walked

around her and crossed the yard into the darkness. With the sound of finality, the entrance door banged behind him as he left. Dragging her feet, Meg went back into the building to wait outside the master's room.

The sound of the beating had stopped, but Isaac was still shouting. 'Get yourself to the cell.'

The door opened and Meg, her eyes widening, gasped in horror. Jake emerged slowly, hardly able to walk. Tears streamed down his face, but still he made no sound.

Instinctively, Meg reached out to him. 'Oh, Jake, I'm so sorry . . .'

The boy shrank from her, avoiding her touch. He turned his head away and moved towards the door. She watched him go, sick at heart to think that he hated her now. But at the doorway, hidden from Isaac Pendleton's view, he turned and smiled. Though his mouth still trembled he winked at her. He glanced back at the door to the master's room and, as Isaac appeared, he turned away abruptly.

'Come in, Kirkland,' the master said. His voice was still stern, but he was no longer shouting.

Trembling and biting her lip, Meg moved forward and entered the room. Isaac closed the door firmly behind her.

'Now, my dear—' Suddenly, his tone was very different. He smiled down at her and put his hand on her shoulder. 'Come along and sit by the fire and we'll have a little chat, shall we?' He guided her towards the sofa and pressed her to sit down. Then he sat down close by, leaning towards her. Putting his fat hand on her knee, he said, 'You've not been here long, so I'm not going to punish you. Not this time, but you must understand and obey the rules we have here.'

Meg stared at him, meeting his gaze fearlessly. She steeled herself not to shrink away from him, though his touch seemed to burn through her skirt. She wanted to push his hand away, to stand up and scream at him to leave her alone. Instead she narrowed her eyes and gritted her teeth.

'You must know by now that men and women are separated. Oh, I know it seems hard, especially if there are husbands and wives in here, but there are good reasons. You see, my dear girl, boys and men of all ages for that matter, especially the sort that we have in here, cannot resist their animal urges. A boy like Jake has to be taught a lesson. One day he'll thank me. Oh yes, he will.' He nodded agreement with himself, a satisfied smile stretching his thick lips. 'Jake Bosley will leave here one day a fine upstanding young man and it will all be thanks to me.'

Meg could bear his touch no longer. She stood up suddenly and his hand fell from her knee. There was a fleeting look of anger on his face, but Meg said swiftly, 'Master, I'm so sorry I broke the rules and I promise you it will never happen again. But you must believe me – we were doing nothing wrong. I swear it. I was very upset and he – Jake – was being very kind to me.'

Isaac smiled sadly. 'Oh, my dear child, how young and innocent you are. But there, there.' He took hold of her hand and patted it. Meg wanted to snatch her hand away; his touch made her flesh crawl. 'I'm here to protect you. Now, you run along and have your supper with the children.' He leant towards her as if sharing a confidence. 'When they're all in bed, I'd like you to do something for me. Just to show me how really sorry you are.' His tone was silky. Meg was silent, holding her breath, afraid of what he was going to say. 'I'd like you to stay up in the dormitory with the children so that Miss Daley is free. And you'll tell her that I'd like to see her, won't you?'

'Oh, but Miss Daley's going to give me some tests tonight. To – to see if I can help teach.'

For a fleeting moment, Isaac's face was like thunder, then he forced a laugh and said, 'Well, well, how very conscientious of our little schoolmarm. But you tell her from me that she can do that another time. Now –' suddenly he pulled her close to him, so that she felt his stale breath on her face – 'you'll do that for me, little Meg, won't you? And we'll say no more about what happened in the yard, eh?'

It was a threat, yet for once there was nothing she could do but nod her head in agreement, even though she hated herself for giving in.

Eight

When Meg burst into the children's dormitory, Louisa Daley put a finger to her lips. Most of the children were already asleep and the others were drowsy, just on the point of falling into a kinder world than they knew in their waking hours.

'I've had to put little Betsy Arnold into my room. She's got the most awful cough. Matron has given me some medicine for her, but it doesn't seem to be doing much good.'

'Miss Daley, Louisa—' Meg began urgently.

'Yes, yes, I know what you're going to say, but I haven't forgotten. We can sit quietly in my room. We'll be on hand for Betsy then. I'll test you on arithmetic tonight. Your written English is very good—'

'No, no, you don't understand—'

'Oh, my dear.' Louisa took Meg's trembling hands in hers. 'Here I am prattling on about schoolwork and I haven't asked how your mother is.'

'She's poorly, but I think she'll be all right. But she – she lost the baby.' For a moment Meg's thoughts were diverted from the message she carried. 'It was a boy too. I think Dad would have like another boy. He was that thrilled when Bobbie was born.'

'Oh, Meg, I'm so sorry. No wonder you don't want to work. I do understand that you really wouldn't be able to concentrate—'

'It's not that. Oh, Louisa, it's the master.'

Louisa paled. 'What – what about the master?'

The words came tumbling out. 'I'm so sorry, Louisa, if it's my fault. You see, I was coming down from the infirmary after seeing Mam and Jake Bosley was in the yard. He – he saw me crying and tried to comfort me and the master saw us.'

Louisa shuddered. 'That man sees everything,' she murmured bitterly. 'From his bedroom and the landing on this floor he can see all the yards. Oh, I can tell you, Isaac Pendleton misses nothing. I only wish I'd thought to warn you, my dear. I suppose he's punishing you both in some way, is he?'

'He – he thrashed Jake.'

Louisa closed her eyes for a moment and sighed. 'Poor Jake, but it's not the first time and I don't expect it will be the last. However many beatings he has, it doesn't seem to dampen his spirit for long.' She paused and then looked into Meg's green gaze. 'What about you? What is your punishment?'

'He – he asked me to look after the children tonight while you – while you—' Meg bit her lip.

Flatly, Louisa finished the sentence for her. 'While I take some time off.'

Wordlessly, Meg nodded.

'It's not your fault, Meg. He's been hounding me for weeks. Ever since I came here, in fact.' Louisa grimaced wryly. 'I think he's got me in mind for the position of Mrs Pendleton number two.'

Meg stared at her in disbelief. 'You wouldn't,' she breathed. 'Oh, you wouldn't marry *him*!'

Louisa laughed and for a brief moment the ridiculous thought drove away Meg's sadness and she began to laugh too. They leant against each other, overcome by a fit of girlish giggles. Drying her eyes at last, Louisa said, 'Well, I'd better go. I daren't refuse. Let's just hope I can keep him at arms' length. Where is he? In his office?' She shuddered and inclined her head in the direction of the master's bedroom across the landing. 'I certainly don't fancy going to his room across there. Now,' she went on more briskly, 'you will look after poor little Betsy, won't you?' Suddenly, there was a spark of mischief in her brown eyes. 'Of course,' she said slowly and deliberately, 'if you're *really* worried about her, you'll have to come and fetch me. Won't you, Meg?' she added pointedly.

Meg giggled again, the conspiracy between them chasing away some of her sadness about her mother and her anxiety over Jake. She didn't like being the cause of the boy's punishment. Especially when he had tried to be so kind to her.

'When shall I come down for you then?'

'Oh, in about an hour.'

'But there isn't a clock. How shall I know the time?'

'I'll leave you my watch,' the young schoolmistress said, unfastening the fob watch she always wore pinned just above her left breast and pressing it into Meg's hand. 'Don't lose it,' she said. 'My father gave it to me. It's all I have to remember him by.'

Louisa hurried away, dreading her mission, yet anxious not to frustrate the master any further.

Meg placed Louisa's watch on the battered chest of drawers and sat down beside the small bed where Betsy lay. The child was restless, her breathing rasping and laboured. Meg poured a little water from the china ewer into the bowl and dipped a flannel into it. Wringing most of the water from it, she dabbed at the child's hot face.

She remembered her mother doing this for Bobbie when he'd had a fever. Betsy opened her eyes and stared up fearfully.

'It's all right,' Meg soothed. 'Miss Daley's had to go down to the master's office. I'm here to look after you.'

The fear faded from Betsy's blue eyes as Meg smoothed the damp tendrils of fair hair back from the young girl's forehead. 'Try to sleep,' she whispered.

'I want my mammy,' Betsy said, her mouth quivering. The girl looked about ten years old. She was very thin and, at this moment, very poorly.

'Where is she? In the women's section?'

Betsy shook her head and bit her lip. 'No, she died.'

'Oh, I'm sorry,' was all Meg could say. After a pause she asked, 'What about your dad? Where's he?'

'He's gone away.'

Meg nodded. 'Yes, so's mine. He's gone to look for work and then he'll come back for us.'

'That's what my dad said.' Betsy's voice trembled. 'But he's been gone two years.'

Meg bit her lip. She didn't know what to say to comfort the child, so she just sat beside her and held her hand. Betsy slept fitfully, dozing for a few moments then tossing and turning with fever and whimpering pitifully. The minutes crawled by. Meg kept looking at Louisa's watch hardly able to believe that the time was going so slowly. Once she held it to her ear to see if it was still going. Reassured by the low tick-tick-tick, she was about to replace it on the top of the cabinet, when Betsy reached out her hand.

'Let me hear it,' she said.

Meg held the watch close to the little girl's ear. Betsy's tiny mouth trembled and tears welled in her eyes.

'My daddy had a watch like that. He – he used to let me listen to it.'

Meg held it there for a few moments until Betsy was asleep once more. She seemed calmer now and her face was not so flushed. Carefully, Meg placed the watch back on top of the chest, noting the time as she did so. Another five minutes, she decided, and then, if Betsy was still asleep, she would creep away and go down to the master's office. Now even the seconds dragged and Meg fidgeted, agitatedly biting the nail of her little finger. When only three minutes had passed, she jumped up, unable to wait a second longer. With one last glance at Betsy, she crept towards the door. Its creaking echoed in the silence and Meg held her breath, sure that it would wake not only the sick little girl, but half the dormitory too. As quietly as she could, she pulled the door to and tiptoed down the centre of the long room. On either side, the children slept on straw mattresses in wooden beds pushed close together. Curled beneath rough blankets, some slept silently, while others snuffled and muttered in their sleep. Bobbie, Meg noticed thankfully, was one of those sleeping peacefully, but in the end bed nearest the door to the landing, she could hear muffled sobs. Meg paused, wanting to comfort the child, yet not liking to linger. She was nervous enough about lying to the master, even if it was to save Louisa from his clutches. What if he insisted on coming up to the dormitory to see Betsy for himself and found her asleep and looking, if anything, better not worse?

Meg moved on, out onto the landing and down the stairs. At the bottom she stood outside the master's office door. She paused a moment, listening for the sound of voices from beyond the door.

She could hear nothing.

Her heart pounding, Meg took a deep breath and rapped urgently on the door. Isaac Pendleton's exasperated voice called, 'Come in.'

Meg rushed into the room. 'Oh, Miss Daley, do come. It's Betsy. I'm sure she's worse. I didn't know what to do.'

Louisa was sitting on the sofa with the master close beside her, his arm around her shoulders. She stood up at once and placed the cup and saucer she was holding on the low table. Then she turned to face Meg. 'I'll come at once.' She glanced down at Isaac. 'I'm so sorry, but I must go. The child is very sick. I really shouldn't have left her . . .'

Isaac struggled to his feet. He put his arm around her again and hugged her to him. 'Your concern does you credit, my dear.' Then he turned frosty eyes upon Meg. 'But you should have fetched the matron, girl. Miss Daley deserves a night off now and again. She works far too hard as it is.' His eyes narrowed and Meg read the threat in them. Suddenly, he was once again the bull-necked, angry tyrant wielding power over all the people in his charge – staff and inmates alike. 'If I'm to allow you to continue as Miss Daley's assistant, you'll have to cope better than this.'

Meg dropped her gaze. 'I'm sorry, sir,' she said meekly for the second time that day. 'I – I was just so frightened. Betsy's breathing. It sounds awful . . .'

Louisa eased herself away from Isaac. 'I'd better go. Perhaps, if she settles again, I can come back.'

'Please do, my dear.' Isaac's voice was husky, but with one last squeeze he released her.

Louisa hurried across the room towards Meg, who dared not meet her gaze, so terrified was she that she would break into nervous laughter. 'Come, Kirkland,' Louisa said sharply, keeping up the pretence of being annoyed at the girl's interruption.

Only when the door had closed behind them and they were hurrying up the stairs, their hands pressed to their mouths to stop their laughter, did Louisa touch Meg's arm and whisper, 'Thank you. Oh, thank you, Meg.'

'I was terrified he'd come with us because she's asleep.'

'Oh, you needn't worry about the master coming to see the children,' Louisa whispered. 'He rarely concerns himself with them, except,' she added wryly, 'to administer punishments.'

'But he came to the school room.' Before Louisa could reply, Meg answered her own question. 'Oh, I see. He came to see *you* – not the children.'

'Exactly,' Louisa said dryly.

They crept down the dormitory and into Louisa's room. The candle was guttering, sizzling and casting eerie, dancing shadows around the room, but Betsy was still asleep.

Louisa lit another candle and then gently felt the child's brow. 'I don't think she's quite so hot.'

'I bathed her face,' Meg whispered and Louisa nodded approval. She straightened up and stood looking down at the child for a moment before saying, 'I think we can leave her to sleep now.' She glanced round the tiny room as she added, 'But I'm afraid we're going to have to leave testing your arithmetic for tonight. We shall disturb her if we stay here and I really daren't go back down to the school room. It's too near his office . . .' Louisa's voice trailed away, but Meg understood. 'Maybe tomorrow.'

'It's all right,' Meg smiled. 'I want to try to see me mam again before I go to bed.'

'Off you go then, dear,' Louisa waved her towards the door, then paused and said, 'Oh, just before you go, where is my watch?'

Meg pointed towards the chest. 'It's on the top there—' she began and then her mouth fell open in horror.

The watch was not there.

Nine

'Where is it? Where's my watch? What have you done with it?' Louisa's voice rose hysterically, no thought now for the sick Betsy or even the sleeping children in the dormitory. 'Have you stolen it?'

Thunderstruck and hurt beyond words that anyone could think such a thing of her, Meg gasped. She felt her face turning fiery red and knew that Louisa would see it as guilt.

'No,' she cried as, in the bed behind them, Betsy stirred and whimpered. But Meg was beyond caring too. 'How dare you accuse me of such a thing? I'd never take a penny that didn't belong to me. I'd starve first.' Dramatically, she held out her arms wide. 'You can search me. Go on, search me.'

'You'd hardly have it on you, would you?' Louisa muttered. 'You must have hidden it somewhere.'

In a moment the blossoming friendship between Meg and the young schoolmistress was torn asunder. Meg shook her head in fear and disbelief. What was happening to her? From living in a cosy cottage with her mother, father and brother she had been brought to this – a pauper cast into the workhouse by her own father, stripped of her clothes and possessions, separated from her family. And now, worse even than all that, she was being branded a thief.

She thrust her face towards Louisa. 'Well, I haven't.'

But Louisa stood her ground. 'Then where is it? You'd better find it and be quick about it.' The schoolmistress's pretty face was suddenly pale with anger, her eyes no longer soft and kindly, but dark with suspicion.

Wildly, Meg looked about her. What could have happened to the watch? Had someone crept into the room whilst she had been downstairs fetching Louisa? Had one of the children—?

Betsy stirred and murmured. 'Daddy – I want my daddy.'

Meg elbowed Louisa aside and wrenched back the covers. There, clutched in Betsy's small hands and held lovingly close to her heaving chest, lay Louisa's watch.

'So that's where you hid it.'

'I did not *hide* it,' Meg almost spat out the words. 'I told you – I left it on the top of the chest when I came to find you. Betsy must have reached for it.'

'Don't try to put the blame on this poor child. She's too ill to have got out of the bed.'

'Well, she can't have been. I did show it to her – I admit that – I held it to her ear and she listened to its ticking. She said it reminded her of her daddy because he had one like it. It seemed to comfort her because she fell asleep then.'

For a moment, Louisa stared at Meg then looked down at the watch and then back to Meg's face. She was struggling with her thoughts. Now that it had been found, she realized she had been far too hasty in her judgement.

'Oh, Meg, I'm sorry. I shouldn't have accused you. Please forgive me. I—'

Meg held up her hand, palms outwards. 'Oh no, don't start that. You called me a thief and I'll never forgive you. And don't expect me to help you any more.

Not—' she added slowly and deliberately, 'with *anything*.' She jerked her head towards the door and her meaning and gesture were clear. *Don't*, she was implying, *expect me to help you with the master*.

'Oh, Meg, please—'

'Don't "Oh, Meg" me!'

'But what about the school? What about you?'

'I wouldn't work for you if they *paid* me,' the girl said vehemently. With that, she moved towards the door.

'Meg, please don't go like this. Let's talk about it.'

'There's nothing to say. Too much has been said already.' With a worldly wisdom beyond her tender years, Meg said, 'You can't unsay what you said, Miss Daley.' She glanced back briefly. 'And don't you be taking it out on our Bobbie, 'cos if you do –' her eyes narrowed – 'you'll regret it.'

'You're hardly in a position to threaten me, Meg.'

'Oh, I'm not threatening you, miss. I'm *promising* you.'

Meg marched through the dormitory and out of the door at the far end, then ran lightly down the stairs. She paused for a moment outside the master's office, wondering if she dared to let him know that the child was not as bad as she had made out and that Louisa Daley was free.

But then she rejected the idea. It would only mean that she had to remain with the children and she didn't want to do that. She wanted to avoid having to see Louisa Daley any more than she was forced.

'Oh, Dad,' she murmured aloud, 'please come back for us soon and take us away from this place.'

*

Sarah's recovery was slow and made more so by the fact that she was sunk in misery and despair. Each day for the following week, flouting the rules, Meg visited her mother in the infirmary.

'I so wanted this baby,' Sarah whispered to Meg. 'I know it's an awful place for a child to be born, but – but I wanted something to remember your daddy by.'

Meg leant closer. 'What do you mean, Mam? You make it sound as if Dad isn't coming back.'

Sarah plucked nervously at the rough blanket covering her, her eyes downcast.

'Mam?' Meg prompted, but still her mother did not answer. She closed her eyes and lay back against the hard, lumpy pillow and sighed.

Meg went on. 'I'm sorry, Mam, but I'll have to go. I'm working in the gardens today.' True to her word, she had refused to enter the school room again. The morning after her quarrel with Louisa, she had marched boldly to the master's office and rapped sharply on the door.

'Come in, come in,' his voice had boomed and Meg opened the door and stepped up to his desk. Standing before him, she felt no fear; she was still smarting with anger from Louisa's unfair accusation.

'I'm sorry, sir,' she began with her most winning smile. She crossed her fingers behind her back at the lie she was about to tell, 'but I don't think I'm suited to teaching. I haven't got Miss Daley's patience.' That part, at least, was true. 'I think I'm better suited to working in the kitchens or even outside, sir. It's what I'm used to.'

Isaac frowned. 'Oh? And what makes you think you can pick and choose what job you do here? If I say you'll help in the school room, then help in the school room you will.'

Meg lowered her head so that he would not see the flash of anger in her green eyes. 'Yes, sir,' she said meekly. She waited, holding her breath. She risked glancing at him through her long eyelashes. He was regarding her thoughtfully. His chair creaked as he leant back in it and laced his fingers across his paunch.

His tone was deceptively mild as he asked, 'Have you displeased Miss Daley? The truth now, girl, because I can ask her, you know. And she –' he paused as if savouring the thought of the schoolmistress – 'will tell me.'

Quickly, as if the very idea appalled her, Meg said, 'Oh, I do hope not, sir. She's a lovely lady and I wouldn't want to upset her.' Meg was shocked by how easily the lies slipped from her lips. She had always prided herself on being truthful and honest, but if she were to be branded as no better than a thief and a liar just because her family had hit hard times, then . . .

Isaac smiled. 'I'm glad you think so, my dear. She is indeed a wonderful, wonderful young woman.' He ran his tongue around his lips. 'Then what is it?'

'It was last night, sir. When she – when you and she – when I was left alone with the children, specially with little Betsy, who was so sick. I – I was frightened of doing something wrong. Of – of displeasing you.'

'But help wasn't far away.' A hint of sarcasm entered his tone. 'As you so ably proved.'

'I know and I'm very sorry for spoiling your evening, sir. I should've fetched the matron, but being new here I didn't know what was the right thing to do and – and Miss Daley'd said that she was responsible for the children.' Meg babbled on, her fingers still tightly crossed, praying that the master would not question Louisa Daley about what had happened and why the new girl now didn't want the best job in the place but would rather scrub floors on her knees or work outside in all weathers. 'And besides,' Meg ended, 'I really don't think I'm clever enough.'

'Oh well.' Isaac shrugged his huge shoulders. 'In that case the guardians would have been unlikely to give their consent to the arrangement. So, we'd better find you something else to do, hadn't we?'

Now Meg explained to her mother. 'There's three of us girls they've let go into the gardens to do the weeding. I've been doing nothing but scrub floors and stone steps all week and it's been so good to be outdoors again today. The men and the boys do the heavy digging and the planting. Mind you, I could do the digging if they'd let me. Do you remember, Mam, how me and Miss Alice used to look after their vegetable patch?' The words were out before she had stopped to think.

Sarah gave a sob and turned her face away, burying it in the pillow.

'Mam – Mam – I'm sorry. I shouldn't have mentioned it.' Meg's voice faltered. 'I shouldn't have reminded you of the times when we were happy.' She touched her mother's shaking shoulder, castigating herself for her thoughtlessness. 'But we'll be happy again, Mam. I know we will. When Dad comes back . . .'

Her mother's sobs grew louder. The door opened and Miss Pendleton bustled in. 'Now, now, we can't have this. Have you been upsetting your mam, Kirkland? What have you been saying to her?'

Meg's expression was all innocence. 'I was just telling her I was working in the garden.'

'Ah yes.' Miss Pendleton pursed her lips. 'I don't approve of my brother making you young girls work out of doors. There's plenty of indoor work for you women.' She sniffed. 'But of course *I* have no say in the matter. But just you mind you keep your distance from the men because Isaac watches from the windows of his room.' She wagged her finger at Meg. 'He'll know if you get up to any shenanigans.' There was suddenly a strange, bitter note in her voice. 'Oh yes, he'll know, all right.'

Meg stood up and eased her aching back. The patch of earth near her feet was clear, though the other two girls were still squatting down, tearing weeds from the ground.

'That's my bit done ready for the men. I'll tell 'em, shall I?' Meg tossed her head towards where a man and a youth were pointing some of the brickwork in the wall. The youth was Jake.

Mary, one of the other girls, stood up. 'You'll get into trouble,' she warned as she glanced nervously towards the windows. 'He'll be watching.'

'Not if he's in his office on the ground floor. He can't see us from there,' Meg said reasonably.

Mary was still nervous. 'Yeah, but you don't know he's in his office, do you? He could be in his bedroom. He can see *everything* from up there.'

Meg gazed up at the first-floor windows in the centre of the building, where she knew the master's bedroom to be. 'Can't see him.'

'Huh,' Mary said scathingly as she picked up her bucket of weeds. 'He'll not let you see him, you daft 'aporth. He'll stand well back, but he'll be up there.

You mark my words. Come on, Kitty, 'ave yer finished? If madam here's going to get 'erself into trouble, I'm off. I don't want to be part of it.'

As the two girls walked away, Meg hid behind the trunk of a tree and beneath its branches. She peered up at the building. *If I can't see him*, she thought with a grin, *then he can't see me*.

'Jake,' she called softly. 'Jake!'

He looked round from where he was kneeling down, smoothing cement into cracks in the wall. She watched him searching for the owner of the voice, but he could not see her behind the tree trunk. Keeping a careful watch on the windows, Meg took a step from her hiding place. 'Jake,' she called again. 'Over here.'

Beneath the wall he, too, was hidden, but if he once stepped away from its shelter he could easily be seen from the second floor of the building.

She saw his quick grin as he got to his feet and moved to the end of the wall. Then he ran swiftly to the first tree and, like her, hid behind its trunk. Then he dodged from tree to tree until he was standing a few feet away from her. They each remained hidden behind a trunk, but they could talk.

'Jake, I'm so sorry about what happened before.'

He shrugged and grinned at her. 'Don't matter. I've 'ad plenty of beatings off of him in mi time. One more meks no difference.'

'Mebbe so,' she countered. 'But I don't like being the cause of you getting another.'

'Forget it. I have.' Then he smiled ruefully, ''Cept I've still got the stripes across mi backside.'

She grimaced in sympathy, then added, 'I just wanted to tell you that I'm getting out of here as soon as I can. I'm going to look for my dad.'

'You'll have to ask permission from the master,' Jake said. 'Do you think he'll let you go?'

Meg's face was grimly determined. 'He'd better 'cos I'm going whether he likes it or not!'

The boy looked envious for a moment. 'Wish I could get out of here an' all.'

'Well, why don't you? Why don't you come with me?'

He stared at her for a moment before a huge grin spread across his thin face. 'D'you know, I reckon I just might at that.'

Ten

'You go and ask him first,' Jake said.

'Getting cold feet?' Meg teased. It had taken them both a few days to pluck up courage to face the master.

'No.' His answer was swift. Too swift, for he avoided meeting her gaze. Meg realized it was a big step for the boy, who had never been beyond the workhouse walls.

'Look,' Meg said, serious now. 'I won't think any the worse of you if you do change your mind—'

'No,' he said firmly. 'I'm coming with you. It's time I got out of here. Don't know why I haven't done it before.'

Meg grinned. ''Cos you needed someone like me to give you a push, that's why.'

Soberly, Jake nodded. 'You could be right, at that.'

'I'm surprised they haven't *sent* you out before now. How old are you?'

'Sixteen.'

'Then why haven't they found work for you in the town?'

Jake shrugged then joked, ''Spect the matron wouldn't let them send her precious boy away.'

Meg laughed. 'Is that what she calls you? Her precious boy?'

'Yeah.' He looked embarrassed for a moment and then added, 'But she makes a fuss of all the little boys – not just me.'

'Perhaps you're special to her, though, if you've been here all your life.'

'Suppose so.' There was a pause before he added, 'Well? Are you going to ask him or what?'

'Please,' Meg began as she stood before Isaac Pendleton's desk, adopting what she hoped was her most winning smile, 'may I have your permission to leave the workhouse on Saturday?'

'Why?' Isaac's tone was not encouraging.

'I want to find my dad and tell him about Mam. I want to see if he's found work yet and I want him to come and see her. He can come to see her, can't he?'

Isaac leant his elbows on the desk and steepled his fingers together. 'We allow visits on Sunday afternoons, but under supervision in the committee room and only for one hour.'

Meg's instinct was to protest, but she nodded sensibly. 'I understand.'

Isaac appeared to be thinking. 'As long as you're not thinking of trying to remove your mother. She's still rather poorly and needs to rest.'

Meg shook her head. 'Oh no. Matron and the doctor are being very kind to her. It's just – just that I think my dad ought to know and – and about the baby.'

Isaac cleared his throat. 'Well – er – yes. Very well then, but you must be back here by six o'clock. Is that understood?'

'Oh yes, sir. Thank you, sir.'

Jake was not so fortunate in his request. 'Oh no, boy,' the master said at once. 'You're not going anywhere. At least, not –' he frowned as he added – 'on the same day as young Meg Kirkland.' He gave a hearty laugh, but somehow there was no humour in the sound. 'Think I don't know what the two of you are up to?'

Jake tried to adopt an innocent expression, but realizing he was failing he decided to be truthful. 'Yes, sir, I admit I did want to go the same day as M—'. He corrected himself quickly. 'Kirkland – because I thought she'd be able to help me. I've never been outside, sir, and – well – I wouldn't know how to go on.'

The big man moved towards Jake, who held his breath, half-expecting a clout around the ears. But Isaac put his hand on the boy's shoulder. 'We haven't always seen eye to eye, Bosley, but it might surprise you to know that actually I admire your spirit. I've felt it my duty to see that you were brought up properly. I've tried to be – well – a father figure for you.' He paused, as if expecting Jake to assure him that he had indeed been like a father and that he, Jake, would be eternally grateful. But no such words of appreciation were forthcoming from the boy. Jake could not imagine that a real father – however strict and stern – would have given him the beatings and sent him to the punishment cell with the same frequency that Isaac Pendleton had done.

'We would miss you if you left, especially,' Isaac added with emphasis, 'the matron. She has always – er – been good to you, hasn't she?' Now Jake was able to say with sincerity, 'Oh yes, sir, yes, she has,' for Letitia had been just what he imagined a mother would be. But Jake's heart sank. Was he expected to stay here the whole of his life?

Isaac cleared his throat. 'Of course the day will come when you must go out into the world and earn your own living. That day is not far away. Indeed, the guardians were only recently discussing the cases of several boys and girls of your age who really should no longer be a burden on the parish. You are fit and healthy and able to do a man's work now. Our only problem is – finding suitable employment for you.' He tapped the side of his nose. 'But never fear, Bosley, that is in hand at this very moment.'

'Yes, sir,' Jake's voice was hoarse. He didn't know whether to laugh or cry. He wanted to leave, oh, how he wanted to leave the workhouse and yet he didn't know what sort of a life awaited him beyond its walls.

Tentatively, he tried again. 'But don't you think, sir, that you could see your way clear to let me go out with Kirkland? Just for a day. Just to get the feel of – of what it's like out there.'

Isaac frowned. 'It wouldn't be right to let you go with a girl, Bosley. And especially, not with her. Not after what I witnessed the other day. Oh no. I couldn't trust you. Either of you. No, I'm sorry. The answer is "no".'

Later Jake told Meg. Her response shocked him. 'Then why don't you just come with me? Run away?'

'Where would we go?'

Meg thought a minute. 'We could go back to the farm where we used to live. Miss Alice would help me.' She bit her lip, unsure for a moment. Part of her did not want to think badly of her former friend. 'I still don't think she had anything to do with us being thrown out. I reckon it was her mam – or her dad. Not Alice.'

'Well, there's one way for you to find out,' Jake said.

Meg nodded solemnly. 'I intend to.'

'So, when are we going then?'

Meg's eyes shone. 'You'll do it? You'll come.'

Jake nodded. 'Even if we have to come back at night, I reckon it'll be worth a beating.'

'Saturday,' Meg said firmly. 'There's a race meeting

this Saturday and I'll bet anything that's where my dad will be.'

'Why?'

Patiently, Meg explained. 'Mi dad worked with horses – farm horses, of course – but Mr Smallwood often used to take mi dad with him to the races. The mester was a great one for the races. Dad used to say that Mr Smallwood wanted to buy a racehorse, but that the missis wouldn't let him. Anyway, Dad got to know a lot of the farmers who liked going to the meetings. He knew one or two of the racehorse owners, an' all. I reckon that's where he'll be trying to find work.'

Jake's eyes shone. 'I wouldn't mind working with 'osses.'

'There you are then,' Meg said triumphantly. 'We'll go to the races on Saturday.'

Jake grinned. 'I say, don't it sound grand?'

Meg thought it best not to tell either her mother or Bobbie what she intended to do. Bobbie might cry and make a fuss and beg to be taken too and Sarah would more than likely forbid her to go.

Very early on the Saturday morning, before it was even light and before anyone else was about, Meg crept out of the women's dormitory. Carrying her clothes, she slipped like a wraith down the stone stairs in her bare feet and into the tiny room where the washing benches were. Shivering, she splashed her face and hands with cold water and dressed quickly. Then she ran silently across the exercise yard at the front of the building to the privies at the far corner. When she had finished she crept along the wall to the door leading out into the gardens and the orchard. She held her breath a moment, fearing that it might be locked against her, but it opened with a creak. Meg glanced back at the windows of the building. No face – that she could see in this light – appeared and no light glowed. The inmates, the staff, and even the master were all still in their beds.

Carefully, she pulled the door shut behind her and narrowed her eyes, squinting through the poor light to see if Jake had yet appeared from the men's yard. The door from which Meg had emerged was at the end of the wall nearest to the path running down at the side of the orchard and leading out onto the main road into the town. Jake would come out of one of the doors furthest away from the path. She was about to move stealthily along the wall when a sound behind her made her jump.

'Psst. I'm here.' Jake hissed and Meg turned to see him peeping round the corner of the wall.

She went to him. 'You ready?'

'Ready as I'll ever be, but I reckon I'll be in trouble tonight. I'll've missed roll-call. I've got one of the lads to answer for me, but if he's spotted, he'll get a thrashing an' all.'

Meg laughed softly. 'Mebbe you won't be coming back tonight. Mebbe you won't ever be coming back again. Come on, let's not stand here chatting. Time we was on our way before anyone else gets up.'

She grabbed his hand and they ran down the path and onto the road. Not until they had turned the corner and were out of sight of the workhouse, did they both breathe more easily.

They turned to each other and laughed aloud.

'We did it. We really did it!' Jake shouted joyously and began to caper along the grass verge at the side of the road. 'I'm free. I'm free. Look at me, I'm free.'

Meg laughed and skipped along beside him. The night

her father had told them that the whole family had to leave their home Meg's life had changed dramatically. But now, as the sun rose behind them, streaking the eastern sky with apricot light, Meg dared to feel happy again.

After Jake's euphoria at being out of the workhouse had settled down, he asked, 'Where are we going first then?'

'The farm,' Meg replied determinedly.

As they walked the five miles to Middleditch Farm, the sun came up.

'Going to be a nice day,' Meg remarked, but all she got out of Jake was a grunt. He was saying little, too preoccupied with looking about him, drinking in the sights and sounds and even the smells of the countryside. A farmer's horse and cart passed them and Jake stood back on the grass verge, as close to the hedge as he could get, eyeing the big shire with trepidation.

'I thought you said you liked horses,' Meg teased.

'Not a big bugger like that!' Jake burst out.

'Language,' Meg admonished playfully. 'What would Miss Pendleton say if she heard you?'

Jade grinned and stepped back into the road as the horse clip-clopped away. 'She'd pat my head and tell me not to be a naughty boy.'

'Wouldn't she report you to her brother?'

Jake guffawed. 'What? The matron? Report me? Or any of the boys? Never.'

'Why not?'

Jake glanced at her. 'You ain't been here long enough to understand the set-up, have you?'

'What do you mean? The set-up?'

'The master likes the ladies – and the girls. All of 'em. He's kind and generous to them, but us fellers, well, he'd take his cane to any one of us or send us to the punishment room soon as look at us. But Miss Pendleton – well – she likes the little boys. Oh, she's no time for the men. Wouldn't give them the time of day, but she loves the lads. Mek a good pair, don't they, the Pendletons?'

The memory of the matron taking Bobbie away, separating the little boy from his family, was vivid in Meg's mind. She stopped suddenly and stared at Jake. She wasn't quite sure why and couldn't have put it into words, but all at once she felt very uncomfortable about the matron's actions. 'What – what do you mean, she *likes* the little boys?'

'Eh?' Jake stopped too and turned to face her. Puzzled, he stared at her for a moment. Then his expression cleared and he laughed. 'Oh, she doesn't do owt funny with them, if that's what you're thinking.'

'I – I don't quite know what I am thinking. It – it just sounded a bit odd. You know.'

Jake nodded. He possessed a depth of understanding that was surprising not only for his age, but also considering the fact that he had spent his entire life within the confines of the workhouse. But, Meg supposed, being in the company of older men he must have heard and learnt a lot. As if answering her unspoken question, he said, 'Funny sort of life, I suppose, being an orphan and brought up in that place, but you meet all sorts. The inmates are mostly nice to us kids and – well—' He looked down and scuffed the toe of his boot on the road in embarrassment. 'I suppose the matron is the nearest us kids've got to a mam.'

Meg was thoughtful for a moment before she said

slowly, 'I suppose so and, if I think about it, that's what mams do.'

'What?'

Meg grinned. 'Protect their kids from the father if he's the strict sort.'

Jake's mouth dropped open. 'Well, I wouldn't like Mester Pendleton as my dad.' He recalled his recent conversation with the master. 'Mebbe that's how he likes to think of himself, but he's not *my* idea of a dad.'

'No.' Meg's agreement was heartfelt. 'Nor mine.' She had mixed feelings about her father at the moment. She still felt very bitter about the way he had deserted his family, but, trying to give him the benefit of the doubt, she thought that perhaps it wasn't his fault. *Maybe*, she thought with dread, *it was mine and I might be about to find out*. As they rounded a bend, Meg said, 'This is it. This is where we used to live. Middleditch Farm.'

Eleven

'What are you going to do?' Jake asked, his eyes wide as he stared around the farmyard.

Hens scratched for food, pigs grunted and squealed in a nearby sty and from the cowhouse came the clanking of buckets, the sounds of morning milking.

'See the missis first.' Meg squinted at the sun to gauge the time. 'She'll be in the dairy by now.' She turned to Jake. 'Come as far as the door with me, but don't step inside. She's a tartar for things being kept clean is the missis.'

Obediently, Jake followed Meg as she marched towards the door of a building attached to the farmhouse.

'Wait here,' she told him as she cleaned her boots on a metal scraper. Then she pushed open the door and peered inside. Mrs Smallwood was already busy with the first batch of warm milk and didn't hear the door open and close. Meg walked towards her.

'Missis—' Meg began. The woman jumped and the heavy container of milk began to slip from her grasp. Meg leapt forward and steadied it, saving it from being dropped and all the precious milk being lost. But she was unprepared for the vitriolic look in the woman's eyes as Mrs Smallwood recovered her senses and realized who had startled her.

'You!' she gasped and snatched the container out of

Meg's grasp, slopping milk onto the floor. 'Get out of my sight. You're not wanted here. You or your blasted family.'

Now Meg gasped with shock. 'What did I do wrong? Please – tell me. What was it I did that was so terrible you threw us all out?'

The woman avoided Meg's direct gaze, but the pleading tone and the genuine bewilderment in the girl's voice must have touched even Mabel Smallwood's hardened heart.

She banged the metal milk churn to the floor. 'I – I didn't like your friendship with our – our Alice.'

It was an excuse, Meg could tell. It was not the truth – at least, not the whole truth – but the young girl could hardly challenge the lie. All she could say was, 'But if only you'd told me, missis, serious like, I mean. I'd – I'd have stopped it.'

Now Mabel met her gaze. 'I doubt it.'

'Then – then why didn't you just sack me? Why did it have to be my dad as well? Did you really have to turn our whole family out of our home just because I was too friendly with your daughter?'

The woman's patience snapped and now she shouted out the truth. 'It wasn't you. It wasn't you at all. It was your father – God rot him!'

'My – my dad? What – what did he do?'

Mabel glared at her, resentment in her eyes, her mouth tight with bitterness. 'You'll find out. Oh, you'll find out soon enough.' She turned her back on Meg in final dismissal.

'But—'

'Clear off.' Mabel waved her hand driving the girl away. 'Just leave. I don't want to talk about it any more.'

Daringly, Meg stood her ground. 'I want to see Alice. I want—'

Mabel whirled round on her, waving her arms above her head and yelling. 'Get out of here, I say. Get out.'

Meg went. Outside the dairy, she stood, white-faced and shaking.

'Whatever was all that about?' Jake asked. 'I could hear 'er shrieking from here.'

Meg bit her lip and glanced back at the closed door. 'I'm not sure. But at least I've found out one thing.'

'What's that?'

'It wasn't me that caused all the trouble. It was mi dad.' She shook her head slowly, as if she couldn't really take it in. 'Goodness knows what he could have done that was so bad. The missis has always had a sharp tongue, but now . . .' Meg's voice faded away.

As they moved away across the yard towards the gate back onto the road, Jake felt a horrible sense of foreboding, as if no good would come of this visit. He was suddenly afraid for Meg and what she might find out.

'So, what do we do now?'

Meg frowned and glanced about her. 'If the mester's about—'

'Oho, you're asking fer trouble now. If the missis is like that, what's he going to be like?'

'He's not as bad as her.' Her face cleared. 'He'll be in the cowhouse, milking. Come on.'

This time, they both stepped into the building. For a moment Meg paused, breathing in the familiar smells. With all that had happened, she hadn't realized just how much she'd missed the farm.

Glancing a little fearfully at the restless cows in the stalls, Jake, close behind her, whispered, 'Is that him?'

Halfway down the row, they could just see the back of a man sitting on a stool, his head resting against the cow's belly, his hands moving rhythmically as he drew the milk.

Meg shook her head. 'No, that's not him.'

The sound of her voice must have reached the man, for he stood up and turned towards them.

'Hey,' Jake said loudly. 'It's Ron from the workhouse. Hello, Ron. So this is where you've been disappearing to every day.'

The man, tall, thin and slightly stooping, grinned and began to move towards them.'

'Best move yer bucket, mister, else she'll have it over, will Buttercup,' Meg advised.

'Oh aye, right you are.' He bent and picked up the bucket from beneath the cow and moved it to safety. 'What you doing 'ere, young Jake? Come fer a job, 'ave yer?'

Jake grinned. 'Wish I had, Ron. No, I've – I've come out without permission. You won't tell, will yer?'

'Course I won't.' He glanced from one to the other. 'But what *are* you doing here?' His face clouded. 'You ain't come looking fer me. There's nowt wrong wi' mi missis back at the house, is there?'

Jake shook his head. 'I've come with Meg. She used to work here. Used to live here till these folks turned her whole family out. She's come to try to find out where 'er dad is.'

The man scratched his head. 'Well, there's no one else here 'cept me an' the mester and the missis, of course. He took me on a couple of days ago and I'm right grateful. He ses if I prove miself, he'll let us have a cottage he's got vacant. Eh, but it'll be grand to fetch me missis and the bairns out o' that place.'

Meg's eyes filled with tears and there was a sudden lump in her throat. 'That'd be our cottage.'

Ron looked awkward and shuffled his feet.

'It's all right,' Meg said swiftly. 'You tek it, if you get the chance. They're hardly likely to let us back. Anyway,' she went on, trying to sound bright and hopeful even though she felt anything but, 'where's Mr Smallwood? I'll talk to him. Or Miss Alice. Is she about?'

'The mester's gone to the races. Went early, he did.' Now a mystified expression crossed Ron's face. 'And Miss – who did you say?'

'Miss Alice. Their daughter.'

Ron shook his head. 'There's nobody else here. Only Mr and Mrs Smallwood. There's no daughter living here. Not that I've seen.'

'Maybe you just haven't seen her if you've only been here a couple of days,' Jake put in.

But it was Meg who shook her head now. 'Oh no, if she was here, you'd have seen her all right.'

Now Meg was more mystified than ever.

Although the racing wasn't due to start until the early afternoon, the ground was already humming with activity.

'I just can't understand what can have happened to Miss Alice,' Meg murmured, still puzzled.

'Maybe she's just gone on holiday,' Jake suggested, trying to be helpful. Not that he had any personal experience of holidays, but he had heard them talked about. Miss Pendleton sometimes went on holiday to visit her sister, who lived in London. At such times Jake had tried to keep out of the master's way as much as possible when his champion was not there.

'The Smallwoods don't have holidays. They hardly ever leave the farm and then only for a day. I've never known any one of them go away for longer than that.'

Jake had run out of suggestions, so they walked on towards the stables in silence.

Horses were arriving early to give their stable lads time to settle them into the surroundings. The trainers would arrive a little later in time to walk the course so they could advise their jockeys on how to run the race.

'Why's this Mr Smallwood come so early if it don't start till this afternoon?' Jake asked.

'He likes to mingle with the trainers and talk to the owners. I told you, he fancies being an owner one day.' Meg bit her lip. 'He always promised mi dad that he'd put him in charge of his racehorse – if he ever got one.'

Wide-eyed with wonder, Jake was staring about him. 'I wonder if there's any jobs as stable lads going?'

Meg laughed. 'You're frightened of horses. What good would you be?'

Jake grinned. 'I could learn. It's only 'cos I've never had the chance to be around them.' He narrowed his eyes and watched a young lad leading a sleek chestnut past. 'Beautiful animals, aren't they?'

'Yeah,' Meg agreed. Her eyes were misty as her gaze followed the magnificent creature. 'Dad once said that if I'd been a boy he'd've tried to get me a job as a stable lad.'

'Would you have liked that?'

Meg nodded and her voice was husky as she answered, 'Yeah. Yeah, I would.'

They wandered around the ground unchallenged. Meg had got them in through a break in the fence she knew about. 'I used to beg mi dad to take me with them when they came to the races, but he never would. Said the master and the missis wouldn't approve. But I used to skive off school and come anyway. It was more difficult when I was working at the farm. There was more work for me when the master and Dad were away for the whole day.' She grinned widely. 'But I managed it a few times.'

'Did they ever catch you?' Jake's life was ruled by the fear of getting caught doing something wrong. The threat of Isaac Pendleton was never far away. Even though he was at this moment enjoying himself as never before in his young life, the day was marred by the thought of the punishment he would get if he was found out. And he was sure that he would be.

Suddenly, Meg clutched Jake's arm. 'Quick, turn round and keep walking.'

'Why? What's—' Jake began but found himself being dragged round and propelled in the opposite direction.

'It's the mester.'

Jake turned pale. 'Not – not Mr Pendleton?'

'No. Mr Smallwood.'

Jake glanced over his shoulder towards the burly figure of the farmer, standing close to the rails. He was talking to two other men and they were laughing heartily.

'But I thought you *wanted* to speak to him? You were looking for him at the farm.'

'Well, yes. And maybe I will. Later. But if I speak to him now he'll likely get us sent out of here. And I want to stay a bit longer.' She thought quickly. 'Look, if anybody ses anything to us – asks us what we're doing here, just tell 'em – just tell 'em that – that you're stable lad for Mr Smith.'

'Who's Mr Smith when he's at home?'

'He's one of the biggest owners and he employs a lot

of stable lads. No one'll know whether you're really one of his or not.'

'Wish I was,' Jake muttered. 'But what about you?'

'Say I'm your sister and you've brought me along for the day.' She grinned. 'With Mr Smith's permission, of course.'

Jake still looked doubtful, but he nodded.

Meg glanced briefly over her shoulder. 'We're out of his sight now, I reckon, and . . .'

She stopped suddenly and clutched Jake's arm again.

'I wish you'd stop doing that, Meg. You ain't 'alf got a grip on you, for a girl. It hurts. Gerroff.'

Meg's gaze was fixed on a figure walking towards them.

'There, look,' she cried excitedly and pointed with a trembling finger. 'That's mi dad.'

She plunged forward, dragging Jake with her. 'Dad, Dad—' she began.

Then suddenly she stopped. She felt as if someone had thumped her hard just below her ribs and knocked all the breath from her body. Her eyes widened in shock and she gasped. The colour drained from her face and her grip on Jake's arm slackened.

Jake pulled free and rubbed his arm where her strong fingers had dug deep. 'Where? Which one is he?' He followed the line of her startled gaze and saw a tall, thin man walking towards them. He was dressed in what was obviously his Sunday best suit and he carried his cap in his hand. His light brown hair was ruffled by the breeze, but he was unaware for he had eyes for nothing and no one except the person walking beside him. He had his arm around the shoulders of a fair-haired young woman and they were looking into each other's eyes as they walked and laughing together. The sound of the girl's tinkling, flirtatious laugh reached Meg and Jake. The man bent towards the woman and touched her forehead with his lips.

Beside him, Jake heard Meg's strangled whisper. 'Miss Alice. It's mi dad and Miss Alice.'

Twelve

As if drawn by Meg's intense gaze, Reuben Kirkland's eyes met hers. He stopped and, puzzled, for she had not yet noticed Meg, Alice looked up at him. Then she too saw what had caught and held his attention. For a moment, all four of them stared at one another and then Meg leapt forward, covering the distance between them in an instant.

She launched herself at her father and pummelled his chest, crying and shrieking. 'How could you? How could you do this? And with her? Of all people, with *her*!'

Reuben caught hold of her flailing fists and tried to hold her, but her rage lent her strength and now Meg turned upon Alice. She grabbed the girl's hair and yanked it from its pins as if she would wrench it from her head.

'You slut! You trollop, you – you—' The vulgar names tumbled from her mouth until there was a small crowd gathering around them. Alice retaliated with a few punches of her own, one catching Meg on the mouth and drawing blood from her lip. At last Reuben pulled his daughter away from Alice, who was now crying and trembling.

Jake did nothing. He certainly wasn't going to help the man. If he'd done anything, he would have waded in beside Meg, but she seemed to be doing very nicely, thank you, on her own. If the scene had not been so obviously traumatic for Meg, it was comical. In fact, several uninvolved onlookers were laughing.

'Better than a peep show, this is,' Jake heard one remark.

'Aye, I like to see two women having a scrap,' another agreed. 'Much more fun than fellers.'

Holding the panting women apart, Reuben glanced about him. 'Show's over, folks,' he said grimly. 'Come on, let's go somewhere quieter where we can talk.'

'Talk?' Meg screamed. 'Talk? What is there to talk about? I see it all now. No wonder me poor mam seemed so – so defeated. All her spirit gone. She must have known and I thought it was just 'cos she was expecting an' . . .' A bitter smile came to Meg's mouth as she added sarcastically, 'Oh, and by the way she had the bairn. But you'll be pleased to know it was born dead.'

Reuben had the grace to wince. 'I never wished that on her, Meggie.'

'Don't call me that,' Meg spat at him. Angry tears filled her eyes and there was a catch in her voice as she added, 'Don't ever call me that again.'

Reuben's eyes were anguished. 'Meg, please try to understand. Alice and I fell in love. We – we have to be together.'

'That's why you got the sack, isn't it? Because of her?'

Seeing she was a little calmer now, Reuben relaxed his hold on his daughter and put his arms around Alice. Seeing his action, Meg felt sick. Alice clung to him, her blue eyes full of tears and her hair wild and fluffy about her face.

'They found out, Alice's mam and dad,' Reuben said.

'And so they threw us all out,' Meg added bitterly.

'And me.' Alice spoke up for the first time. 'They threw me out an' all.'

'My heart bleeds for you,' Meg fired back. For a moment she closed her eyes and shook her head, still hardly able to grasp the truth. 'I thought you were my friend, Alice. How could you do this to me? To all my family? To my mam and to little Bobbie? How could you stand by and see us put in the workhouse? You were my one hope. It was really you I came looking for today. I thought if there was anyone who would try to help us, it'd be you.'

'Like your dad says, we fell in love. I love your dad and he loves me and we want to be together, no matter what.'

Slowly Meg nodded. 'No matter who gets hurt, eh? You don't care about anybody but yourselves, do you? Well, I hope you rot in hell, the pair of you.'

Rage carried her through, held her up whilst she turned her back on them and marched away. With one last glance at them, Jake turned and followed Meg.

It wasn't until they had reached and crawled through the hole in the fence that Meg sat on the ground. She drew her knees up, wrapped her arms around them and dropped her head, hiding her face against her skirt. Her shoulders heaved with racking sobs.

Jake could think of nothing to say so he sat beside her and put his arms about her. They stayed like that until Meg's weeping subsided. At last she raised her face, ravaged by tears, and whispered, 'I'll never trust anyone ever again.'

*

A little later, Meg, calmer now, said, 'We might as well go back. There's nothing else to stay out here for.'

'Suppose not,' Jake agreed reluctantly. 'But I was enjoying miself. At least,' he added swiftly, 'I was until that happened.'

Meg tried to smile, but it was a feeble effort. At this moment she felt as if she would never smile properly again.

'Come on then,' Jake said, scrambling up. 'If we can sneak back in before dinner time, we just might get away with it.'

'I needn't sneak in. I had permission,' she reminded him.

Jake wrinkled his brow thoughtfully. 'Tell you what, I'll go in through the hole in the hedge into the orchard and start working there.' He grinned swiftly at her. 'You're not the only one who knows about holes in things to get in and out.'

There was no answering smile from Meg, but she did ask, 'I thought you said you'd never been out before?'

'*I* haven't, but I know a few who have.' He paused and then asked, 'Do – do you think you could leave it a bit before you come back in? Just – just so it doesn't look as if we've been out together. If I have been missed, then—'

'Course I will. I don't want you to get another thrashing. I feel bad enough about the one you did get.'

'Don't.' Jake grinned and squeezed her arm. 'You've got more than enough to worry about without thinking about me.' He bit his lip and looked at her uncertainly, then away.

'What?' she asked, realizing that there was still something on his mind.

'Look, Meg, would you mind . . . ? I mean, while we've been sitting here, I've been thinking—'

'While I've been making a complete fool of miself,' she said bitterly.

'No.' Jake's tone was gentle. 'You haven't made a fool of yourself. You could never do that. Not to me.' He pulled her close and for a moment she rested her head against his shoulder.

'Good job old Pendleton can't see us now,' Jake murmured as he bent his head. With the awkwardness of youth and the clumsiness of the first time, he kissed her. Startled, Meg drew back and stared at him.

'Sorry,' Jake mumbled, his face fiery red.

'No.' Meg took his hand. 'Don't say that,' she whispered. There was an awkward pause between them before Meg prompted, 'What was it you wanted to ask me?'

On safer ground, Jake's embarrassment subsided. 'I just wondered if you'd mind if I had a talk to Ron when he comes home tonight. See if there's any jobs going at that farm.'

'Why should I mind?'

'It just seemed – well – a bit unkind to be trying to get a job there when the only reason there might be one going is because you got the sack.'

Meg's mouth was tight as she said, 'Don't you worry about that, Jake. You go ahead. Don't bother about me or anybody else. You look out for yourself.' Her tone was icy as she added, 'It's what I'm going to do from now on. Me, miself and I – that's who I'm going to look after,' she declared and, as a hasty afterthought, she added, 'And mi Mam and Bobbie, of course.'

*

On her return to the workhouse, Meg worked with a fury. She scrubbed the stone steps of the staircases and the flags of the passageways until her knees were sore and her hands bleeding. Her tears were gone. She refused to cry over her father ever again, but there was a heavy feeling in her chest as if a huge lump was stuck there.

When she walked into the women's day room for her supper, she was surprised yet gladdened to see her mother sitting beside the fire. Miss Pendleton was bustling around Sarah, tucking a rug around her knees and handing her some socks.

'We have to do all the mending for the men. Not much use at that sort of thing – men. You're not fit to do heavy work yet, but you can darn these.' At that moment, Miss Pendleton caught sight of Meg. 'And look who's here. Your girl's back.' She raised her voice. 'Had a nice time out, Kirkland? Did you find yourself a job?'

Meg bit her lip and shook her head.

'Ah well, not to worry. Tell you what,' the woman added as a thought came into her mind, 'next time you get permission to go out, go into the town to the tailor's shop. It's owned by a Mr Rodwell. He's walking out with a friend of mine – Miss Finch.' The woman paused and laughed loudly. 'Mind you, they've been engaged for five or six years and there's still no sign of wedding bells. Anyway, I hear he's looking for a young woman to work in his shop. He's started to stock ladies' underwear and finds a lot of his customers are too embarrassed to be served by a man. Tell him I sent you, Kirkland.'

Meg tried to smile as she thanked the matron politely.

Letitia Pendleton nodded. 'You can sit and talk to

your mam for a bit, but,' she added, handing Meg a pile of socks too, 'you can make yourself useful while you're doing it. And now I must see to my little boys.'

As she began to move away, Sarah looked up with pleading eyes. 'Matron, how is Bobbie? Please – can I see him?'

'Not today, Kirkland. You'll see him tomorrow when the chaplain comes to hold the Sunday service in the committee room – your little lad can spend the rest of the afternoon with you.' Letitia's eyes softened. 'He's a grand little chap. I've quite taken to him. Don't you worry. I'll look after him.'

As soon as the woman had left the room, Sarah whispered, 'Meg, have you seen Bobbie? Is he all right?'

Meg shook her head. 'No, Mam, not today. I – I've been out.'

Sarah nodded, 'Yes, I heard the matron say so. You've been looking for work?'

'Well,' Meg said slowly, 'not exactly. I – I went looking for Dad.'

Sarah seemed to slump in her chair and some of the socks slid from her lap. She closed her eyes and gave a low moan. 'Oh, Meggie, I wish you hadn't done that.'

There was silence and Meg bit her lip as she watched the anguish on her mother's face. Sarah was silent, asking no questions. If she had been in her mother's place, the questions would have been tumbling out of her mouth. *Did you see him? Has he found work? When is he coming back for us? And when – oh, when – can we get out of this place?*

But Sarah asked nothing and sat with her head in her hands. Now Meg was sure. 'Mam? You knew, didn't you? You knew about – about *her*?' Meg couldn't even bring herself to speak her former friend's name, so great was the hurt of Alice's betrayal.

Sarah sighed heavily and admitted, 'Yes, yes, I knew.'

'How long has it been going on?'

'I don't know. I've known for about a month, but it must have been going on a lot longer than that.' She paused and then whispered, 'Oh, Meggie, I wish you hadn't found out. Don't hate him—'

'Don't hate him?' Meg's voice rose and some of the other women looked up, but the girl was oblivious to their curious glances. 'Oh, I hate him all right. And her. I hate them both. But don't you worry, Mam. I'll get a job and I'll get us out of here. You, me and Bobbie.'

She jumped up and piled the socks she had been given to darn onto her mother's lap. 'I'll go right now and see the master.'

'Oh, Meg—' Sarah began, but her daughter was paying no heed.

She planted a kiss on her mother's forehead and patted her hand. 'Don't worry, Mam. I'll take care of everything.'

She turned away and was about to hurry across the room when the door was flung open and the man she sought stood there, filling the frame.

'Good evening, ladies, good evening. And how are we all on this fine night?'

Feet shuffled and chairs scraped as all the women stood up and chorused, 'Good evening, Master.' Even Sarah struggled to her feet, the socks spilling from her knee.

'Sit down, sit down, ladies, do,' Isaac boomed and glanced around the room. His gaze came to rest on Sarah as she sank back into her chair. Meg bent and retrieved the socks from the floor.

Isaac pulled up a chair and sat down beside Sarah.

'Sir,' Meg began, 'I was just coming to see you. Please – may I have your permission to go out again on Monday?'

'Ah, well now, I don't know about that. We can't have you going out too often, Kirkland. Your poor mother needs you here.' He took hold of Sarah's hand and held it.

Meg was sure she heard stifled laughter from the women behind her, but the girl was too intent on her goal to worry about it at the moment. 'Matron has given me the name of someone who might give me a job.'

Isaac turned his watery blue eyes on Sarah. 'What do you say, my dear?' he asked smoothly, still holding her hand. 'Shall we let her go, eh?'

'If you please, sir,' Sarah said softly, 'I'd be very grateful. Meg is a good girl and is only trying to look after us.'

Isaac started back, pretending shock. 'Oh, my dear lady, you wound me deeply. Don't you think that is what we're trying to do here? To look after you?'

Sarah lowered her head and said huskily, 'Yes, yes, of course, I didn't mean . . .'

Isaac patted her hand and laughed. 'No, no, of course, you didn't. I was only teasing. Of course, she can go.'

Despite the turmoil of the day, Meg rewarded the master with her widest smile, which lit up her green eyes and dimpled her cheeks. 'Thank you, Master.'

The master gazed at her and, as she dipped a curtsy and moved towards the door, Isaac murmured, 'By, but she'll be a beauty one day and no mistake.'

Hearing him, the girl's mother shuddered.

Thirteen

After supper most of the women, weary from their day's work, began to drift up to the dormitory.

'I'll just get some more coal in, Mam,' Meg said. 'You go on up. I shan't be long.'

Carrying the coal bucket, Meg slipped down the stairs and across the yard towards the coal store. It was the one building in the row that stood between the men's and women's yards and was accessible from both. She and Jake had arranged to meet there under cover of darkness.

'There you are.' His voice came out of the blackness. 'I thought you weren't coming.'

'The master came to the day room and then there was supper. I couldn't get away.'

'Like I told you. He likes the women.'

'He seems to have taken a fancy to me mam. He was sitting beside her, holding her hand.'

'You want to watch him.'

'But I thought he was after Miss Daley.'

Jake laughed softly. 'He's after owt in skirts. But I don't reckon he'll get far with the schoolmarm. She's sweet on the doctor.'

Meg was thoughtful. 'Mm. I noticed that.'

Side by side they shovelled coal.

'Look, we still might get caught meeting here,' Jake whispered. 'Next time, let's meet in the dead room.'

Meg was startled. 'The what?'

'It's a room right at the end of this row of buildings in the men's yard, where they put the dead 'uns.' She saw his white, even teeth shining through the gloom as he grinned. 'There's only empty coffins in there.'

Meg shuddered. 'You sure?'

'Well, not *all* the time. If someone dies—'

'Ugh!'

'But it's safe. No one'll go in there.'

'Don't blame 'em,' she muttered, with feeling. She paused and then added, 'All right then. Anything to save you another thrashing. Did you get into trouble today?'

'No, I was lucky. I slipped into the orchard and started working and nobody seemed to have missed me.'

'Not even Miss Pendleton?' Meg asked saucily.

She heard his low chuckle. 'No, though she did say, "I haven't seen you all day," at suppertime. Gave me a right scare. I thought she was going to ask where I'd been. And I can't lie – specially not to her.' He leant closer. 'They reckon the reason she makes such a fuss of the lads is 'cos years ago, when she was a young girl, she had a baby boy.'

Meg gasped. 'What? You mean – you mean she wasn't married?'

'Yeah.'

'What happened to it?'

'Don't know. Mebbe it died or was taken away from her. You know, adopted.'

'Or maybe,' Meg said thoughtfully, 'it was sent to the workhouse.'

Jake stared at her through the darkness. 'I'd never thought of that.'

'So that's why she loves all the little boys who come in here.' Meg felt a sudden surge of sympathy for the woman. 'Poor old Letitia.'

Jake chuckled softly. 'Daft name, isn't it? What parents in their right mind would call their daughter "Letitia"?'

Meg was defensive. 'I think it's quite a pretty name. Besides, Isaac's not much better.'

'Yeah, but his name does suit him. Look, I'll have to be off. Don't want to get caught now, seeing as I got away with mi little expedition into the big wide world.'

'Did you enjoy it?'

He was solemn now. 'I would have if it hadn't been for meeting your dad and you being so upset.'

'Seems mi mam has known about his carryings on for a month or more,' Meg said bitterly and added incredulously, 'And she doesn't seem to blame him.'

'What? Do you mean she doesn't *mind*?'

'Oh, she minds all right, but she said to me, "Don't blame him, Meg." I can't understand her. I really can't. If I was her, I'd want to kill 'em both.' Beneath her breath she muttered, 'I felt like it anyway.'

There was silence between them for a while, the only sounds the scraping of the metal shovels on the stone floor and the tumbling of pieces of coal into the buckets.

'Anyway, I'm going out again on Monday. Miss Pendleton's given me the name of someone who might give me a job.'

'Well, good luck. Wish I could find one.'

'Have you spoken to Ron yet?'

'No.'

'Why not?'

'I – I dunno, really.'

'Jake,' Meg said firmly, 'just do it.'

'Matron –' Meg stood before Letitia Pendleton on the Monday morning and adopted her most docile and pleading expression – 'do you think I could be allowed to wear my own clothes? Just today. The master has given me permission to go and see Mr Rodwell and – and seeing as he's a friend of yours, or rather a friend of your friend – I do want to be a credit to you.'

Letitia laughed and her chins wobbled. 'I see. Workhouse uniform not good enough for you, eh?'

Meg caught the twinkle in the older woman's eyes and said coyly, 'But I scrub floors in these clothes, Matron.'

'No disgrace in honest hard work.' Letitia pondered for a moment and then said, 'Very well, then. See Waters and tell her you have my permission.'

'Oh, I don't know about that. It's most unusual.' Ursula pursed her thin lips with disapproval.

'But matron said I could.'

'Strikes me you're trying to hide the fact that you come from the workhouse. Trying to fool a would-be employer into thinking you're better than you are.'

'Of course I'm not,' Meg replied heatedly. 'Miss Pendleton's recommended me to go and see this Mr Rodwell. That's hardly hiding the fact that I'm here, is it? Ask her, ask the matron if you don't believe me.'

Ursula sniffed. 'She's not here to ask. She's gone out for the day.' She made no move to find Meg's belongings.

'Well, who would you believe? Mr Pendleton?' Meg persisted.

'We mustn't worry the master about such a matter.'

'Yes, we must, if you're not going to let me have them.' Meg reached out and grabbed hold of Ursula's thin arm. 'Come on. We'll go and see him this very minute.'

To the older woman's consternation, she found herself being dragged out of the storeroom, across the men's yard and into the door leading directly to the master's office. 'Kirkland, I don't think we should—'

'You should have thought about that before you refused to obey the matron's orders.' Meg paused briefly and stuck her face close to Ursula's. 'And they *were* her orders.'

'Oh well, in that case—'

'No, no. Too late now. We'll ask the master and we'll do what he says. Whatever it is.' Meg had already raised her hand to knock on the door, but now Ursula reached up and grasped hold of it.

'No – please – don't. I don't want to cause trouble.'

'You don't want to cause trouble for yourself, you mean. You couldn't care less about me. But I bet you've suddenly realized that the master – new though I am here – will take my side.'

Suddenly, Ursula's face twisted into ugliness. 'Of course he will. He can't resist a pretty face. Well, let me tell you something. When I first came here, I was young and pretty too. Oh yes, you can hardly believe it, can you? Well, it's true. And he couldn't resist *me*. But now I'm older, he's cast me aside and he's after the younger ones.' Now it was Ursula who hissed in Meg's face. 'You want to watch out for yourself else you'll end up like me. But why should I care? I'll get you your clothes and much good may they do you.'

She twisted her arm out of Meg's grasp and went back the way they had come, with Meg following her more slowly.

It felt wonderful to Meg to be dressed in her own clothes again; to feel soft underwear against her skin instead of the rough, scratchy garments the workhouse provided. She'd lost weight since coming here and her dress hung loosely on her, but beneath her shawl it didn't show too badly. The clothes had been crumpled when Ursula handed them to her, but the use of a hot iron in the wash house had made them look much better.

Meg paused at the porter's lodge. 'Albert, I have permission to go out. I'm going after a job.'

The old man hauled himself out of his chair and limped to open the gate for her. He remembered the lass coming in with her mam and her little brother. The poor woman had been heavy with child and now, by all accounts, she'd lost the bairn.

'You look as pretty as a picture, mi duck,' he told Meg, knowing she would not sneer at him daring to compliment her. Not like some of the women in here who laughed in his face if he even spoke to them. Trollops, the lot of 'em, to his mind, but not this lass and her mam. They were a nice family. 'Mind you're back by six o'clock, won't yer? Shouldn't like to see you in trouble.'

Meg smiled at him, dimpling prettily. 'I will, Albert.'

As he closed the gate behind her, she turned and waved and he called, 'Good luck wi' yer job.'

There was a spring in Meg's step as she walked down

the long cinder path to the road. She breathed in deeply, savouring the fresh morning air. Oh, what it was to be free, out in the open. She hadn't realized just how much the workhouse confined her. How damp and cold and oppressive it was to be inside those thick walls and behind the iron bars of the huge gates. She felt like a caged bird within its confines, but out here she could fly free.

Meg found herself sending up an ardent prayer. *Please let me get this job! Please let me get it and then I can get Mam and Bobbie out of that place.*

Fourteen

Meg walked down the High Street in the centre of the town. Already the street was busy: ladies in long skirts and white blouses were moving from shop to shop with baskets on their arms. Two young girls, carrying school books, stood chatting in the middle of the road, whilst a youth with a bicycle stood leaning on it, trying to catch the eye of one of the girls. He raised his cap to Meg, but she put her nose in the air in haughty rejection, tossing back her long red hair beneath the beribboned straw boater.

Outside the General Stores stood the proprietor, in a white jacket and a long white apron that reached down to his ankles.

'Good morning, good morning . . .' Meg heard him greeting the folk passing his shop.

She walked on, past the newsagent's with a rack of the day's papers hanging to one side of the door, past the ironmonger's with pots and pans, buckets and mops in the window, to the shop next door, where the sign read 'T. RODWELL & SON, Tailor and Outfitter'. It was a double-fronted shop, with the door in the centre between two windows.

Meg paused and peered in. Her heart was beating fast and her hands felt clammy. Inside she could see a man standing behind the counter. He was thin with receding dark hair and dressed in a sober suit with a waistcoat, a stiff-collared white shirt and a plain tie. He was serving a customer and as Meg glanced at the man in front of the counter, she gasped. It was Theobald Finch, the chairman of the board of guardians at the workhouse. Meg bit her lip, uncertain what she should do. Should she wait out here until Mr Finch had left or should she go inside and stand quietly at the rear of the shop until Mr Rodwell was free?

Deciding that the latter course of action was perhaps the safest – she didn't want to be accused of hanging about in the street in a suspicious manner – Meg opened the shop door. The bell clanged loudly and both men turned to look at her. Meg closed the door carefully, though the bell clanged again. She turned to face them.

'Good morning.' She smiled. 'I've come to see Mr Rodwell. Would you like me to wait outside?'

Closer now, she could see that the tailor was younger than she had expected him to be. She had imagined an elderly man, but Mr Rodwell looked to be in his early forties. He had a sallow complexion and his pale hazel eyes were large behind thick spectacles.

He blinked several times, but did not smile. 'No, no,' he said in a soft voice. 'That won't be necessary. Just wait over there, if you please, and I'll be with you shortly.'

'Thank you, sir.'

She moved to the far end of the long shop, aware that Mr Finch was still watching her. 'I know you, don't I? I've seen you before somewhere.'

Meg thought it politic to drop a small curtsy. 'You interviewed me and my family, sir, a week or two back. We – I'm from the workhouse.'

'Ah, yes. I remember you now. Your mother fainted, did she not?'

'Yes, sir.'

'And is she recovered now?'

'She is getting better, thank you, sir. But she – she lost the baby.'

'Ah.' The large man said again, but without a word of sympathy. He lost interest in her and turned back to choosing the material for his new suit. Meg waited, trying to curb her natural impatience. She watched how Mr Rodwell flicked through a swatch of fabric, giving his customer details of the make-up of each piece. 'Now this one is a fine worsted. And this one a coarser weave but very hard-wearing and this one . . .' And so on until Meg's head spun. There'd be a lot to learn, she thought, and wondered if she wouldn't be better to seek employment on another farm. At least she understood that work and there might be a cottage for her family . . .

At last Mr Finch made up his mind. 'That one, Percy. That's the one.'

'A wise choice, if I may say so.' The tailor inclined his head. It was almost a bow – but not quite. 'I'll order the cloth. Now, would you like me to take your measurements?'

'Not today, Percy. I'm in a hurry.'

Who'd have thought it, Meg thought, amused, *considering the time he's taken to choose? I must have been standing here for ten minutes or more.*

'I'd like to see the material again,' Theobald said. 'You know, in a full piece, just to make sure I like it. You can take my measurements then. Good day to you, Percy.'

'Good day, Theobald.'

Theobald opened the shop door with a flourish and then turned back. 'I'll see you later. I believe you're dining with us tonight.'

'That is so.'

Theobald's smile broadened. 'Clara is looking forward to it.'

Percy Rodwell gave a thin smile and dipped his head once more.

When the door had closed behind his customer, the tailor turned towards Meg. For a few moments he scrutinized her, taking in her appearance from head to toe. When his gaze finally met her green eyes, he seemed a little startled and blinked rapidly.

'You – you wanted to see me?'

Meg moved forward. 'Yes, sir. Miss Pendleton sent me. She said she's a friend of yours. Or rather,' she added hastily, 'a friend of Miss Finch's.'

'I hadn't realized they were friendly. I rather thought—' He paused and then asked, 'Why did Miss Pendleton send you to see me?'

'She thought you might have a job for me.'

Percy frowned. 'A job? For you?'

'She thought you were going to start stocking ladies' – er – garments and that perhaps your customers might prefer to be served by a woman.'

Percy allowed himself a small amused smile. Meg had the feeling it was because she had referred to herself as a 'woman'.

'That is correct,' he said in his soft voice. He cleared his throat and now he avoided her direct gaze. 'But I had it in mind to employ someone a little more – er – mature than yourself.'

Meg made sure that disappointment showed keenly on her face. 'I see,' she whispered and hung her head. Then she gave a huge sigh and glanced around the shop. 'What a shame! I'd've loved to work here. To have learnt all about fabrics and such. It must be so interesting.' She turned her brilliant eyes upon him and sighed again. 'But, of course, if I don't suit—'

'Well, now –' Percy was flustered – 'I didn't say that exactly.' He cleared his throat nervously. 'We – er – could discuss it. Yes, yes, we can discuss it.'

For the next half an hour, Percy Rodwell questioned Meg closely about herself, her family and her background. When he heard that her only experience of work had been as a dairymaid, doubt crossed his face once more.

Meg leapt in quickly. 'I realize you might prefer someone with experience in this kind of work, but I am honest and reliable and quick to learn and –' she ran her tongue around her lips and suggested craftily – 'and you could train me in *your* ways, couldn't you?'

He glanced at her. 'Well, there is that, I suppose.' He pondered for what seemed to the anxious girl an interminable time. At last he said, 'Very well, then. I'll speak to Miss Pendleton about you and if her comments are satisfactory, I'll take you. But it will be for a trial period, mind.'

Meg's eyes shone. 'I understand. And thank you, sir. I won't let you down, I promise.'

'We shall see, we shall see,' Percy said. 'Present yourself here at eight thirty sharp next Monday morning – one week from today – and we shall see.'

As she left the shop, Meg glanced back at the building. Two dummies, fully clothed in men's suits, stood in one of the windows. The other window displayed shirts, ties and socks. She glanced upwards and saw that the smaller windows on the first floor were very dirty. It was obvious that the upper floor was used only as a storeroom or perhaps a workroom. She wondered if there were enough rooms to make some into living quarters.

Meg skipped all the way back to the workhouse. She couldn't wait to tell her mam and Bobbie. The only thing worrying her was whether Miss Pendleton would speak well of her. But she had not upset the matron. Waters would have been a different matter and maybe even Mr Pendleton would not give her a glowing reference exactly, but she was sure that Miss Pendleton would speak well of her.

Albert was waiting for her when she rang the bell at the back gate to the workhouse. 'How did yer get on then?'

'Mr Rodwell's going to give me a trial. I'm to start next Monday.'

'He's a decent sort.'

'Mr Rodwell? Do you know him, Albert?'

The old man sniffed. 'I know most folks round here. Used to be an oddjob man in these parts, till I couldn't work any more.'

'And you . . . you . . .' Meg hesitated. She couldn't imagine that Albert had ever bought a suit at the tailor's. Albert finished her sentence for her. 'I worked for him now and again. Not in the shop, o' course. At his house.'

Meg kept her face the picture of innocence. 'Oh, so he doesn't live above the shop, then?'

'Used to do. Years ago.' This was the most talkative that Albert Conroy had been in years. But this pretty young girl had shown him such respect, kindness even. 'When his dad had the shop before 'im the whole family lived upstairs. But Percy moved into a little cottage near the church a few years back.' He sniffed. 'When he got hisself engaged to Miss Clara Finch.'

Meg smiled back at him and leant closer to share a secret. 'Mr Finch was in the shop when I got there. I had to wait for him to leave and as he went he said –' she mimicked Mr Finch's cultured tones – '"I believe you're dining with us tonight," and when Mr Rodwell nodded, Mr Finch said, "Clara is looking forward to it."'

Albert's smile widened, stretching his face more than it been for years. 'Been hengaged for six years or so, they have.'

'Six years!'

Albert chuckled, a wheezing sound. 'Aye. Not one to rush into anything, isn't Percy Rodwell.'

'But six years! I wouldn't wait six years,' Meg declared. 'Not for any man.'

Albert eyed her. 'Shouldn't think you'd 'ave to, mi duck. Have you seen Miss Finch?'

Meg shook her head and Albert chuckled again. 'Well, wait till you do and then you'll see why Percy's in no hurry to tie the knot.'

Laughing, Meg skipped on her way feeling more light-hearted than she had done since the day they had entered the workhouse. She went into the wash house and took off her own clothes. As she dressed once more in the workhouse uniform, she smiled to herself. She wouldn't have to dress in these awful garments for much longer. Soon she would be handling the fine fabrics in Mr Rodwell's shop.

She focused her thoughts on the future and refused to think about her father and Alice. Now she had new hope. Her mother was getting better. Sarah would be sad for a little while about the loss of her baby but soon . . .

Waters was standing in the doorway of the bath

room. 'You'd better come, Meg. Miss Daley is asking to see you.'

'Well, I don't want to see her,' Meg said abruptly.

'I think you should, Meg.'

The girl looked at her in surprise. Waters's tone was kindlier and she had called her Meg. Her attitude was so out of character that Meg was alarmed.

'What is it? What's wrong?' But the woman had turned away and all she said was, 'Miss Daley's in the children's dormitory. You'd better hurry.'

Cold fear clutched at Meg's heart.

Fifteen

Meg ran up the stairs and burst into the dormitory. The children were getting ready for bed, the bigger ones helping the little ones. Meg glanced around wildly, but she could not see her brother.

'Where's Bobbie? And where's Miss Daley?'

She knew some of the children by name now from her brief time spent in the school room. One of the older girls came towards her. 'Miss Daley's in her room.' She pointed to the far end of the dormitory to the room where Meg had looked after the sick child.

'Is she with Betsy?' Meg asked.

The girl shook her head. 'No. Betsy's better. Look, she's in her bed over there.'

Now Meg could see the thin, pale little girl sitting up in bed. Betsy held out her arms towards Meg and tears welled in her eyes. 'Meg,' she called, her voice trembling.

Sighing inwardly, Meg crossed the room to stand by her bed.

'I'm so sorry I caused trouble. I didn't mean to steal the watch. I – I just wanted to hear its tick. It – it reminded me of me dad.'

'It doesn't matter,' Meg said. She had neither the time nor the patience to listen to Betsy. There was only one thing on her mind. 'Do you know where Bobbie is?'

'In there. Miss Daley's looking after him. He's poorly.'

Meg's heart pounded anxiously. She had been right to be fearful. She ran down the long room to the closed door, ignoring Betsy's pleading, 'Meg, say you forgive me . . .'

Meg didn't even knock, but rushed straight into the schoolmistress's bedroom. The room was stifling and Meg's gaze went at once to the bed where Bobbie lay. His face was flushed and though his eyes were closed he was writhing and moaning. His nose was very sore and looked as if it had been bleeding. Miss Daley was bending over him, sponging his face. She glanced round at Meg but all she said when she saw who it was, 'You shouldn't be here. It might be infectious. He's quite sick.'

'What is it? What's the matter?'

'I don't know.'

'Has matron seen him? Have you called the doctor?'

'Meg,' Louisa said gently, 'they don't call the doctor for every minor childish ailment.'

'That's not a minor illness,' Meg said heatedly. 'Just look at him!'

'Well, yes. His pulse is weak, I have to admit, but then children can be terribly sick one minute and fine the next.'

Meg's mouth was a grim line as she whispered, 'If anything happens to our Bobbie, I'll know who to blame, won't I?'

'Meg—' Louisa began, but the girl whirled around and was gone from the room. She had to find her mother.

As she neared the women's day room, Meg could hear her mother's hysterical crying. When she rushed into the room, she saw Sarah in the middle of the room wringing her hands and wailing. The other women were clustered around her, but standing beside her was Isaac Pendleton. He was holding her hand and patting it.

'Now, now, my dear. Don't fret. Matron will take care of little Bobbie. He'll be good hands.'

Catching sight of her daughter, Sarah wailed afresh. 'Meg, oh, Meg. What are we to do? Bobbie's ill.'

'I know. I've seen him.'

Isaac Pendleton looked round, a flash of annoyance in his eyes. 'You had no right to go anywhere near the child. If it's something infectious, we could have an epidemic on our hands.'

'Then why isn't he in the infirmary with the matron?' Meg flashed back.

Surprise flickered briefly across Isaac's face. Before he could open his mouth to refute Meg's statement, she said, 'He's in Miss Daley's room at the end of the dormitory and I don't think the matron has even seen him yet.'

'But I thought—' Isaac began. He looked back at Sarah. 'I thought it was matron who told you.'

Sarah shook her head. 'No, no, it was Waters.'

'Waters! She had no right . . .' He broke off, gave Sarah's hand a final pat and added, 'Leave this to me.' He took hold of Meg's arm roughly and propelled her across the room. 'And you, young lady, had better come with me.'

'Why won't they let me see him?' Sarah wailed. 'I'm his mother.'

Meg glanced back over her shoulder to see that some of the other women in the day room were clustering round her mother and one was putting her arms about

Sarah's shoulders. At least, she thought, her mother was being comforted.

'Where – where are you taking me?' Meg was a little afraid to be alone with the master. He was a strange mixture. One moment he was charming and benevolent, the next a frightening, vengeful figure.

'To see if what you say is true. I've been hearing about you, miss. How you throw folks' kindness in their faces.'

Meg gasped. 'Me? I'd never do that.'

He stopped suddenly and pulled her round to face him. 'Then what's this I hear about you refusing to do the nice little job I found you in the school room? Where's your gratitude for that, eh? I had thought it was that Miss Daley found you unsuitable, but she tells me that it is you who have the gall to refuse to work with her.'

'I—'

'Don't bother trying to drum up some fancy tale.'

'But you don't understand—'

'I understand only too well, my girl. Ungrateful little chit that you are.'

'No, I'm not,' Meg was stung to retort boldly. 'I'm not ungrateful.'

Suddenly his attitude changed and he stood gazing down at her. 'By heck,' he murmured, 'but you're a bonny wench and a fiery one. I'd like to have the taming of you. If only you were older I'd let you show me just how grateful you can be—' He frowned and seemed to shake himself. 'Come along,' he said more briskly, but now the anger had gone from his voice. 'Let's find out what's to do with the little chap and see if we can put your poor mam's mind at rest. She's a bonny little woman, your mam.'

Isaac strode through the children's dormitory and opened the door into Miss Daley's room. Meg peered beneath his arm, her glance going at once towards the bed. But she could not see Bobbie, for now Miss Pendleton was there and bending over him.

'What's to do, then, Letitia?' Isaac boomed. His sister turned an anxious face towards him and Meg caught her breath. There were tears in the matron's eyes.

'I think it could be diphtheria, Isaac. He's very poorly, the poor little mite.'

'Then we must have him moved at once to the infirmary and you must isolate him and yourself, Letitia. There's no other course of action. We don't want an outbreak. The guardians would be most displeased . . .'

The hours dragged by. Darkness fell and supper passed, though Sarah and Meg could eat nothing. The other women were silent, leaving them alone with their worries.

'If only they'd let us see him,' Sarah moaned constantly and Meg bit her lip. Several times, Meg went outside and through the gate into the men's yard to stand in front of the long row of buildings across the yard from the main workhouse. She stared up at the dimly lit windows of the infirmary on the first floor above the bake house. She knew that was where they had taken Bobbie.

On her fifth visit outside, when she had been standing in the darkness for some time, a soft voice spoke behind her in the shadows. 'Meg? Meg, is that you?'

It was Jake. He had slipped out of the men's quarters and along the side of the wall. He was standing near the door into the room at the end of the row. 'Come on. Quick.'

With one last glance up at the windows, Meg ran lightly towards him.

'In here.' Jake took her hand and pulled her into the small room and closed the door. As her eyes became accustomed to the dark, Meg could just make out the shape of three coffins lying across trestles. 'Is there – is there anyone in them?'

'Nah. No one's died lately.'

Meg breathed more easily.

'Now, tell me – what's going on?' Jake whispered.

'It's Bobbie. He's sick and – and they won't let us see him.'

'That's usual, Meg. They won't let any of the mams see their kids, even if they're ill.'

'But if only they'd let Mam go to him. She could nurse him. She needn't mix with the other women until – until he's better again.'

'But that'd mean she didn't work, wouldn't it?'

'She's not working anyway. Not really. She's not well enough yet.'

'There you are then.' He tried to comfort her with common sense. 'They don't want her catching summat, do they?'

'But no one can look after him better than his own mam,' Meg cried passionately.

There was a long silence until Jake mumbled, 'I wouldn't know about that.'

Her mind on Bobbie, Meg didn't notice the sadness in his tone. Instead she said, 'I mean, you'd think they'd be glad of the help. You'd think they'd prefer the mother to look after him instead of the matron having to devote all her time to one child.'

'But it's what Miss Pendleton always does.' Jake paused significantly before adding, 'Specially if it's a little boy.'

'They've not even let us know if the doctor's been,' Meg ranted. Suddenly she made up her mind. 'I can't stand this. I'm going to see the master.'

'Meg . . .' Jake called after her, but she had wrenched open the door and was running across the men's yard. Moments later she was knocking urgently on the master's office. There was no reply, so she rapped again. Nothing.

She hesitated only a moment before running up the stairs to the master's bedroom. Before she could lose her nerve, she knocked on that door and Isaac's voice boomed, 'Come in.'

Meg opened the door and stepped into the room. Immediately, she understood the reason for Isaac's impatience. He was sitting on the sofa before a blazing log fire with his arm along the back of the sofa around a woman, whose head rested on his shoulder. The sound of weeping reached Meg and, as she recognized the woman's dark brown hair, she gasped aloud. 'Mam – what are you doing here?'

Gently, Isaac disentangled himself and stood up. Though irritation still showed in his eyes, he managed to say smoothly, 'Come in, my dear. Come and sit down. We didn't know where to find you.'

'I – I've been in the yard. I was trying to – I wanted to feel as close as I could to Bobbie.'

She moved forwards stiffly and sat down, her gaze going to her mother. But Sarah was sitting hunched up on the sofa, her hands covering her face.

'Mam – what are you doing here?' The sight of her mother with the master's arm around her had disturbed

Meg. But at Isaac's next words any qualms she had about her mother were driven from the girl's mind.

'My dear,' he said in a solemn tone, 'we have bad news, I'm afraid. Little Bobbie died an hour ago.'

Meg felt as if her heart had stopped beating. She began to shiver uncontrollably. 'Oh no, no. Not that. Not Bobbie too.'

Sixteen

They were used to death in the workhouse. It happened to the young as well as in the dormitories for the old and infirm, where death was to be expected. Indeed, many elderly folk, too infirm to work, knew that they were entering the workhouse to die.

And, amongst the young, many were undernourished and weak when they arrived. In such conditions, infectious diseases spread rapidly and there was little care available beyond a perfunctory visit from the doctor and the ministrations of the matron. One whole section of the local cemetery, where paupers were buried, gave testament to this fact. A flat area, broken only by gentle mounds with no marked graves, no headstones erected by loving relatives, spoke of the desperate circumstances of the departed. No one mourned them, no one had cared enough about them in life to give them shelter and now no one cared about them in death.

But Meg cared. She was incensed that her little brother should have been allowed to die. For the first time since the misunderstanding over the watch, Meg sought out Louisa Daley. She found her alone in the classroom before the start of morning lessons.

'You killed him,' she cried passionately. Fists clenched, she stormed towards the young schoolmistress. 'You *let* him die.'

Louisa blanched. She stepped back behind the desk,

trying to put a barrier between herself and the distraught girl. 'Meg, there was nothing that could have been done. It – it was diphtheria. Philip – Dr Collins – said so.'

'Ah yes! Dr Collins!' Meg's eyes blazed. 'Too busy paying court to you to attend to his patients.'

Louisa gasped. 'That's not fair.'

'Not fair? Not *fair*? Is it fair that my poor mam has lost four babies and now her little boy? And I've lost my Bobbie.' Tears threatened to choke her, but anger carried her on. She shook her fist in Louisa's face. 'First, you call me a thief and then you let my brother die. I won't forget this. I swear – one day – I'll make you pay.'

She turned away but then swung back to deliver one last salvo. 'And don't you dare to think of coming to his funeral.'

It was the custom for the matron and the schoolmistress to attend the funeral of any child who had been in their care. But this time Meg made sure that Louisa Daley knew she was not wanted.

Sarah and Meg stood beside each other after the brief and soulless committal of the pathetically small rough wooden coffin into the cold earth. Only one other person attended the brief service held at the graveside: the matron. She stood on the opposite side of the deep hole, holding a handkerchief to her face.

'Another of my little boys gone,' she wept.

Meg wanted to shout: *He wasn't yours. He was ours. Mam's and mine*. But she said nothing. The woman's sorrow was genuine and, strangely, the fact that someone else was grieving for little Bobbie seemed to comfort Sarah. It was she who stepped around the grave and took Letitia's arm to lead her gently away. Poor Sarah had become so used to heartache in her life that she expected it now.

With one last glance down into the grave, Meg whispered, 'Goodnight, my darling little brother. Sleep tight.' It was what she'd always said to him when she'd tucked him in bed at night. She was heartsore that even that small, loving action had been denied to her, and to Sarah too, during the past few weeks. Only the matron – or Louisa Daley – had had that privilege. Meg turned away, tears blurring her vision, and stumbled after the two women.

It was only then that she remembered. Today was her sixteenth birthday.

On their return to the workhouse, Jake was hovering near the gate leading from the men's yard into the women's.

Letitia put her arm around him and hugged him to her, even though he was as tall as she was now. Her little Jake. She'd cared for him since the day he was born. She wouldn't lose him. Jake would always be with her. 'What are you doing here, Jake? If the master sees you—'

'Sorry, Matron, but – but—' He nodded towards Meg and her mother, now crossing the yard towards the back door into the women's quarters. 'I wanted to see how Meg and her mam were.'

Letitia shook her head. 'Ah, poor souls.' She glanced across the yard and then up to the windows of her brother's rooms. Then she smiled at the anxious boy in front of her. 'You're a good boy, Jake.' She patted his cheek and seemed to come to a swift decision. 'I know. Walk across the yard with me. You can have a few minutes with the lass just inside the back door. If he sees you with me, he'll not say anything.'

Jake grinned at her. 'You're a diamond, Matron.'

The woman's round cheeks flushed and for a moment tears sparkled in her eyes. Then she smiled fondly. 'And you're a rogue, Jake Bosley. You know how to twist me round your little finger, don't you? Always have done.' But she turned and walked across the yard, Jake falling into step beside her. 'Now, don't let me down,' she murmured as they walked. 'Only a few minutes, mind.'

The two young people were left alone just inside the back entrance.

'You all right?' Jake asked softly. Meg nodded, unable to speak for a moment.

'And – and your mam?'

Meg sighed. 'Sad. We both are. But—'

'What?' Jake pressed gently.

'It was funny, really. Miss Pendleton seemed even more upset than us.'

Jake shrugged. 'She always is when one of the little ones dies.'

There was silence between them until Jake asked hesitantly, 'Shall you – shall you try to find yer dad again? To tell him about Bobbie, I mean?'

Meg gave an explosive snort. 'No, I shan't. He doesn't care about us. Any of us. Made that plain, hasn't he? I don't care if I never set eyes on him again.'

'I just thought – well – he is Bobbie's dad and I thought he ought to know.'

Meg thrust her face close to Jake's. 'He doesn't deserve to know anything,' she hissed. 'And if you want me an' you to go on being friends, then shut up about him. As far as I'm concerned, I haven't got a dad. Not any more.'

Jake blinked at her vitriolic words. Then, despite himself, he grinned. 'By, no wonder you're a redhead. Fiery, aren't yer?'

But Meg could not share his attempt at fun. She glowered at him. 'Yeah, I'm fiery. Looks like I'm going to have to be to get anywhere in this world. I'm on me own now, aren't I?'

'You've still got yer mam.' The wistfulness in his tone was lost on Meg, who was too wrapped up in her own tragedies. She pulled a face. 'By the look of things, it's going to be me looking after her, not the other way about.'

Jake gave a weak smile and shuffled his feet in embarrassment. 'You – you can count on me, Meg. I'll always be there for you.'

Meg stared at him for a moment and then softened enough to touch his arm and say huskily, 'Thanks, Jake, but let's face it, you don't know much about the world outside these walls, do yer? And I'm damned if I'm staying in the workhouse the rest of me life.'

Jake squared his shoulders and puffed out his thin chest as far as he could. 'Neither am I,' he declared boldly. 'I've talked to Ron and I'm off to see the mester at the farm come Monday. And if he teks me on, Ron says I can move in with him and his family in the little cottage—' He stopped suddenly, appalled to realize that he was talking about Meg's former home. 'Oh, I'm sorry.'

'Don't be,' she said harshly. 'Look after yourself, Jake.' She smiled wistfully as she added, 'Try and get the little room above the kitchen. It was mine and it was always warm from the chimney above the range. And – and think of me.' She turned away to run up the stairs, her hobnailed boots clattering on the stone steps.

Jake gazed after her. 'Oh, I will, Meg,' he whispered, even though she could not hear him. 'I'll think of you all the time.'

Meg was waiting outside Mr Rodwell's tailor's shop well before opening time the following Monday. It was a wet morning and cool for July. The wind whistled round the corner, making her shiver. She hopped from one foot to the other, trying to keep warm, and was thankful when at last she saw a figure hurrying up the street, his umbrella held low in front of him against the driving rain. He didn't see her until he was almost at the door and lifted his umbrella, searching in his pocket for the keys to his shop.

'Ah, there you are,' Percy said.

'Yes, sir. Here I am.'

'Dear me, you must be soaked. Come in quickly . . .' He fumbled with the keys, dropping them to the ground in his haste. Meg bent and picked them up, handing them to him with a smile. She was about to say: *Don't worry about me, Mr Rodwell. I'm used to working out in all weathers. A bit of rain doesn't bother me.* But then she thought better of it. Instead, she smiled shyly. 'It's very kind of you to be so concerned, Mr Rodwell.'

At last he got the door open and held it for her to step inside ahead of him. 'Have you been waiting long?'

'A bit,' she said, as if reluctant to admit it. 'I didn't want to be late.'

'Very commendable, my dear,' Percy said, a smile creasing his thin face. 'But I don't like to think of you standing in the cold waiting for me.'

He moved about the shop opening the window blinds and letting in what early-morning light there was on this dull day. Then he beckoned her to the back of the shop and ushered her through a door and into his workroom. Meg glanced about her.

The place was very untidy. Bits of fabric were scattered all over the floor. A length of cloth, marked with chalk lines, lay on the long table with a huge pair of scissors waiting to be used. A yardstick and measuring tapes were thrown down haphazardly and cottons and threads were heaped on a shelf nearby. A tailor's dummy stood in one corner, draped with a half-finished jacket, and at one end of the table was a Singer sewing machine, the gold lettering gleaming against the black of the machine.

Before she stopped to think, Meg cried out, 'Oh, you've got a sewing machine!'

'Er – well – yes,' Percy murmured. 'The tools of my trade, you know.' He cleared his throat. 'Now, first of all, I must light the stove. I like it lit most days – even in summer. This is a cold building and I like my customers to have a feeling of warmth when they step into the shop.'

Meg had noticed the stove in the back corner of the shop as she had walked through. It was similar to the one at the workhouse, which she had learnt how to light and keep stoked.

'I'll do that for you, Mr Rodwell,' she offered, taking off her outdoor coat.

He glanced doubtfully at the white cotton blouse she was wearing. She had ironed it so carefully the previous evening. 'It's a very dirty job,' he warned.

Meg smiled sweetly at him and was gratified when Percy blinked rapidly. 'I brought my apron just in case,' she told him. 'And I'll be sure to roll my sleeves up.'

'Well, if you're sure, it would be a help. I have to

admit,' he confided, 'it's a job I hate doing. My hands get so rough and then – when I have to work . . .' He gestured towards the table and the tailor's dummy.

Meg nodded. 'I understand. You must keep your hands nice.' She glanced around. 'Just tell me where I can find paper, kindling and coal.'

Percy gestured towards a door at the far end of the workshop. 'That leads into a backyard, Miss – er – Kirkland. The coal store is out there and you'll find all you need.' He seemed about to say more, but then glanced away from her. 'Please – er – have a look around while you're out there. So – so that you know where everything is.'

Meg opened the back door and stepped outside. On either side high walls separated the tailor's backyard from the next-door premises. To the left would be the ironmonger's, Meg realized, and on the right – by the appetizing smell that was already wafting over the wall – there must be a bakery. Immediately to her left in the yard was a wooden lean-to used as a scullery. As Meg pushed open the door, it scraped on the dusty floor. *The whole place wants a good scrub*, she said to herself and couldn't prevent a wry smile as she thought of Mrs Smallwood's face if she were to see this place. Meg's smile faded. She didn't want to be reminded of the past – not any of it.

At the end of the yard were two doors into brick-built outbuildings and a gate in the wall, which led into the alley running between the backyards of this street and the next. One door was the coal store. The other, Meg found, was the privy. Now she understood Mr Rodwell's suggestion that she should familiarize herself with the premises. He had been too shy to tell her directly where the privy was, but knew she would find it for herself. She smiled as she picked up newspaper, kindling and a bucket of coal and returned to the shop.

'Find everything?' Percy enquired, hovering near the stove.

'Yes thank you, sir,' she said, demurely dropping her eyes and making no reference to the delicate matter of the whereabouts of the privy.

'Good, good,' Percy said, rubbing his long-fingered hands together. 'I'll – erm—' He paused, not quite knowing what to do with himself now that Meg had taken over his usual first task of the morning. 'I'll sort out the money for the drawer.'

Very soon Meg had a good fire going in the stove and the shop began to feel warmer. She washed her hands in the tiny scullery and hung up her apron on a hook behind the door, pulled down her sleeves, smoothed her hair in the cracked mirror on the wall and went back inside.

The first customer of the day had entered the shop and was standing in front of the counter talking to Mr Rodwell. Meg went to stand behind the counter, keeping a discreet distance from both Mr Rodwell and his male customer. But she was close enough to do his bidding should he need her. She waited patiently until the satisfied customer left the shop, a parcel under his arm.

Mr Rodwell turned and smiled at her over his steel-rimmed spectacles. 'Well done, Miss Kirkland.'

Meg glanced back at the fire. 'It's quite an easy stove to light,' she said. 'Not so temperamental as the one at the—'

'Now, now, there's no need for us to mention – ahem – where you are obliged to reside at this moment in time. No need at all.'

'You're very kind, Mr Rodwell.'

There was a pause before Percy added, 'Actually, I wasn't referring to the fire at all. No, I meant you were right to wait quietly whilst I served my customer. It was well done, my dear. Very well done indeed.'

Now Meg lifted her face and gave Mr Rodwell the full benefit of her most dazzling smile.

Seventeen

Later in the morning, when the shop was empty, Percy cleared his throat and said tentatively, 'I – erm – heard about your loss. Your little brother. Miss Pendleton called in on Saturday and she told me. I was very sorry to hear it.' He glanced at her, his pale eyes sympathetic behind his spectacles.

Meg wanted to ask what the matron had said about her. Had she given her a good reference? But at the mention of her brother, tears filled her eyes. She only had to think of little Bobbie and the tears came all too readily. There was no need for pretence now – her grief was all too genuine. 'Thank you,' she said huskily.

'I – erm – would have quite understood if you'd needed a few more days before starting your employment with me.'

Meg shook her head firmly. 'No – thank you – it's very thoughtful of you, but it's best to keep busy.'

'I just thought that perhaps your mother might need you . . .' Percy's voice trailed away.

'There are plenty of people at the – plenty of people *there* to comfort her.' For some reason that Meg could not quite understand, the vision of Isaac Pendleton with his arm around her mother's shoulders flashed into her mind. The picture made her feel uncomfortable.

Percy was nodding. 'Quite so,' he murmured. 'But

it's not quite like having a member of your own family close by, is it?'

Carefully, Meg rolled fabric back onto a bolt of cloth that Percy had had on the counter to show to a customer. Meg took a deep breath. In control of her emotions once more and now pretending innocence, she asked, 'Have you any family, Mr Rodwell?'

'What?' He was startled as if he was unused to having anyone ask personal questions. 'Who? Me? Oh well, no, not really. I – erm – did have once. Of course I did. But I was an only child and since my parents died there has been no one.'

Now Meg feigned surprise, even though she knew the answer well enough. 'You mean – you're not married?'

Percy blinked rapidly, took off his spectacles, polished them vigorously with a tiny cloth he carried in his waistcoat pocket and then perched them back on his nose. 'Oh, dear me, no. Certainly not. Well, that is to say, I – erm – may one day decide to – erm – embark upon the sea of matrimony.' He shook his head. 'But it's a big step. A very big step.'

Meg smiled coyly. 'Well, she'd be a very lucky lady to have you as a husband, Mr Rodwell.'

Percy blinked again.

During the hour the shop was closed for lunch, Percy explained his reasons for wanting to employ a female assistant. 'I've found it increasingly difficult to do my work in the back room and look after the shop too. Interruptions, you know. If I have to stop the machine in the middle of a long seam, it can spoil it completely.'

Meg smiled and nodded. Percy Rodwell was obviously

a perfectionist in his work if not in the cleanliness and tidiness of his premises. But if he let her stay . . .

He was speaking again. 'And I want to expand – well – alter things round a bit. It was Miss Finch's idea that I should stock women's apparel. She suggested that I should make the right-hand side of the shop into the ladies' section, whilst this side –' he waved his arms about, demonstrating – 'should stay as the men's.'

Meg glanced around her. 'Are you going to put a counter this side too? For me . . .' She hesitated then, with a coy tilt to her head, went on, 'I mean – for your assistant to serve at?'

'Yes, yes, that's a very good idea.' He was all enthusiasm. 'Miss Pinkerton . . .' He broke off to ask, 'Do you know Miss Pinkerton?'

Meg shook her head.

'She's a dressmaker and milliner. She lives in a little cottage just by the church, near where I live, actually. Well, she has always made garments for Clara – Miss Finch – and my fiancée has persuaded her to make dresses and costumes – even coats – to order for me.'

'And hats?'

'Oh yes, eventually, hats too, I'm sure.'

'Ladies like nice hats,' Meg volunteered and again Percy's pale eyes rested thoughtfully upon her.

About mid-afternoon, a woman entered the shop. Meg looked up and smiled, ready to offer her services and eager to show Mr Rodwell what she could do. But Percy hurried forward at once, his hands outstretched towards the woman. 'My dear, I'm so glad you've called. There's someone I'd like you to meet.' He put his arm around the woman without actually touching her, but shepherding her towards the counter, where Meg was standing. 'My dear, this is Miss Kirkland. She's – erm – on trial for a month and I am proposing to train her to serve the – erm – ladies' items I am planning to stock.' Now he smiled at Meg. 'Miss Kirkland, this is Miss Finch.'

Meg smiled and bobbed a respectful curtsy. In a quiet, demure voice, she said, 'I'm honoured to make your acquaintance, Miss Finch.' *So this*, Meg was thinking, *is Miss Clara Finch, Mr Rodwell's fiancée and Miss Pendleton's friend.* Meg had expected Mr Rodwell's fiancée to be a pretty young woman, slim and dressed in fashionable clothes with a sweet smile and adoring eyes when she looked up at her intended. But the woman before her was nothing like Meg's romantic imaginings. Clara Finch was thin and angular with cold grey eyes, a beak-like nose and a small, pursed mouth. She was dressed in a dark purple costume that admittedly was well made and expensive, but it was drab and unbecoming. The woman – *she must be forty if she's a day*, Meg thought – carried her hands folded neatly in front of her at waist height. Meg felt Clara's hard gaze appraising her. When she spoke, Clara's tone was shrill and sharp, her words clipped. 'I don't know why you wanted a woman working here at all, Percy. Haven't I promised to help you out now and then if you need it? And you most certainly don't want –' she nodded at Meg with a swift pecking movement of her head – 'a young girl and one from *that place*.' The last two words were spoken scathingly.

Meg felt the colour rising into her face, but defiantly she lifted her chin. Though her green eyes sparked with anger she kept her tone submissive and courteous. 'My family have fallen on hard times, ma'am, through no fault of their own.'

Mentally, she crossed her fingers, praying that Miss Finch did not know the truth about their misfortune. But Mr Finch was a crony of Mr Smallwood's. They went to the race meeting together . . .

Meg's heart fell as she saw the gleam of malice in Miss Finch's eyes. 'Indeed?' Clara said, her tone laced with sarcasm. 'That's not what I heard.'

Beside her, Percy began to fidget. 'Oh, now come, my dear, all that is merely idle gossip and speculation.'

Clara whipped round to face him, making Percy blink rapidly. 'Percy, I have never indulged in idle gossip. You should know me better than that.'

'Of course, my dear. I'm sorry, I did not mean to imply—'

A little mollified, she nodded. 'Very well.' Then she turned her attention back to Meg. 'Your father, girl, brought shame to a decent, well-brought up young woman, Alice Smallwood, besides causing his family to become an expense on the parish.' She leant across the counter, closer to Meg. 'Your father, girl, should be horsewhipped.'

Meg stood her ground and returned the woman's gaze steadily. 'I entirely agree with you, ma'am. And I'd cheer on any person who cared to do it.'

Now it was Miss Finch who looked startled and, for a brief moment, nonplussed. But she recovered herself quickly and took refuge in finding fault. 'You are too bold, miss. You have too much to say for yourself.' She turned to her fiancé. 'If you want my opinion, Percy, you'd do better to look elsewhere for your counter assistant. Someone more mature would be far more suitable.'

'Oh, but Clara – my dear – Miss Pendleton herself

recommended the girl. I thought – she being your friend – that you would approve.'

Clara sniffed dismissively. 'Letitia Pendleton would like to class herself as my friend, but I have no wish to be associated with such a person. She has tried before to ally herself to my family. But it won't work. Oh, dear me, no. No, Percy, be guided by me. The ladies you hope to attract to your establishment would much prefer an older person to serve them and someone more refined. This girl was nothing but a milkmaid. What can she hope to know about fine fabrics and the kind of garments that *ladies* wear?'

Percy blinked. He glanced in embarrassment towards Meg and then took hold of Clara's arm and drew her away from the counter. He leant closer to her to whisper, but Meg's sharp ears still caught his words. 'But my dear, the child has suffered most grievously. The family was turned out of their home. Oh, I know, I know, he – the father – no doubt deserved it, but it is hardly his poor wife's fault, is it? And certainly this girl is not to blame. You've heard for yourself how bitter she is. And worse than that, the mother lost the child she was expecting and only this week the little boy died in the – in the – in *that place*.'

Clara's eyes shifted towards Meg and then widened. 'What of?'

'What?' Percy was mystified.

'What of? What did the boy die of?'

Percy shrugged. 'I don't know . . .' Now they both gazed at Meg.

Meg bit her lip. She knew only too well that her brother had died of diphtheria, but would Miss Pendleton and her brother want the fact known? An epidemic in the workhouse was something to be feared. Already there were two more suspected cases amongst the children, but the matron had isolated them at once and Dr Collins visited daily. But Meg didn't want Mr Rodwell or Miss Finch to hear about it any more than Isaac wanted it known beyond the workhouse walls. She faced them squarely. 'I don't know. You'd have to ask the doctor – or the matron.'

'Well, I hope it was nothing infectious, girl,' Clara said and took a step backwards. 'I think I'll be going, Percy. I'll see you tonight.'

'Thank you, my dear. I shall look forward to it.'

'Don't be late. Theobald hates unpunctuality.'

As the shop bell tinkled at her departure, Meg busied herself with tidying the shelves. She could not trust herself to meet Percy's eyes. She knew her runaway tongue was in danger of saying far more than it ought to.

The work was not as physically hard as farm work and yet, for some reason, Meg found it very tiring. Maybe it was having to be quiet and polite all day long, with a smile permanently plastered on her face. She was constantly alert, trying to anticipate Mr Rodwell's every need. There was so much to learn, much more than she had ever dreamed. All the different garments, the different sizes, different fabrics and qualities. And when the new stock began to arrive – stock that was new even to Percy and something of a mystery to him – Meg was busier than ever. He was already looking to her to take charge of it. To price it and put it away. Even to display it, although he was still embarrassed to have ladies' undergarments on show. A new counter had been installed on the right-hand side of the shop and all the drawers and shelves behind were given over to women's wear. Meg lost count of the number of times she climbed the stairs to the cluttered rooms above the shop to dump piles of men's vests, long johns, socks and shirts to make room for the ladies' garments. But at least now she could see the rooms on the first floor for herself. She had been right; they were only used as storerooms and untidy, higgledy-piggledy storerooms at that! They weren't even proper stockrooms, Meg realized. Oh, she'd taken plenty of old stock up, but she had never once seen Percy bring anything down into the shop. The rooms were just a dumping ground for rubbish, she was sure.

She would ask him, Meg determined, if she could tidy the rooms out, give them a good clean and sort out all the stock. If she worked hard and pleased him, he would take her on permanently as his assistant and then she could ask him if she and her mother might live above the shop. She would tell him how much better it would be to have someone living on the premises. She could light the stove before he even arrived. She could sweep and dust and clean the shop after it closed. He wouldn't have to stay late at night to do these tasks, as she knew he often did.

Percy was speaking to her, dragging her back from her plans. 'When you serve the customers, Miss Kirkland, you must let them know – delicately, of course – that we now stock such – erm – items.' He waved his hand towards the drawers containing ladies' underwear.

Meg smiled to herself and was crafty enough not to explain every little detail about the new stock to her employer. The less he knew about ladies' apparel the more he would need to rely upon her.

She was enjoying the work, but every night her head whirled until it ached with all the information she had tried to absorb. And there were still chores in the workhouse awaiting her at night.

On the Saturday evening at the end of her third week working in the tailor's shop, Meg trudged wearily home. *Home!* she thought in disgust as the huge building loomed out of the dusk. *Fancy having to call the workhouse 'home'*. They had been in the workhouse now for almost seven weeks and Meg was even more desperate to leave it than she had been when they had first been admitted. Then she had truly believed that they would only be there for a few days at the most.

'If I ever meet up with him again,' she vowed, thinking of her father, who had caused all this, 'I'll kill him. And *her*.'

She still wasn't sure which betrayal hurt her the most: her father's or her friend's.

But tonight, as she opened the gate into the yard, her steps quickened. Something was banishing her tiredness and unhappy thoughts. She couldn't wait to tell her mother. She had left the shop that evening, calling, 'Goodnight,' to Mr Rodwell and leaving him to close up. In the street she had paused for a moment to glance up at the windows above the shop. If they were all cleared out, as she planned, there was plenty of room for her and her mother to live up there. She hugged the idea to herself, feeling more positive and hopeful than she had for weeks. As she hurried through the workhouse gate and across the yard, she was vaguely aware of someone calling her name. But, intent on sharing her wonderful idea with her mother, she paid no heed and ran inside and up the steps into the women's day room.

'Mam,' she cried, flinging open the door. 'Mam,

where are you? I've had the most marvellous idea. If only . . .'

She stopped, hesitating in the doorway as her gaze swept around the room. Several faces turned towards her, others did not look up, and Meg had the strange feeling that it was deliberate. No one spoke.

'Where is she? Where's my mam?' she asked of no one in particular. Now everyone lowered their gaze and turned away. Only one woman stood up and stumbled across the room towards her.

Ursula Waters stood before her. Her thin, bony hands clasped Meg's shoulders, her fingers digging painfully into the girl's flesh. Young and strong, Meg quickly shook her off.

'You ask where she is?' Ursula shrieked, her eyes wild, spittle showering Meg's face. 'As if you didn't know. You've planned it, I bet. You're a scheming little hussy and she's no better than she should be.'

'Waters, I don't know what you're on about.'

But Ursula continued to scream at her, tears now coursing down her thin, lined cheeks. 'Fancy, a mother who's just lost her child, two, if you count the miscarriage. And look at her now. Carrying on like a common trollop off the streets. I felt sorry for her. I did. I did. But not any more. Oh, not any more.'

Now it was Meg who gripped the woman's shoulders firmly. 'Waters, I don't know what you're talking about. Just tell me – where is my mam?'

Waters's face contorted into an ugly grimace. 'With *him*,' she spat. 'With the master.'

Meg blinked, still unable to understand why Ursula was so upset. 'She's gone to see him, you mean? What about? Is something wrong?'

'Oho, there's something wrong all right, but not the

way you mean,' Ursula said bitterly. 'Oh no, everything's all right for her. Very "all right" now.'

'I don't understand.'

'She's gone to him.'

'Yes, you said that, but—'

'Moved in with him. Moved her belongings into his room. She's – she's *with* him. Your mother is Mr Pendleton's new – new *fancy woman*.'

Eighteen

Meg's mouth dropped open and she stared at the woman in front of her in horror. 'Wha— what do you mean?'

Ursula's lip curled. 'You know exactly what I mean! A girl of your age and brought up on a farm too. Oh, don't play the innocent with me.'

Vaguely, Meg heard a movement behind her. Someone else had come into the room, but she hardly noticed. She was so caught up by the terrible things this vindictive woman was saying about her mother. 'But – but my mam would never – she wouldn't . . .' Meg was incensed. Her green eyes blazed and she raised her hand as if to strike Ursula. But before the blow could land, someone standing behind her caught hold of her wrist and held it fast.

'Don't, Meg.' Jake's voice was soft in her ear. 'It'll cause you more trouble. Come away. Leave her.'

Meg struggled against his grasp, but Jake held on grimly. He put his arm about her waist and dragged her bodily from the room, whilst Meg still shouted and cursed at Ursula. She shook her fist. 'You wicked, evil woman to say such things. I'll – I'll . . .' But she could think of nothing bad enough to threaten.

'Come away, Meg,' Jake urged, all the while pulling her out of the room. Once in the passageway, he pulled the door shut and leant against it, barring her way back inside. 'Just calm down, will yer?' He spoke firmly now. 'And I'll explain it all.'

'What is there to explain? She's got it wrong. My mam wouldn't . . .' She fell silent, her mouth open. She squinted in the half-light of the passageway to see Jake's face more clearly. His expression was sober, pitying almost. 'She wouldn't . . .' she protested again, but now her voice was feeble and cold uncertainty was stealing over her. She shivered and Jake drew her close. Her head resting on his shoulder, neither of them caring for once who saw them, Jake whispered, 'What she says is true.' As he said the words Meg stiffened and would have pushed away from him, but he held her firmly. 'Not – not perhaps like she's making it sound. That dried-up old prune is jealous. That's what's the matter with her. Just 'cos your mam is young and pretty and old Isaac is taken with her. Who can blame him, eh?'

Now Meg sobbed against his neck and clung to him. 'Oh, Jake, it's not true, is it? She wouldn't – couldn't – take up with a man like Mr Pendleton.' She paused and then added in a pitiful tone that tore at the boy's heart, 'Could she?'

Jake stroked her hair tenderly. 'Isaac likes the ladies. Always has. But he's kind to 'em. Even when he – well – when he moves on to the next, he sees that they're well cared for. He finds them a job in the town or even a job here.'

Slowly Meg raised her head and looked at him. Her mind was working again. 'You mean – that Waters was once – you know?' It was what the woman herself had implied, but Meg hadn't believed it possible.

Jake nodded. 'It was before I can remember, but that's what they say. After, he tried to set her up with a nice little job in the town. Working in a little shop, they said. Ever such a nice, genteel sort of job, but she wouldn't go. She wanted to stay here in the workhouse. Can you believe it?'

Meg swallowed and said huskily, 'Yes, yes, I can. I see it all now. I see why she's – she's so bitter. She still loves him and it must hurt her to see him take up with younger women.' She felt a fleeting pity for the lonely spinster. Then another thought struck her. 'But I thought Mr Pendleton had his eye on *her* . . .' She couldn't bring herself to say Louisa Daley's name but there was no need, for Jake laughed softly. 'The schoolmarm, you mean?'

Meg nodded.

'Oh aye, well he had. But the young doctor's got in there first and I 'spect old Isaac doesn't want to upset him. Dr Collins does the workhouse quite a few favours. He attends folk here without sending in a bill a lot of the time, but I reckon it's because he can see Miss Daley when he visits.'

Meg sighed and shook her head. 'It's all too much for me. I can't take it in. Me mam. How could she? How *could* she?' She shuddered at the thought of her mother lying beside Isaac Pendleton in his bed. 'It's disgusting. *She's* disgusting.'

'Aw, don't be like that, Meg. Your mam must be feeling so bad, what with losing her baby, then her little lad . . .' Jake bit his lip, not wanting to refer directly to her father's desertion, yet the thought was in both their minds. 'And Isaac will be kind to her. He's a good man, really.'

'How can you say that after the way he beat you? That was cruel.'

Jake shrugged. He had known no other life than within the walls of the workhouse. He had no means of comparison. 'I've sometimes thought he's a bit harder on me than the other lads, but then –' he grinned – 'I'm more trouble to him than they are. And I've always got the matron on my side.'

'She likes you,' Meg murmured absentmindedly, her mind still in a tumult of emotions concerning her own problems. 'She's not what I imagined the matron in the workhouse would be. I thought she'd be horrible. More like Waters.'

'Aw, come on, Meg. Poor old Waters is an unhappy woman.'

Meg stared at him. 'How is it,' she asked slowly, 'that you seem so – so sensible and – and knowing, when you've never hardly been outside the workhouse?'

Jake tweaked her nose playfully. 'I've always kept mi eyes and mi ears open. I've met lots of fellers in here and they all had a story to tell and they've liked talking to me. About their lives, their families and how they'd come to be in here. Well, I listened, Meg, and I learned. I learned a bit of readin' and writin' in the school room but I learned a lot more about life by listening to them fellers.' Now his ready smile widened. 'And now I'm not going to be here for much longer. That's why I came looking for you, to tell you.'

Meg suddenly realized that Jake should have been nowhere near the women's quarters. His news must be important for him to take such a risk.

'I've got that job on Smallwood's farm. I start on Monday.' His eyes were shining. 'Only one more day, Meg, and I'm out of here. And it's all thanks to you. If you hadn't taken me out wi' you that day, I might have been stuck in here for the rest of mi life. But now I'm getting out and I ain't coming back. Not ever.'

Meg felt a lump in her throat that had nothing to do

with the news about her mother. She touched his shoulder. 'I'm glad, Jake. Real glad for you. But I'll miss you.'

He laughed aloud. 'Oh, you'll still be seeing me. I'll be down to that there shop you're working in to get the mester there to mek me mi first proper suit. You see if I don't.'

Meg couldn't bring herself to seek out her mother. She didn't want to speak to her or even see her. And she certainly didn't want to encounter Isaac Pendleton. That night she lay in the narrow bed in the women's dormitory. The empty bed beside her, where her mother had slept, taunted her. Meg stared into the darkness, listening to the breathing, snores, even murmurings of the other women in the room. Sometime during the early hours of the morning she must have dozed fitfully, but when it was time to get up she awoke with a blinding headache. She was sorry it was Sunday. She wanted nothing more than to escape to the sanctuary of the tailor's shop. But she had to endure the glances and the whisperings of the other women, the long walk into the town to morning service and another long, restless night.

Unable to face breakfast on the Monday morning, she was about to slip out of the gate when she heard Albert's voice.

''Morning, lass. Now, you weren't going off wi'out saying ta-ta to me, were you?'

Meg sighed inwardly and turned to face the old man limping towards her. She tried to smile, opened her mouth to speak, but before she could utter a word, he said, 'Aw, lass, what's wrong? You ill?'

Meg bit her lip and shook her head. 'No,' she said huskily. 'I didn't sleep too well.'

'Ah!' was all the old man said, but somehow he managed to put such a depth of understanding into that one sound that Meg's eyes filled with tears. Impatiently, she dashed them away with the back of her hand, determined not to let anyone see her cry. At least, anyone other than Jake.

She glanced at Albert and saw the sympathy in the old man's rheumy eyes. 'You – you know, don't you?'

Albert nodded.

Bitterly, Meg said, 'I suppose everyone knows.'

'Aye well, you can't keep secrets, lass, in a place like this. But look at it this way, yer mam'll be well looked after. I'll say that for 'im, if he teks to a young woman, he treats 'em well, treats 'em fair. And I'll tell you summat else an' all, he doesn't cast 'em aside when he's done wi' 'em either. He sets 'em up in some nice little job that should see them all right for the rest of their days, so to speak.'

'That's what Jake said,' Meg murmured.

'Well, 'e's right.'

Meg bit her lip, but the words would not be held in. 'But it's the shame, Albert. How could she? My *mother*? That's not how she's always brought us—' She pulled in a shuddering breath when the appalling truth hit her. She was now the only child left. 'It's not how she's always brought *me* up to behave.'

'No, lass, I don't expect she did. But life has dealt her a lot of bitter blows lately, hasn't it? She's down there –' he pointed towards the ground – 'in the depths of despair and old Pendleton can be very kind when he wants to be.'

Meg turned away. They all seemed to be on Isaac

Pendleton's side. No one seemed to understand how she felt. But she answered Albert politely. 'Thank you for talking to me, Albert.'

'Tha's all right, lass. Any time.'

As she walked away from the shadow of the workhouse towards the town, the young girl's mind was in a turmoil. She could scarcely take in all that had happened. And she still couldn't believe what they were saying about her mother.

Her little family had been hard-working, honest, trustworthy and loving towards one another. And now, in the space of only a few weeks, her father had deserted them for a pretty face and a flighty nature. Because of his betrayal, not only of his family, but of his employers too, they had lost their home and their livelihood and faced the shame of the workhouse. Another baby had been lost and then poor little Bobbie had died. Yet Meg knew she could have faced all that if only she still had her mother. But what Sarah had done was beyond forgiveness. Meg had felt bitter and unforgiving towards her father, but it was nothing compared to how she now felt about her mother.

As she neared the shop and saw Mr Rodwell opening up the door, Meg made herself a promise. *I'll see mi mam tonight and, if it's true what they're saying, then that's it. I don't want anything to do with her ever again.*

And I'll tell her so.

Nineteen

Meg worked hard that day, throwing herself into each task with a kind of desperation. She was aware of Percy's anxious glances and knew he could sense that something was not quite right. But he said nothing; perhaps he thought the cause was 'women's troubles', a subject far too delicate for any man, especially a bachelor, to approach.

Meg worked on, never pausing to give herself time to think, to dwell on the hardships and disappointments life was throwing at her. The only person she spared a brief thought for was Jake, but even thinking of him starting his new job at the farm revived her own bitter memories. She unpacked all the new stock as it arrived and arranged it. She dressed the right-hand window, which Percy had now given over to ladies' wear. She stayed on long after the shop had closed to sweep and tidy up and she even made a start on the storerooms above, in the hope that she could persuade Percy to let the rooms to her. If only she had a proper home for her mam to come to, she was sure that she could persuade Sarah to leave Isaac Pendleton. Meg still hadn't given up hope entirely.

'There's a lot of stuff up there, Mr Rodwell. Is it to be thrown out?'

'Oh, dear me, no. I couldn't throw any of it away. I mean, someone might ask for something one day . . .'

Despite her inner unhappiness, Meg found herself smiling. When pigs might fly, she thought, but said demurely, 'How about offering some of the things for sale at less money? I mean, you could even put some in the window showing the marked-down price. You know how the farmers who come into the town on market day love a bargain. And they're not the sort to want fancy clothes.' She giggled mischievously and her green eyes twinkled at him. 'Some of those long johns I've carted upstairs to the storerooms are just what the old farmers still wear. I used to see Mr Smallwood's hanging on the line on wash day.'

Percy stared at her. 'Do you know, Miss Kirkland, I think you could be right. How clever of you to think of it. We'll do it. Yes – yes – we'll do it.'

Late in the afternoon the shop bell clanged and Meg looked up, hoping that it was a female customer for her to serve. In spite of her own worries, she really enjoyed serving in the shop, guiding the customers towards their purchases, giving an honest appraisal, handing out compliments when something was just right, a tactful, 'Perhaps you might like to try this instead . . .' when something really didn't suit.

'Always try to be honest with your customers, but do it in such a way that they hardly notice that you're really saying, "That looks absolutely dreadful and I wouldn't let you walk out of my shop wearing it in a hundred years,"' Percy had taught her. It had made her laugh when he had said it. Today she didn't feel like laughing, but she plastered a welcoming smile on to her face as she glanced up to see who had entered the shop.

Her smile faded when she saw Clara Finch advancing towards the counter, her hands folded neatly in front of her, her lips pursed to nothingness.

'My dear,' Percy greeted her, hurrying out from behind his counter. 'What a nice surprise.'

'I don't think it will be, Percy, when I've said my piece.'

Percy gave a nervous laugh. 'Oh dear, that sounds ominous. What have I done now?' His tone was jovial and yet Meg had the feeling that there was a hint of truth in his statement, as if he often did things that displeased his fiancée.

'It's not so much what *you've* done, Percy, but you are perhaps guilty of a lapse in common sense.'

He looked perplexed. Miss Finch's gaze was fixed on Meg's face and slowly Percy followed suit. Under their scrutiny, Meg could not prevent the colour rising into her face, but she lifted her chin defiantly and stared back at the woman.

'Look at her, Percy. Just look at that bold, brazen look. My goodness, girl, you've a lot to learn. But, if I have any say in the matter, you won't be learning it in this establishment. Oh, dear me, no.'

'Clara, my dear, whatever's the matter? And what has it to do with Miss Kirkland?'

'I've just had a visit from Miss Pendleton.' The lips pursed even tighter. 'The wretched woman seems to think that she has some right to be called a friend of the family, when really –' she broke off and muttered – 'but that's another matter.' She cleared her throat and said loudly, 'My brother has some standing in the community and I pride myself too that I am a respectable, God-fearing woman—'

'My dear, of course you are. Who could doubt that fact?' Percy murmured. He had now looked away from Meg and was anxiously scanning the face of his intended.

Clara turned her eyes accusingly upon Percy for a moment, and under their steely gaze he blinked rapidly. 'You seem to have forgotten that fact when you brought this – this hussy to work in your establishment. It reflects on me as your future wife whom you employ, you know.'

Percy gasped. 'Oh, now come, my dear. Miss Kirkland is doing very nicely. The customers – the lady customers, that is – seem most pleased with how she—'

'Do they indeed? You surprise me, Percy. But then, perhaps I ought not to be surprised. Perhaps they do not know what *I* know.'

'What – what you know, Clara?' Percy stuttered, any composure he'd tried to cling to now draining away.

'Yes, Percy. What I know. I don't suppose she has told you herself, has she?'

Percy glanced briefly at Meg and quailed afresh. The girl's face was fiery with embarrassment, but there was now a spark of defiant anger in those fine green eyes. He felt trapped between the two of them and feared an unseemly scene. Respectable though his fiancée claimed to be, he'd once witnessed her screaming like a fishwife when one of her housemaids had committed some offence. The experience had unnerved him and made him unwilling to set a firm date for their wedding.

'No,' Clara continued, 'I see that she has not.'

'Erm,' Percy began, glancing worriedly from one to the other, his greatest fear that a customer would enter the shop. 'Perhaps you would like to go into the workroom to talk together. It would be better—'

'What I have to say can be said here, Percy. I don't mind who hears me.'

'That's what I was afraid of,' Percy muttered.

'What did you say?' Clara flashed at him.

'Nothing, my dear,' Percy said mildly, but the worried frown did not leave his forehead.

'Well, then.' Clara turned her attention back to Meg. 'What have you to say for yourself, miss?'

Meg took a deep breath and willed herself to speak calmly and respectfully. This was her employer's fiancée. Percy would side with Clara. It was natural. So, she, Meg, would have to be very careful what she said and how she said it. 'Miss Finch, I can hardly bring myself to speak of it, it pains me so much. To think that my own mother would act in such a way.' Meg hung her head as if she bore the full burden of guilt. 'How am I ever to hold my head up again in respectable society?' she whispered, trying desperately to give the impression that she was throwing herself upon the other woman's mercy. For a moment it seemed as if she might have succeeded, for Miss Finch appeared nonplussed by the girl's dignified answer. But Clara was not yet finished. Her mouth twisted into a sneer. 'And then, of course, there was your father running off with a girl half his age.'

Meg kept her eyes downcast and her chin trembled. She nodded and allowed tears to splash onto her hands, which she gripped tightly in front of her. Her voice husky, she said, 'I know. Oh, Miss Finch, I hardly know how to bear it all. If it hadn't been for the kindness of Mr Rodwell putting his trust in me, then – then I truly believe I would not have wanted to live any longer . . .' She raised her eyes, brimming with tears. 'But surely a Christian woman like yourself can see that none of it is my fault. What can I do? What *can* I do?'

'There, there, my dear girl,' Percy interposed. 'We'll say no more about it. Erm – whatever it is.' Percy was still partially in the dark. He had no idea what the two women were talking about. He could only murmur, 'Please, don't distress yourself.'

Clara whirled around to face him. 'Her mother has become Isaac Pendleton's latest – latest *paramour*.'

Percy blinked and stared down at her for a moment. Then he glanced at Meg and back again to Clara.

'Well?' Clara demanded. 'What have you to say about *that*?'

Percy frowned and shifted his weight from one foot to the other. 'Erm, well. I don't really think it is any of our business, my dear. Not really.'

'Not – our – business?' Clara's voice was rising shrilly and Percy put out his hands, palms outwards, trying to placate her.

'What I mean is – as Miss Kirkland says – it is not her fault—'

'One is judged by the company one keeps,' Clara said piously. 'People will talk, Percy. Believe you me, people will talk and your customers, at least all the *lady* customers you are hoping to attract, will go elsewhere.'

For a moment Percy looked helpless and then, gripping the tape measure that always dangled around his neck during working hours, he straightened up and declared, 'Well, I'll just have to take that risk, won't I, my dear? I am not prepared to punish this poor girl for something that she hasn't done. She is to be pitied, not blamed.'

Now it was Clara's face that coloured, so vividly her complexion was almost purple. 'Well, really!' was all she could utter for a few moments. Then the tirade began. 'You disappoint me, Percy. I would have hoped for better things from you, really I would—' The shop doorbell clanged and a woman entered the shop, but Clara, in full flow now, did not notice. 'How can you even consider employing a girl with such connections? Bad blood will out, Percy. Mark my words, it's in the breed.' On and on she ranted until even the woman who had entered the shop began to look embarrassed and seemed about to leave.

Meg moved around the counter, eased her way past Clara and stepped towards the newcomer. 'May I help you, madam?' she asked politely as if nothing untoward was going on behind her.

The woman glanced towards Clara. 'I – er—' she began hesitantly. 'I was looking for a new hat. I understand that Mr Rodwell is beginning to stock ladies' fashions and I wondered . . .'

Meg shook her head apologetically. 'I'm sorry, madam. At the moment we don't stock hats although we may do so in the future.' Meg spoke carefully, smoothing out the local dialect from her speech. 'But we do have a wonderful selection of undergarments, if you would care to take a look,' she added hopefully.

But the customer shook her head, stepped backwards and fumbled for the door handle. Casting one last look towards Clara, she murmured, 'Perhaps another time . . .' turned and hurried out.

'There, you see?' Clara said at once, gesturing towards the shop door through which the potential customer had just disappeared. 'That woman didn't want to be served by a chit of a girl. Really, Percy, can't you see further than the end of your nose? Ladies want to be served by an older woman. Someone who is discreet and *respectable*. The kind of woman you need to employ is a genteel kind of woman who has become impoverished through no fault of her own.'

'Surely Miss Kirkland fits that description?'

'I said, "impoverished", Percy. Not a pauper from

the workhouse!' She glared at him, but when he made no reply, she gave an exasperated 'Huh!' and turned towards the door. She pulled it open and looked back to launch one last parting shot. 'You haven't heard the last of this, Percy Rodwell. If you won't listen to me, then perhaps you'll listen to my brother.' Her face twisted into a sneer as she added, 'After all, he does own these premises.'

With that, she swept out, slamming the door so hard behind her that the bell shuddered on its spring for several moments.

Meg was appalled at what she had heard. In her view the woman was hysterical – mad. Even if she disapproved passionately of her fiancé's employment of Meg, she herself had shown a surprising lack of decorum. But Meg knew she must be careful what she said to Percy. Clara was still his fiancée. She must not forget that.

Now that the shop was empty, she turned tearful eyes towards him. 'Oh, Mr Rodwell, I hadn't realized how my family's troubles might reflect upon you.' She pulled in a deep breath and took a risk. 'I should leave at once. I'd hate to lose you custom because of – because of—' Now she allowed the tears to flow freely down her face. She pulled out her handkerchief and covered her face, sobbing uncontrollably into it.

She felt Percy move to her side and his tentative touch on her shoulder. 'There, there, my dear. Please don't cry. I wouldn't dream of you leaving. You're doing very nicely here. Very nicely. Don't worry any more about – about Miss Finch. I will talk to her. Yes – yes, I will talk to her again. She has my best interests at heart. I know that, but – well – perhaps . . .' His voice trailed away but then he added more firmly, 'But there must be no more talk of you leaving.'

'Oh, thank you, Mr Rodwell. You are good. Thank you.'

He patted her shoulder again and murmured, 'There, there.'

Behind her handkerchief, Meg smiled.

Twenty

Her heart in her mouth, Meg knocked on the door of Isaac Pendleton's office. Trying to keep her anger, disgust even, in check, she adopted a docile image. When his voice boomed out telling her to enter, she opened the door and smiled as she stepped into the room.

'Ah, Meg, my dear girl.' Isaac rose from behind his desk and came towards her, his arms outstretched.

Meg shuddered but managed to hide her revulsion. 'I wondered, sir,' she began meekly, 'if I might see my mother, if you please?'

'Of *course* you can, my dear. You don't need to ask. My door is always open to you.' He put his arm around her shoulder and pulled her against the bulge of his stomach. 'After all, we are almost family now, aren't we? I expect you've heard that your mother has made me the happiest of men by agreeing to become my – er – um – *friend*?'

Meg had to clamp her mouth tightly shut to prevent the vitriolic words that were tumbling around in her mind from spilling out. 'Where – is she?' she managed to stammer.

'In my room upstairs. Run along and see her, my dear. I'll be along shortly.'

Meg managed a weak smile as she pulled herself away from him and left the room.

The stairs leading to the first floor were just outside

the master's room. As Meg put her foot on the first step, she heard a movement above her and glanced up to see Louisa Daley coming down towards her. Meg stood aside and waited until the schoolmistress passed by. At the foot of the stairs, Louisa paused. She smiled uncertainly. 'Meg,' she began hesitantly. There was a pleading tone in her voice but Meg only glared back at her, her expression frosty and unforgiving. 'Meg, please – can't we be friends again? I am so sorry. What more can I say?'

'There's nothing you can say that can undo what happened.'

'But I've apologized about the watch. And as for Bobbie – well – Philip – Dr Collins said there was nothing he could've done even if he'd been called in earlier.'

'There might have been,' Meg insisted. 'You shouldn't have tried to look after him yourself. You should've told matron sooner. At least she really cares about the children.'

'How can you say that? *I* care, Meg. Really I do.'

The girl was stony-faced and unforgiving.

'Won't you believe me, Meg? I truly am so sorry. I know you don't want to come back to the school room – that you've found a nice post in the town. Do you like it? Are they kind to you?'

'What do you care if they're kind to me or not? We're just paupers to you. Not even worth your precious doctor's attention. And I'm just a common thief, aren't I?'

'Oh, Meg, please—'

'Let me pass.'

Louisa remained where she was, blocking Meg's path to the stairs. 'You're going to see your mother?'

'That's none of your business.'

Louisa touched Meg's arm, still trying to make amends. 'Things will be better for her now. For you both, now that you're under Mr Pendleton's protection. You needn't think of yourselves as being in the workhouse any more.'

Meg's face contorted. 'You don't think I condone what she's doing, do you?'

'But you'll be set for life now. Isaac – Mr Pendleton – looks after his – his ladies. He—'

Meg thrust her face close to Louisa's. 'Then why didn't you climb into his bed?'

Louisa gasped and drew back. Meg pushed her aside. 'I've nothing more to say to you.' Without looking back she lifted her skirts and ran up the stairs.

'How could you, Mam? How could you do it? After all you've taught me.'

'Oh, Meggie, please don't judge me.' Sarah came towards her daughter, beseeching her for understanding. But Meg refused to reach out to her mother. She couldn't bear to touch her. Even when Sarah put her arms about her and laid her face against Meg's shoulder, she did not move, but held herself rigid, refusing to return her mother's embrace.

'I feel so alone,' Sarah whispered. 'I need someone to take care of me. Of us.'

'You've got me. I'll take care of you. I've got a good job in town—' Mentally, Meg crossed her fingers, hoping that this was still the truth now Miss Finch had made clear her disapproval. Maybe, with the hold her family had over her fiancé, in more ways than one, Clara might yet persuade Percy to dismiss Meg. The accusation was out of her mouth before she could stop herself. 'But I might not have now because of what you've done.'

Astonished, Sarah pulled back and stared at Meg. 'What – whatever do you mean?'

Unable to hold back her frustration, Meg blurted out, 'Mr Rodwell's fiancée is Miss Finch and she's friendly with Miss Pendleton and she knows that you – that you've become what she calls Mr Pendleton's latest "paramour". And all them down there—' Momentarily, in her anger, her care for her grammar deserted her as she flung out her hand in the vague direction of where the women's day room was on the floor below. 'They all know. You should've seen them last night when I came home. And as for Waters, she nearly attacked me.' She forbore to tell her mother that if it hadn't been for Jake, it would have been she who attacked Waters, not the other way about. 'One way or another the whole town will know soon,' she went on, sparing her mother nothing. 'And if what Miss Finch says is true, then the ladies will stop frequenting Mr Rodwell's shop.' She paused and then drove the knife home. 'And then they might persuade their menfolk to stop too and then where will he be? Not needing an assistant, that's where.'

'But Isaac's kind and generous and he says he'll look after you too. He'll look after us both. He wants you to go back into the school room with Miss Daley.' Sarah gripped Meg's arm, pleading desperately. 'Oh, Meg, please, do what he asks. He'll set us up for life. He's got contacts. He can arrange for you to become a teacher. Just think about that, Meg.'

The door opened quietly behind them, but they were

both so caught up in their conversation that neither of them noticed who was standing there.

'No, I won't think about it. I don't need to. I'm not letting that man rule our lives. Oh, Mam—' Now it was Meg who took hold of her mother's shoulders and gave her a gentle shake as if trying to instil some sense into the distraught woman, who, in her view, was making a tragic mistake. 'I do understand how you must feel, truly. After everything that's happened, but please don't do this. Don't become Isaac Pendleton's mistress. He'll cast you off eventually, just like he did Waters. Then where will you be?'

Sarah shook her head. 'He's not like that. He – he looks after – even if . . .' Her voiced trailed away.

'Look, I was going to tell you last night. There's some rooms above Mr Rodwell's shop that I'm sure aren't used. I'll ask him if we can live there. Just you and me. I'm sure he'll say "yes".'

Slowly, Sarah shook her head and whispered, 'Meg, I'm sorry, but I need—'

Meg pulled away from her mother. Her green eyes filled with disgust. 'Then you're no better than a – than a *whore*. If you stay here with him, I want nothing more to do with you. Do you hear me?' Though her voice broke on the final words, she cried, 'If you stay here, I don't want to see you ever again.'

The figure in the doorway moved into the room. This time it was not Meg's ally, Jake, but Isaac Pendleton, who had heard every word of Meg's final outburst. 'I think, young lady, you've said quite enough.'

Sarah gasped in horror, realizing what he must have overheard, but Isaac moved forward to stand beside her and put his arm around her. 'Your mother's quite right.

I intended to look after you both. But not now. Oh, I'll take care of your mother, but not you. From this moment on, my girl, you're on your own.'

Sarah clutched at the front of Isaac's coat. 'Oh, please, Isaac, don't cast her out into the streets.'

For a moment, he said nothing and Meg could see his internal struggle on his face. 'Very well, since it is you who ask, my dear, she can stay in the workhouse for the time being.' He turned back to Meg, his face purple with rage, his eyes bulging. 'But you will have none of the special privileges you *might* have enjoyed.'

'I don't want them,' Meg spat back. With one last glance at her mother, she whirled around and ran from the room. As she did so, all she heard was her mother's pleading, 'Oh, Meggie, please don't go. Not like this . . .'

Twenty-One

'Oh, Mr Rodwell, what am I to do? I'm so ashamed of my mother.'

Meg had told Percy everything that had happened the previous evening. Now she covered her face with her hands, but she peeped through her fingers to watch his reaction. Percy was agitated. He removed his spectacles, polished them and replaced them. He cleared his throat. 'Well, my dear. I can see how you're placed. It is unfortunate. Most unfortunate.'

Meg sobbed.

'Now, now, don't take on so. I didn't mean to imply that it was your fault. But, of course, whilst you are still at the – still *there* . . .'

Now was the moment. It had come sooner than she'd dared to hope. Meg took a deep breath. 'Sir, I know it's a dreadful imposition and if you say no then I will quite understand. As you say, whilst I am still living at the workhouse . . .' She gulped back a sob, her mouth trembling. 'And now I've stood up to the master, he's – he's going to make life so difficult for me – I wondered . . .' She allowed the words to come tumbling out, erratic and desperate. 'I just wondered – the rooms above the shop. Could I perhaps live in one of them? I'd only need one. And I could keep an eye on the shop all the time, have the stove lit every morning for you and do the cleaning at night after we've closed.

Oh, Mr Rodwell, sir, please – please would you consider it?'

Percy stared at her as if she had taken leave of her senses. 'But – but they're not suitable. I mean, they're in a dreadful state. They're not habitable.'

Meg hung her head and was at once full of pretended contrition. 'I shouldn't have asked. You haven't even said you're keeping me on. I haven't completed my trial period. I was taking too much for granted. I'm sorry.'

Percy was still staring at her as if he was suddenly seeing something that he hadn't noticed before. Nervously, he cleared his throat. 'No – no, it's not that. Miss Kirkland – Meg – I am quite satisfied with your work. Very satisfied, in fact.' He gripped the tape measure hanging around his neck. 'It's just . . .' He stopped and stared at her again.

In a small, pathetic voice, Meg said, 'It's just that Miss Finch wouldn't agree.'

Percy shook his head emphatically. 'No, it's not that either. Miss Finch has nothing to do with the running of my business.' He paused and then added, almost grimly, 'Not yet, anyway.'

'But it would make it very awkward for you, I see that. I'm really sorry, I shouldn't have asked you. I wouldn't have done if I hadn't been so desperate.' Tears filled her eyes again. She made a great play of dabbing her face, squaring her shoulders and smiling bravely through her tears. 'I'll think of something. Now, shall I make us a cup of tea and tidy the workroom? You must have worked very late last night, Mr Rodwell. I see the suit for Mr Pickering is almost finished.'

Percy nodded absently. 'He wants a final fitting today,' he murmured, 'And the suit finished as soon as possible. I think he plans to wear it for the next race meeting.'

'Oh yes,' Meg murmured. Unbidden, the memory of her last visit to the racecourse and the picture of Alice clinging to her father's arm pushed its way into her mind. Banishing it swiftly, she widened her smile and was gratified to see Percy blinking in its radiance. 'Then you'll be needing that cup of tea and, if you want to carry on working on it, I can hold the fort in the shop.' Seeing his mouth open to protest, she added at once, 'I can always fetch you if a gentleman requires you particularly.'

The morning passed with Meg's mind in a turmoil. Every time Percy emerged from the workroom, she looked up eagerly to see if he was going to say anything. But he avoided meeting her gaze and only spoke to her when he required her to do something. By the middle of the afternoon Meg was losing heart and by the time for her to leave came he had still not said any more about her idea.

Dispirited, she trudged towards the workhouse. Albert met her at the gateway. 'I'm sorry, lass, but mester's given orders you've to be sent straight to the punishment room.'

Meg gasped. 'Why?'

The old man shrugged his shoulders. 'Search me, lass. I'd go there miself instead of you, if I could, but—'

'Oh, Albert.' Now genuine tears filled her eyes. She was touched by the old man's thoughtfulness.

He patted her shoulder with rough kindness. 'There, there, lass. You've done summat to upset him and you'll have to pay. Thing is, old Isaac's fine and dandy, generous to a fault, when we'm all doing his bidding.

But cross him –' the old man shook his head – 'and there's hell to pay.'

Meg's eyes widened. 'He's not going to keep me locked up so that I can't go to work, is he?'

Albert looked at her sorrowfully. 'Three days, he said. On bread and water.'

Meg stared at him, her mind working quickly. She glanced round the deserted yard and then up at the windows of the master's rooms, which overlooked the back of the main building. There was no shadowy figure standing there. *Too busy with me mam*, Meg thought bitterly. She stepped closer to Albert. 'Go back into your lodge. You haven't seen me, right?'

'Aw, lass, what're you up to now? It won't do no good, yer know. Yer'll only get yersel' into more trouble.'

'Don't worry about me, but I don't want him taking it out on you. Just do one thing for me.'

'What's that, lass?'

'Tell Jake I've gone.'

'He's not here no more, mi duck. He's living in at the farm now.'

'Well – when you do see him, then.'

Albert sighed. 'All right. But what are you going to do?'

'Best you don't know.'

'I wouldn't tell—' he began indignantly.

'I know you wouldn't,' Meg said swiftly. 'It's not that it's just – well – I don't want him even *thinking* you know.'

The old man sighed. 'All right – but you will take care of yoursel', won't you?'

Meg grinned at him through the dusk. 'Oh, I'll do that

all right, Albert. And – and thanks for – for everything.' Briefly, she gripped his hands in hers.

'I ain't done nowt,' the old man sniffed, sounding suspiciously tearful.

'You've done more than you know.' Impulsively, she leant forward and kissed his cheek. Then she was gone, running across the yard and up the stairs to the women's dormitory. She held her breath as she opened the door. She was lucky – the room was empty. The women would all be at supper. That was where she should be. If anyone missed her . . . Then she remembered. She would not be missed, for they would probably all know by now that she'd been banished to the punishment room. If no one but Albert had seen her come back from work, then there was still time for her to escape.

Hurriedly, she gathered together her belongings. It didn't take more than a minute or two – there was precious little to gather – and then she was creeping back down the stairs and scurrying across the yard, afraid that at any moment the master's voice would boom out. Thank goodness she'd been allowed to wear her own clothes to go to work in. At least she had those. She reached the gate out of the yard again. Albert had gone back into his lodge and closed the door. She looked briefly through the window and saw him sitting at the table, a plate of food in front of him, but he wasn't eating. He was just sitting, his arms resting on the table and staring into space. He didn't even glance towards the window.

Meg crept out of the yard and into the lane. She slipped like a silent wraith along the side wall and then began to run as fast as she could away from the workhouse.

She ran and ran until her lungs were bursting and she could run no more. When she reached the shop, the premises were in darkness. Percy Rodwell had gone home. Meg crept down the passageway at the side of the shop and let herself into the yard at the back. She tried the door into the workshop, but, as she'd expected, it was locked and bolted. But she found that the door to the lean-to scullery was unlocked. There was little in there worth stealing and Percy didn't bother to secure it. Meg shivered as she felt her way around in the darkness. Even though the August night was balmy and warm, it would get colder in the early morning, but she had her thick shawl and all the clothes she possessed, though they were pathetically few. She did not want to lie on the brick floor, so she spread a layer of clothing on the top of the table and curled up on it with her shawl covering her. She wished now that she'd been brave enough to steal a blanket from the dormitory, but she had not dared. Isaac would have her sent to prison for theft. He'd do anything, she thought, to get back at her for the things she'd said.

Meg slept fitfully, waking every so often, cold and shivering. She was pleased to see the pale light of dawn creeping in through the grimy windows. She sat up and climbed stiffly down from the table. Her feet were like blocks of ice and had no feeling. She stamped them and threw her arms about herself, trying to get warm.

She opened the door and listened. Already she could hear movement from the other yards in the row of houses and shops, so she went out to the pump in the middle of Percy's yard. The handle squeaked and icy, fresh water streamed from the spout. She splashed her face, shivering anew as she did, and then took a long drink. Next she visited the privy and then returned to the scullery to try to make herself look presentable. It was fortunate, she thought, that she had taken to coming round to the back entrance each morning. Percy would see nothing unusual when he opened the back door to find her standing there.

Meg had no idea what the day would bring. How long could she stay in the scullery without Percy finding out? And what would he do when he did?

One thing Meg did know: no matter what happened, she would never, ever go back to the workhouse. She would sooner die of starvation and cold.

Twenty-Two

Meg spent four more nights in the scullery before she managed to take the spare door-key from the hook behind the back door on the Saturday evening. Each night she left as usual by the front door, calling out a cheery 'Goodnight' to Percy and set off in the direction of the workhouse. But she only went as far as the end of the street, where she waited until Percy left the shop, carefully locking the door behind him. Then, in the darkness, she crept back into the yard and let herself into the workroom by the back door. Not daring to light a lamp or even a candle in case someone should see the light, Meg felt her way through to the shop and huddled down by the stove. Though the floor was uncomfortable, at least she was warm throughout the night now.

She was awake early each morning. She'd washed and tidied herself and was standing outside the back door when Percy arrived for the day's work.

'Good morning, Meg – Miss Kirkland.' As he held open the door for her and she passed close to him to step inside, he touched her shoulder. 'You look tired, my dear. Are – are things still the same?'

Meg nodded. 'I haven't seen my mother since – since that night.' It was the truth, if not the whole truth. She did not tell him that she hadn't been back to the workhouse since then, for he would surely ask questions. As it was, she lived in dread that Miss Pendleton would have told Miss Finch that Meg Kirkland had left the institution.

'Dear, dear,' the kindly man murmured. 'What a state of affairs, to be sure.' He went through to the front of the shop, shaking his head sadly and leaving Meg to start the day's work.

The stove was soon revived each morning for now Meg was able to keep it going through the night. She just hoped Percy wouldn't notice that the shop was warmer than usual when he arrived. Later that day she was able to sneak upstairs to fetch a man's woollen vest and a pair of long johns from the old stock. These would keep her warm during the nights. It could still be surprisingly cold at two o'clock in the morning. She'd look a strange sight, but she didn't care. There was no one to see her. She also found two moth-eaten blankets and stowed these and the garments near the top of the stairs, where she could easily find them in the dark when she returned each night.

Meg had no means of washing and drying her clothes and by the end of two weeks her dress was decidedly grubby. Percy must have noticed. Late one afternoon he handed her a parcel and, avoiding her eyes, murmured, 'I thought it would be nice for you to wear some kind of uniform. I . . . er . . . hope these . . . um . . . garments will fit.'

'Oh, *thank* you, Mr Rodwell,' Meg said as she unwrapped a long black skirt and a white cotton blouse. Her gratitude was heartfelt, but even Percy could not guess just how much the gift of the clothing meant to her.

Meg managed to remain undiscovered for almost four weeks. Sundays were the worst. Then she wandered the streets, her stomach rolling with hunger, for she had no money to buy anything. The small wage that Percy paid her was soon gone. She was relying now only on the bread rolls that Percy bought from the bakery for their midday meal.

'It's too far for you to go home in the middle of the day,' he'd said when she had first begun working for him. 'But you'll get a good meal at night, won't you?' Meg had smiled, wondering what he would think to the workhouse supper of bread and porridge. The best meal of the day there was the one at midday which she was now missing: boiled meat, peas and potatoes.

After four weeks the strain of living in such harsh conditions was taking its toll. One morning, exhausted by a fitful night's sleep, she awoke with a start to find Percy bending over her as she lay on the floor near the stove.

'Meg?' His tone was more concerned than angry. 'Whatever are you doing here? And – and how did you get in?' Then he straightened up and, staring down at her strange garb and the makeshift bed of old blankets on the floor by the stove, realization spread across his face. 'Oh, my dear girl, you've been sleeping here, haven't you?'

Meg scrambled to her feet with difficulty. Her limbs were stiff and cold. 'Oh, please, Mr Rodwell. Please forgive me. I've done no harm, honestly. Please don't be cross—'

'I'm not, my dear. I'm just so sorry you didn't trust me enough to tell me. If I'd known then . . .' He took off his spectacles, polished them and replaced them on the bridge of his nose.

'I had to leave the workhouse, Mr Rodwell. Mr Pendleton was going to shut me in the punishment room on bread and water for three days. He wasn't even going to let me come to work.' Meg said, standing now and trying to smooth her hair. She knew what a ridiculous sight she must look, with an old man's woollen vest pulled over her own clothes and a pair of long johns peeping out from beneath her skirt. Percy looked her up and down and the corners of his mouth twitched. He tried to control himself, but he smiled and then he chuckled and finally he was laughing out loud. Meg joined in and they were both shaking with laughter until tears ran down their faces.

'Oh, Meg, what a sight you look!'

'I know,' she spluttered. 'But they are warm. I found them upstairs. It's not your best stock. I wouldn't have used that.'

'Oh, my dear girl,' Percy said, wiping his eyes, 'I wouldn't have minded if you had. It'd've been worth it. I don't know when I last laughed so much.' And they dissolved into laughter afresh.

'Now,' Percy said at last, 'go and make yourself presentable through the back and then you must go next door to the bakery and buy whatever you would like to eat. I don't suppose you've had any breakfast, have you?' He looked down at her with mock severity, but there was still a twinkle in his eyes. Then the twinkle faded as he added, 'In fact, if I'm not much mistaken, you haven't been eating properly for some time, have you?'

Meg shook head.

'Right, you go and get whatever you want. Tell Mr Wilkins to put it on my account. And then we'll talk.'

'Yes, Mr Rodwell,' Meg said meekly, hanging her head.

*

Later in the morning, when there was a lull in the number of customers coming into the shop, Percy once more went through his spectacle-polishing routine. Meg had noticed by now that this was a nervous habit of his when he was anxious. He seemed to do it a lot, she thought, when Miss Finch came into the shop.

'Now, we must decide what we are going to do.'

Meg waited, chewing her little finger, her heart thumping painfully. Was he going to dismiss her and send her back to the workhouse? The punishment room awaiting her was, to her mind, far worse than the discomfort she'd suffered recently sleeping on the floor of his shop.

'Don't send me back there, Mr Rodwell, please . . .'

He looked at her and blinked rapidly. 'My dear girl, nothing was further from my mind. I wouldn't dream of sending you back – there.'

'You're – you're not going to dismiss me then?'

Percy shook his head. 'Certainly not. You're doing very nicely here and the ladies seem to like you.' He paused, then glanced away as he murmured, 'Well, most of them anyway.' And Meg knew that he was thinking about Miss Finch. 'No, no, I was just wondering where we could find lodgings for you in the town. I mean, I'd take you home with me, but – well – it wouldn't be right. You do understand, don't you?'

Meg nodded. She bit her lip and then plunged in, repeating her previous request. 'Mr Rodwell – please – would you let me use the rooms above the shop? I'd clean them out and make them habitable and – and I'd be on hand to look after the shop. I could keep the stove going all night in the winter—'

'Ah, so that's why the shop has been so warm every morning,' Percy said thoughtfully. 'I see now.'

'And it would be good to have someone living on the premises, wouldn't it?' Meg rushed on, but her heart sank when Percy shook his head. 'It wouldn't be right, a young girl like you living on her own here.'

'I'd be all right. Really I would. Oh, please, Mr Rodwell, won't you think about it?'

'Well . . .' he seemed to be wavering and Meg pressed home her point. 'I could clean the shop after hours and sort out all the stock. I'd enjoy that, really I would. Oh, please, do say yes.'

He stared at her for a several moments before slowly he nodded. 'Very well, then, but –' he wagged his forefinger at her – 'there's just one thing.' Meg held her breath as he continued, 'You're not staying here any longer. Until we've got those two rooms upstairs habitable, you are coming home with me.' He smiled archly at her. 'I'll risk my reputation, if you'll risk yours.'

Meg laughed and thanked him prettily, but she did not voice what she was thinking.

Whatever was Miss Finch going to say about that when she heard? As hear she surely would.

Twenty-Three

Clara Finch had plenty to say. From the workroom, where she was carefully sewing buttons onto the jacket of a suit, Meg heard it all.

'Percy Rodwell, have you taken leave of your senses entirely?' the woman almost screamed at him. 'You mean to tell me that you're going to let that slut of a girl live over the shop? You're trusting her to be alone here? Well, I declare I've heard everything now.'

Percy's tone was calm. 'The girl is no slut. She and her family have hit hard times.'

'No slut, you say. Like mother, like daughter, I say.'

In the workroom, Meg winced and her resolve against her mother hardened.

'I really couldn't pass comment on her mother, Clara,' Percy was saying, his voice low. 'I've never met the poor woman, but just remember she's lost her husband and two of her children. Can't you find it in your heart to be a little more sympathetic?'

Clara snorted in a most unladylike manner. 'You make it sound as if her husband died. Well, I don't know what that chit of a girl has told you, but he didn't.' By now Meg had crept closer to the door leading from the workroom into the shop. It was ajar and she peeped through the open slit to see Clara prod Percy in the chest with a sharp, bony fingertip. 'He ran off with another woman. Morals no better than a tomcat's, if you ask me. And now the mother has taken up with Isaac Pendleton.'

'Clara,' Percy cut in, 'nobody is asking you.'

There was a moment's stunned silence and then her voice shrilled. 'Percy Rodwell, how dare you speak to me like that?'

'My dear—' Percy began.

'Don't you "my dear" me,' Clara shot back. 'The scheming little hussy is taking you for a fool, Percy. But if you're too blind to see it, then so be it. But don't come running to me for sympathy when she runs off with all the takings.'

'She won't do that,' he said confidently and the listening girl felt a warm glow of gratitude flood through her.

'Don't my opinions count for anything with you, Percy?'

There was the slightest of pauses before Percy answered. It sounded to Meg as if he was having to force the words out. 'Of course, my dear,' he said mildly, 'but I think I am a better judge of character than you give me credit for.'

Clara's laugh was hard and brittle. 'You're a fool, Percy. A fool over a pretty face. Just like a lot of men. Though I'd've thought better of you. But . . .' She paused deliberately, then added, 'If you won't listen to me, your fiancée, then perhaps you'll listen to my brother.' Percy did not respond this time and Clara added pointedly, 'Don't forget, *my dear* –' the endearment was heavy with sarcasm – 'that he owns these premises. I think he has a right to say who occupies them, don't you?'

Meg heard the swish of the woman's skirts as she moved and then the sound of the shop doorbell. Now, through the crack, she could see Clara standing near the door, her hand on the doorknob, about to leave. Then she saw the woman turn back to deliver one last parting shot. 'Don't force my brother to do something we might all regret, Percy.'

She left the shop, slamming the door behind her so that the bell bounced crossly.

Meg pulled open the door and stepped into the shop. 'Oh, Mr Rodwell, I couldn't help overhearing. I'm so sorry. I should leave at once.' She moved closer to him and looked appealingly up into his face. Huskily, she said, 'I can't bear to be the cause of trouble between you and your fiancée.'

Percy was still staring at the closed door through which Clara had departed. 'Don't concern yourself, my dear,' Percy murmured.

Behind the round, steel-rimmed spectacles, Percy's hazel eyes had a thoughtful, far-away look.

For the rest of the day there was a tense atmosphere in the shop. Customers came and went and were served with the usual polite efficiency, yet between Percy and Meg there was constraint. They were both waiting for the arrival of Theobald Finch. Meg didn't know what to expect and Percy did not share his thoughts with her. Yet they were both jumpy, and each time the shop doorbell clanged they turned towards it, holding their breath until they recognized the newcomer.

Mid-afternoon, Meg was alone in the shop whilst Percy worked in the back room. The bell clanged and Meg looked up to see Jake standing in the open doorway, grinning widely. There was no one in the shop to see, apart from Percy, so she hurried towards him, her hands outstretched.

'Jake – how are you? How are you getting on at the farm? Have you settled in with Ron and his family? Oh, do tell me everything.'

'It's great,' he began, closing the door and coming further into the shop. 'They're really nice people, the Smallwoods.' He sounded surprised after what Meg had told him.

Meg sighed. 'I suppose they are. It was my dad and Alice caused the trouble, if I'm honest.' She changed the subject, away from painful memories. 'Tell me what you're doing.'

'All sorts. I like the milking the best. Never thought I'd tek to cows, but they're nice creatures when you get used to 'em.'

'Do – do you help in the dairy?'

'A bit, if the missis is short-handed. She's got a girl working there, but Mrs Smallwood ses she's useless. I reckon she's going to get rid of her before long.' There was a pause before he said, 'I was thinking I might tell her about Betsy.'

'Betsy! But she's not old enough.'

'She's twelve – nearly thirteen.'

'Is she? I thought she was only about ten.'

'She's very small for her age. But she's wiry and stronger than she looks.'

'She'll need to be to work in Mrs Smallwood's dairy,' Meg said tartly. Her feelings towards the young girl were mixed. She knew she shouldn't blame Betsy for the mix-up over Louisa Daley's watch – the girl had been very ill and had hardly realized what she was doing. But if it hadn't been for Betsy, Meg might now have been training to be a proper teacher with Louisa as her friend. But then, of course, there had been Bobbie . . .

Jake broke into her thoughts. 'I've moved in with Ron and his family and I've got the little bedroom you told me about.' He touched her arm. 'I think about you when I'm lying in bed at night. Was it your bed? Is – is that where you slept.'

Meg nodded, a lump in her throat. 'I 'spect so. I shouldn't think the Smallwoods have refurnished the place.'

Jake laughed. 'No, they haven't.' Then his voice softened as he said, 'But I'm glad they haven't if I'm sleeping in your bed. It – it makes me feel closer to you.' Colour crept into his face as he added. 'I – I miss you, Meggie.'

It was the endearing pet name her father had called her. When her family life had fallen apart, she had vowed never to let anyone else call her that. Yet for some reason she didn't mind Jake using it.

'And I miss you, but I'm glad you like it there,' she said brightly. Then she added wryly, 'Mind you don't do anything to upset the missis and get yourself thrown out, that's all.'

Jake's face was sober now, the wide grin gone. 'I've been up to the workhouse.'

Meg dropped her gaze and began to turn away, but Jake caught hold of her arm and held on to her, forcing her to remain where she was. 'Meg, I've seen your mam. She's desperate to see you – to know if you're all right.'

Meg glared at him. 'She should have thought of that before she got into Isaac Pendleton's bed.'

'Oh, Meggie, don't be so hard on her. What else has she got left?'

'She's got me,' Meg said passionately and struck

herself in the chest with her clenched fist. 'I'd never've let her down. Not like she's let me down.' Meg was leaning towards him now, shouting in his face. 'She brought me up to believe that I shouldn't let a man – any man – touch me before I'd got a wedding band on me finger. And then just look what she does.'

'Well–' Jake shifted uncomfortably from one foot to the other – 'that's different.'

'Why is it?' she shot back.

'Because – because it just is. I mean – when you're a young girl and it's your first time an' that.'

'When you're a virgin, you mean?'

Jake's face flamed as he nodded.

Meg's face twisted. 'It's no different. She's – she's a whore.'

Softly Jake said, 'She's still yer mam and she loves you.'

Now Meg pulled herself away from him. 'Well, I don't love her any more. I hate her and I never want to see her again. And you can tell her that.'

Jake shook his head. 'I'll do no such thing.' He sighed and said gently, 'Look, I can understand why you're feeling hurt, but in time you'll feel different.'

'No, I won't. I never forgive and I never forget.'

She turned away and went to stand behind the counter, but there was more between them now than just the physical barrier. Jake stood awkwardly, still near the door, whilst Meg stood behind the counter glowering, and that was how Percy saw them as he came in. He glanced from one to the other.

'Jake's just leaving, Mr Rodwell. Goodbye, Jake,' she added pointedly and picked up a bolt of cloth, turning her back on him as she replaced it on a shelf behind the counter.

Jake nodded to Percy, pulled on his cap, and opened the door just as someone else was about to enter. He stood aside and allowed Theobald Finch to step inside, then left without another word.

'Now, Percy, what's all this about? You've quite upset the old girl, don'tcha know.' Theobald said the last three words as if they were one. His glance alighted on Meg. 'And – er – is this the young lady in question?' He frowned as he added, 'I know you, don't I? Weren't you the lass at the workhouse whose mam fainted?' This was the second time that Theobald Finch had recognized her by remembering that incident. Meg bit her lip.

Percy leapt to her aid. 'That's beside the point, Theo. Meg has come to work for me here in the shop. As you know, I am expanding my business into ladies' – erm – apparel and I need a female assistant.'

'But surely, Percy, old man, someone a little older would be more suitable.' They were talking about her now as if she wasn't there, but Meg stood her ground, wanting – needing – to know just what was being said.

'Meg is quick and willing to learn. I can teach her my ways. The way I want things doing.'

'Well, yes, I can see that might have its advantages,' Theo conceded.

Percy removed his spectacles, polished them and replaced them. 'I really can't see what Clara is so upset about.'

Theobald cleared his throat, glanced briefly at Meg and then dropped his gaze. 'Give us a moment, girl—'

'Her name is Miss Kirkland,' Percy almost snapped.

Theobald Finch stared at her. 'Ah,' he said, 'now I do recall. Your family used to work for Smallwood. Is that right?'

Reluctantly, Meg nodded.

'And your father seduced their young daughter?'

Rashly, and not knowing really why she did when her own feelings for him were so bitter, Meg leapt to her father's defence. 'Alice Smallwood was a flirt. It wasn't all his doing. She – she led him on and – and he fell for a pretty face.'

Theo eyed her and nodded slowly. 'And that's not all, is it? Your mother's taken up with Isaac Pendleton, I hear. And what about you? Are you setting your cap at Percy here? Think he's a good catch, do you?'

'Now, look here—' Percy began, but Theobald held up his hand.

'Percy, old chap, I think perhaps – in all the circumstances – it might be best if you dispensed with this girl's services.'

Percy was quite calm and all hesitation gone as he said, 'No, Theo. I'm sorry, but I will not. Meg is to remain here and she is to live in the rooms upstairs and if that doesn't suit you then . . .' He left the sentence hanging in the air between them, an unresolved contention.

'Well now, let's not be too hasty. Think the matter over, Percy, there's a good fellow.' Theo patted his future brother-in-law on the shoulder and, completely ignoring Meg, turned and strode towards the door, pausing only to say, 'Think it over, I'm sure you'll come round to our way of thinking, Percy, if you know what's good for you.' Then he pulled open the door and was gone.

Before the sound of the shop bell had died away, Meg said, 'There's nothing else for it.' She looked up at Percy with soulful eyes. 'I'll just have to go back to the workhouse.'

'I won't hear of it. I'm not going to be bullied into doing something I don't want to do.'

'Oh, Mr Rodwell,' Meg breathed, a catch in her voice, 'you don't know how much that means to me.' She turned her bright gaze on him and Percy blinked.

Then she dropped her gaze and gave an exaggerated sigh. 'But Miss Finch is your fiancée. I don't want to cause trouble between you.'

She felt him touch her shoulder lightly and when she looked up at him again, she saw that he was smiling. Softly, he said, 'I think the trouble was already there long before you arrived, my dear. You've just made me see things so much more clearly. Oh yes – so *much* more clearly.'

Twenty-Four

Late that evening they left the shop together, Meg walking beside Percy along the street, clutching her belongings. They were pathetically few and Meg felt ashamed.

'Here we are,' Percy said, opening the gate into the tiny front garden of a cottage in a row of similar houses. He opened the front door and stood aside for her to enter. 'Please,' he said, smiling down at her, 'come in.'

Meg stepped into a small, dark hallway and waited whilst Percy closed and bolted the door. 'Wait here,' he said, 'whilst I light a lamp and then I'll show you round.'

The cottage was small, but clean and neat and tidy. It could have been cosy, but to Meg's eye it lacked a woman's touch. There were no pretty cushions on the sofa, few ornaments, and what pictures there were on the plain, whitewashed walls were dark and dreary. Meg itched to place fresh flowers on the sideboard and to light a cheery fire in the grate in the small front parlour. The room looked as if it was never used, merely dusted once a week, the square of carpet in the centre brushed and the hearthrug shaken. But as she followed Percy through the hallway again and into the long, narrow kitchen at the back of the house, she realized that the front room was the only sitting room. *He must use it*, she thought, yet *it looks so forlorn, so unloved*.

The kitchen, too, was sparse, adequate only for a

single man's needs. The feeling of loneliness made Meg shudder. Used to family life and even to the workhouse, where it was impossible to be alone for more than five minutes in the day, Meg couldn't imagine coming home to an empty house and a cheerless grate. It must be awful, she thought, to have no one to talk to, no one with whom to share the day's news.

A tiny twisting staircase led up out of the kitchen to two bedrooms.

'The first one's mine, but this is a spare room. There are sheets in the cupboard. I hope they'll not be damp,' Percy added worriedly. 'No one's been in here for a long time.'

Meg smiled and glanced around her. It was the largest bedroom she had ever slept in. 'It'll be fine, Mr Rodwell. I'm very grateful.'

'Please –' he gestured towards the small fireplace – 'light a fire. I had both chimneys swept only last month, so you shouldn't have any trouble getting it going.'

'It doesn't seem right to be lighting a fire in a bedroom in summer,' Meg murmured.

'Well, we're into September now.' Percy smiled. 'And nights start to turn a little autumnal. Besides, it feels cold and musty in here. Not being used, I expect. No, no, Meg. Light a fire, do – it'll help air the room. There are sticks and coal in the backyard. You do that and make up the bed while I find us something to eat.'

Half an hour later, Meg sat on the bed watching the shadows cast by the flames dancing on the ceiling. She felt herself growing drowsy. The bed felt so comfortable and she was warm . . . She shook herself awake, yawning and rubbing her eyes, then went down the stairs, opening the door at the bottom and stepping straight into the kitchen.

Meg gasped in surprise. The table to one side of the narrow kitchen was laid and Percy was placing steaming dishes of meat and vegetables on top.

'Come and sit down, Meg.'

'Oh, Mr Rodwell. I never thought – I mean – of course, living on your own . . .' Her voice trailed away, not quite sure if she was saying the right thing.

'Needs must, my dear. Of course, it would be nice to be married. To have a wife to come home to . . .' Now it was Percy's voice that faded away and he bowed his head and clasped his hands together to say grace.

He began to serve the food, but Meg jumped up. 'Please – let me.'

When she had finished serving them both, she sat down again opposite him and they smiled at each other. They ate in silence, yet it was a companionable silence. At the end of the meal, Meg stood up. 'Now, I'll do the washing up. You go and sit in the front room and read your paper. That's what—' She stopped suddenly. She had been about to say, 'That's what my father liked to do,' but she bit back the words that reminded her so cruelly of happier times.

'That's very thoughtful of you, Meg,' Percy said, 'but it's chilly in there and it's hardly worth lighting a fire at this time of night just for one. I usually sit in here until bedtime.' Meg glanced around, but there were only the two wooden chairs that they had sat on at the table. There was no easy armchair for the man of the house. 'I always light one on a Sunday, but we can light one tonight if you like, now that you're here too,' he added. There was suddenly an eager note to his voice and he even half rose out of his chair, as if to go this very minute to fetch paper, sticks and coal.

'No, no, please, don't trouble on my account. If you don't mind, when I've washed the pots, I'll go to bed. I – I am rather tired.'

'Of course,' Percy said, understanding. 'You can't have been sleeping very well for the past few nights.' He put his head on one side. 'Just how long have you been sleeping at the shop?'

Meg bit her lip. 'Nearly four weeks. For the first two nights I slept in the scullery.'

'You must have been frozen out there.' Percy was appalled. 'Even summer nights can be very cold. Why ever didn't you tell me?'

'I wish now I had, but – but—'

Gently he said, 'You thought I would send you back to the workhouse.'

Meg nodded and Percy sighed. 'Well,' he said slowly, 'if I'm honest with you, that's very well what I might have done. At least, I would have encouraged you to go back there until we could have sorted out somewhere for you to live.'

'I was – I was going to ask you if we could *both* live above the shop. My mother and me. But when I got back to the workhouse, on the very night I was going to tell her of my idea, well, she'd – she'd—'

Percy patted her hand. 'There, there, don't distress yourself. Now, you get to bed. I'll see to the pots—'

'No, no, please let me do them.'

'Very well. But then you must get some rest.'

The following morning Meg awoke with a sore throat and a throbbing head. Her nose itched until she sneezed again and again and her eyes watered.

She dressed and went downstairs.

'My dear girl,' Percy said at once when he saw her. 'You look dreadful.' Then swiftly he rephrased his tactless remark. 'Oh, I'm sorry, but you do look ill.'

'I think I have a cold cubbing,' she said thickly and sneezed again.

Percy stepped back quickly. 'Oh dear, I do hope the sheets weren't damp. Look, you must stay at home today.'

'No, I'll be all right,' Meg said, wiping her eyes and sniffing loudly.

'No, no, I insist. Besides,' he added swiftly as he saw she was about to argue once more, 'it doesn't do to be in the shop with a heavy cold. I know because I've had to be there on a couple of occasions when I really should have stayed away. The customers don't like it.' Then hastily, lest she should think that all he cared about was his customers, he added, 'And you'll get better much quicker if you rest. Have a day in bed, Meg.'

'A day in bed!' Meg squeaked. Usually a healthy child, she could not remember ever having stayed in bed during the daytime.

Percy smiled and nodded. 'Yes, go on. Spoil yourself. Tell you what, before I go to the shop I'll fetch you some fresh lemons. Put the juice in some hot water and drink it as hot as you can. And I think –' he went towards a kitchen cupboard and pulled open the door – 'ah yes, I thought so.' He picked up a jar and held it out to her. 'There's some honey here. Hot lemon and honey. That'll help.'

Meg wiped her eyes. Whether her tears were a result of her cold or sprang from his thoughtfulness, even she could not tell.

*

Meg slept most of the day away, but towards late afternoon she had two visitors. The first was Clara Finch, who banged on the door until, woken from a deep sleep, Meg staggered downstairs to open the front door. Bleary-eyed, her hair hanging unkempt about her face and dressed only in her nightgown, Meg opened the door, to be pushed roughly aside as the other woman barged her way in.

Slamming the door behind her, Clara leant against it and surveyed the barefoot girl before her.

'This is a fine how-de-do.' Her mouth tight, her cold eyes raked Meg from head to toe. 'No wonder Percy was reluctant to tell me where you were. Well, you might fool him, miss, but you don't fool me. You can get your things together and get out of this house this minute.'

Meg sneezed, loudly and juicily. Clara pressed herself back against the door, but there was nowhere to go. 'Really, girl,' she admonished, 'haven't you a handkerchief?' Meg sniffed and Clara answered her own question with an exasperated sigh. 'No, I don't suppose you have. Here, take mine.'

Meg took the clean delicate lace handkerchief that Clara held out to her. She blew her nose, saturating the tiny square of linen in seconds.

'Thank you,' she said politely. All her 'ems' sounded like 'bees' as she added, 'But I'b not going anywhere. Mr Rodwell gave be perbission to stay in bed today. I'b sure I'll be a lot better toborrow. I'b only staying here till the roobs above the shop are ready.'

Clara's mouth turned down at the corners. 'If you think I'm going to stand by and let you move in over the shop, you'd better think again.' She took a step towards Meg and then, remembering the girl's cold, pulled back. 'The workhouse is where you belong, girl. You and your kind. And I'll see you back there, no matter how long it takes me. I know what you're up to. You think you can wheedle your way into Percy's affections. Getting him to feel sorry for you and bringing you home with him. What will people say? Have you stopped to think what harm it might do to his reputation? To his business, even? When folks get to know you're here – alone in this house with him – his business will suffer. Specially, this new venture of his with ladies' apparel. What self-respecting lady is going to frequent his establishment with a little slut like you behind the counter to serve them?' Her beady eyes narrowed. 'I can see your game. You think he's a good catch, don't you? A bachelor with a nice little business. You're no better than your mother.'

'I'b not like by bother,' Meg cried thickly. She sneezed and, to her frustration, tears ran down her face. She didn't want Clara Finch to think she was crying, but this heavy cold was making her feel wretched.

'No?' Clara raised her eyebrows. 'So you intend to try to get a ring on your finger, do you?' She held out her bony fingers, on one of which was a solid gold band inlaid with the blue enamel initials CF and PR. Between the two sets of letters were two tiny stones, a ruby and an emerald. 'Well, this is his ring and that's where it's staying. On *my* finger.'

Before she could stop herself, Meg said, 'He doesn't seeb in buch of a hurry to get the wedding ring to go with it onto your finger, though, does he?'

Shocked, Clara gasped. 'How dare you? Just wait till I tell Percy how rude you've been to me. You might as well pack your bags this very minute. You'll be out on the street by nightfall.' She smiled maliciously. 'Back in the workhouse even quicker than I could have hoped.' With that, she pulled open the door and left, slamming it behind her.

Meg sneezed and groaned aloud. How could she have let her foolish tongue run away with her? She went into the kitchen and cut one of the two lemons which Percy had left on the table. Then she squeezed the juice into a mug and added a teaspoonful of honey and poured hot water into it from the kettle that was kept permanently on the hob. Carefully, she carried the mug back up the stairs and snuggled back beneath the bedclothes. Sipping the liquid, she found that the tang of the lemon cleared her blocked nose and the honey eased her sore throat. The fire, built up that morning by Percy before he left for work and added to by Meg with the coal he had left, was still casting a warm glow about the room. It crackled comfortingly and shadows danced on the ceiling and walls as the daylight faded.

Meg leant back against the pillows and sighed. Warm and drowsy, she was about to drift into sleep when another knocking at the front door roused her.

'If it's that old biddy back again, I'm just not answering it,' she muttered, frowning, and pushed herself further beneath the bedclothes. But the knocking persisted and then she heard a voice calling – a young voice, a voice she recognized. 'Meg? Meg, where are you?'

'Jake!' She sat up, flung back the covers and swung her feet to the floor. 'I'm coming,' she called. 'I'm coming.'

'What are you doing here? Shouldn't you be at work?' she asked as she opened the front door. 'Come in, quick, before all the gossiping old biddies down the street see you.'

Jake stepped inside and pulled off his cap. He glanced

around the small hallway and peered through the half-open doorway into the front room. 'Nice little place, Meg. Getting your feet under the table, are you?'

Did she imagine it, or was there a trace of sarcasm to his tone?

'Don't you start,' she pouted. 'I've just had that dragon of a fiancée of his round here telling me to pack mi bags.'

'Can't blame her. News travels fast – half the town's talking about the pretty young lass old Mester Rodwell has taken on in his shop and moved into his house an' all.'

'He's not that old,' Meg retorted.

Jake stared at her, his face sober now. 'I was only joking. Oh, Meg, you're not really setting your cap at him, are you?'

Meg stared back. The thought hadn't entered her head. Oh yes, she'd made up to him, but only to get a job, to get the rooms over the shop to live in. She'd never thought about anything further than that.

But now she did. First Miss Finch and now Jake was suggesting so much more. Meg's eyes narrowed thoughtfully and a slow smile began to spread across her face.

'And what if I am?' she said softly.

Disgust flitted across his face. 'You're not serious?'

Her only answer was to shrug.

'How can you even think of doing such a thing? Specially after the way you've treated your own mam. You've called her all sorts and yet now you're thinking of climbing into an old man's bed. Ugh!'

'I wouldn't do what mi mam's doing,' she cried hotly. 'Oh no! If I get into Percy Rodwell's bed – or any other man's – there'll be a wedding ring on mi finger first. You can take bets on that, Jake Bosley!'

Twenty-Five

'You have today off as well,' Percy insisted the following morning.

'But I feel much better.'

'And you look much better, but I'd be happier if you had at least another day's rest. We don't want it turning into a nasty cough.'

Meg giggled. 'Well, you could always rub my chest for me.'

Percy blinked and stared at her for a moment.

'I'm sorry – I shouldn't have said that. It – it was a family joke if anyone got a bad cough. Mam used to rub goose grease on to our chests and – and—' She let tears fill her eyes and she turned away, saying in a husky, trembling voice, 'I forgot where I was for the moment. I'm so sorry.'

Yet again, he patted her shoulder awkwardly. 'There, there, don't let it upset you.'

Meg was not upset. She was angry – with herself. She had been too forward, too bold. Percy wasn't the sort of man she could joke with like that. Not like Isaac Pendleton, she thought wryly. He'd've been only too ready to take her up on the offer! The thought made her shudder. She still could not believe that her pretty young mother could become the mistress of such a man.

'You stay here – just for today, at any rate, and we'll see how you are in the morning.'

'All right,' she agreed meekly, but her mind was busy. She'd had a restless night that was not altogether caused by her cold. Nothing had been said about Miss Finch's visit either to the shop or to the house. Percy had not remarked on it and Meg had no intention of telling him about either of her visitors. But their remarks, their insinuations, had given her ideas. Ideas she meant to put into practice that very day.

Percy Rodwell opened the door to his home in the evening and thought he had stepped into the wrong house. An appetizing smell of cooking drifted into the hallway from the kitchen and through the open door into the front room he could see a fire blazing in the grate. On the small table in the window stood a vase of flowers. Percy blinked and reeled, momentarily unsteady on his feet. It felt as if he had stepped back into his childhood and he half expected, when he stepped into the kitchen, to see his mother bending down to take a crusty brown loaf out of the range oven. But, as he pushed open the door, it was Meg who straightened up, her face flushed – not with fever now but from the heat of the oven. In her hands she held a tin of sizzling roast potatoes. A stew bubbled in a pan on the hob.

'Oh,' she said, catching sight of him. 'I'd hoped to have it all on the table by the time you came in. But it's all nearly ready. Sit down.'

'Meg – what . . .?'

'I wanted to thank you for all you've done for me. All I could find was a bit of stewing beef and a few vegetables. But there was flour and fat in the pantry and some fallen apples. Did someone give you those?'

Mesmerized, Percy nodded absently, but he did as she bade him and sat down at the table.

'I've made some pastry so there's apple pie for afters.'

In a dream, Percy picked up his knife and fork and began to eat. Then, blinking as if to bring himself back to reality, he said, 'I'm sorry, I haven't asked how you're feeling.'

'Much better,' she said, sitting down opposite him. 'How was your day? Have you been busy in the shop?'

'Mm,' he nodded, his mouth full. 'Two or three ladies came in and asked specifically for you.'

Meg looked up at him, her eyes wide. 'Did they really?'

'Mm,' he said once more and did not speak again until his plate was clear. 'My, that was good. I never seem to get my stews to taste like that. Whatever do you put in it to give it that . . . that . . . ? Oh, I don't know. It's just got a special taste.'

'Ah,' said Meg, gathering the dirty plates together and bending down to bring the apple pie out of the oven to the table. 'Now that would be telling. We women have to have our little secrets,' she said coyly. 'Or you'd be able to do very nicely without us, wouldn't you?'

Percy smiled. 'I don't think so, Meg,' he murmured appreciatively as the smell of hot apple pie assailed his nostrils. To his surprise he heard himself saying rashly, 'I don't think I'd even want to try to manage without you now.'

Meg hid her triumphant smile. 'I feel so much better, I'll come back to work tomorrow. I can't have my lady customers kept waiting.'

'There's no hurry. I told them you might not be back until the beginning of next week. They all said they'd call again then.'

Carefully, Meg said, 'So – er – who were these ladies?'

Percy wrinkled his forehead as he recalled their names. 'Miss Robinson – you know, the fussy little spinster?' Meg nodded. 'She didn't want me to serve her. She was blushing as she came into the shop, and when she saw there was only me behind the counter she got very flustered.'

Meg laughed. 'Oh, poor thing. Who else?'

'Let me see – Mrs Newton and – oh yes – there was that young woman who's the schoolmistress at the – erm – at the workhouse.'

Meg's head shot up. 'Louisa? Miss Daley? She came into the shop?'

'Yes. She asked for you, but she didn't say why she wanted you. I supposed it was to buy something.'

'Maybe,' Meg said thoughtfully.

'Unless, of course, it was a message from your mother.'

Meg's mouth hardened. 'Whatever it was, I don't want to know. I don't want messages from my mother and I certainly don't want to see Louisa Daley.'

'Why? I thought she seemed quite a nice girl. The sort that might be a nice friend for you.'

'I thought she was my friend – once upon a time. But she betrayed me.'

'Betrayed you?'

Meg bit her lip, wondering whether she dared to confide in Percy. Was she taking too much of a risk? Would he believe her or begin to think that perhaps his fiancée was right after all?

She took a deep breath and the words came spilling out. She told him how she had been left in charge of Betsy and all that had happened.

'She accused me – me! – of taking her father's watch,' Meg finished indignantly and her eyes blazed. 'And no one – *no one* – accuses me of theft.'

In the face of her vehemence, Percy blinked.

The following morning, Percy said, 'Why don't you have another day off?' He smiled sheepishly. 'It – it was rather nice to come home to a warm house and a meal ready and waiting.'

Meg laughed. 'I'll do the same for you tonight. It'll be a pleasure, but—' She bit her lip.

'But what?' Percy asked anxiously.

'There's not much food left and – I'm sorry – but I haven't any money—'

'Oh, good heavens. What am I thinking of? Wait a moment . . .'

He went back up the stairs and Meg heard him opening a drawer in the chest in his bedroom. Moments later he returned and pressed several coins into her hand. 'Buy whatever you need.' He put his hand up. 'Don't tell me. It'll be a nice surprise.'

'Is there anything you don't like?'

Percy wrinkled his brow. 'I can't think of anything. I'm not a fussy eater.'

They smiled at each other.

Percy opened the door of his house eagerly that night. For the first time in years – not since before his mother had died – it felt like a home. He sniffed the air appreciatively. Something smelt good, but he couldn't decide just what it was . . .

'Roast pork, sage and onion stuffing and apple

sauce,' Meg told him moments later as he stood in the kitchen watching her. 'I used the rest of those fallen apples.' Her cheeks were rosy, her eyes bright. And, he realized with a jolt, she looked completely at home in his tiny kitchen.

'Sit down. I won't be a minute . . .'

'Not before I've put this outside the back door to chill.' Percy smiled as he produced a bottle of white wine from the bag he was carrying.

Meg's eyes widened. 'Oh! How very grand we'll be tonight. I know the posh folks drink wine, but I never have. Oh, Mr Rodwell, what a treat.'

'Please,' he said hesitantly, 'won't you call me Percy?' Then he added hastily, 'Not in the shop, of course, but when we're here. On our own.'

Meg's green eyes sparkled and Percy Rodwell was lost.

Twenty-Six

'Hello, lad, what yer doing here?' Albert Conroy greeted Jake on Sunday afternoon as he opened the gate for him. 'Can't keep away from us, eh?' He laughed wheezily.

Jake grinned. Like Meg, he had always had time for the old man whom many ignored. 'Something like that, Albert. You all right?'

'Oh ar, same as ever,' Albert said, resigned to his lot. He would never leave the workhouse, but there was no use in railing against what he couldn't change. He closed the gate and limped painfully back to the door of his lodge. 'Like a cuppa, would yer? Kettle's on the boil.'

Jake laughed. 'I don't remember a time when your kettle wasn't on the boil. Go on then.' Still chuckling, Jake followed the old man into the tiny room that was old Albert's home. Carefully, Jake laid a package on the table. 'I've brought you some eggs. Don't worry, I ain't pinched 'em. The missis said I could.'

Tears filled Albert's eyes. 'Aw, lad, that's kind of yer. A' yer sure? Don't you want to give 'em to – well – to someone else?' It was a long time since anyone had thought enough about him to bring him a gift.

Jake wrinkled his brow, pretending to think. 'No, can't say as I do. Go on, you daft old devil. I brought 'em for *you*.'

Albert sniffed and touched the package with trembling fingers. 'Thanks, lad.'

Moments later they sat together, Albert in the dilapidated armchair, Jake perched on a stool with a loose leg. Jake stirred the tea in the cracked mug, looking down into the swirling, dark brown liquid.

'Penny for 'em, lad.'

There was a silence before Jake said dolefully, 'I don't reckon they're worth a penny, Albert.'

'Wha's up? Don't tell me you're missing this place.'

Jake smiled, but it wasn't his usual wide grin. 'No. I miss some of the people, but no, not the place, even though it's the only home I've ever had.'

'Are they good to you, these folks you're working for?'

Jake nodded. 'Aye, the mester's all right. She's a bit of a tartar, but Meg warned me about her . . .' His voice trailed away and Albert watched his face.

'Ah,' the old man breathed. 'It's that lass, is it?'

Jake's head shot up. 'What?' He met Albert's steady, knowing gaze and realized denial was futile. He glanced away and sighed as he nodded. 'I don't know what to do. She won't listen to me.'

'How d'yer mean?'

Jake sighed. 'She's run away from here—'

'I know that. I saw her the night she came back when he –' Albert jerked his thumb towards the master's room – 'was going to lock her in the punishment room. She took off then and I ain't seen or heard from her since.'

There was a long silence between them until Jake blurted out, 'It's because of her mother. Meg doesn't . . . approve of her mother being with old man Pendleton.'

Albert shrugged philosophically. 'Can't blame the poor woman for seeking a bit of comfort. Had enough sorrow in her life just lately to turn her mind, if you ask me.' He sniffed. 'I like that little lass, but I reckon she ought to be grateful that someone's being kind to 'er mam and looking after her. And he does look after his lady friends, yer know. I'll say that for 'im.' Albert sniffed. 'Though I ain't got much else to say in his favour.' There was a pause before the older man pressed Jake to say more. 'Why's she so upset about it?'

'She – she says it's not how her mother brought her up. Meg feels betrayed, I suppose.'

'Aye, aye,' the old man murmured. 'And so soon after her dad ran off. Must have hit the lass hard. They've both brought her up to believe one thing, then she sees 'em doing the opposite. Both of 'em. It's a lot for a young lass to come to terms with. And, aye, mebbe to forgive an' all. You'll have to understand that, Jake.'

'I do, but – but she's doing the same thing herself now.' His mouth tightened. 'Talk about pot calling kettle black!' When Albert looked puzzled, Jake went on. 'She's gone to work for Mr Rodwell, the tailor and – and she's moved into his house.' Jake's face was tortured as he added, 'She's living with him, Albert. She's *living* with him.'

The old man could find nothing to say except, 'Aw, lad. Aw, lad.'

'How is she? Have you seen her? Where is she living?' The anxious questions tumbled out of Sarah's mouth.

Jake perched nervously on the edge of the sofa in Isaac Pendleton's office. The only occasions he had ever visited this room were when he had been in trouble. Usually such visits had ended with a thrashing or being sent to the punishment room across the yard, 'for his own good' as Isaac always put it.

'It hurts me far more than it hurts you, boy.' Isaac had always made a great play of being in loco parentis. 'You have no father to guide you and so it falls to me to fill that role. It pains me, really it does, boy, but if you're to make something of yourself in this world then one day you will thank me.'

At the time Jake couldn't imagine that he would ever have reason to thank the big man who seemed to wield the cane with such relish.

'It's what your father – whoever he was – would have wanted me to do. He'd have wanted me to make a man of you.' And the cane would swish through the air, landing on the thin trousers that offered no protection. The only solace Jake had ever had was that after Isaac's 'ministrations', Miss Pendleton would seek him out and clasp him tightly to her ample bosom, promising that she would have words with her brother. 'He's too harsh on you,' she would sob, stroking Jake's hair. 'You must try to be a good boy and not make him angry. He thinks it's his job to mould you into a fine young man. And you will be a fine young man, Jake. Oh, you will be.' And she would hug him all the tighter.

It was not lost on Jake that neither Letitia nor Isaac ever made reference to his mother. Perhaps, he thought sorrowfully, a young, unmarried girl giving birth in the workhouse and then dying and leaving her child to their tender mercies was not even worth a second thought.

'Is she all right?' Sarah prompted again.

Jake sighed. He hated having to be the one to tell the poor woman what her daughter was doing and, even worse, that Meg didn't want to see her own mother. He tried to soften the blow, but without deliberately lying. 'She's been ill. Had a heavy cold and – and Mr Rodwell's let her stay at his house.'

Sarah stared at him. 'But – but – he lives alone, doesn't he? I mean – he's engaged to Miss Finch, isn't he? *She* doesn't live there, does she?'

Jake was obliged to shake his head.

Sarah was silent for a moment as the implications unravelled themselves in her mind. Then she covered her mouth with trembling fingers. 'Oh no!' she breathed. 'You mean – you mean that Meg is living there alone with Mr Rodwell.'

Again Jake just nodded.

'But what will people say? I mean, they're saying enough about me. I don't matter, but Meg—' She paused again and her eyes widened. 'This is all my fault, isn't it? She's doing this to pay me back.' Sarah closed her eyes and rocked backwards and forwards. 'She was disgusted at me and yet now she's harming herself. No one will believe that nothing's going on between them.' Her eyes flew open again as she asked breathlessly, 'Does Miss Finch know?'

''Fraid so.'

Sarah groaned, then she brightened visibly. 'But maybe that's just as well. She'll either put a stop to it or – or give her approval and if his fiancée approves then people can't think . . .'

Her voice trailed away as she saw Jake's solemn expression. 'Nothing will stop the talk, missis. It's already started.'

'Now, Percy, I've come to get this matter sorted out once and for all.' Clara appeared at the shop the following morning and faced Percy across the counter. 'About this girl—'

At that moment Meg appeared from the workroom. Hearing the woman's shrill voice, she came through at once. 'You mean "this girl", Miss Finch?'

'I'm talking to my fiancé. This has nothing to do with you.'

'I think it has everything to do with me, Miss Finch. Mr Rodwell was kind enough to give me a bed in his spare room for a couple of nights whilst I get the rooms above the shop cleaned out. Then I'll be moving in here.'

'Over my dead body,' Clara spat. 'You should be back in the workhouse, where you belong.' Her lip curled. 'I'm sure you could usurp your mother's place if you smile nicely at the master. He likes young flesh. Only trouble is, he can't often get it.'

'Clara! Really, that's quite enough.'

She rounded on Percy. 'There's no one here. None of your precious customers, who, let me tell you, will soon stop coming in here when they hear about your carryings on.'

'And what carryings on would those be, Clara? And from whom are they going to hear it?' Percy's tone was deceptively mild, for there was a warning glint in his eyes. But if she saw it, Clara took no notice.

'Percy, I'm warning you. Get rid of this girl. If you don't – then – then—'

'Then what, Clara?'

'Our engagement is at an end.'

Meg stood still, hardly daring to breathe. She had not expected matters to come to a head so quickly. It was what she wanted, but not like this. Miss Finch – and her brother – could do untold harm to Percy and his business. And that was not what Meg wanted at all.

She moved forward to stand beside Percy. It gave the impression that the two of them were ranged on one side, facing Clara together.

'Oh, please, Miss Finch. If you really don't want me to live here, then . . . then . . .' She forced the tears to fill her fine eyes and spill down her cheeks. 'Then – I'll go back to the workhouse. But, please, don't ask Mr Rodwell to dismiss me. I'm trying so very hard and I do want to better myself.'

Now Clara turned her vitriol against Meg. 'Oho, I've no doubt you want to better yourself, girl. But don't think I can't see through your schemes, even if Percy here is too blind. I know what you're up to.'

As if mystified, Meg shook her head and widened her eyes innocently. 'I don't know what you mean, Miss Finch. All I know is that my father has betrayed his wife and family and now my mother . . .' She gulped and pressed her fingers to her mouth, as if the shame was too much to be spoken of aloud.

'Exactly. Your mother is no better than she should be. And you, I've no doubt, are going down the same path to ruination. Well, you're not dragging my Percy with you. Not whilst there's breath in my body, you're not.'

Percy's voice was calm, yet there was an unusual firmness in his tone as he said, 'No one is dragging me anywhere. I can make up my own mind, especially about my business. Meg—'

He got no further for Clara interrupted him with a wild screech. 'Oh, "Meg", is it now? So I was right all along.'

Percy continued as if she had not spoken. 'Meg will remain in my employment and she will continue to live in my house. In my opinion,' he went on, his steady gaze meeting Clara's hostile glare, 'the rooms above here are quite unsuitable for anyone to inhabit.'

Clara gave a gasp and tottered backwards. She seemed about to fall, but she recovered herself. Pressing the palm of her hand to her chest as if she had a terrible pain there, she rasped, 'I do declare, Percy, you've quite taken leave of your senses.'

When he made no move to go around the counter to her or even to say anything further, her eyes narrowed and she nodded. 'Very well then. You leave me no alternative. I will not be a party to this – this disgrace. As I said, Percy, you may consider our engagement to be at an end.'

They stared at one another for a few moments before he nodded slowly and said quietly, 'As you wish, Clara.'

With one last surge of energy, Clara Finch shook her fist at him. 'You've not heard the last of this, Percy Rodwell. Wait till my brother hears. Then we'll see if you will still have a business.'

As the sound of the shop bell died away after Clara's indignant departure, Meg said, 'Oh, Percy, I didn't want that to happen. Go after her. Make it up with her. Please. I couldn't bear to be the cause of you being unhappy.'

Slowly, Percy turned to look down at her and there was a note of surprise in his tone as he said, 'Don't worry yourself about that, my dear. In fact, all I am feeling at this precise moment is an overwhelming sense of relief.'

Twenty-Seven

Percy closed the shop and they set off along the street.

'I'll just call in at the General Stores,' he said. 'Get a bottle of wine. This calls for a celebration.'

Meg looked up at him. 'A celebration?' Even she was surprised. 'You mean – I mean – I thought you'd be devastated.'

'Do I look devastated?'

'No,' Meg agreed, trying to keep her face straight. Percy was smiling, but then that was his right. She must not let her own feelings show, the flutterings of excitement in the pit of her stomach as her plan began to form and take shape and, yes, began to happen.

'When we get home . . .' He savoured the words. 'When we get home, if you make the meal, I'll light the fire in the front room and we – we'll have a nice, cosy evening together.' Suddenly, he was unsure. 'Is – is that all right?'

She smiled radiantly. 'Of course it is. Just what we both need.' *Thank goodness*, Meg was thinking, *that I had already planned a special meal tonight.*

Percy stopped outside the grocer's. 'What wine should I get? White or red?'

'But we've some left from last night—'

He waved aside her protest. 'I want to celebrate,' he said firmly.

'Well, it's roast chicken.'

His eyes sparkled. 'My favourite,' he murmured. 'White, then.'

Left alone outside the shop for a few moments, Meg began to feel less confident. What if Miss Finch made real trouble for Percy? What if her brother was so incensed that he threw Percy out of his shop? What then?

'Here we are.' He was back beside her and her doubts faded. In the short time that she had known him, she had never seen him look so happy or relaxed.

Some time later as they sat opposite each other across the narrow kitchen table, Percy confirmed her thoughts. He raised his glass to her in a toast. 'That was a lovely meal and I'll tell you something, Meg, I don't know when I last felt as happy as this. I feel as if I've been let out of prison.'

Huskily she said, 'I know just how you feel. That's how I felt the day I left the workhouse. And I owe all that to you. I'm only sorry that it's caused trouble between you and your fiancée. You – you will make it up with her, won't you? I mean her brother owns your shop premises. What if – what if he turns you out?' At last, she was voicing her greatest fear.

'I don't think he'll do that. He knows it would be difficult to find another tenant. The building needs a lot spending on it and Theobald Finch doesn't like spending money.'

'Haven't you ever tried to – to buy it from him?'

'My father – he started the business – tried to years ago, and I tried too, but the only way I was ever going to get it was to . . .' His voice faded away.

'What?' Meg prompted. 'Go on.'

Reluctantly, Percy admitted, 'Theo promised to give me the title deeds to the shop on my marriage to Clara. It – it was to be our wedding present.'

Meg gasped. 'And now you've lost that all because of me.'

'No, no,' Percy assured her. 'You mustn't think that. You've done me a favour. I think I always knew marriage between Clara Finch and me wasn't right, else why would I have kept putting off the wedding date every time she tried to suggest one? She would have had us married four years ago but I –' he smiled sheepishly at Meg – 'but I kept finding excuses.'

'Did you?' Meg said and smiled at him, her wonderful, breathtaking smile. It took poor Percy Rodwell's breath away and left his senses reeling. 'No,' he said, shaking his head slowly. There was a new-found certainty in his tone. 'No, I won't be trying to make it up with Miss Finch.' He raised his glass. 'I'm glad it's happened. Truly I am. So, I want to make a toast, Meg. To my new assistant, to the new ladies' wear and – and to freedom. Our freedom.'

Smiling, Meg touched his glass with her own. 'Here's to us, Percy,' she said softly.

'He's broken off his engagement to Miss Finch. The missus heard it in town.'

On the following Sunday afternoon, Jake brought the news to the workhouse, to Meg's mother. Sarah gasped. 'Why? Is it anything to do with Meg?'

Jake's face clouded as he shrugged. 'Who knows?'

'What have you heard?'

'Just that Miss Finch was so angry about Mr Rodwell employing Meg and then taking her to live with him that she threatened him. If he didn't get rid of Meg, their engagement was off.'

'And?'

'He insisted he wasn't going to sack Meg and that she was going to continue living at his house. Meg'd asked him if she could live in the rooms above the shop, but Miss Finch wouldn't hear of that either.' Jake glanced at Sarah and debated whether to tell her the whole story.

'You know the last time she came here?' he began tentatively. Sarah nodded, tears filling her eyes. 'The night after she found out about me and – and Isaac?' she whispered. 'That's the last time I saw her.'

'Yes. Well, she was coming to tell you that she'd had the idea of asking Mr Rodwell if you could both live above the shop. You and her. She said she wanted to look after you.' As Sarah covered her face with her hands, Jake said swiftly, 'I'm sorry, I shouldn't have told you that.'

'Yes, yes, you should. Oh, poor Meg. No wonder she's angry with me. Do – do you think she will ever forgive me?'

'Of course she will. Give her time. You're her mam.' He tried to make his voice sound hopeful and positive, but in his heart he wasn't sure. Although he thought Meg was wrong, a tiny part of him could understand how she must feel.

'I don't think so,' Sarah murmured sadly. 'First her dad and then me. We've both let her down. I don't think she will ever forgive either of us.'

Jake said nothing.

'Now, Percy, this is a fine how-de-do. Let's see if we can sort it out, man to man, eh?' Theobald Finch stood in the centre of the shop first thing on the Monday morning a week after his sister had arrived home to tell him that Percy had broken off their engagement. Hating confrontation, Theobald had deliberately left the matter for a few days, hoping that Percy would see sense and beg Clara's forgiveness. But a week had passed and there had been no sign of Percy coming, cap in hand, to the Hall.

Meg, serving a lady at her own small counter, had glanced up when he entered. It was the moment she had been dreading. There was only one other person she feared seeing more than Theobald Finch – Jake. But he hadn't been near the shop, even though by this time she believed he must have heard the gossip. Ron's wife came regularly to the bakery next door. There was no doubt she would have carried home the news with great glee. And Meg could imagine Mrs Smallwood's reaction. 'Aye well, I allus said she'd come to a bad end, that one. Blood will out.'

Oh yes, Jake would know by now, and if he knew, then everyone at the workhouse would soon hear of it too.

'Would you care to step into the workroom, Theo. We shall be more private there.'

Theobald gave a loud guffaw. 'I don't reckon there's anything I have to say that half the town don't know already, Percy.' He glanced towards Meg and her customer. 'Morning, Mrs Cartwright. Fine morning for a juicy bit of gossip.'

The woman glared at him, two pink spots appearing suddenly in her cheeks. 'Well, really!' She gathered her belongings and stormed from the shop, leaving Meg calling after her. 'But, madam . . .'

Mrs Cartwright paused at the door to turn and say, 'I have never been treated so abominably in my life. I shall never set foot inside this shop again.'

The shop bell clanged huffily as she slammed the door behind her.

'Oh, dear me,' Theobald remarked, his tone heavy with sarcasm, 'the lady seems somewhat offended. You'll have to be more careful, Percy, else you'll soon have no customers left, my dear fellow.'

Percy sighed. 'Please, Theo, come through—'

'I'm quite comfortable here, thank you. Now, about this other little matter. Look here, Percy, I don't want there to be trouble between us. Make it up with Clara, there's a good fellow. Now, what do you say?'

There was a long silence whilst the two men stared at each other. Meg held her breath. Quite calmly, but very firmly, Percy said, 'No, Theo. I'm sorry, but I no longer think marriage between Clara and me would work.'

'You mean – you're jilting her? My sister is being jilted by a penny-pinching upstart like you?'

Percy did not answer, but continued to meet Theobald's hostile eyes with a steady gaze. At last he spoke. 'So,' he asked slowly, 'are you going to give me notice?'

'I've a good mind to . . .' Theobald began but then, glancing about him, he seemed to think better of it. 'But this is business. I'm not a man to let private matters interfere with business. You've always been a good tenant, Percy. No, no, we'll keep business entirely separate.' Slowly Meg let out the breath she seemed to have been holding for ages. 'But,' Theobald warned, 'you've not heard the last of this. Oh, dear me, no.'

When he had gone, Meg said, 'I thought he was going to turn you out.'

Percy, his gaze following the portly man down the street, said slowly, 'No, he's more got more business acumen than that.'

'Does – does he own a lot of the shops?'

'The four shops in this row – the bakery, this one, the ironmonger's and the greengrocer's beyond that.

And then he owns several other properties about the town. Houses and cottages mainly. A whole row of them in Mint Street and one or two near the church, including . . .' He had been about to say more but at that moment the shop bell clanged and one of Percy's best customers entered. Percy hurried forward.

'Good morning, sir, good morning. Your suit's ready for you. If you'd care to step this way into the workroom . . .'

'Why don't you go down to the shop and see Meg yourself?' Jake suggested to Sarah.

'Oh no, I couldn't. If she doesn't want to see me, then . . .' She closed her eyes and sighed heavily. 'Besides, I don't want to embarrass her. If she's well settled in a good job, it's – it's better that I keep out of the way.' Sarah's voice was forlorn as she murmured, 'I'd only shame her.'

Jake took Sarah's thin hand as he declared stoutly, 'You couldn't shame anyone. She's being very silly and unkind and I'm going to tell her so.'

'Oh no, Jake, you mustn't. You're a good, thoughtful boy, but you really mustn't.'

'I shall. She should be grateful to have a mother like you. I – I would be.'

Sarah smiled sadly and stroked his hair. 'No wonder everyone here likes you so much. We all miss you.'

'Even old man Pendleton? I bet he misses the exercise with his cane.'

Sarah laughed for the first time in months. 'Oh, Jake, you bad boy. But it's Miss Pendleton I feel sorry for. She really misses you and weeps when you don't visit.'

'She's the same with all the boys.'

Sarah shook her head. 'No, I don't think so. You're special to her.'

'Well, I was here the longest.' He grinned, delighting in his own newly found freedom. There was only one thing marring his complete happiness. Meg.

'Is it true what they say?' he went on, trying not to think of her.

'What about?'

'That the matron had a little boy of her own once.' His voice dropped to a whisper. 'Even though she was never married.'

'Oh, I don't know about that, Jake. And I wouldn't dare to ask. Mr Pendleton is very kind to me, but I wouldn't like to pry into his private life.' She leant closer to Jake and whispered. 'I asked about his wife once and he snapped my head off and told me never to mention her name again.'

'Perhaps it's too painful for him to talk about her.'

'What happened to her? Did she die?'

Jake wrinkled his brow. 'That's what they say, but it happened about the time I was born. They say that's why Miss Pendleton came here to take her place as the matron. It's not usual, you know. A brother and sister being master and matron. It's usually man and wife, but after his missis died the guardians let Miss Pendleton come.' He stood up. 'And talking of her, I'd better go and see her.' He grinned. 'Don't want her in tears 'cos I didn't see her while I was here.'

Jake was as good as his word. The following day he asked George Smallwood for a little time off during the afternoon to go into the town.

'Aye, lad. Tek the pony and trap. He could do with

an outing and that way –' the big man laughed – 'you'll be back quicker.'

When Jake entered the tailor's shop, there were three customers and he was obliged to wait to speak to Meg. She was serving two customers at once, running along the counter from one to the other, whilst on the other side of the shop Percy was unrolling a piece of suiting to show a gentleman.

By the time the place was empty, Jake had been kicking his heels for ten minutes and his irritation with Meg had grown.

'Hello, young man,' Percy, the first to be free, greeted him jovially. 'Come to be measured for a new suit have you?'

'I've come to see Meg,' Jake replied curtly.

Percy glanced across at the one woman customer left in the shop and saw Meg carefully writing in the customers' ledger. Most of the townsfolk had accounts at the shop and paid at the end of each month. 'I don't think she'll be much longer.'

As the woman left, Percy said, 'Take Jake into the back. You can make us all a nice cup of tea, Meg. I'm parched after all that talking. We've been quite busy this afternoon, haven't we?'

As soon as the door closed between them and Percy, Jake could contain his anger no longer. 'Oh, "Meg" now, is it? When's the wedding set for then?'

Meg glared at him. 'Don't be stupid, Jake.'

'If anyone's being stupid, it's you, Meg Kirkland. Why haven't you been to see your mam? You're making her so unhappy.'

'*I'm* making *her* unhappy? What about what she's done to me? You only seem to think about her. What about me?'

'You seem to be doing very nicely for yourself. I don't think you need my help or my sympathy. But she does.'

'Then you can be her son. Hers and her fancy man's.' She thrust her face close to his. 'Because I'm no longer her daughter.'

Twenty-Eight

'Meg, are you happy here?' Percy interrupted her thoughts as they sat together in the cosy front room after a superb Christmas dinner, which Meg had cooked: goose and all the trimmings followed by plum pudding and mince pies. It had been a quiet day with just the two of them, but a welcome one, for the days and weeks leading up to Christmas had been busy at the shop. But now, in the quietness of the little house, her work done, Meg couldn't stop the memories intruding: pictures of the Christmases they'd spent at Middleditch Farm when Mrs Smallwood had invited the Kirkland family to the farmhouse. Her table had always been laden with all manner of food and, for once, she'd not minded Meg's friendship with Alice. The girls had helped her in the kitchen in the morning and then, later in the afternoon, the two families would join in the games that Meg and Alice devised. There had been warmth and laughter, but, Meg wondered now, had that been when her father had first cast his eye at Alice? And Jake – she hardly dared to think of him. It would be the first Christmas he'd ever known outside the workhouse. He'd be at the farm with the Smallwoods and Ron's family.

For a moment an acute longing to be with Jake threatened to overwhelm her. Then she heard Percy's tentative voice asking her, 'Are you happy here?'

Meg plastered a bright smile on her face. 'Of course I am. Who wouldn't be? Living in a nice little house like this and I love working in the shop. Handling all those lovely clothes—'

'You can have anything you want, you know. From the shop. If there's anything – anything at all—'

'Oh, I didn't mean it to sound as if I was asking for anything,' Meg said hurriedly. 'Please don't think I was dropping hints. You've given me such a beautiful shawl as a Christmas gift. It's far too good for me.'

Percy smiled and shook his head. 'Nothing's too good for you, Meg.' His gaze never left her face. 'And I would never think – for one moment – that you were dropping hints. You're not that sort of girl.'

Meg dropped her gaze and for a moment shame swept through her. How guileless he was. Could he really not see through her schemes?

There was a long pause before he said, 'Meg—' and then stopped again.

'Yes, Percy?'

'I . . . erm . . . just asked because . . . I . . . erm . . . wondered if our . . . well . . . our arrangement is causing you any embarrassment. I mean, we know that people are talking. I'm just concerned for your reputation, that's all.'

Meg put her head on one side and said coyly, 'And what about your reputation?'

Now Percy laughed. 'I don't think mine will suffer too badly, do you? I expect half the men in the town wish they were in my shoes.'

Meg lowered her head to hide her smile, but to Percy the action appeared to be one of modesty. 'You're a lovely young woman, Meg, and I wouldn't want to be the cause of making matters worse for you. You've suffered enough this past year. All I want to do is to take care of you.'

She looked up. 'You are doing, Percy. You've been wonderful, but I'm only sorry that me coming here seems to have caused trouble for you.'

'Don't ever think that. I'm – I'm pleased it happened. Pleased you came and – yes – I'm pleased my engagement to Miss Finch is at an end. I saw her in her true light in her treatment of you.'

Suddenly, he launched himself out of his armchair and fell on his knees in front of her. 'Oh, Meg, Meg,' he cried passionately, 'you must know how I feel about you. How I care for you. How I – love you!'

'Oh – oh! I had no idea,' Meg squeaked and widened her green eyes. She hoped she sounded suitably surprised and with just the right amount of pleasure. But in truth it was neither sudden nor a surprise. It was what she had planned to happen. 'Oh, Percy.' She leant forward and took hold of his hands. 'Do you – do you really care for me?'

'I've never felt this way about anyone before in my whole life,' he said ardently.

Meg couldn't resist saying saucily, 'Not even Miss Finch?'

'Especially not Miss Finch. I know I'm a lot older than you, but – but I just want to look after you. Would you . . . oh, Meg, will you marry me?'

'Don't you know I care for you too?' She was careful not to use the word 'love'. 'You've been so kind to me, so generous. I'd be honoured to be your wife.'

Behind the thick spectacles Percy blinked his surprise. 'You would? Are you sure? Really sure? I mean – I thought – perhaps that young man who comes to the shop. Jake—'

'Him!' Her tone was scathing, trying to blot out the sudden image of Jake beneath the mistletoe at Middleditch Farm. Oh, how she wished—. No, no, she didn't. She mustn't even think of Jake. She was on the verge of getting exactly what she had planned for these last few months. She must not think of Jake – not now. 'He disapproves of me. He's taken my mother's side. He doesn't realize how much she's hurt me.'

Percy, his eyes wet with happiness behind the thick spectacles, patted her hand. 'You don't know how happy you've made me, my dear. I want everyone in the world to be as happy as I am at this moment. When we're married, Meg, your mother can come here. She won't have to stay with Isaac Pendleton. She can live with us. Would that make you happy?'

Now Meg's tears of gratitude were genuine and she felt a surge of guilt, suddenly ashamed of her scheming. 'Oh, Percy, thank you. Thank you.' She flung her arms about his neck and kissed his cheek. In that moment she silently vowed that she would be a good wife to this kind and generous man. She could trust Percy Rodwell not to hurt her. He would take care of her. It was all she wanted, she told herself as she closed her eyes and buried deep inside her any feelings she had ever had for Jake Bosley.

Jake burst into the master's room without even knocking. He stood in the doorway, panting. It was New Year's Day and he had run all the way from the farm, rage and frustration spurring him on.

From her place on the sofa in front of the fire, Sarah looked up, and Isaac rose from behind his desk.

'What's this? What's this? Bursting in here without a by your leave? Is the place on fire, boy?'

Gasping, Jake's glance went beyond the master and found Sarah's startled gaze. 'She's only going to marry him, that's what!' he blurted out.

Sarah's mouth dropped open and she fell back against the cushions, her hand to her chest as if, suddenly, she found it difficult to breathe.

'Who? What?' Mesmerized, Isaac glanced round at Sarah and then back to Jake. 'Who are you talking about, boy?'

'Meg! She's going to marry Percy Rodwell.'

'Meg is? But – but he's engaged to Miss Finch.'

'He broke it off. Weeks – months – ago. And now . . .' His voice broke and he was unable to carry on.

Isaac leant on the desk towards Jake, resting on his knuckles. 'You mean to tell me,' he said slowly, frowning heavily, 'that Percy Rodwell broke off his engagement to Miss Finch in order to marry Meg?'

Jake nodded, his own expression as grim as the older man's.

Isaac sank down into his chair again and leant back, his hands clasped in front of his ample stomach. 'Well, well,' he said as he recovered from the surprise. 'All I can say is that he'll rue the day he married that little slut instead of Miss Finch, who is a fine woman of some standing in this town. And let me tell you, boy –' Now he wagged his forefinger at Jake as if he were somehow responsible – 'her brother, Mr Theobald Finch, will not stand by and see his sister slighted in such a way. Oh, dear me, no. Mr Percy Rodwell had better watch out, that's all I can say.'

Behind him, Sarah wept silently into her handkerchief.

The banns were read in the local church on the first three Sundays in May. Because Meg was under the age of consent, the vicar had sought Sarah's permission. She was reluctant to give it, but believing it was what her daughter wanted, she signed the form. Percy and Meg were to be married early in the morning on the last Friday of the month. The wedding was only three days away when Meg put on her best hat and coat and walked up the road towards the workhouse.

She couldn't help remembering the first time she had approached it. Though it was barely a year ago so much had happened since. She was almost seventeen now, yet she felt so much older and painfully wiser. With that knowledge had come bitterness and resentment. But today, at Percy's insistence, she was going to see her mother. Where Jake had failed, Percy – and all that he had to offer – had persuaded her to heal the breach.

'Hello, lass. Come to see yer mam, 'ave yer?' Albert greeted her at the gate. 'And what's this I hear about you getting wed? I thought you was waiting for me.'

Meg laughed. 'Oh, Albert, I'm far too old for you.' The old man laughed wheezily, but then his face sobered. 'I 'spect you'd like a word with yer mam without *him* earwigging, wouldn't yer?'

Meg nodded.

'Right. You wait in my little room here and I'll go and find one of the young 'uns to tek a message to yer mam.'

The old man limped away and Meg sat down in his lodge to wait. Peering out through the open door a few moments later, she saw a little girl skip across the yard towards the main building and old Albert returning.

'There, that's done. You can have this place to yerselves for a nice little chat. I'll make mysel' scarce.'

He brewed tea, hot and strong, and then said, 'She'll be along in a minute so I'll go and have a chinwag with one or two of the fellers in the orchard. Little walk'll do me good and I can still keep me eye out for folk coming up the path.'

After Albert had gone, Meg waited, her nervous fingers twisting her gloves. She rehearsed the words she intended to say to her mother. *If you come with me now, we'll say no more about you and* him. *Folks'll forget in time and living with Percy and me . . .*

A shadow appeared in the doorway and Meg looked up. It was not her mother who stood there, but Ursula Waters.

'So,' she said, stepping into the tiny room, 'you want to see your mother, do you? Well, I'm very sorry, but your mother does not want to see you.'

Meg rose slowly to face her. She tried to tell herself that no one in the workhouse had any power over her now, but still she found she was trembling. Then anger strengthened her resolve and swept away her fear. 'I've come to take her away from here. She's coming to live with me.'

'To live with you and your new husband, you mean. Oh, I think not. The master . . . wants her. He won't let her go.'

Meg raised her eyebrows. 'I'd've thought you'd have been only too pleased to be rid of her.' She paused and then added, with deliberate cruelty, 'There might be room in his bed again for you, then.'

Ursula's face worked as she struggled to control her emotions. She clenched and unclenched her hands. 'I want . . .' she gasped, 'him to be happy. That's all I want out of life now. Him to be happy. And if she – if she makes him happy – then—'

'And what happens when he tires of her? When a younger, prettier woman comes into the workhouse and he casts her aside? Just like he did to you?'

Even as the words left her lips, Meg knew she had said too much. The woman flew at her with flailing fists, catching her a glancing blow on the side of the head. But the young girl was much stronger and fitter. She caught and held the hysterical woman's wrists and, though Ursula writhed and twisted in Meg's grasp, she could not break free.

'Now, listen to me. You just go and tell my mother I want to see her.'

'No,' Ursula screamed at her. 'He won't want her to see you. *She* doesn't want to see you. She told me.'

For the first time, Meg was unsure. 'Is – is that true?'

'Of course it's true.' Ursula was calming down a little now, though Meg still kept tight hold of her.

'Is he going to marry her?'

'Marry her?' Ursula sneered. 'He'll not marry her – or anyone. Besides, she's not free. She's still married to your father, isn't she?'

'But if she wasn't, would he marry her then?'

Slowly, Ursula shook her head. 'He can't.'

'Can't? Why can't he?'

'Because . . . because,' the woman blurted out, 'he's still married.'

'Still married? But – but I thought his wife died.'

'No. She ran off. Couldn't stand it in the workhouse. She was the matron before – before Miss Pendleton came – but she hated it. She ran off with one of the fellers that was in here. That was when . . . that was when the master turned to me. I looked after him. I cared for him. I would never have left him.'

Meg stared at her. 'Do you know, Waters,' she said slowly, as she released her grasp, 'I feel sorry for you, I–'

Ursula's face was ugly again. 'Don't you feel sorry for me,' she spat. 'I could have left this place years ago – if I'd wanted. He'd have set me up in the town, but I couldn't bear to leave him. Just to be near him. That's all I ask and to see that no one – *no one* – ever hurts him again.' She thrust her face close to Meg's. 'I won't let them. Do you hear?'

'Yes,' Meg answered quietly, 'I hear.'

'Save your pity for yourself. You're going to need it if you marry Percy Rodwell. You're stealing another woman's man, with your green eyes and flaming hair. Seducing him with the promise of your young body.' Ursula glanced Meg up and down and her mouth twisted with jealousy. 'You mark my words.' She stood back, a smug expression on her face. 'You'll live to regret the day you marry Percy Rodwell.'

Twenty-Nine

Jake hovered at the door into the dairy, waiting for Mabel Smallwood to glance up and see him. He'd finished helping Ron with the evening milking and should, at this moment, have been making his way back to the little cottage for his evening meal with Ron's family. But there was something more important on his mind than eating. In fact, his thoughts were tearing him apart and robbing him of his appetite.

Meg was getting married tomorrow and he had to try and prevent it. She wouldn't listen to him, but she might listen to her mother. If only he could persuade Sarah to make the first move, to go and see her daughter in the shop, then maybe . . .

'Hello, lad, what're you after?'

'Sorry to bother you, missis, but I need to go into town. Urgent, like. And the mester's not about to ask.'

Mabel sniffed. 'Ain't that just like him. Never about when you want him. What's so urgent then?'

'I – er – have to see someone.'

Mabel glanced at him sharply. 'You seem to be needing to "see someone" a lot just lately. Got a girl, have yer?'

Jake shook his head, but he felt the colour creeping up his face. 'I want to see someone at the workhouse.'

Mabel sniffed her disapproval once more. 'Should've thought you'd've been pleased to shake the dust of that place off yer feet. Can't understand why you still want to keep going back.'

'I don't really, missis. It's just . . .' He sighed. 'Well, there's just something I have to do and if I don't do it today, it'll be too late . . .' His voice trailed away as if already he was anticipating failure.

Again, Mabel's glance seemed to bore into his soul and read his mind. 'Ah, I know. It's that wretched girl, isn't it? You're seeing that Meg creature.'

'She's not a creature,' he flashed back, unable to stop himself.

'Oho, so that's it, is it? You've got yer eye on her yourself, 'ave yer?' Suddenly her face softened. 'Look, Jake, you're a good lad. Me and the mester have taken to you, but don't get yourself mixed up with that family, if you'll take my advice. They're trouble. The lot of 'em. There's bad blood there. It's in the breed.' She paused, glanced away and then, coming closer, said in a low voice, 'You'll get hurt by them, lad. Same as me and the mester have been hurt. I don't often talk about it and I'll skelp the lugs off yer if I hear you've breathed a word about it to anyone, but it near broke our hearts when that bugger seduced our daughter. Oh, she could be a bit flighty, our Alice, I know that, but she wasn't a bad girl. But 'im.' She cupped her hands, thumbs touching as if encircling someone's neck. 'If I ever see him again, I'll swing for him.' She took a deep breath, calming herself. Then she turned away, shrugging her shoulders. 'But, it's up to you, lad. I'll not stop you going. Do what you have to do, but I'm warning you, it'll bring you heartache being involved with that family.'

'Thanks, missis. I'll be as quick as I can . . .'

Before she could say any more, he turned and ran

across the yard and into the road towards the town and the workhouse. He ran most of the way, stopping only to catch his breath when he could run no more. At last he was hurrying through the gate, pausing only to greet Albert briefly, then across the yard and in through the back entrance. He halted near the clerk's office door, cocking his head on one side, listening intently. He didn't want to run into the master: he wanted to catch Sarah alone. There was no sound coming from inside the clerk's office, no murmur of voices. No doubt the clerk was in there busily writing in all the numerous ledgers, keeping all the official records of the workhouse up to date. The door of the master's office was directly in front of Jake as he stood hesitating, whilst to his right the stairs led to the first floor. He put his foot on the bottom step, debating where the most likely place to find Sarah was. He bit his lip. During the daytime, she would probably be downstairs in the office, but there was also more likelihood of Isaac being there too. He took a step up the stairs and as he did so something – a movement perhaps – made him glance up.

Ursula was standing at the top of the stairs. 'What do you want here? You've no business here now.'

She descended the stairs until she was standing three steps above Jake, effectively barring his way. 'I expect it's matron you've come to see, is it? Can't keep away, can you?'

'None of your business,' he retorted boldly. As an inmate, he would not have dared to speak to Waters in such a way. She still had influence over the master and she was a tittle-tattle, if ever there was one. 'I've come to see Mrs Kirkland.'

There was a sudden malicious gleam in the woman's eyes. 'About that trollop of a daughter of hers, is it?

Well, I can save you the trouble. Mrs Kirkland wants no more to do with her daughter. And the master agrees with her. The wretched girl has made her bed. She can lie in it.'

The picture Ursula drew was in Jake's mind too – Meg in Percy Rodwell's bed, lying beside him, him turning to her . . . Jake shuddered.

Ursula's keen eyes were boring into his thoughts. 'No,' she whispered. 'Not a pretty thought, is it? Specially not for you. Sweet on her, aren't you? I saw you together when you were here. Sneaking around at night, meeting in the dead room—'

'Please, just let me see Mrs Kirkland. We might still be able to stop her—'

Ursula took two more steps down and grasped Jake's coat. 'Be off with you, else I'll call the master. She doesn't want to see her daughter – or you.'

'I don't believe you—'

Jake never finished his plea for, with a violent push that caught him off balance, Ursula sent him flying off the step to land sprawling on the floor. 'Be off with you and don't come back here again, or you'll find yourself in the punishment room . . .'

At that instant, a figure appeared in the entrance door: a figure who gave a cry of alarm and bent over Jake at once.

'Waters! What are you doing?' Letitia cradled Jake in her fat arms. 'There, there. Are you hurt, my precious boy?'

'He's trying to make trouble. I was telling him to let well alone, but he slipped and fell off the step. He'd do best to stay away from here, wouldn't he, Matron, or he might hear things he didn't ought to.'

'Hold your tongue, woman.' For once Letitia was in command. 'Or it'll be me telling the master.'

Ursula sniffed and pushed her way past the pair of them. 'Suit yourself, but just remember – I've been here a long time. A very long time . . .'

As the woman walked away, the matron muttered beneath her breath, 'Too long,' but then her attention came back to Jake. 'Are you sure you're not hurt?' Letitia's face crumpled, tears filled her eyes and ran down her plump cheeks and she held on to Jake even more tightly as if she would never let him go . . .

A little later Jake walked away from the workhouse, his thoughts in tumult. He had failed in his attempt to see Meg's mother, yet he could not believe that it was Sarah who'd said she did not want to see her daughter. On the occasions he had spoken to her, she had been desperate for news of Meg and longing for the rift between them to be healed. Jake sighed heavily as he trudged along. There was one last thing he could do, though he didn't hold out much hope of success.

He would go and see Meg one more time and plead with her not to marry Percy.

Jake held his breath as he knocked on the door of Percy's cottage. Meg might be at home now preparing their evening meal whilst Percy was still at the shop. Suddenly the door opened and she was standing before him.

'Jake!'

He couldn't tell from her expression if she was pleased to see him.

'Meg – I must talk to you.'

She frowned. 'If you've come to try to persuade me to change my mind, you're wasting your time.'

'Look, let me come in. We can't talk here on the doorstep.'

Meg glanced up and down the street. 'No, I don't want the nosy beggars round here gossiping about me.'

'Huh,' Jake muttered wryly. 'I should think there's plenty of that going on already. A bit more won't make a ha'porth of difference.'

'Oh well, if you're going to be like that.' Meg glared at him and Jake sighed. 'I'm not. Oh, Meggie, please – please let me in. There's something I must say to you.'

'If it's about Percy—'

'Just let me in, will you?'

'All right,' she said grudgingly and held the door a little wider for him to step inside.

'Meg, please don't do it,' he began at once. 'Work for him, live with him if you must.' His agony at the very thought was plain on his face, yet he pressed on. 'But please – don't marry him.'

'Give me one good reason why I shouldn't.' Facing him in the tiny hallway, Meg ticked off her own reasons on her fingers. 'He loves me, he's kind to me, he's got a nice little home and a good business. What more could I –' her face twisted with bitterness – 'a girl from the workhouse, hope for?'

Jake's face was white. 'But you don't love him, do you?'

'Love?' She was scathing. 'What do you know about love?'

'I know I love you,' he said simply and she gaped at

him. He caught hold of her hands and held them fast. 'Don't do it, Meg. Don't marry him. Marry me.'

'You?'

'Yes, me. Is that such an awful thought?'

'No,' she whispered. 'It's not an awful thought at all. It's just that I – I hadn't realized.' Her eyes filled with tears and she squeezed his hands in return. 'Oh, Jake, I can't.'

'You mean you don't love me,' Jake said harshly.

'I – I – oh, Jake, you shouldn't ask me that. You really shouldn't – not now.'

'Come away with me. Come now. Ron and his missis'll take you in . . .'

Meg was shaking her head and laughing, a little hysterically, through her tears. 'If they did, they'd soon find themselves homeless when the missis found out. We'd all end up back in the workhouse, Jake. She'd see to that.'

'So – it's no, is it? You're really going to marry him.'

Meg bit her lower lip so hard that she drew blood, but she nodded, tears splashing down her cheeks as she did so.

'Then it's goodbye, Meg, 'cos I shan't see you again if you marry him.'

'Oh, Jake,' she cried, 'don't say that. Please – I thought you were my friend.'

'I am your friend. More than you will ever know.'

'Then don't desert me. Please, Jake.'

Slowly, he shook his head. 'I can't stand to see you marry him,' he said huskily. 'And I don't like the way you're treating your mother.'

'But I went to see her. I did. Honestly. I waited for her in Albert's lodge. But Waters came and told me that

Mam didn't want to see me. That she never wanted to see me again.'

Jake's face softened a little. 'You went to see her? You really went?'

'Percy said I should.'

Jake's expression hardened again. He snatched his hands away. 'Oh, so it wasn't because of what I said, because *I* asked you to go and see her? Only because *Percy* –' he spat out the name – 'asked you.'

'Oh, Jake, don't – please don't be like this. I can't bear it.'

He pushed past her and opened the door, almost falling out into the dusk of evening in his haste to get away.

'Jake, Jake, please don't go. Not like this.'

But he did not answer her, did not even look back as he stumbled away, tears blinding him.

He had never been so hurt. Nothing in his life in the workhouse, not even the master's beatings, had hurt this much. Meg's arrival had brought him such hope, made him see that he could escape from the shame of his birth. It had been she who'd encouraged him to seek a life outside the workhouse. But for her, he would still be locked away behind the high walls with no kind of future. Her will, her determination, had given him courage, had given him hope and, yes, had given him someone to love, someone with whom he had dreamed of sharing the rest of his life.

And now, by some reasoning of her own that he would never understand, Meg was tying herself to a man old enough to be her father. Jake's mouth twisted. He was sure that the only reason she was marrying Percy Rodwell was for security. A security that he, Jake

Bosley, a lowly paid farm labourer, born and raised in the workhouse, could never give her.

No one came to their wedding early the following morning. There was no best man, no bridesmaid, and the verger and a churchwarden were obliged to act as witnesses. As Percy and Meg made their vows, their voices echoed eerily in the cavernous surroundings of the vast church. But Percy smiled down happily at his young bride, oblivious to the absence of relatives or friends. Only, as they walked down the pathway after the ceremony, did Meg fancy she saw the figure of a woman hovering beneath the shadow of some trees and wondered – for a fleeting moment – if it was her mother.

'Percy . . .' she began, turning to him to catch his attention, but when she looked back the figure – if it had ever been there – had disappeared.

There was to be no honeymoon – Percy decreed that the shop could not be closed – so they returned home, ate a hasty breakfast and went together to the shop.

About mid-afternoon, a stranger dressed in a black morning suit with a top hat and ebony cane entered the shop.

'Mr Percy Rodwell?' he enquired in a superior voice.

'Yes, sir. What can I do for you?' Percy hurried forward, almost rubbing his hands at the thought of the custom such a gentleman might bring to his shop.

The man produced a long, brown envelope, which he held out towards Percy with an exaggerated flourish.

'I am from the firm of Baggerley, Snape & Proust, solicitors, and I am requested by one of the partners, namely Mr Snape, to hand you this letter personally.'

Percy blinked, glanced at the envelope and then at the man and then back to the envelope before stretching out trembling fingers to take it.

'Good day to you, Mr Rodwell.' Having accomplished his task, the man raised his hat and left the shop, leaving Percy holding the envelope as if it might burn him.

'What is it?' Meg asked, moving forward.

'I – er – don't know.'

'Then hadn't you better open it?' she said practically. She slid her arm through his. 'Perhaps some rich old aunt has died and left you a fortune. Have you got any rich old aunts?'

Percy shook his head. 'I – er – don't think so.' He was still staring at the envelope.

'Go on, Percy. Open it. Do.'

He pulled open the flap and took out a single sheet of headed paper. As he read the letter, the colour drained from his face. When he looked up, his eyes were shocked. 'It's Clara, Miss Finch. She . . . she's suing me. For breach of promise.'

Thirty

'How can she?' Meg demanded when the initial shock had worn off a little, though Percy was still trembling. 'It was her who broke it off. I heard her myself threaten that, if you didn't sack me, the engagement was at an end. You didn't break it off, Percy. She did.'

'Well, yes, I suppose so, but . . .' His diffidence had returned. It seemed as if the very mention of Clara's name robbed him of every scrap of self-confidence.

'But what?'

He shrugged and said flatly, 'I don't know.'

'What're you going to do?'

'See my solicitor, I suppose.'

'It's not one of them, is it? Snape and what's 'is name?'

Percy shook his head. 'No, no. I go to a Mr Henderson the other side of the town. It's the firm my father always used. I was going to see him anyway soon about changing my will, so I suppose—'

'Go now, Percy. This minute. I can mind the shop.'

'Oh, I don't know about that, Meg.'

'It's almost dinner time and we don't get many customers between one and two. Go on, Percy.'

'But he – Mr Henderson – might be at lunch too.'

'Well, at least go to his office. If he's not there, make an appointment for when he is.'

'Yes, yes, you're right, my dear. Of course you are. It was just – just—'

'Just what?'

He took her hand. 'This is our wedding day and I planned to close the shop early so that we could go home. Have a nice long evening together . . .'

He said no more, but she understood his meaning. Involuntarily, she shuddered and was mortified that Percy noticed.

He touched her cheek. 'Oh, my dear, there's nothing to be afraid of. I wouldn't hurt you for the world.'

'I know that,' she told him. It was the part of getting married to him that she'd tried to blot out of her mind. She would do her duty to her husband, she would submit to him, but not for her the joy of giving herself to the man she loved . . .

Her mind shied away from what she knew she must endure later. Now she said, 'Do go, Percy. The sooner you go, the sooner Mr Henderson will be able to put your mind at rest.'

Mr Henderson was unable to put Percy's mind at ease.

'He thinks she has a case,' Percy told Meg worriedly when he arrived back at the shop later in the afternoon. He'd waited through the firm's lunch hour for an appointment at two o'clock. By the time he'd talked to the solicitor and trudged back across the town, it was already four thirty.

'Oh no,' Meg breathed, her eyes wide and anxious.

'We'll close now and go home. I'll tell you all about it there. But –' Percy shook his head sadly – 'it's not going to be the kind of evening I'd planned.'

Indeed, it spoilt their day. Neither of them could eat the special meal that Meg prepared and later, in their bed, Percy's lovemaking was fumbling and over so quickly that he wept against her neck.

Sleepless, Meg stared into the blackness and knew she had made the most terrible mistake of her life.

'Oh, Jake,' she whispered into the silence of the night, 'what have I done?'

The case was the scandal of the district. Several months had passed since their wedding and now the case was due to be heard in the imposing courthouse in the town during the first days of November.

Meg felt sick every time she thought about it.

At the workhouse Sarah was kept in ignorance of the events in her daughter's life. Isaac threatened everyone who came into contact with Sarah that, should they breathe a word about it to her, he would make their life utter misery. Since life in the workhouse was not easy by any standards, their tongues were stilled. So Sarah lived in blissful ignorance of Meg's troubles, believing her daughter happily married and well cared for. There was no doubting that the last of Sarah's hopes was true: Percy cared for Meg deeply and refused her nothing. And Meg was careful to play her part. She was a good and dutiful wife. She cooked, washed, ironed and cleaned his house and helped him in the shop. To their delight, the number of customers entering the shop had increased rather than decreased as they had both feared might happen.

Despite the worry of the impending court case, Percy was amused. 'Nothing like a bit of scandal to get the ladies of the town through our door.'

'As long as they keep coming once all this is over,' Meg said wryly.

'Oh, they will. We sell good-quality merchandise. They'll keep coming back for more.'

Meg glanced at him but said nothing. She believed it was curiosity that, for the moment, brought the good ladies of South Monkford into Percy's shop.

It seemed that Meg was right, if the number of women who crowded into the public gallery on the first morning of the case was anything to go by. By half-past nine the gallery was crowded and several people were already having to stand to watch the proceedings when Judge Henry Ashton, an elderly, severe-looking gentleman, took his place.

Meg sat in the front of the public gallery. Percy had not wanted her to attend and they'd almost had their first argument over the matter.

'I need you to stay at the shop,' he had said.

'Believe me, Percy, there'll be no customers that day. They'll all be at court and so,' she had added firmly, 'shall I.'

Although he said no more, Meg had the feeling that the real reason behind Percy's request that she stay away arose from the embarrassment he might feel at her hearing all that would be said in court.

She'd put her hand on his arm and said gently, 'Percy, whatever happens in that court, I know the truth. I could see for myself that a union between you and Miss Finch would have brought you nothing but unhappiness. Even if I hadn't come along, I believe you should not have married her, though I can see that you would probably have done so eventually.'

Percy gripped her hand. 'All I want you to know, my

dear, is how very much I love you. You will remember that, won't you?'

'Of course I will, Percy.'

If Meg had been in love with Percy herself then Mr Snape's opening speech on behalf of the plaintiff might have caused her considerable heartache. He spoke with theatrical eloquence of the romance between his client and the defendant.

'Here, your honour, we have something of a novel situation. This is the first time that such an action has been brought in the County Court in South Monkford. But, just in case any of you are in any doubt, I can assure you that these proceedings are right and proper under section 64 of the County Courts Act of 1898, giving County Courts jurisdiction in such a case with the consent of both parties.' Mr Snape puffed out his chest, grasped the lapels of his gown and continued.

'Your honour, I represent the plaintiff. Miss Clara Finch is a lady of genteel birth living under the protection of her brother, Mr Theobald Finch, a much-respected pillar of the society of this town. He and his family have lived at the Hall in South Monkford for four generations. During that time the family has served this community in a variety of ways. I will not take up your valuable time with all the positions of trust and authority which Miss Finch's family has held over the years. Suffice it to say that Mr Theobald Finch is a town councillor and has served as mayor on one occasion, with his sister, Miss Finch, acting as his lady mayoress. He is the chairman of the board of guardians of South Monkford workhouse and he is a churchwarden at St Michael's as well as a member of the board of governors for our local school. So, gentlemen, you see the kind of family of which Miss Finch is a much loved and respected member. She has involved herself in good works in the town, supporting her brother in all that he does and being a devoted member of the church.

'Now, as for – er – Mr – er—' Here, Mr Snape paused and shuffled his papers as if the name of the defendant was not even worth remembering. 'Ah yes – Mr Percy Rodwell . . .' He grimaced and spoke the name as if it pained him to do so. 'His family has lived in the town for a much shorter period of time. His parents moved to the town, I understand, in the year of 1868, shortly before Mr Rodwell's birth. He was born, I understand, in the rooms above the tailor's shop which his father rented, mark you, from the Finch family. Eventually, Mr Rodwell followed his father into the tailoring business and became the sole proprietor on his father's death in 1898. His mother, with whom the defendant continued to live, died in 1903, and since that time he has lived alone in a small house on Church Street. Mark you well, then, gentlemen –' Mr Snape made another extravagant gesture around the courtroom towards Percy and his eyes came to rest with a benign smile upon his client, Miss Clara Finch – 'the difference between the backgrounds of these two people. The one, my client, coming as she does from a genteel, upper-class home, being a property owner and landowner in her own right with a comfortable income as well as the sole beneficiary of her brother's will. The defendant –' again the man's tone changed rapidly from deference to derision – 'is a man of – trade.' The last word was spoken as if its utterance left a nasty taste in his mouth and there was a ripple of laughter around the courtroom. The judge looked crossly over the top of his spectacles at the sound and the noise subsided.

'About eight years ago –' Mr Snape gripped the lapels of his gown again – 'Mr Rodwell, who of course was known to the family through his tenancy of Mr Finch's properties, began to pay court to Miss Finch.' There was the sound of laughter, quickly stifled.

'At this stage, it has to be said—' Mr Snape's tone made it sound as if he were reluctant to say this – 'it has to be said that the defendant conducted the courtship with decorum. He approached Mr Finch for his permission and, this being given, he began to call at the Hall on a Sunday afternoon and sometimes on a Saturday evening after the close of – er – his business to dine with the family. During the first two years he observed the proprieties, the niceties, of such a courtship, their meetings always being in the presence of a third party.'

Again, from the public gallery came the sound of muffled laughter.

'Six years ago the couple, with Mr Finch's approval, became officially engaged. An announcement was made in the newspaper informing the whole world of the impending nuptials.' Mr Snape waved a newspaper in the air. 'And a small dinner party was held at the Hall to celebrate the event. If necessary, I can call several witnesses who were present on this happy occasion.'

He paused, cleared his throat and continued. 'The defendant purchased a ring. Not a ring of any great value, I hasten to add, though Miss Finch—' he inclined his head towards his client with an ingratiating smile – 'declared herself happy with the token of their betrothal.' He cast a baleful glance at Percy, who was sitting with his head bowed and hands clasped before him. 'Of course, my client would not say so for herself, but she is a modest soul, not of a grasping or a self-seeking nature. Miss Finch,' he declared resonantly, 'was most certainly not attaching herself to the defendant for his money.'

Now for the first time Mr Snape turned slowly and deliberately raised his eyes to seek out Meg, sitting in the front row of the gallery and it seemed to her that every eye in the vast room turned to look at her.

Thirty-One

Mr Snape's opening speech continued until the judge adjourned for lunch.

By the time Meg had struggled through the throng, ignoring the nudges and whispers around her, and fought her way to Percy and Mr Henderson, she was seething. 'It's not what he's saying,' she ranted, pacing up and down the small room, 'it's the way he's saying it. He's so scathing, so . . . so . . .' She couldn't think of the words to describe the way in which Mr Snape was besmirching poor Percy's character. 'So . . . awful,' she finished.

She sat down beside Percy and took his hand in hers. 'Oh, Percy, this is all because of me. I'm so sorry.' Whilst she knew, deep in her heart, that she was not in love with Percy Rodwell and never would be, she was very fond of the man who had been so kind to her. Watching her, Mr Henderson recognized her concern as being genuine. About Percy's regard for his young wife he had never been in doubt, but until this moment he had been unsure of the young woman's. Now Mr Henderson smiled, knowing that later on that day – if Mr Snape ever finished his opening speech – he would be able to stand up and speak just as eloquently as his adversary, safe in the knowledge that there was real affection between the couple.

After lunch the courtroom filled up again, buzzing

with excited chatter. Many there had never been inside a court before and none had ever seen a breach of promise case.

'She's a hard-faced shrew, that Clara Finch,' the few men there muttered to one another, their sympathies all with the defendant when they compared his former fiancée with his pretty young bride. 'Only thing is, I can't see what that young lass sees in him.'

'Money, that's what. He may not be in Theobald Finch's league, but he's a good catch as far as that young 'un's concerned. She's from the workhouse, they say.'

'Wasn't it her father who ran off with farmer Smallwood's daughter . . . ?'

And so the gossiping and the tittle-tattling went on, the men siding with Percy, whilst the women, for the most part, found themselves siding with the jilted woman.

As the judge entered the room, all present rose as the whispering subsided and every eye turned eagerly towards Mr Snape. What juicy morsels would he reveal this afternoon?

Mr Snape resumed his demolition of Percy's character subtly but effectively. He went into lengthy detail about the courtship's progress. According to his client, every attempt on her part to set a date for the marriage had been met by prevarication from the defendant. 'His excuses ranged –' here Mr Snape waved his hands expressively – 'from being too occupied with building up his business – a business in which, I might add, your honour, my client made it only too obvious that she would be willing, nay happy, to help. The defendant –' not once, Meg noticed, did Mr Snape refer to Percy by his name now – 'also gave the excuse that his home was not suitable for a lady of Miss Finch's standing in the community.' Here Mr Snape paused and smirked. 'For once, your honour, I find myself in agreement with the defendant.'

Though the judge did not even smile, this time he made no move to quell the ripple of laughter that ran around the court.

'So we come to the events leading up to this unhappy breach of promise action. The defendant, in his wisdom,' Mr Snape added sarcastically, 'decided to employ a young girl from the workhouse. Perhaps –' he spread his hands again – 'he wished to act charitably, to give a pauper the chance of a lifetime. Perhaps we should not condemn him for that action.' It was the closest the man had come to praising Percy, yet Meg could still detect the sarcasm in his tone. At his next words, she realized his intention. 'And oh, your honour, what a chance of a lifetime that turned out to be.'

'This young . . .' he paused, searching for the right word to describe Meg. 'This scheming hussy –' a startled gasp echoed through the courtroom – 'played upon the defendant's sympathies. She seduced him, your honour. There is no other way to describe—'

'That's not true!' Meg was on her feet, shouting at the prosecuting solicitor. 'Don't listen to him, your honour. It's not true what he's saying about me or about Percy – Mr Rodwell.'

An excited buzz ran through the public gallery and the judge banged on his bench with his gavel.

'Young woman, sit down or else I shall have you put out of court.'

'But, sir—'

Another angry bang. 'It'll be a charge for contempt of court if you utter another word. Sit down and be quiet.'

Meg glanced towards where Percy was sitting with his head in his hands. Mr Henderson was looking at her and frowning. He gave a little shake of his head and patted his hand in the air, indicating that she should sit down. Then he put his fingers to his lips. Meg subsided back into her seat, her face red. Now everyone was looking at her. She could feel their stares on the back of her neck and hear the whispers. The judge banged again and there was silence.

'Pray continue, Mr Snape.'

Mr Snape gave a little bow towards the bench. 'Thank you, your honour.' He glanced towards his opponent and Percy and then briefly up to the front row of the gallery towards where Meg was sitting. Smirking, he said, 'May I crave your indulgence, your honour. The girl is, of course, so *very* young!' It was neatly done, turning Meg's impetuous outburst against her.

The judge, whose white bushy eyebrows were almost meeting above the bridge of his nose in a frown, merely grunted and nodded to the plaintiff's lawyer to proceed.

Mr Snape droned on for another hour, extolling the virtues of his client as a woman of independent means, of a certain standing in the community who would bring nothing but respectability and stability to her future husband in both his personal and business life. In comparison, he painted a lurid picture of Meg as a woman who would bring disgrace and eventual ruin to the defendant.

At last he sat down and the court buzzed again, until Mr Henderson rose slowly to commence his opening speech.

'Much has been made of the plaintiff's standing in the community, but let us, for a moment, consider the position of my client. Mr Rodwell' – Mr Henderson stressed the use of Percy's name – 'was born here, in this town, in the rooms above the premises where he now conducts his business. He now lives in a small town house on Church Street. A modest dwelling by some standards –' he glanced towards the prosecution – 'that is true. Mr Rodwell is not a wealthy man. He makes no claims to be. He is, indeed, a modest man in all ways. Modest in wealth, modest in character. And, following in his family's footsteps, he runs a modest enterprise in, as we have heard, rented property. Rented, as we have also heard, your honour, from the plaintiff's brother. I'm sure there is no one in this courtroom' – Mr Henderson's glance swept the public gallery and around the court – 'who would deny that my client runs a respectable, though modest, tailoring business' – his voice became a little louder and his tone firmer, 'in a fair and honest manner. But consider for a moment, if you will, the position my client must have found himself in some eight years ago. We are led to believe that it was my client, Mr Rodwell, who began to court the plaintiff. In fact, your honour, it was the plaintiff who made the first – er – shall we say – approach to my client. Of course, there is no shame in this. Was it not our late and much lamented Queen Victoria – correct me if I am wrong – who was obliged to make the proposal of marriage to her beloved Albert because of her superior position?'

Now there was a gale of laughter around the courtroom and the judge banged his gavel irritably.

'As we have heard, the plaintiff is a genteel and respectable lady. But when she invited Mr Rodwell to dine at the Hall with herself and her brother, was that not placing my client in something of a dilemma? Apart from not wishing – quite understandably – to upset this genteel and respectable lady, he is also her brother's tenant and would feel, no doubt, under some kind of obligation to accept their kind invitation.' He paused to allow these thoughts to filter into the minds of all those listening. Meg glanced at Clara and saw her whispering urgently in her solicitor's ear, but Mr Snape was shaking his head and patting her arm as if to quieten her. Meg smiled wryly. Miss Finch wanted to argue with the opposition's statements just as she herself had done so rashly.

'Events moved on,' Mr Henderson continued, 'and the invitations to dine, to parties, to Sunday afternoon outings became more frequent, so frequent, in fact, with refusal unthinkable, that in the eyes of the community there must be some kind of – er – *understanding* between the plaintiff and my client. This modest and unassuming man found himself drawn into a relationship with the plaintiff that had really not been of his making. But let us be fair – we must not forget that the plaintiff is a genteel lady. I have no doubt that her motives were *most* respectable.'

Again a ripple of laughter ran through the courtroom, quickly silenced by the judge's frown.

'Perhaps at this time the plaintiff's brother – my client's landlord – took a hand in moving matters forward by pointing out to my client that his frequent visits to the home of the lady in question were putting her reputation at risk. Now, imagine my modest and unassuming client's feelings at this point. He has no wish to offend his landlord. The lady in question is . . .'

Here Mr Henderson paused and turned to look at

Clara. He regarded her for some moments, his silence drawing the attention of everyone present to her: to her gaunt face, to her hooked nose, to her hard, beady eyes, to her thin and shapeless figure. He cleared his throat and continued, '. . . as we have been repeatedly told, is a genteel and respectable lady. And Mr Rodwell had, at that time, no other – er – prospect.'

There was a titter from the gallery.

'He lived alone and ran his business alone. His only social life was comprised of invitations from the plaintiff. And so he becomes betrothed to this lady of means, of standing in the community, and the event is duly celebrated and becomes common knowledge. But this engagement, your honour, lasts six years. It would appear to an outsider, would it not, that there was nothing to stand in the way of the nuptials between these two – er – young lovers?'

More laughter from those present and even the judge allowed his lips to twitch.

'But if the prosecution is to be believed it was my client who prevaricated, with the weak excuse that he had nothing to offer his lady love. And indeed –' Mr Henderson puffed out his chest and gestured towards Clara – 'in comparison with this lady of independent means, of superior standing in the community, what has a modest tailor in rented business premises and living in a tiny cottage got to offer her?

'But in all this, your honour, we have not heard one word of the emotions between the plaintiff and my client. Oh, much has been made of the plaintiff's suitability. Who could argue that she is an undoubted catch?'

Now there was loud, insulting laughter from the gallery. The judge bowed his head as if to hide his face.

Then he banged his gavel, but there was still stifled sniggering from the gallery.

'We have heard no mention of love between them, of unbridled passion that could not wait for blissful union—'

'Mr Henderson,' the judge warned, and Percy's solicitor bowed, acknowledging that his turn of phrase might be becoming indelicate.

'Your honour,' he murmured. 'But then,' he continued, 'into my client's life comes this young woman – an impoverished young woman, your honour, with not a penny to her name, with nothing to offer a prospective husband. She has no standing in the community, she comes from the workhouse.' He paused to allow this information to sink in. 'But one day, in an effort to pull herself out of the mire, she dresses herself in the only clothes she has and walks all the way into town to Mr Rodwell's shop. She has been told, by a friend of the plaintiff's I might add, Miss Pendleton, the matron at the workhouse' – Clara whispered urgently into Mr Snape's ear, but Mr Henderson continued – 'that Mr Rodwell might be looking for a female assistant to serve his lady customers with . . .' Mr Henderson coughed delicately, 'underwear. And so, with a hopeful heart, this young girl sets out to better her circumstances with no further thought in her pretty head than that of securing a respectable, though lowly, position and being able to support herself and her poor mother.

'My client, altruistic and kindly, takes her on trial. On trial, mark you. But the young woman rapidly proves her worth. She is lively, warm-hearted, has a natural empathy with the customers and she is willing to do anything that is asked of her.'

There was a loud guffaw from a man standing at the

back of the public gallery. 'I bet she is!' He was quickly shushed by those around him. Ignoring the interruption with a look of contempt, Mr Henderson continued, 'But this young woman's strong instinct to be independent, not to be a burden on the parish any longer than she must, leads her to seek shelter at night in the shop.' Cleverly, the solicitor glossed over Meg's reason for leaving the workhouse. 'When he finds out, her kindly employer, far from dismissing her as his fiancée demanded he should, takes this girl to his home and gives her shelter. In return for his kindness, his trust in her, the young woman brings comfort and affection into his life. His world is suddenly a sunnier place and he falls hopelessly in love with her. But his love is not hopeless for, to his great surprise and delight, the young woman returns his affection.'

Mr Henderson stood for a moment shaking his head sadly. 'But now, of course, we come to the crux of the matter and why we find ourselves here in this courtroom today. The engagement that we are led to believe existed between the plaintiff and my client.'

At this there was an explosive snort of rage from Clara and nervous laughter from the public gallery. Again Meg noticed Mr Snape patting Clara's hand to quieten her.

'The truth of the matter is, your honour' – Mr Henderson rested on his knuckles on the table in front of him, leaning towards the judge and looking directly at him as his sonorous voice echoed round the room – 'that it was, in fact, the plaintiff who broke off the so-called engagement when my client refused to accede to her wishes. Wishes, your honour, which included the dismissal of the young woman from both his home and from his place of business. The plaintiff' – he now waved his hand dramatically in the direction of Clara Finch – 'cared nothing for the welfare of this young woman. Where she could have helped and supported her betrothed in giving the poor girl a chance in life, the plaintiff was vindictive and jealous. She resorted to emotional blackmail. Her very words, your honour, were—' Here he paused dramatically and held up a piece of paper from which he read, "'If you do not dismiss the girl, Percy, then our engagement is at an end."'

He threw the paper down on the table in disgust. 'Your honour, I appreciate the difficulty facing you—'

'Thank you for your concern, Mr Henderson,' the judge remarked dryly. 'I am sure I shall rise to the occasion.' He allowed himself a small smile and glanced over the top of his spectacles towards the gallery. He was rewarded by laughter and someone even dared to clap.

'Quite so, your honour, but if I may be permitted to stress the point, it was the *plaintiff* and not the defendant who terminated their betrothal because he would not obey her. Now' – he straightened up and smiled benignly – 'if I am not mistaken, the vows contained in the marriage service do contain the word "obey". But am I not right in thinking that this particular vow is made, not by the man, but by the woman, who promises to "love, honour and obey"?' Mr Henderson paused again as if waiting for someone, anyone, to contradict him. When no one did, he added in silky tones, 'Not a very auspicious start to married life between the plaintiff and the defendant, eh?

'And one last point, your honour—'

The judge glanced at the huge clock on the back wall of the public gallery. 'Do you anticipate this taking very long, Mr Henderson?'

'No, your honour, just a few moments more.'

'Very well,' the judge said resignedly and settled back in his chair, his fingers linked in front of him.

'And my last point is this. My client is an honourable man – the sort of man who would have sacrificed his own happiness for the sake of keeping his word and his promises. But would it not have been the act of a *dishonourable* man to have continued in this relationship, to have gone through with marriage to a woman he no longer loved, purely for the sake of keeping his word? *When all the time he would have been in love with another*. Some might say he's a fool. A fool to throw away all that marriage to the plaintiff might have brought him.' Mr Henderson ticked the items off on his fingers. 'A fine house to live in, ownership of his business premises, which, we have heard, was to form part of the marriage settlement. And, last but not least, no doubt he could look forward to a step up the ladder in the social life of this community. He gave up all that, your honour' – his tone was husky with emotion as he gestured towards Clara and then let his arm continue in a sweep until it came to rest pointing in Meg's direction – 'to follow his heart.'

Thirty-Two

That evening Jake read the newspaper avidly, where the case was being reported in detail.

'Look,' he burst out. 'Just look what they're saying about her. It's not true! Someone ought to tell them—'

'Oh aye, and what would you tell 'em, eh?' Mabel Smallwood said grimly. 'That she's whiter than white, 'cos let me tell you if she's anything like her father – and her mother by all accounts – then she isn't.'

Jake stared at her. Then his manner softened a little. Craftily, he said, 'What was she like before her father – went off?'

Mrs Smallwood sniffed and admitted grudgingly, 'All right, I suppose, though she was always a bit of a flirt. Eyeing all the lads and chatting to them.'

'But was there any real harm in her?'

'She was only a lass when she was here. She's grown up a bit since then.'

'She had to, didn't she?' Jake was being greatly daring, defying his mistress in such a way.

Mrs Smallwood glared at him and then dropped her gaze. 'Aye well, you could be right. But we couldn't keep the family on here. Not after . . .' She fell silent.

'I know,' Jake said, gently now. 'I do understand.'

She looked at him and said slowly, 'For a young 'un, you're a very understanding sort of lad.' Then, unusually, she smiled at him. 'But just you be careful with that little madam. She's a heartbreaker, that one.'

Jake turned away. He didn't answer her, but what he could have said was: *Thanks for the warning, missis, but it's too late. Meg's already broken mi heart.*

'I suppose you'll be wanting time off to go to the court tomorrow to hear the verdict?' When he made no response, she answered herself, flapping her hands at him. 'Oh, go on with you, then. Though what the mester'll say, I daren't think.'

Mr Smallwood said nothing. Like his wife, he had taken to the young lad. They both liked Ron and his family, but they were a family unit, complete in themselves. Jake was alone in the world and the couple – though they would never have admitted it, not even to each other – were missing their daughter. The following morning, George Smallwood appeared in the yard dressed in his going-to-town suit. Without preamble he said bluntly, 'The missis reckons you want to go into the courthouse today. That right?'

'I . . .' Jake began hesitantly and then decided to be bold. 'Yes, I do, sir. But only if I can get mi work done first. I wouldn't go otherwise.'

'You'll not get it all done afore you go, else you'll miss all the excitement.' The tall, rotund figure beamed down at him. 'I've a mind to go myself. Bonfire night last night and the verdict today. Reckon there could be a few fireworks in that courtroom if the verdict goes the wrong way. I've known Percy Rodwell all his life and his father before him. A quieter, more docile fellow you couldn't wish to meet. I just can't believe he's in the middle of such scandalous goings on.' He stroked his chin. 'And as for that lass . . .'

Jake waited, holding his breath, willing the man not

to say anything unkind about Meg because, if he did, then Jake might just forget himself and likely lose his job.

'As for that lass, she was a pert little thing when she worked for us, but I don't believe all the things they're saying about her in the papers.'

'No,' Jake told him solemnly. 'Neither do I.'

'Right then, run along home and put your better clothes on.'

'I – er – haven't got any other clothes than these.'

'What?' The farmer looked scandalized. 'Is that so?' When Jake nodded, George murmured, 'Oh aye, I was forgetting where you'd come from, lad. That old skinflint Pendleton wouldn't give you a decent suit to your back, I'll be bound.' He put his hand on Jake's shoulder. 'Tell you what, m'lad. When Percy Rodwell's back in his shop we'll have you kitted out with a new suit, eh? How about that then?'

Jake managed to summon a smile and thank him politely. He didn't want to tell his employer that he had vowed never to set foot in the shop again. Not while Meg was still there.

Unaware of the young man's dilemma, George boomed, 'Let's be off then. Get the pony and trap harnessed, Jake lad, and we'll be off. Don't want to miss the fun, eh?'

The fun, as George called it, had already started by the time they reached the courthouse. All the seats were taken in the public gallery and George and Jake were obliged to stand just inside the door, squeezed in at the back.

'Not a minute too soon,' George muttered. 'They've stopped anyone else coming in now.' Jake heard him with half an ear. He was craning his neck to catch sight of Meg. And then he saw her, sitting in the middle of the front row of the public gallery. But he could not see her face.

They had scarcely got settled before the judge came in and the proceedings began. It seemed that only the prosecution wished to call any witnesses and there was only one: Mr Theobald Finch.

'Why won't you let me speak up for you, Percy?' Meg had begged him. 'I heard her say it. I was there. She threatened to break off the engagement if you didn't sack me.'

'I don't want you involved, Meg dear.' Percy was firm. 'And besides, I'm not sure whether a wife is allowed to testify on her husband's behalf.' He patted her hand. 'You just sit in the gallery – quietly, mind. Mr Henderson says you could jeopardize whatever chance I have got if you anger the judge.'

Meg was contrite. 'Yes, I know. I'm sorry for my outburst yesterday. If I could apologize to the judge, I would. I was just so angry at all the lies that horrible Mr Snape was telling about you.'

'Well, that's what the prosecution and defence is all about. Though how the judge is going to make up his mind through it all, I don't know. Mr Henderson isn't exactly telling the plain, unvarnished truth either, now is he? He's angling things the way he wants them to look.'

Despite the seriousness of their situation, Meg giggled. 'No, he's very clever, isn't he? But surely the judge can see by just looking at Miss Finch that she's a dried-up old spinster, who's just out for revenge?'

And now, in the courtroom once more, Meg, completely unaware of Jake's presence a few paces behind her, was crossing her fingers and hoping that Mr Henderson's cleverness would win the day for Percy.

Theobald Finch gave his testimony precisely, clearly and, strangely, quite impartially. When responding to questions it was obvious that he was trying to be entirely truthful and would not allow himself either to be led by Mr Snape or trapped by Mr Henderson.

'My family has always found the Rodwells to be excellent tenants. I have nothing against the defendant in a business sense.'

Mr Snape was quick to leap in. 'But you have in a personal sense, haven't you, Mr Finch?'

Theobald cleared his throat and glanced briefly at the judge. 'All I can say is that the engagement between Rodwell and my sister was a definite fact. Rodwell came and asked for my permission and we held a party.'

When it came to Mr Henderson's turn to cross-examine Theobald, he asked, 'Why do you think it was that there was such a long delay between the couple becoming engaged and setting a date for the wedding?'

Theobald shrugged. 'I expect Rodwell felt unable to provide for my sister in the manner to which she had always been accustomed, as they say. I expect he was trying to get a bit more capital together. Buy a better house, perhaps. I don't really know. It was never discussed with me.'

'Do you mean to tell us, Mr Finch . . .' Mr Henderson glanced around the courtroom, surprise on his face. 'Do you really mean to tell us that your sister never discussed these matters with you?'

'Ar-humph,' Theobald shifted uncomfortably and ran his forefinger around his collar as if it was too tight. He was growing redder in the face with every minute. 'Well, she might have said something of the sort. That – that she didn't like his poky little house.'

Laughter rippled around the court and, hearing it for the first time, Jake was startled.

'Ah,' said Mr Henderson, satisfied. 'His poky little house, eh?'

'But we offered for him to live with us – at the Hall – after their marriage.'

'At the Hall? Really? And you also offered to give Mr Rodwell the deeds to the property where he conducts his tailoring business? Is that not so?'

'It is so,' Theobald replied.

'Then why do you suppose – with all this on offer to him – that a date was never set?'

'You tell me,' Theobald shot back. 'I don't understand it myself.'

Mr Henderson leant forward on his knuckles as he said slowly and deliberately, his gaze boring into Theobald's eyes, 'Do you suppose it could possibly be because – even before this young girl appeared on the scene – Mr Rodwell was unsure of his true feelings for the plaintiff? He was having doubts about committing himself to her – *for life*?'

'Yes – no – I mean – I – er – um – suppose it's – it's possible.' Poor Theobald was obliged to admit the fact and for a brief moment, Meg felt quite sorry for him. 'But then,' he volunteered, regaining his composure, 'he shouldn't have got engaged to her, should he?'

'No.' Mr Henderson nodded solemnly. 'I am obliged to agree with you there.' He paused and Meg held her breath. Was Mr Henderson giving up? Whatever was he thinking of, agreeing with Mr Finch?

But then Mr Henderson's smile was deceptively

benign. 'But is it not possible, Mr Finch,' he went on smoothly, 'that in the early days of their – er – romance, my client did have a genuine fondness for the plaintiff? Perhaps, it was only when she found that his poky little house – the place that had been Mr Rodwell's home for the greater part of his life – wasn't good enough for her to live in, when she began to make demands about whom he should or should not employ in his business, when she began to threaten . . .' He paused and then said quietly, 'Need I say more?'

Theobald Finch did not answer.

When all the speeches had been made, the witness heard and the plaintiff and the defendant had each appeared in the witness box to be examined and cross-examined, the judge adjourned the case over the weekend whilst he made his decision. As Meg stood to leave, she glanced up and her gaze met Jake's. She climbed the steps towards him, pushing through the chattering crowd who were filing out.

Her immediate reaction at the sight of him was to smile, but that faded when she saw his solemn face, the censure in his eyes. By the time she reached him, her mood was belligerent. There were enough people blaming her – she could tell by all the whispering and nudging – without Jake joining their number.

'What are you doing here? Come to gloat, have you?'

Jake opened his mouth to make some biting retort, but then he closed it again. He was shocked by the look on her face. She seemed genuinely distressed as she pushed her way past him, down the stairs, through the entrance hall and out onto the wide steps at the front of the building. She stood there, pulling in great gulps of fresh air as if she had not been able to breathe in the confines of the courtroom.

'He doesn't deserve all this,' she said as Jake came to stand beside her. 'He's a good man – a kind man – and that – that bitch is dragging his name through the mud.'

'And yours,' he murmured.

She gave a wry laugh. 'Mine? Oh, what does my name matter? My name's in the mire already. But his? Like I say, he doesn't deserve it.'

She turned and hurried away from him but not before Jake had seen the tears in her eyes. Perplexed, he stared after her and one of old Albert Conroy's sayings crept into his mind. 'Funny creatures, women. They take some understanding, lad.'

Well, Jake thought, his Meg did. He still thought of her as 'his' and probably always would. But had he misjudged her? Had he really got it all so very wrong?

Thirty-Three

On the day that the judge was to sum up the case and give his verdict, the public gallery was crowded again. Jake and George Smallwood were once more squeezed in at the very back. The hubbub in the courtroom ceased abruptly as the door below opened and the judge entered to take his place. He shuffled his papers and cleared his throat.

'This has been a difficult case,' he said at last. 'By the evidence presented, I am convinced that an engagement did exist between the parties and that that engagement was subsequently broken. But who broke it off? That is the question.' He cleared his throat and glanced around as if enjoying the suspense he was creating. *Get on with it*, Meg wanted to shout, but she kept her lips pressed together.

'We are told that the plaintiff threatened to end the engagement if her fiancé did not comply with her wishes in the matter of the employment of the young woman. One could' – he spread his hands expressively – 'deduce from this that, because her fiancé did not comply, then it was she who broke off the betrothal. The defendant took her at her word, so to speak. Now, mindful of the vagaries of a woman's mind . . .' At this there was heartfelt laughter from the men in the gallery and the judge allowed himself a small smile, 'we could assume that the lady did not mean what she said. That she was, indeed, only using it as a threat to get her own way.' He paused and seemed lost in his own thoughts for a moment. 'But the defendant *did* take her at her word. Called her bluff, as you might say. But what follows makes us think that even if we believe the so-called threat, then the defendant used this threat to break the engagement for his own ends. He had taken up with the girl and wanted to marry her and here, presented to him on a plate, was his excuse. He could, he thought, release himself from the now unwanted entanglement of his engagement in order to marry the girl.'

The courtroom was silent now, hanging on the judge's every word. He recapped at some length what had already been ably said by the two solicitors. One moment he seemed to be in favour of Clara, the next on Percy's side.

'After much deliberation,' he said at last, when the folk in the gallery were beginning to get restive, 'I feel bound to accept the plaintiff's story.' He paused to wait whilst the excited whispering from the women onlookers in the gallery subsided. Clara Finch's face was a picture. Eyes narrowed, she smirked with satisfaction, and glanced across towards where Percy was sitting with his head in his hands. Vindicated, she was almost preening.

'And . . .' The judge looked slowly round the whole courtroom before he said in ringing tones, 'I award her the sum of – one farthing.' He banged his gavel and stood up to leave.

There was a stunned silence and then a loud guffaw of laughter from all the men present whilst the ladies twittered with indignation.

'What does it mean?' Jake asked George Smallwood. 'I don't understand.'

'It means, lad, that the judge felt compelled to find in her favour, as they say.' When he saw that Jake was still frowning, he explained in simpler terms. 'That he believes Miss Finch's story. That Percy Rodwell did break their engagement to marry Meg. But in awarding her only one farthing in damages he's indicating that he doesn't really blame Percy one bit.' George laughed loudly. 'And I bet there's not a man here who wouldn't agree with him. Why, you've only got to look at that skinny spinster with her vicious tongue and your Meg to side with Percy. He's a lucky feller. That's what we're all thinking. Lucky to have escaped that biddy's clutches and lucky to be married to that young lass.'

Aye, my Meg, Jake was thinking bitterly. *But she's not 'my Meg' any longer. She's Percy Rodwell's.* And yes, Percy was a lucky fellow.

The unusual court case, the way it had been conducted and its surprising outcome were the gossip of the town for several days. Gradually, however, folk settled back into their normal routine and other matters took their attention. But for some life had changed dramatically. Clara Finch rarely ventured out of the Hall. She had been humiliated in front of the whole community and she felt she could never hold her head up again.

'I told you not to be so daft, bringing an action against him,' was her brother's comment. 'What can you expect when it's men making the judgement?'

'I expected justice,' Clara replied through clenched teeth. 'And I expected a little more support from you – my own brother. It was you who lost the case for me. Standing up there and sounding as if you sympathized with – with – *him*. I'll never forgive you for that, Theo. Never!'

'Well, it wasn't my idea to bring the case.' Theobald paused and eyed her speculatively. 'Where did you get the idea from anyway?'

'Why do you assume I got the idea from someone else?' she snapped back. 'Don't you think I've got a mind of my own? Don't you think I'm capable of thinking for myself?'

Theobald's answer was a disbelieving grunt. 'Well, *did* you think of it for yourself?'

'Not – exactly.'

'So?'

'Oh, if you must know I was taking tea in a cafe in the town with Letitia and—'

'Letitia?' Theobald was startled. 'Letitia Pendleton?'

'Of course Letitia Pendleton. How many other Letitias do we know?'

'Well! You do surprise me.' He cast her a keen look. 'I thought,' he said, and there was a pointed edge to his tone, 'that she wasn't good enough to be in your company.'

'No more she is,' Clara snapped, 'but if the wretched woman has the effrontery to join me at the table – without being asked, I might add – I can hardly make a scene in a public place.'

'Mm, well, you made quite a scene in a public court, didn't you, my dear?' If he hadn't been her brother, Clara would have thought he was revelling in her humiliation. 'But she's not the vindictive sort,' he murmured mildly. 'Not Letitia. Now, if you'd said it had been Isaac's idea—'

'Oh, and you'd know that, wouldn't you, Theo. If anyone'd know that, you would.'

Brother and sister glared at each other and, though not another word was spoken, ghosts from the past lay between them.

At last, Clara sighed. 'It wasn't Letitia.'

'Ha!' Theobald let out a sound of great satisfaction. 'I thought not. Then who was it? Was it Isaac?'

'No. She'd brought some woman with her from the workhouse. She works for Letitia – has quite a good position there, so I believe.' Clara was at pains not to let her brother think that she had been taking tea with a workhouse pauper. 'It was this woman's birthday. I forget her name. Walters or Waters or something like that. Letitia had brought her into town as a treat. Well, it was her suggestion. "If it was me," she said, "I'd sue him." And I'll tell you something, Theo. I'm not sorry. No, I'm not. In spite of that horrible judge, I'm glad I let the women of this town know just what men are capable of. They'll be on my side, I can assure you. And when I've finished with Percy Rodwell and his fancy piece, he'll wish he'd never been born!'

Percy and Meg settled into a contented routine. Each day they worked together in the shop until mid-afternoon, when Meg went home to the little cottage to prepare an evening meal and to do her housework. On Monday evenings she washed. On Tuesdays she ironed. On Wednesdays she cleaned the bedrooms and on Thursdays she cleaned the downstairs rooms. On Saturday evenings she lit a fire in the front room and they sat together companionably, Percy with his newspaper and Meg with her sewing and mending. On Sundays, when the shop was closed, they attended morning service at church and then after lunch they went for a walk, if the weather was good, or again sat together in the front room. And at night in the privacy of their bedroom, Meg would open her arms to Percy and submit herself to his trembling lovemaking.

It was a quiet, well-ordered life and Meg told herself it was what she wanted. She closed her mind to her former life. She determined never to think of her father or of her lost little brother. And she hardened her heart towards her mother.

If she doesn't want to see me, she told herself, *then I don't want to see her. I'll never think of her again. I won't even think about that place and the people she's chosen to live with. I shall wipe them from my mind.* The master, the matron, Louisa Daley, Waters – all of them. Even poor old Albert had to be banished from her thoughts, for if she were to allow herself to think about him, then unbidden memories of the others at the workhouse would creep into her mind.

But there was one whom, try as she might, she could not banish from her mind or her heart. Jake Bosley refused to be forgotten.

Though she was unaware of it, Jake was finding it just as hard to put Meg out of his thoughts. He buried himself in his work at the farm, labouring from dawn to dusk and falling into his narrow bed in the little room in Ron's cottage. But even there he could not forget her. Where he slept had been her room, her bed, even. Her head had rested on the very same pillow he now used. Her young, lithe body had made the hollows in the mattress where he now lay. Her hand had touched the doorknob. She had washed in the bowl and ewer on the washstand, and she had brushed her hair, staring at herself in the cracked mirror. And his pledge to keep away from her, to let her get on with the life she had chosen, was thwarted by the kindness of his employer. Mr Smallwood had not forgotten their conversation about Jake's clothing – or rather the lack of it.

Just before Christmas, he said, 'Now, lad, I promised you a Sunday best suit and the missis has agreed. We hadn't realized that you'd only got the clothes you stood up in.' He made a sound of disapproval. 'What that place is coming to, I don't know.' He nodded his head in the vague direction of where the workhouse stood across country from his farm. 'You'd think the parish could run to equipping a young lad out when he ventured into the world. Anyway, ne'er mind about that. We don't mind forking out for a new suit for you.' He smiled and nodded. 'You're a good lad and we're pleased with the way you're shaping up, so we hope you'll stay with us.'

Jake, feeling suddenly happier than he had done for months – ever since Meg had married Percy Rodwell in fact – beamed. 'Oh, I will, sir. You and the missis have been very good to me.'

'There's just one other thing. I know you like living with Ron – and they like having you – but he tells me his missis is expecting another bairn.' For a brief moment there was an expression of envious longing in the older man's face, but it cleared quickly as he went on. 'And they're going to be a bit short of room. We wondered if you'd consider moving into the farmhouse with me and the missis. There's . . . there's . . .' again a fleeting glimpse of deep pain, 'only the two of us now.'

Jake hesitated, torn between wanting to stay with Ron and his family in the house where Meg had once lived and yet at the same time longing to be freed from her ghostly presence in his room in the long night hours.

He smiled up at his employer. 'I'd be glad to, sir. I'll try not to be a trouble to you and your wife.'

'Oh, you won't be, lad, no more than . . .' George cleared his throat and swiftly changed the subject. 'Just one other thing. The missis will expect you to go to church with us every Sunday. You'd do that for her, lad, would you?'

Jake grinned. 'Of course, sir. I'll be able to show off me new suit.' As they walked across the yard together towards the house to tell Mabel Smallwood what had been arranged between them, George put his arm across the young man's shoulders and they laughed together.

Watching them from the window, Mabel, for all her hard exterior, felt a lump in her throat. 'Aye,' she murmured. 'He's the son you've never had, George. Let's hope he's a mite more biddable than that good-for-nothing daughter of ours.'

So, two days later, Jake stepped into Percy's shop to be measured for a new suit. It seemed as if his path and Meg's were destined to cross. It would not be possible for him never to see her, for he knew she attended church on Sundays and now he was expected to do the same.

Forget it, Jake told himself. *It's in the past. She's married and nothing can change that. She's lost to you and you'd better get on with your own life.* So Jake buried his feelings deep inside himself and when he walked into the shop, it was with a bright smile plastered on to his face and a cheery word on his lips, as if all that had gone before was forgotten – and forgiven.

Thirty-Four

'Do you know of anyone who'd come as a dairymaid?' Mabel asked Jake. He had been working at Middleditch Farm for almost two years and during that time he had longed to ask the missis if Betsy could come and work at the farm, but he had never quite been able to pluck up the courage. 'Ron's eldest lass might be all right in a year or two's time,' she was saying, 'but she's a mite young at the moment.' Mabel sighed. 'And I really need someone now.'

Jake grinned at her. For all the sharpness of her tongue, he had become very fond of the missis and the mester too. He was as happy as he could be living with them. It was the closest he would ever come, he thought, to having a real family. He felt – though he could never really know – that they treated him as they might have done their own son, and had treated their daughter, he supposed. Though how, Jake asked himself, Alice Smallwood could have run away from such a kind and loving home, was beyond him.

'I just might,' he answered Mabel now as his grin widened. 'That's if you don't mind having another workhouse brat under your roof.'

Mabel stared at him for a moment and then laughed aloud. 'Well now, I'll have to think on that 'cos I don't know if I could put up with another young 'un like you.' As their shared laughter faded, she said more seriously, 'What's she like, this lass you've got in mind? 'Cos I can see you've got someone. How old is she?'

'Nearly fourteen.'

She looked at him for a while with her head on one side and her tone sharpened. 'Got yer eye on her, have you? 'Cos I won't have any hanky-panky under my roof.'

'I don't think of little Betsy like that.' He wrinkled his forehead. ''Spect she's more like a sister to me than anything.'

'Mm.' Mabel sounded none too sure. Little Betsy would grow into a young woman and then what? Still, she could keep a sharp eye on them both. A much keener one, Mabel reminded herself bitterly, than she had on her own daughter.

'Tell her to come and see me then.'

'Aw, thanks, missis.'

He turned away as if to go to the workhouse that very minute, but Mabel asked, 'Who was your mam, then?'

'Dunno, really.' He shrugged. 'Some poor lass who got herself into trouble and I 'spect her family didn't want to know. That's if she had any.'

'What happened to her?'

'Eh?' He stared at her, mystified by her question.

'Well, I mean, did she die? Or – or did she – just leave you there?'

'Is that – is that what they do? Just – just leave their bairns there? As if they've never existed?' Despite his years in the workhouse, that thought had never entered his mind.

Mabel did not answer him but asked another question. 'Do you know her name?'

Slowly, Jake shook his head, his eyes still fixed on

her face. 'Never thought to ask. I – I just took it that she'd died having me – or soon after. And I supposed her name was Bosley.'

'And your father?'

'Huh! Some bastard who didn't want to know when he'd had his way. Sorry, missis, but you know what I mean.'

Mabel hid her smile. 'You're probably right. And maybe you're right not to want to find out. But if you ever did, there'd be your birth certificate. I expect the master has it at the workhouse.'

'Birth certificate?' Jake looked puzzled for a moment. 'I've heard the other chaps in the workhouse talk about them, but I didn't know I'd got one.'

'It's the law. Every birth, death or marriage has to be registered legally and a certificate issued.' She glanced at him. 'If you wanted me to, I could ask Mr Pendleton for it. I'd have a right to see it as your employer. But only if you wanted me to, Jake.'

'Oh, well. I dunno. I've never really thought about it.'

'Well, if you ever decide you'd like to find out a bit more, let me know. All right?'

'Mm. Yes, well, thanks, missis.'

'And in the meantime, go and tell Betsy to come and see me tomorrow afternoon.'

Now Jake was smiling once more.

'Hello, Dr Collins. What are you doing here? Somebody ill? I hope it's not Betsy, 'cos I might have found a job for her.'

As Jake opened the gate into the workhouse yard, he came face to face with the young doctor on his way out.

Philip Collins smiled and stood aside. 'My word, Jake, farming life certainly suits you. You've filled out in all the right places. I do believe you've grown taller too.'

Jake laughed. 'Fresh air and all that good food the missis piles on my plate.' He rubbed his stomach and licked his lips. 'By heck, but she's a fine cook.'

Philip laughed. 'I can see that. It's not a place I have to call very often. They're too healthy by half.'

'So who's ill here then?'

'Thankfully, at the moment, no one. Oh, the usual sniffles, but nothing serious. No, I – er – came to see my fiancée. She's only got another month to work here. Miss Daley and I are getting married in six weeks' time, at the end of August.'

'Congratulations.' Jake grinned. 'I had me eye on her miself. If I'd've been a bit older, you wouldn't have got a look in.'

Philip smiled, knowing that the young man was only teasing. Jake had not an ounce of conceit about him and wouldn't realize just what a good-looking fellow he had become. His dark brown eyes were the same as ever, mischievous and yet with a depth of compassion for others that had perhaps come about because of his own unfortunate start in life. Jake's face was still thin, but now weather-beaten to a healthy tan and his brown hair was streaked by the sun.

'I can believe that,' the doctor murmured, smiling too, but there was a hint of seriousness in his tone.

They side-stepped each other and were about to say goodbye, when they both turned back and began to speak at the same moment.

'There's something you could—'

'How's Meg's mother?

They both stopped and Philip gestured that Jake should say his piece first.

'I just wondered how Meg's mother – Mrs Kirkland – is. Is she – is she still with *him*?'

Philip allowed himself a wry smile. 'She is.' He seemed about to say more, but decided against it. Jake nodded briefly. He understood the young doctor's unspoken words. If the master was taken up with Sarah, he was less likely to be bothering Louisa Daley. And that suited Dr Collins. Now, answering Jake's first question, Philip said, 'She's not too good, really. But I think her problem . . .' he hesitated, not sure if he should be divulging this to a third person, 'is more emotional than physical. Oh, she's not robust at the best of times, but I think she misses Meg terribly. She's so hurt by Meg's rejection.'

Jake stared. 'But – but Meg came to see her, the day before she married Percy Rodwell. She was told that her mother didn't want to see her. Meg did try. And I tried to see her – Mrs Kirkland, I mean – too. But I got the same answer.'

Philip stared at him for a moment and then let out a long 'Ahhh'. He was thoughtful for a moment before saying slowly, 'Next time I see Sarah alone, I'll tell her that. In the meantime, could you do something for me?'

'Anything, doctor.'

'Louisa is also very distressed by her estrangement from Meg. She became very fond of the girl, even though they worked together for such a short time. Louisa has no close relatives now. Her mother died two months ago. She would dearly love Meg to be her matron of honour at our wedding. Would you ask Meg to let bygones be bygones, Jake? It would mean so much to Louisa.'

Jake pulled a face. 'I'll try.' But his tone lacked hope.

Philip nodded. 'You can only do your best. Good day, Jake. And I hope all goes well for Betsy. She's a sweet child.'

The doctor turned away and as Jake began to cross the yard Betsy herself came skipping towards him, a happy smile on her face. 'I saw you from the dormitory window. I was making the beds. I don't go to school any more now, you know. And guess what?' She jumped up and down excitedly in front of him, clapping her hands. 'Miss Daley's asked me to be her bridesmaid.'

Jake smiled at the little girl's joy. To him, he thought, Betsy would always be a little girl.

'That's wonderful.'

'She's having such a pretty dress made for me. And afterwards' – Betsy's eyes shone – 'she says I can keep it.'

Jake held out his arms to her and Betsy skipped into them to be enveloped in a bear hug.

'Now, I've got some even better news for you.'

Betsy giggled and looked up at him. 'Whatever could be better than being bridesmaid and wearing a pretty new dress?'

Jake looked down into her upturned face, into her dancing blue eyes. For the first time he saw how pretty she was, with small, delicate features, perfectly shaped. Her face was too thin and her skin too pale, but fresh air and Mrs Smallwood's cooking would soon alter that.

'How would you like to work as a dairymaid?'

Betsy's eyes widened and her mouth dropped open. Against him, Jake felt her heart thud. Her voice was an ecstatic squeak. 'With you? At your farm?'

Jake chuckled. 'It's not my farm, though I wish it was. No, the missis is looking for a young dairymaid and she asked me if I knew anyone. And I thought of you.'

'Oh, Jake, thank you, thank you, thank you.' She hugged him tightly.

'Hey, don't thank me yet. You'd only be on trial to start with. And she's quite a tartar when she wants to be, the missis. Mind you.' His grin widened. 'I get on with her all right.'

'You get on with everyone, Jake. Everyone likes you.'

Except the one person I want to like me, Jake was thinking, but he kept this to himself.

'You should hear matron going on about you and how she misses you.' Betsy leant closer and lowered her voice, even though there was no one else in the yard to overhear. 'You should see her while you're here.'

'Of course I will. Come on, we'll go together and tell her the good news.' He took hold of her hand, not caring now if the master was watching. At last he was out of Isaac Pendleton's clutches for ever. But out of habit he glanced up towards the upper-floor windows.

'You're quite safe,' Betsy said, her eyes sparkling with mischief. 'He's not here today.'

The smile spread across Jake's face. 'Right,' he said. 'I'll see matron and then I'll see Meg's mam. See how she is and then I can tell Meg. I've to see her later anyway.'

At the mention of Meg's name, Betsy let her hand fall away from Jake's. She stepped back and the sparkle was gone from her eyes.

Thirty-Five

Meg stared incredulously at Jake. 'She must be joking! Me be her matron of honour? And with that – that child – of all people – as her bridesmaid? Oh no. Never. Never in a million years.'

They were standing in the workroom at the back of the shop, talking in heated whispers for Percy had an important customer in the shop choosing some of the best fabric he stocked to be made into a suit. Ironically, it was for a gentleman who was to be one of the doctor's guests at the wedding.

'I don't understand you, Meg, honestly I don't. You're the most unforgiving person I've ever met. And whilst we're on the subject, your mam is making herself ill with worry about you and not seeing you.'

'I went,' Meg hissed back, justifying herself angrily, 'but *she* didn't want to see *me*.'

'I don't think that was true. I reckon it was the master who didn't want you seeing her.'

'Why?'

Jake shrugged. 'How should I know?'

There was a pause whilst they glared at each other.

'So,' Jake prompted at last, 'what are you going to do?'

'Do? What about?'

'About either of them? Both of them?'

'Nothing.'

'So, you're going to refuse to be Miss Daley's matron of honour and you won't go and see your mother?'

Meg stretched her mouth into a sarcastic smile. 'Correct. Now, if you'll excuse me, I think my husband' – her accent on the word was unmistakable – 'requires my help in the shop.'

Jake flinched and stared at her. Where was the lovely girl he had met when she had first come to the workhouse? Where had she gone?

He turned away, sick at heart. Without another word he marched through the shop and out of the front door, slamming it behind him with such force that the bell bounced and the glass rattled.

In the back room, Meg stood chewing her fingernail and fighting back the tears.

Meg did not tell Percy that Miss Daley wanted her to be her matron of honour, but when the card arrived inviting them both to the wedding, Percy was adamant that they should attend.

'Of course, I don't know Miss Daley all that well, but the doctor has been very good to me. He was very kind one winter when I was ill. We should go to his wedding when we've been invited.'

'But it's on a Saturday. We'd have to close the shop if we both went. Why don't you go, Percy, and I'll mind the shop?'

Percy pursed his lips. 'Oh no, my dear, that would never do. It would be most unseemly.'

Meg looked at him, her mind working quickly. 'But surely you don't want to go.' She paused significantly and then added slyly, 'Won't Miss Finch be there? And her brother? Surely you don't want to run into them?'

Percy blinked. 'Oh, I hadn't thought of that.'

Meg lifted her shoulders. 'I'd've thought it stood to reason that the doctor would invite them. They're such prominent figures in the town. Or so we were led to believe, weren't we?'

Percy looked worried. 'Well, yes. I suppose you're right. Perhaps it would be rather awkward if they were there too.'

'Of course it would. And we wouldn't want anything to spoil the doctor's wedding day, would we?'

'No, no, of course not.'

'Then I think it better if we politely decline owing to business commitments. They know that the shop is always open on a Saturday.'

'I suppose so.' But Percy was still frowning anxiously.

Meg patted his arm. 'Don't let it worry you. You can explain to the doctor when you see him. He'll understand.'

She turned away, a satisfied smile on her lips, knowing that once more she had got her own way.

On the day of the wedding not one customer entered the shop and Percy fretted. 'We could have gone. We should have gone.'

'It's too late now,' Meg said briskly, carefully folding a pair of ladies' bloomers. She was amused to see Percy averting his gaze. 'I expect there are a lot of our customers at the wedding if the number of hats I've been asked for this last two weeks is anything to go by. Really, Percy, we should begin to stock hats, you know. We'd do a brisk trade, I'm sure.'

'Mm.' Percy's mind was elsewhere.

'And it's so hot today. We never get many customers

when it's such good weather. They stay indoors out of the heat.'

Percy glanced out the window at the bright, sunlit street. 'At least she's got a nice day for her wedding,' he murmured. 'She's lucky after all the rain we've had recently.'

'Yes,' Meg said flatly. Deep in her heart, she was envious of Louisa. The doctor was a good catch and young and handsome too. And he was kind. It would be very easy to fall in love with Dr Philip Collins. Meg's eyes had a faraway look.

If she hadn't met him in the workhouse, if she hadn't been wearing that awful, degrading uniform, then perhaps . . .

'Do you want to go home, my dear? I can manage here.'

'Yes, I will.' Meg dragged herself back from her daydreaming and flashed him a brilliant smile, the smile that had bowled him over and still did. 'I've some shopping I'd like to do and then I'll go home and cook your favourite meal.'

She knew that the day would end with Percy's awkward lovemaking. But she could always pretend . . .

Back from his honeymoon and looking fit and not so tired as he normally did, Dr Collins called into the shop. Meg hurried towards him and held out her hands. She smiled and kissed him swiftly on both cheeks. Philip seemed a little startled and the colour crept into his face.

'We were so sorry not to be able to attend your wedding. You do understand, don't you? It would have meant closing the shop. I tried to persuade Percy to come alone, but he wouldn't hear of it.'

'Of course not,' Philip murmured, his gaze still upon her face, her hands still in his.

She leant closer, sharing a confidence. 'And it might have been very embarrassing if Miss Finch had been there. We didn't want anything to spoil your lovely day.'

Before Philip could answer, Percy came through from the back room, a tape measure dangling round his neck, pins sticking out from his lapel. 'Doctor – Philip – how are you? Did you enjoy your – er – honeymoon?'

Meg pulled her hands away.

'Yes, thank you. We went to the Lake District. The weather was perfect. It didn't rain once.'

Percy gave a small, embarrassed laugh. 'That's unusual for there, so they tell me. I mean, I've never been.'

'You should go, Percy. Take Meg. It would do you both good.'

Percy shook his head, glancing away. 'Oh, I – we – couldn't leave the shop.'

'I've explained to Philip,' Meg said, forcing gaiety into her tone as, boldly, she used the doctor's Christian name for the first time – Percy did, she told herself, so why shouldn't she, as his wife? – 'why we could not attend the wedding.'

'Yes, yes, we were very sorry.'

'We were too.' The doctor's glance rested on Meg again. 'Especially Louisa. She particularly wanted you there, Meg, even if you didn't feel able to be her matron of honour.'

'What?' Mystified, Percy glanced from one to the other.

'Louisa asked Meg to be her matron of honour.'

'Oh, Meg,' Percy was reproachful. 'Why ever did you

refuse? That was a great favour Miss Daley was bestowing upon you.'

Meg thought quickly and then she put her hands to her face, her eyes wide with surprise above them. 'Oh no, I'm so sorry. I didn't believe him.' She turned from one to the other. 'I thought Jake was teasing. You know what a tease he can be. Well, perhaps you don't. But – but Miss Daley – Louisa – didn't come herself. Nor even you, Philip, and I never thought for a moment it was true. Oh, how dreadful! What must she think of me?'

Tears filled her eyes and she covered the whole of her face with her hands, peeping between her fingers to gauge their reaction.

Philip put his arm about her awkwardly and she pretended to sob against his shoulder. 'Please, don't distress yourself. There's obviously been a misunderstanding. I see it now. We should have come ourselves. Not sent messages. Don't think about it any more. Tell you what,' he said, brightly, 'you must both come and have dinner with us one evening. After the shop has closed. There, what do you say?'

Meg pulled back a little and smiled tremulously, looking up into his face. 'You're so kind to me. I don't deserve it.'

His gaze was on her face. Seeing the tears shimmering in her eyes, her soft mouth trembling, the just-married young doctor was appalled to find that at that moment he wanted nothing more than to kiss that mouth. To gather this young girl into his arms and hold her close.

With a leap backwards, he snatched his arm away, as if the touch of her ignited something in him that made him tremble with fear and longing. 'That's fine, then. I'll – I'll speak to Louisa about it. And – and we'll arrange something.'

But the invitation to dine with the doctor and his bride never arrived. Percy was disappointed and, though he never voiced it, Meg felt he blamed her. More than once she caught him looking at her, reproach in his eyes.

Thirty-Six

'So, what do you think, missis? Will she do?'

Betsy had been at Middleditch Farm for over a month now and Jake was eager to know if the mistress planned to keep her. Already the thin, wan child was blossoming into a healthy young girl, with a bloom on her smooth cheeks and new roundness to her body. And all day long Betsy had a sparkle in her eyes, the sparkle of real happiness. Jake couldn't know – wasn't conceited enough for the thought ever to cross his mind – that Betsy's happiness had as much to do with his nearness as with her new life.

Mrs Smallwood, her back to him as she kneaded bread dough on the kitchen table, took a moment to answer, whilst Jake's heart began to drop. 'Aye,' she said at last. 'She'll do.'

'Aw, missis, thanks.' Jake put his arms around the woman's waist and rested his head against her back. 'You don't know what it'll mean to Betsy.'

'Oh, go on with you, you daft ha'porth.' She waved him away, wafting flour into the air. 'I just hope I'm not bringing trouble on myself having you two under the same roof.' Her voice dropped as she muttered, 'As if I haven't had enough in my time already.'

Jake stepped back, hurt by her insinuation. He moved round the table to face Mabel. 'I'd never do anything to hurt Betsy. She's like a little sister to me. Always has been.'

Mabel eyed him wryly. 'Really. Well, I don't think that's how she sees you. As a brother, I mean.'

Jake blinked. 'Eh?'

With fond impatience, Mabel said, 'She's besotted with you, lad. She idolizes you.' Pointedly, she added, 'And I wouldn't want to see you taking advantage of the lass.'

Gaping at her, still unable to believe what he was hearing, Jake shook his head. Hoarsely, he said, 'I wouldn't, missis. I promise you I wouldn't.'

'Mm,' Mabel's tone still held doubt. 'Mm, well, let's hope so.'

Recovering a little, Jake asked, 'So you're going to keep her on?'

Mabel nodded. 'If she carries on as she is now and – she behaves herself – then yes, I'm keeping her on.'

'Can I – can I tell her?'

Now Mabel smiled one of her rare smiles. 'Aye, all right then.'

'Just one thing—'

'What is it now? More favours?'

Jake grinned. 'I suppose so, yes. It's Betsy's birthday next week – on the fifteenth of September. She's fourteen. Would you make her a cake? I don't reckon she's ever had a birthday cake in her life.' He didn't add that he hadn't either. 'They didn't do that sort of thing in the workhouse.'

Mabel stared at him. Into her mind flashed the pictures of her own daughter. Alice at five, six, seven and then – jumping the years – at fourteen, blowing out the candles on her cake, surrounded by her friends. First little girls from school and then bigger, older girls as they all grew up together, filling the farmhouse with their chatter and laughter.

'Aye.' Mabel's voice was husky. 'I'll make her a cake. It's on a Sunday, so we'll have a surprise party for her. Don't you go telling her, though.'

His eyes shining, Jake shook his head at the wonder of it all. Just how had workhouse brats like him and Betsy fallen on their feet like they had? 'You're a good 'un, missis.'

'So get your thinking cap on and decide who you're going to invite. Kids from the workhouse, I suppose.'

Jake wrinkled his forehead. 'Maybe one or two, but I reckon she'd like Miss Daley, I mean Mrs Collins, to come. And the matron. Miss Pendleton was always kind to her.'

'Aye well, invite who you like lad.' She looked up sharply. 'As long as it's not *her*. I won't have that girl in my house.'

Jake's heart was heavy. Without her name being mentioned, he knew she was referring to Meg. 'No,' he said sadly. 'She wouldn't come anyway.'

'Good job an' all,' Mabel muttered, as she pounded the dough almost as if she wished it was Meg's head beneath her strong hands.

Jake didn't hurry out of the kitchen in search of Betsy. He walked slowly, deep in thought. Was it really true what the missis had said? Did little Betsy really like him? A smile began at the corners of his mouth and spread slowly into a broad grin. He squared his shoulders and felt as if he had grown an inch as he went in search of her.

*

'Now, you've got to blow out all the candles at once and make a wish. That's what my mam used to tell me to do when I was a little girl.'

Letitia was enjoying herself. Her round face was red from the heat in the farmhouse kitchen and with pleasure in the day. She was sitting between Jake and little Betsy – her two favourite children from the workhouse. Though Betsy wasn't so little any more. She'd filled out and looked so happy and contented that it brought tears to the matron's eyes. And as for her beloved Jake – it was taking her all her time not to keep putting an arm around him and hugging him to her – he was growing into such a handsome young man. A son that any mother would be proud of.

I haven't done such a bad job with these two, she thought. Though a workhouse was not the ideal place for children to grow up in, she'd always done her best for all the little ones. Tried to be the mother to them that they'd lost. Tried to take their mother's place. Especially with Jake . . . And now look at their happy, healthy, smiling faces. The sight brought a lump to her throat and tears to her eyes, but she dashed them away impatiently and said again, 'Come on, Betsy, all at one blow.'

Pink with excitement and happiness, Betsy took a deep breath and blew and everyone around the table clapped: Philip and Louisa Collins, two younger girls from the workhouse, the matron, Ron with his wife and their children, Mr and Mrs Smallwood and, most important of all to Betsy, Jake. They had each given her a little gift: a hair ribbon, a lace handkerchief, and a brush-and-comb set. The two younger girls had picked bunches of wild flowers on their way to the farm. Jake had given her a prayer book to carry on Sunday mornings now that they were both expected to attend church with the Smallwoods. She would treasure that most of all because it came from him. But the best gift of all was this party.

'Put your bridesmaid's dress on for your tea,' Jake had urged her earlier in the day.

'Oh, I couldn't. It's far too grand. I'd get it messed up helping the missis get the tea ready.'

'I'll help her today. It's your birthday. You can just sit and look pretty in your posh dress and watch.'

'But what will the missis think? What will she say?'

'Oh, I'll make it right with her,' Jake said vaguely, knowing already that it was fine with Mrs Smallwood. They had planned it together.

'How are we going to get her to dress up in her finery?' Mabel had asked and it had been Jake's idea that he should make out he would help with the tea whilst Betsy had a little time off on her special day.

Now, as she cut the cake with Mabel's help, Betsy was thinking: *I'll never have another party better than this. Not as long as I live, I won't.* She glanced up and caught Jake watching her. The fact that he was there, that they were living and working together, made her life perfect.

Modest, unassuming little Betsy dared not hope for any greater happiness.

After tea they played party games in the parlour. Blindfolding Betsy, Jake spun her round and she moved carefully around the room, arms outstretched, trying to find Jake and have an excuse to put her arms around him.

They almost didn't hear the knock at the back door for their noisy laughter.

'I'll go,' Mr Smallwood said, heaving his bulky frame out of the easy chair.

Philip grimaced. 'It'll be for me, I expect.' So it was no surprise that George's glance went directly to the doctor when he came back into the room.

'It's old Albert from the workhouse.' He glanced at his wife before saying. 'He ses Sarah Kirkland's very ill.'

'Did you know about this?' Philip asked the matron at once.

Letitia shook her head. 'No. I had no idea. Isaac's never said . . .' She glanced around, her eyes fearful that they were somehow blaming her for Sarah's illness. Then she added more briskly, 'I'll come with you, Doctor, if I may.'

'Of course. Come along, my pony and trap are in the yard.' He glanced at the others, all turned to stone by the news. 'Does anyone else want a ride back to the workhouse? You'll have to be quick.'

The two young girls scurried to get their shawls and Letitia bustled after them to find her own as Philip turned to his wife. 'My dear—' he began but Louisa interrupted, laying her hand on his arm. 'I can see myself home. You must go at once with Albert.'

Jake moved stiffly as if coming back to life after the shock. 'I'll – I'll see Miss – Mrs Collins home, Doctor.'

'No, really—' Louisa began, but Jake interrupted. 'It's all right. I'll have to go into the town anyway. I'll have to tell Meg.'

No one spoke and the happiness fell away from Betsy's face.

Thirty-Seven

'I don't believe you. It's all a tale to get me to come and see her.'

Jake eyed Meg with disgust. 'Do you really think I'd joke – play a game – with your mother's life? She's ill, I tell you. Old Albert came to the farm to fetch the doctor.'

'What was the doctor doing there?'

Jake sighed. 'If you must know, we were all there. At a party. Betsy's fourteen today.'

'Oh, very nice,' Meg said sarcastically, her eyes flashing. 'Very cosy.'

Jake's mouth hardened but he couldn't hide the hurt in his dark brown eyes. 'Well,' he said sharply. 'Are you coming?'

'I can't. Percy's going to Nottingham tomorrow to order stock. I've things to do.'

'I'll wait for you.'

'No need. I'm quite capable of walking up to the workhouse by myself.'

'But I want to make sure you go.' Jake was belligerent.

'Don't you trust me?' Her tone was skittish, but Jake's was blunt. 'No, I don't.'

Her face darkened. 'Well, you're right. I'm not going. I've Percy's meal to prepare and his suitcase to pack. He's staying overnight.'

Jake stepped forward and gripped her arm roughly. 'You're just making excuses. Percy Rodwell's not the sort of man to make a fuss when he knows your mam's ill. You can't fool me, Meg. You don't want to go. That's the truth of it, isn't it?'

She thrust her face close to his, spitting the words out. 'Yes, yes, yes. That's the truth. I don't want to go. I don't *want* to see her and I'm not *going* to see her.'

'And what,' he asked her quietly, 'happens if she dies? How will you feel then?'

There was silence between them as, close together, they glared into each other's eyes. Then she shook off his grip and turned away. 'Then I'll have to deal with it, won't I?'

There was nothing more he could do, nothing more he could say to persuade her. Jake turned away from her, sick at heart. He did not go home to the farm but trudged towards the looming shape of the workhouse, the place he had once called 'home'. He marvelled at how different his life was now and wondered how he had stuck it in that place for so long. But then, he reminded himself, he had known no different. He still might not have done, if it hadn't been for Meg.

He groaned and tried to close his mind to her. He didn't want to think of Meg now.

Albert was back in his lodge and he opened the gate to Jake. 'I've come to see how Mrs Kirkland is.'

The old man shook his head. 'She's badly. They've moved her across to the infirmary. Matron's with her, but they reckon—' He wiped his mouth with the back of his hand, glanced at Jake and then looked down at the ground. 'See, lad, I didn't like to say back there – at the farm – but it seems she tried to take her own life.

Slashed her wrists, they say. There's blood everywhere – up in his room.'

'Oh no,' Jake breathed and stood just inside the gate, uncertain what to do next. He glanced up at the windows of the master's rooms. 'Is *he* here?'

'Nah. Been away all day.' He gestured with his head. 'She knew when to pick her time to do it. Thought with him out all day and the matron off to the party, then she wouldn't be disturbed. It's lucky one of the women took her up a cup of tea and found her.'

'Is she – is she going to be all right?'

Old Albert shook his head sadly. 'It's touch and go, I reckon.'

Jake glanced beyond the old man, across the yard towards the door leading to the stairs up to the infirmary. As if reading his mind, Albert said, 'I wouldn't go up there, lad. The doc's still with her and the matron. Leave 'em to it, lad. Leave 'em to it. They'll do their best . . .'

It seemed that the combined efforts of the doctor and the matron were still not enough. Before Isaac had returned, red-faced from merrymaking and looking forward to a night of passion with his woman, Sarah had slipped away, sinking into a peaceful oblivion, released at last from all the heartache and sorrow her short life had brought her. Jake, sitting with Albert, heard the news from Ursula Waters.

She stood in the doorway. 'Well, he's got rid of his latest paramour, then.' Her tone was almost gleeful. Jake felt sickened. 'She thought he was going to cast her off. That's why she did it. There's a younger woman just come in here. He's been eyeing her up. I can tell.

Kirkland must have thought she was going to be cast aside, so she saved him the trouble. She couldn't bear it. Sooner slash her wrists than live without him.' She nodded knowingly, her eyes bright, a satisfied smile on her thin lips. 'That's how it would be. Oh, I know that's how it would be.'

Jake stared at her. 'Do you mean – she's gone? She – she's died?'

Ursula nodded.

Behind him, Albert sighed deeply and murmured, 'What a waste! A nice little woman. What a shame!'

Suddenly Jake launched himself at Ursula, knocking her backwards against the wall. 'You bitch. You're glad, aren't you? Glad she's out the way. You reckon you've still got a chance with him. You dried-up old hag! As if—'

With surprising strength, Albert grasped Jake around the waist and pulled him away. Ursula was gasping in fear, her eyes wide and frightened.

'Nay, lad, that's not the way,' Albert said, holding him firmly. 'It won't bring her back, more's the pity. And you –' His eyes were hard as he glared at the woman holding her hand to her flat chest – 'you can get out of my lodge.'

'You . . . you . . .' she gasped, 'have no right to speak to me like that. You're only the porter.'

'Oh, aye? And what great authority have you in the place, eh? Oh, get out, woman, else I might be tempted to let this lad have a go at yer.'

Ursula scuttled out, but before he relaxed his hold Albert asked softly, 'All right now, lad?'

Jake gave a muffled sob and nodded. With his arm still about him, Albert gently guided Jake to a chair and pushed him into it. 'Now then, what we need is a strong cup of tea with a drop of summat in it.' He tapped the side of his nose. 'But don't you go letting on to *him* that I've got a bottle of the hard stuff here, will yer. Else I'll end up in the punishment room.'

Jake said nothing, but dropped his head into his hands and groaned. 'Fancy her doing that. Poor, poor woman. She must have been heartbroken. Just wait till I see Meg. Wait till I get me hands on Meg.'

Jake's loud banging on the door of Percy Rodwell's cottage was enough to waken the street.

'Your mother's dead.' When Meg opened the door, the words came out far more bluntly than he had intended. 'She took her own life.'

Meg gasped and stared at him, the colour draining from her face. She stood rigidly as if turned to stone. She held her breath, waiting for the news to hit her. And then it came. Realization flooded through her like a tidal wave. 'Oh – oh – oh!' she gasped like a person drowning. She wrapped her arms around herself, bending over, doubled up as if in terrible pain.

Jake watched, his heart hardened against her. He could not bring himself to go to her and put his arms around her, could not comfort her, could not even touch her. At her next words, his disgust deepened.

'How could she? Oh, how could she do that?' Meg gasped. 'The shame!'

It was, of course, a criminal act to commit suicide and even though the criminal was beyond reach, society still exacted a cruel penalty. Sarah would be buried in unconsecrated ground with no stone to mark her grave.

'The shame is that her own daughter judged her and found her guilty and then deserted her. Even now you're not thinking of her, of how she must have felt, are you, Meg? Just yourself. It's always *you*, isn't it?'

Slowly, like an old woman, she pulled herself up to face him. 'Why? Why did she do it?'

He lifted his shoulders, a jerky, angry movement. 'Waters reckoned the master had his eye on a younger piece. If I'd thought for one moment that it wasn't the sort of thing yer mam'd do, then I might even think—'

'But she wouldn't do that. My mam wouldn't kill herself,' Meg blurted out.

Jake stared at her. 'Are you sure? I mean, she must have been so unhappy.'

'Was she? The last time I saw her – with *him* –' still, Meg was bitter – 'she looked much better. The only thing that was upsetting her was . . . was . . .' She dropped her gaze.

'Yes, go on, say it. Face it, Meg. The only thing upsetting her was – you!'

They glared at each other, breathing heavily, their eyes hostile.

'To think I once thought I loved you,' Jake whispered. 'And now you sicken me. You really do. And this caps it all. Even now you haven't got a kind word to say for her. Your own mother.'

'What about me? Did she think about me when she took up with him? She was just the latest in a long line of his – his – *whores*. You want to think yourself lucky, Jake Bosley. You want to be thankful you haven't got a mother to do that to you.'

It was the cruellest thing she could have said to him and it broke his heart. The instant the words were out of her mouth, Meg regretted them. But it was too late.

Thirty-Eight

'Dr Collins – can you spare me a moment?'

Seated in his pony and trap, Philip looked around to see who had called his name. 'Jake! How are you?' he said, stepping down and holding out his hand towards the young man hurrying towards him.

As they shook hands, Jake said, 'I'm fine.' His look belied his words, for there was a worried frown creasing his face and his eyes were dark with anxiety. 'But I need to talk to you. When could you spare me a few moments?'

Philip took the watch out of his waistcoat pocket and glanced at it. 'Not now, I'm afraid. I'm due up at the workhouse for a medical inspection.'

Jake's lips pressed together grimly. The mention of the workhouse only increased his worries. 'Later on today, then,' he persisted. 'I can meet you anywhere you say. Only not there. Not at the workhouse.'

Philip smiled, thinking that the young man's reluctance stemmed from his years within its walls. He wouldn't blame Jake for a moment if he never wanted to set foot in the place again. 'Is it a medical matter? Can you come to the surgery?'

'No, it's not. Not really.'

'Then come to the house after evening surgery. Say, eight o'clock. All right?'

'Fine. We'll have finished the evening milking by then, an' all. Thanks, Doctor.'

Louisa opened the door to Jake's knock.

'How nice to see you, Jake. Are you well? Are you happy at the farm? And how's little Betsy doing? Oh, dear me, what a lot of questions I'm throwing at you before you've hardly got through the door!' She laughed. 'Come in. I'm just about to serve coffee in the drawing room. Go on through. Philip's in there and I'll join you in a minute.'

The doctor and his wife now lived in a double-fronted detached house in an elegant area of South Monkford. Philip had one of the bay-windowed front rooms as his surgery, with the room behind it as his dispensary. Patients waited in the vast hall for their turn to see him. On the opposite side of the house was the Collinses' private sitting room and behind that the dining room, with a kitchen to the rear of the house.

Louisa now opened the door on the right-hand side of the hallway and ushered Jake into the sitting room. From a deep chair beside the fire, Philip rose and gestured towards a sofa. 'Come in, Jake, come in. Sit down, do. It's good to see you – and looking so well. The outdoor life certainly agrees with you.'

Jake smiled. For a moment some of the worry lining his face was chased away. He'd always liked the doctor and Louisa, too, and had it not been for the sombre reason for his visit, he would have been delighted to spend an evening in their company. But Jake was hardly aware of his surroundings: the oil paintings on the wall, the cabinet with its delicate china, the bulky sideboard, the heavy ruby velvet curtains . . . He was too anxious about the reason for his visit to notice any of it.

They had only just exchanged polite pleasantries by the time Louisa came back into the room, bearing a tray with coffee and a selection of fancy cakes and biscuits. Setting it down on a low table in front of the crackling log fire, she asked, 'How do you like your coffee, Jake?'

His rueful smile flickered briefly. 'I've never had any, Miss – Mrs Collins. They're tea drinkers at the farm and before . . .' He needed to say no more. Coffee was never served in the workhouse, at least not to the inmates.

'I'm sorry,' Louisa said at once. 'I didn't think. I'll put milk in for you, but try it without sugar first. I can always put some in if you find it bitter.'

When they were all settled, Philip leant back in his chair and said, 'Now, what is it you wanted to see me about?'

Jake glanced briefly at Louisa and then looked away again. Quick to understand, Louisa said, 'If you want to talk to Philip privately, then I'll go.'

'As long as it's not a medical matter, Jake, I have no secrets from my wife,' Philip said, glancing fondly across the hearth at her. 'You can speak freely.'

'It's – it's about Mrs Kirkland. Meg's mother.'

Again the doctor and his wife exchanged a glance – a concerned look now – before Philip prompted gently, 'Yes? What's troubling you? If it's about where she has to be buried, then I'm afraid there's nothing anyone can do. As a suicide, she had to be—'

'That's just it,' Jake burst out, relieved at last to be able to share his darkest fears. 'That's it exactly. *I don't think she committed suicide.*'

Philip sat up straight in his chair so suddenly that his

coffee slopped into the saucer. 'What? What did you say?'

Louisa gave a startled gasp and her eyes widened. She said nothing, but her horrified glance went from one to the other.

'I just don't think she's the type to have committed suicide. That's all.'

'Why not? What makes you think that?'

Jake took a deep breath. He was gratified that the doctor was taking him seriously and not dismissing his thoughts out of hand as wild imaginings. 'She wasn't the sort. Oh, I know she'd had an awful lot of tragedy in her life. Enough to make anyone give up hope, but – but – look, maybe I'm being stupid. Will you just tell me, where was she found? *How* was she found?'

Philip relaxed back into his chair. With a deep sigh, almost as if he shared some of the responsibility himself, he said, 'She was in bed. In the master's room, of course. He was late coming back home. She'd cut her wrists.' His eyes were dark with the memory of it. 'They called me, but there was nothing I could do. There was blood everywhere. I called the police. I had to, Jake. I couldn't cover up something like that even if I'd wanted to. It'd've jeopardized my career.' He paused and then muttered. 'But I did want to, if truth be known. Poor woman.'

Jake licked his lips. He didn't want his next words to sound as if he was accusing the doctor of not doing his job properly. 'And were you quite, quite sure that she had – had done it herself?'

Philip stared at him. 'Well . . .' he began and then stopped. He was staring at Jake and yet he was not seeing the young man in front of him. He was visualizing again the distressing scene in the bedroom as he'd found her. 'She'd cut her wrists.'

'But could someone else have done it? Done it to her?'

'Not without her fighting them off. And there was no indication of a struggle.'

'Could someone have done it to her while she was asleep?'

'No, no, she'd have woken up.' Philip shook his head and then, suddenly, he was very still as he added slowly, 'Unless she'd taken a sleeping draught.'

Jake leant forward now. 'Did she take sleeping draughts? Did you prescribe them for her?'

'Not since she lost the baby. No – no, I tell a lie. The last time I gave her some was when her son died. Little Bobbie.'

'Might she have had some left?'

'I don't think so. Matron has charge of all the drugs on the premises. She keeps them locked in a cupboard in the infirmary. She is very strict about that.'

'Who had keys to that cupboard?'

'The matron, the master, of course, and myself. As far as I know, no one else.' He looked keenly at Jake. 'Surely you're not suggesting one of them did it, are you?'

Jake stared at the doctor, but did not reply.

'My God!' Philip was shocked. 'You are!' He paused briefly and then asked bluntly. 'Who?'

'The master.'

'The master?' Philip and Louisa both spoke at once, then the doctor shook his head firmly, 'Oh no, Jake. I think you're wrong.'

'I just can't think Mrs Kirkland would do it,' Jake went on. 'Even Meg . . .' He faltered over her name and then his tone hardened as he added, 'Even Meg, who hasn't a good word to say for her poor mother, doesn't think so. Waters said Mrs Kirkland had done it because she was afraid the master was going to cast her aside. Like he did all his women eventually,' Jake went on bitterly. 'But I just can't believe it. Not Mrs Kirkland.'

The doctor sat forward in his chair and placed his cup on the table. Resting his elbows on his knees, he linked his fingers together and leant towards Jake. 'Let's just suppose for a moment that you're right. That there was foul play involving – as they say – a person or persons unknown. How do you think it could have been done?'

'I've been going over it in my mind and apart from believing that she wouldn't kill herself, I just thought it was an odd place for her to do it. I mean, if I wanted to kill myself by cutting my wrists, I'd've done it in the bath. I'd have gone to the bath room and done it there.'

'But you'd have risked being found.' Philip was playing devil's advocate.

'She risked being found in the master's bedroom. She didn't know what time he'd be coming home.'

'Maybe she did it hoping he'd find her in time,' Philip suggested. 'Maybe it was a cry for help.' He paused, and guilt swept through him that he had not noticed whether the poor woman was so depressed that she had been driven to suicide. 'Perhaps he was later than she thought in getting home and he was *too* late.'

They were bandying ideas between them, testing out Jake's terrible theory. Philip looked across at Louisa. 'Come on, love, help us out here. What would you – God forbid that you ever should – have done? *How* would you have done it?'

Louisa thought for a moment. 'Of course, you can't

tell how terrible she must have been feeling,' she said slowly, still not quite able to discount it as a suicide and unwittingly adding to her husband's sense of guilt. 'She'd lost her husband, her baby, Bobbie.' As she remembered the little boy, Louisa's eyes filled with tears. 'And then, when she opted to take what security she could as – as the master's –' she ran her tongue around her lips – 'the master's friend, her own daughter condemns her and deserts her.'

Philip sighed. 'Yes, when you put it like that, the poor soul had reason enough, didn't she?'

'And yet,' Louisa went on slowly, 'I have to agree that over the last weeks I was working there, she did seem happier. Oh, there was a sadness deep in her eyes, a sadness, I suspect, that would never have gone, but she looked better – she'd put on a little weight.' She glanced at Jake and explained, 'She'd gone so terribly thin after little Bobbie died, I feared for her then. But after the master took her in, well, she seemed better. If only Meg . . .' She stopped and glanced up at the two men. 'I'm sorry – I shouldn't be blaming poor Meg. She must be feeling dreadful.'

'Huh! Only for herself. She says her mother has humiliated and shamed her. Again!'

'That's just bravado. She's covering up her true feelings, I'm sure,' Louisa said gently. 'She must be feeling torn apart.'

Jake cast a disbelieving look at her. 'You're being too kind. Maybe you don't know Meg now like I do. She's changed. Become ruthless. She's just out for herself. Out for what she can get. Look how she duped poor old Percy Rodwell into marrying her.'

'Oh now, Jake, I think you are being unfair,' the

doctor put in. 'Percy is devoted to her. You only have to see him with her to know that.'

'I don't deny that, but is *she* as devoted to *him*?'

Philip stared at him.

Jake nodded and smiled grimly. 'No, you can't say she is, can you?'

Now there was silence between the three of them until Philip said slowly, 'So you really think there might be cause to doubt the apparent suicide?'

'Well, it's been bothering me. I just needed someone to talk it over with and I thought you'd be the best person. You'd seen her and you'd know if something hadn't seemed quite right.'

Philip frowned. 'It's strange you should say that because there was something at the very back of my mind niggling me and yet I couldn't quite put my finger on it. Look, do something for me, will you, both of you?'

Jake and Louisa looked at him, eager to help in any way they could. Philip grimaced. 'It's a bit of a gruesome thing to ask you, but can you make the action of cutting your wrists? I want to see how you would do it.'

They stared at him, then at each other and shrugged. But they each picked up one of the small cake knives, which Louisa had brought in on the tray.

'You first,' Jake nodded towards Louisa.

She held her hands in front of her, the knife in her right hand. Then she pretended to cut into her left wrist with a downward stroke so that, in reality, a cut would have appeared diagonally from the base of her thumb to just below her wrist bone. She switched the knife to her left hand and repeated the stroke, against with a diagonal, downwards gash.

'Mm, good,' Philip nodded. 'Now you, Jake. You're left-handed so it will be interesting to see if there's any difference.'

There wasn't. Jake made the stroke in the same direction and in the same place on each wrist as Louisa had done. When he had done, he looked up expectantly. Again, Philip nodded and picked up a knife himself. The result was still the same; a diagonal, downward stroke on the inside of his wrists. Jake and Louisa were watching him. Carefully, he laid the knife back on the table and linked his fingers once more before looking up at them to say quietly, 'That's what was niggling at me. The cuts on her wrists didn't seem right. They were diagonal, all right, but the other way. And the natural way to do it is the way we've demonstrated.'

'So – so you think someone else could have done it?' Jake said. 'If she'd taken a sleeping draught—'

'Or worse still, if she'd been *given* a sleeping draught.'

Louisa covered her mouth with trembling fingers. 'Oh, Philip, how dreadful. You really think someone might have killed her?'

Solemnly, Philip said, 'I don't like even to think it, but Jake has raised doubts in my mind too now and I'll have to take it further. I shall have to share my suspicions with the police. Now, Jake, I shall need your help. You, more than anyone, know the internal workings of that place. Who does what and who has access to different places? For instance, could anyone else at all have got hold of a sleeping draught from the infirmary?'

'I suppose anyone could if they'd had the chance to get hold of a set of keys. They could have got into the cupboard when matron wasn't looking, though Miss Pendleton,' he added swiftly, anxious that the woman who had always been so kind to him should not be blamed in any way, 'was always very particular about it being kept locked. And she always kept the keys with her. Had 'em on a chain around her waist.' Despite the seriousness of their conversation, Jake smiled. 'We always used to reckon she slept with it still on her.'

'What about the master? Was he so particular – so careful?'

Everything led back to Isaac Pendleton.

Jake shook his head. 'I – I don't know.' He was trying desperately to be impartial, to put aside the memory of the beatings he had suffered at the hands of the master.

Thirty-Nine

It was Percy who persuaded Meg that she should at least attend her mother's funeral.

'So you'd have me humiliated all over again, would you? You're as bad as Jake.' She pouted truculently.

He sighed. 'You won't be humiliated. It's not your fault she – she did what she did.'

'She committed suicide. Why don't you say it outright?'

Percy winced. 'Like I say, it's not your fault.'

'Jake thinks it is. He's blaming me because I didn't go to see her.'

Percy stared at her. 'But you did go. I persuaded you to go. You did go, Meg, didn't you?'

'Yes, yes,' she waved him aside impatiently. 'Of course I went, but Waters came and told me that my mother didn't want to see me.'

Percy blinked. 'Oh.' He was puzzled. He had never met Sarah, but he couldn't imagine any mother not wanting to see her own child.

But Meg's mind was no longer on her mother. She was filled with indignation against Jake. 'I don't know what he's trying to do to me. Stirring up trouble. Having the police come here to question me and then having to stand up in court and answer that man's questions. What do they think I've done? Murdered her?'

Ironically, it had been Mr Snape who had posed the questions to the witnesses.

'There had to be an inquest after a suicide,' Percy commented reasonably. 'And if Dr Collins wasn't happy, then the police had to look into it, didn't they?'

'But it was Jake who stirred it all up.'

'Well, they haven't found anything, have they? Nothing that proves any different. The police couldn't come up with any evidence of foul play. Nor could the doctor.'

'Of course they haven't. All that stuff about the cuts being the wrong way.' She made an angry gesture as if slashing her own wrists, first one way and then the other. 'As if that proves anything. You can do it either way.'

'I hope you'll never think of doing such a thing.' He was worried now. If the tendency was in Meg's blood . . .

'I wouldn't dream of shaming my family like that. Oh no, nothing will ever get me so down that I do away with myself.'

On the morning of the funeral Percy saw to it that Meg was dressed in black from head to toe. He himself wore a black suit and tie and insisted that the shop be closed all day as a mark of respect.

'She doesn't deserve any respect,' Meg glowered.

'Oh, Meg, show a little compassion for your poor mother.'

'And besides,' she went on as if he hadn't spoken, 'I thought folk round here didn't like women attending funerals.'

'I don't hold with that. I never have. We're going together.'

So Meg found herself obliged to go, but she was the only woman standing alongside Percy on the cold, windswept patch of ground just outside the churchyard boundary. The vicar intoned the words monotonously, his voice clearly indicating his own disapproval. He had no words of forgiveness or understanding for the dead woman or of comfort for her daughter. On the opposite side of the grave stood the only other three people to attend: Isaac Pendleton, Jake Bosley and Dr Collins.

Isaac's face was stony. He had taken it as a personal insult that Sarah had so hated her life with him that she preferred death. He glared accusingly across the grave at Meg, seeming to blame her as the plain wooden coffin – a pauper's – was lowered into the ground.

As the few mourners moved away, Isaac caught hold of Meg's arm and roughly swung her round to face him. 'Had you anything to do with this? Was it your meddling that caused it?'

Meg glared back at him. 'I could ask you the same question. What did you do to her to make her life so unbearable that she didn't want to live it any longer? She didn't show any sign of doing anything like that before. No, not even when my father went off and she lost the baby.' Meg was aware that both the doctor and Jake were near enough to overhear the conversation, as well as Percy, who was standing protectively by her side.

'She was depressed because the only member of her family left to her – you,' Isaac went on, 'refused to come and see her.'

'I came,' Meg was almost shouting now. 'I came to see her, but Waters told me that she didn't want to see me and that you didn't want me to visit her either. Not ever. Waters was adamant.' Unbidden, tears sprang to her eyes and though she tried to dash them away, Jake had seen them. His heart twisted. Had he been misjudging his beloved Meg all along? Did she – under all that bravado – really care?

'I'd never have said such a thing,' Isaac answered indignantly. 'In fact, I sent Waters down into the town – to the shop – to ask you to come and visit your mother.'

Meg stared at him. 'You did? Well, she never came.'

The doctor and Jake glanced at each other and stepped away from the others a little.

'He's lying,' Jake muttered. 'I bet he never did any such thing. Waters idolizes him. She'd do anything he asked – whatever it was. I bet he never asked her.'

'I think,' Philip murmured, 'that the master has some questions to answer. Have the police seen him? D'you know?'

Jake shrugged. 'I've no idea.'

'Then I'll have another word with Sergeant Donaldson.'

It all came to nothing.

Several weeks later Sergeant Donaldson told Philip, 'We can't find firm evidence that anyone other than the deceased had anything to do with her death. Oh yes, I grant you there's room for suspicion, but what we need is proof.'

'And we can't give you that?'

The sergeant shook his head. 'Sadly, no. I don't like to think of that poor woman being accused of suicide if it wasn't and, even worse, I don't like to think of a murderer still being at large. But . . .' He spread his large hands helplessly.

'I understand,' Philip said heavily. 'Thank you for trying, at least.'

'Aye well, Doctor, keep me posted. If you see any funny business going on at that place, you let me know, and we'll take another look.'

'Tell me, was the master interviewed?'

The sergeant nodded. 'The only thing he said of interest was that Mrs Kirkland had seemed listless and depressed when he left that morning. He tried to cheer her up, he said, promising to bring her a present back from the city. He was in Nottingham that day on business, it seems.'

'What about some of the others at the workhouse? Did you speak to them?'

'Oh yes. The matron, of course, and a woman called – now what was her name – Waters. Yes, that was it. Even old Albert. We asked him if anything unusual had happened. You know, had there been any visitors – that sort of thing.' The sergeant cleared his throat. 'We couldn't disregard anyone. Not even her daughter, seeing as there was some sort of estrangement between them.'

'What did Albert say? Had he seen anything out of the ordinary?'

The sergeant shook his head.

'And Waters – what about her?'

'She said she'd taken up a cup of hot milk at about eight o'clock and that Mrs Kirkland had said she was going to take one of the sleeping draughts you'd left her.' He leant forward and lowered his voice. 'But do you know what that woman, Waters, said then?'

Philip shook his head. The sergeant straightened up and sniffed disapprovingly. 'Well, I never thought to hear such things from a woman's mouth. I mean, it's not the sort of thing a lady would mention.'

'But you were conducting an enquiry,' Philip reminded him mildly. 'Maybe she thought she had to tell you everything.'

'Oh aye, I don't deny that. But it's what she said she'd said to Kirkland that – well, speaking frankly, Doctor – disgusted even a tough old nut like me. I thought I'd heard it all, seen it all.' He shook his head wonderingly.

'What was it she said?' Philip prompted.

'She told me that she'd said to Kirkland – that's what she called her – "Kirkland". Not *Mrs* Kirkland or even Sarah.'

Philip nodded. 'They call everyone by their surname in there.'

'Humph!' Sergeant Donaldson grunted disapprovingly. 'Take away every last shred of dignity, do they?'

''Fraid so.'

'Anyway, she'd said to the poor woman, "You'll not get any sleep when he gets home. He'll be wanting your services." Have you ever heard the like, Doctor? Spoke to her as if she was a common woman of the streets, and bold as brass she was an' all when she was telling me. Now, I know Mrs Kirkland was living with the master and that's nowt to do with me, but if there's summat going on up there that I ought to know about—'

'I'm sure there isn't, Sergeant. Mr Pendleton isn't keeping an immoral house, if that's what you're implying.'

'Well, it makes you think, doesn't it, when someone makes a remark like that. And she seems such a prim and proper woman, that Miss Waters, an' all.'

Philip smiled. 'Well, once upon a time she was Mr Pendleton's – er – lady friend, if you get my meaning.'

The sergeant nodded, understanding at once. He'd been a policeman a long time. Nothing surprised him and it took a great deal to shock him. 'A case of the green-eyed monster, is it?' For a moment there was silence between them before the sergeant sighed and said sadly, 'But I don't know what else we can do.'

Heavily, Philip agreed, 'No, I don't think there is anything.'

In the early evening of the same day, Philip made a house call next door but one to the Rodwells' home. It was his last call and though he knew Louisa would be waiting dinner for him, he felt obliged to call to see Meg. She opened the door and when she saw who was standing there, she smiled her wonderful smile, which made even the happily married doctor's heart miss a beat.

She drew him inside.

'I just called to break the news to you . . .' he began, but she was pulling him into the front room, where a welcoming fire burned, and pushing him gently onto the sofa.

'Let me get you a drink. You must be so tired after a long day. What would you like? Beer? Whisky?'

Philip held up his hands in protest. 'Oh no, no, I shouldn't.'

'But haven't you finished for the day? You don't hold an evening surgery on a Thursday, now do you?'

'Well, no, but I still shouldn't. If I get a call out—'

She laughed gaily. 'I'm not suggesting that you get

rolling drunk. Only a little nip to keep out the cold on the way home.'

'I really shouldn't. Louisa will be waiting dinner for me.'

'Half an hour won't hurt. Come on, take your coat off, else you won't feel the benefit when you go out.'

Suddenly feeling weary after a long day, Philip gave in and allowed her to take his coat and fetch him a tot of whisky. She sat down opposite him.

He leant back, relaxing into the comfortable chair, the weariness of the day washing over him in waves.

'I only came to tell you that the police are taking the matter of your mother's death no further. I am sorry.'

Meg shrugged. 'I didn't really expect they would. It was only Jake trying to salvage her reputation.' She still wasn't sure whether she was touched by Jake's concern or irritated by it.

There was a long silence before Philip murmured, 'I shouldn't keep you. You must be preparing dinner for Percy coming home.'

'Percy won't be coming home tonight. He's gone to London on business. We're going to begin stocking hats and he's gone to one of the well-known fashion houses. Of course, Miss Pinkerton is going to make them for us. She's such a clever little woman – even if she is a bit of a fussy old spinster.'

Meg was chattering as if she hadn't seen anyone to talk to for weeks and Philip suddenly realized how lonely she must be for company nearer her own age. If only, he thought, she would make it up with Louisa. He knew his wife would dearly love to be Meg's friend again.

He felt exhausted and was struggling to keep his eyes

open in front of the warm fire. The tot of whisky she had pressed upon him was already beginning to take effect. 'Shouldn't you have gone to London if it was to see ladies' hats?' he asked drowsily.

'Oh no,' Meg said softly, as she watched the doctor's eyes close completely and his head droop. 'Percy is much better at choosing ladies' apparel than ever I would be. He has such an eye for quality.'

She rescued the glass before it slipped out of his hand to the floor and then, smiling down at him, she rose quietly and fetched a blanket from her own bed to cover him.

She closed the door behind her gently, leaving him to sleep. As she went back to the kitchen, Meg was smiling to herself.

Now let's see how you like it, Louisa Collins, when your precious husband gets accused of something he didn't do.

Forty

When Philip woke, it took him a few moments to remember where he was. The fire in the grate had burned away and the room was cold. He glanced at the window and saw that it was dark outside. He pushed off the blanket and struggled to his feet, still half asleep. Then he pulled the watch from his pocket and blinked at it in the soft light from the gas lamp which Meg had left burning.

It was five minutes past midnight.

'Oh my goodness,' he said aloud. 'Louisa will be worried sick.' He stumbled towards the door and was about to pull it open and shout Meg's name, when he realized she would probably have gone to bed and be asleep by now. He went back and turned out the light and then tiptoed across the room, opening the door as quietly as he could. In the hall, everything was in darkness. He bit his lip, trying to remember where the coatstand was. He didn't want to blunder about in the darkness, knocking into things. His eyes slowly became accustomed to the gloom and in the light from the street lamp shining through the coloured leaded window he began to discern shapes. He reached out and felt for his coat on the pegs opposite and then found his hat on a shelf. He struggled into his coat and rammed his hat onto his head. Then he felt about for his doctor's bag. He had brought it into the house with him. He never left it unattended in the trap. His fingers closed around its handle and he picked it up.

Then another dilemma faced him. The front door was locked and bolted. If he were to go out that way, he would be leaving the sleeping girl upstairs with an unlocked front door. He felt near the doorknob and found the heavy key in the lock. Then he made sure that there was a letterbox cut into the door. Finding it, he breathed a sigh of relief, unlocked and unbolted the door and let himself out. He relocked the door and posted the key back through the letterbox. It dropped with a clatter onto the tiled floor.

Upstairs, Meg lay awake smiling into the darkness and listening to the sound of the pony's hooves ringing through the still night air as Dr Collins drove his trap away from her house.

Louisa was still up, dozing in the armchair by the fire's dying embers.

'Oh, poor you,' she murmured soothingly as she hurried into the hallway to help her husband out of his coat. 'I'll get you some hot milk with a little something in it. It'll help you sleep.'

Philip shuddered. How ironic her words were. If only she knew . . . And then he shivered again, praying that she would never know.

Seeing him shaking, Louisa asked, 'Are you cold, my dear? I can light the fire in the bedroom.' She did not ask what had kept him out so late, but took it for granted that he had been with a very sick patient or attending a difficult birth. Her implicit trust made Philip feel even more guilty.

'No, no.' He reached for her hand and held it to his cheek. 'We'll go straight up.'

She patted his hand. 'You get into bed and I'll bring your hot milk up. Do you want anything to eat?'

Philip shook his head and stumbled tiredly towards the stairs. He should tell her the truth, tell her exactly what happened. There was nothing to be ashamed of, nothing had happened between him and Meg.

Then why, he castigated himself, could he not bring himself to tell his wife about it?

The following morning, as soon as he had finished his surgery, Philip went out on his rounds. His first call was to the tailor's shop. As he entered the shop and closed the door behind him, he was startled when Percy appeared from the back room, the ever-present tape measure around his neck, his steel-rimmed spectacles perched on the end of his nose.

The tailor smiled in welcome and immediately Philip felt even more guilty than before. 'Dr Collins – how nice to see you in pleasanter circumstances.' The last time the two men had met had been at Sarah's burial.

'Yes, yes,' Philip said swiftly. 'I – er – need some new gloves. Very cold driving the trap, you know.' The truth was that he hadn't been able to find them that morning and feared he had left them at Meg's house.

'Of course,' Percy was saying. 'And you have to be out in all weathers, even at night.'

Philip jumped. Did he know? Had Meg told him? Had Percy found his gloves in his house? But the tailor's next remark was innocent enough. 'Meg will be sorry to have missed you. She's taken the morning off, now I'm back. She had to hold the fort alone yesterday and first thing this morning, but I caught an early train home and arrived about an hour ago.'

'You must be tired.'

'No, no. The hotel I stayed at last night was very comfortable. I slept surprisingly well.'

So did I, thought Philip ruefully. *Too well and in the wrong place.*

The gloves, which he didn't really need, purchased, Philip made his escape. Not knowing whether he was being extremely foolish or not, he went straight to see Meg at her home.

She opened the door wide, silently inviting him to step inside.

'No, no, I mustn't come in,' Philip began, but Meg smiled at him archly.

'Don't you trust me, Doctor?'

He did not reply, but inside his own mind he was saying: *It's myself I don't trust*. Instead he smiled thinly and asked, 'Did I leave my gloves here?'

'Yes.' She pulled the door wider. 'Come in while I fetch them.' She leant forward, glanced up and down the street and then whispered, 'I hid them, just in case Percy saw them and asked awkward questions.'

As he stepped into the hall – he could do no other if he wanted to retrieve his gloves – he said, 'You – you didn't tell Percy, then?'

Meg closed the door and leant against it, watching him. She widened her eyes. 'Of course not. Now,' she said briskly, 'have you time for a drink?'

'Oh no! No more of your drinks, Meg.' He held out his hand as if to ward her off. 'Besides, I must be on my way. I've patients to see.'

She moved closer to him and, though she wore no perfume, the smell of her enticed him. It was a natural, womanly smell. Earthy and inviting. She put her hands, palms flat, against his chest. 'What is more natural than that you should feel able to rest at a friend's house when you were so desperately tired? You told Louisa where you were, of course?'

'Well – no – I – er – no, I didn't.'

'Then it will be our little secret.' She made it sound as if there was much more to hide than what had actually happened. 'We must think of Louisa and Percy.'

Without another word being spoken, she fetched his gloves and handed them to him. He left the house, but as she closed the door after him, Meg was still smiling.

I'll get my revenge on you yet, Louisa Collins.

Another Christmas came and went and life in South Monkford settled into a routine. Percy and Meg worked side by side in their shop. To the surprise of them both – though neither of them ever voiced their private thoughts to the other – the number of their customers grew steadily as they increased the range of their stock. Meg had secretly worried that the scandal of the breach-of-promise court case would seriously affect their business. And, though he said nothing to her, Percy had been concerned too. But their fears had been unfounded. Even Theobald Finch continued to frequent the shop, though they never saw Clara. In fact, very few people of the town ever saw Miss Finch. She ventured out rarely and when she did she travelled to Nottingham, where, incognito, she could shop away from the nudges and whispers. That the townsfolk of South Monkford had better things to think of now never occurred to the embittered woman.

Meg threw herself into work at the shop and at

home. She learnt as much as she could about the business and persuaded Percy to teach her tailoring. At first he was reluctant. 'Oh no, it's no job for a woman. How would you do the measuring? No gentleman would like that.' But Meg was insistent and at last he allowed her to learn how to use the sewing machine. She filled her days deliberately. That way she had little time to think. She refused to dwell on the past, nor would she plan the future. She just lived from day to day, being a good wife to Percy and helping him to build the business.

That way, little time was left for her to think of Jake.

At the farm Jake couldn't believe his luck. Every morning he woke to marvel at his good fortune. He was well fed and doing a job he loved. And best of all, little Betsy – who had always been one of his favourites at the workhouse – blossomed before his eyes. And if his nights were disturbed by haunting dreams of a fiery red-haired girl with a wonderful smile, no one would have guessed it from the wide grin that was permanently on his face. Only if they had thought to look a little closer would they have seen the sadness deep in his brown eyes that would never quite go away.

At the workhouse, for the first time in many years, Isaac slept alone in the vast double bed. Much to Ursula's glee, no one replaced Sarah Kirkland in the master's affections and the lonely, obsessed spinster began to cherish hopes once more.

I knew he always loved me best, she told herself. *He needs me. I was right to stay here – to devote my life to caring for him. He'll turn to me again. I know he will. I just have to be patient and wait . . .*

So it was Ursula who took the master his meals, who ran errands for him, who whispered tales about the inmates into his ear. Things, she said, that he ought to know, had a right to know. Yet to her chagrin he hardly seemed aware of her existence. And certainly he never invited her into his bed again.

'I know what you're up to.' The matron was not so blind as her brother.

'Up to?' Ursula assumed an innocent expression. 'Whatever do you mean?'

'Pandering to him. Running after him. Well, it won't work. He was fond of Kirkland. Really fond. And he's missing her.'

'He'll forget her.' Ursula smirked. 'And when he does, I'll be there.'

Letitia cast her a disbelieving glance, but said no more. She was not a cruel woman though at that moment she was tempted to say: *He'll never take up with you again in a month of Sundays*. But Letitia held her tongue. If anything, she felt sorry for Waters. The woman had wasted her life, choosing to stay in the workhouse instead of making a life for herself outside its walls as Isaac would have helped her to do. But no, she'd rejected his offer, preferring to stay near him, forever hoping that one day he would . . .

Well, he wouldn't, Letitia knew, but she would say nothing against her brother. They were bound together by shared secrets from the past. And there were things, too, that Ursula Waters knew, so it would not do to cross her. Letitia was obliged to be content with her lot – she had made her bed and she had to lie in it. Isaac had been good to her and she was grateful to him. She was lucky – she knew she was. And she had her little boys to love and cherish.

There was only one thing that saddened her these

days. She didn't see Jake as often as she would have liked and even less since Sarah's death. He hadn't been to the workhouse since then and she missed him. Oh, how the matron missed seeing her special boy.

Forty-One

When Britain declared war on Germany in August 1914 the news came as a shock to the people of South Monkford. Events outside the town rarely troubled the serenity of their lives, but now events in a far-off country, which should have had nothing to do with them, had turned their cosy world upside-down. In a fever of patriotism young men, and even not-so-young men, rushed to volunteer. Sons, husbands and fathers – all were swept up in the fervour to enlist.

At Middleditch Farm Betsy and Mrs Smallwood were in a permanent state of anxiety lest Jake should be caught up in the excitement.

'He won't go, will he?' Betsy said a dozen times a day.

'I hope not.' Mrs Smallwood was unusually patient with the young girl's fears and constant questions. Betsy was only voicing Mabel's worries.

At last it was George Smallwood who dared to speak out. 'You'll not do anything daft, lad, will yer? Like joining up?'

Jake's face was sober. 'I've decided . . .' he paused and George, Mabel and Betsy stared at him, 'not to volunteer, but of course if they bring in – what do they call it?' He looked at George, who said, 'Conscription.'

'Yes, that's it. If they bring in conscription, then of course I'll have to go.'

'Mebbe you'll not have to, lad,' George said. 'They'll need workers to stay on the land. There'll likely be food shortages if it goes on for very long.'

'But they say it won't,' Mabel put in. 'They say it'll be all over by Christmas.'

'Aye well, I wouldn't hold mi breath, love, if I was you,' was George's only reply.

Jake said no more, but silently made up his own mind. If conscription did come in, he would go then – even before they sent for him. He would answer his country's call.

'We'll never cope with all these orders for suits, to say nothing of the underwear they're buying,' Percy said worriedly. Nothing was too good for their menfolk when they went to war, and wives and mothers flooded into the tailor's shop demanding the very best for their loved ones. 'What on earth they want new suits for to go into the army, I don't know. Mind you, folks are very particular round here, but they'll not be given a chance to wear them. Once they're given their uniform, that'll be it. They'll not see their own clothes again until . . .' His voice faded away. Already news of the carnage at the Front had reached the town.

'Just be thankful they do, Percy,' Meg said. 'And we've nearly sold out of ladies' hats. Poor Miss Pinkerton is working through the night sometimes just to keep up with the demands.'

Percy sighed. 'I expect the ladies want to look their best when they wave their menfolk off. To give them a pretty memory to carry with them.'

'Is there any chance we could get a contract for making uniforms?' Meg was thinking of their own business, thriving in spite of – or rather because of – the war. 'I could help you.'

'Oh no.' Percy shook his head. 'That's very specialized and besides –' he shuddered, the thought abhorrent to him – 'I wouldn't want to.'

'Wouldn't want to?' Meg repeated, surprised. 'But there must be a lot of money to be made.'

'I wouldn't want to make money out of such a tragedy as this war is going to be,' Percy said righteously.

Then you're a fool, Meg wanted to say, but for once she held her tongue. She was revelling in the turn of events. Her recent life had been just a dull routine of housework and working in the shop. Even learning tailoring skills had palled. But now there was some real excitement. 'We'll have to take on more staff. Can't you advertise for a tailor? It's you who needs the help making the garments. I can cope with serving the customers. But you've been working every night for weeks.' She stepped closer to him and smoothed back a lock of his hair – hair that was thinning prematurely, she noticed.

Percy looked askance at her. 'Take on someone else? Oh no, I couldn't do that. Besides, this rush is only temporary.'

But the demand for new suits, new clothes of all description was a surprisingly long time in diminishing. After weeks of working late into the night every night, by November Percy was looking tired and even thinner.

'I'm calling the doctor,' Meg declared and refused to listen to Percy's weak protests. 'You must stay in bed all day tomorrow and I'll get Ph— Dr Collins to call to see you.'

It had been almost two years since the night he had

fallen asleep in her home. She had seen Philip rarely since, and then only in public, when she would smile at him coyly and be gratified by the look of embarrassed confusion that coloured his face. He was a nice man, she told herself, and she shouldn't make sport of him. Yet, it was so tempting. Her life was so dull and what harm could a little flirtation with Louisa's husband do? It would just serve her right, Meg thought, still unable to forgive.

And now, with Percy's exhaustion, there was an excuse – a genuine reason – to send for him, but she had to make sure he would come. She wrote a polite note and sent it by an errand boy to Philip's surgery asking him to visit. *I will not be at home*, she wrote, *as I must keep the shop open. The front door will be unlocked.*

Meg smiled to herself as she folded the note and handed it to the grubby urchin to deliver for her.

The following morning Percy insisted, 'You must go to the shop. You must be there to explain to Mrs Heane why her son's suit isn't ready. The poor woman was in tears when she ordered it. "It might be that last suit I ever buy for him," she said.' Percy sighed heavily. 'I suppose I can see now why they're wanting the best for their boys. It might be the last chance they get. Tell her I'll have it done tomorrow without fail.'

'I'll do no such thing,' Meg countered. 'I'm waiting here until the doctor comes and as for you working today or tomorrow, well, we'll see what he says.'

Meg was gratified by the startled look on Philip's face when she opened the door.

'I thought—' he began.

'I know,' she said quickly. 'I didn't mean to be here, but I didn't like to leave him. Once my back is turned, he'll be out of that bed and struggling to the shop. And he really isn't well. He's been working so hard.' Her tone softened as she noticed the dark circles beneath Philip's eyes. 'As you have too, I can see.'

He stepped into the house with a sigh. 'There's a lot of illness about,' he murmured, as he pressed himself back against the wall of the narrow hallway to allow her to lead the way up the stairs. He was overwhelmed by the surge of emotion that coursed through him at her nearness. And worse, as she lifted her skirts to climb the stairs in front of him, he caught a glimpse of her neat ankle and the curve of her calf. He closed his eyes and paused for a moment, catching hold of the banister rail to steady himself. Then he took a deep breath and followed her, keeping his gaze firmly on each tread of the staircase.

At first, Percy refused to obey the doctor's advice. 'I can't stay in bed. I have work to do. Meg can't cope alone in the shop and there are suits to finish and . . .' He groaned, closed his eyes and lay back against the pillows.

'Two days in bed, that's all I'm asking,' Philip said. 'If you feel better, then you can get up, but I would still advise you to stay at home for at least another two days after that.'

'It's impossible,' Percy moaned.

'If you work yourself into an early grave, the suits won't get made, will they?' Philip said bluntly. 'And you're not being fair to Meg,' he added, though he kept his gaze firmly on his patient, not daring to meet her eyes. 'She can no doubt manage the shop alone for a day or two, but if you get really ill, how would she cope then? Have you thought of that?'

Percy sighed. 'I hadn't looked at it like that.'

'Then I think you should.'

'All right.' Percy capitulated with a weary smile. 'I'll do as you say, Doctor.'

'Good. And I'll make you up a tonic.' Now he was obliged to glance at Meg. 'Perhaps you could collect it from the surgery later. I'd offer to drop it in, but I'm so very busy.'

'Of course,' Meg said evenly.

It was almost dark by the time Meg left the shop and made her way towards the doctor's house. She raised the heavy brass knocker and let it fall with a loud thud that echoed through the house. She waited several moments before she heard light footsteps beyond the door. When it opened, she saw Louisa holding out both her hands in welcome.

'Oh, Meg, I'm so glad to see you. Come in.'

'I've only called to pick up some medicine for Percy,' Meg said stiffly as she stepped into the hallway.

Louisa closed the door and stood facing her. 'Meg,' she began tentatively, 'can't we let bygones be bygones? Can't we be friends again? I am more sorry than I can ever put into words about what happened between us.'

Meg's mind was working rapidly, calculating. Suddenly, she smiled her brilliant smile and even Louisa gasped at the swift transformation from sulky pout to friendly warmth. She had forgotten just how beautiful the young girl was.

Meg took her hands and squeezed them. 'Nothing would give me greater pleasure. And I – I'm sorry now that I wasn't at your wedding. When Jake told me you wanted me to be your matron of honour, I thought it was him trying to bring us together again. I'm sorry I didn't believe him.'

'I was hurt at the time, but let's put it all behind us. Just one thing: Jake Bosley is the most honest boy I know. You can trust him with your life.'

Meg's mouth hardened and Louisa suddenly feared that she had just lost the tentative beginning they had made. Then Meg shrugged her shoulders and it was as if she was shrugging Jake off too. 'I never see him now.'

'Don't you?' Louisa was surprised. 'Then you won't know.'

Meg's eyes were sharp with an interest she could not hide. 'Know what?'

'About him and Betsy?'

Unable to speak, as a sudden inexplicable fear tightened her throat, Meg shook her head, her wide eyes fixed on Louisa's face.

'They've got engaged.'

After a moment, Meg found her voice, but it was a high-pitched squeak. 'Engaged? But – but Betsy's only a child.'

Louisa was smiling. Betsy had been one of her favourites at the workhouse and was a regular visitor to Louisa's home now. She shook her head. 'Not any more, she isn't. She was always small for her age and looked a lot younger than she really was. She's sixteen now.'

Meg's mind was in a whirl. Jake – her Jake, for he *was* her Jake – was going to marry Betsy. The depth of the emotion that swept through her startled her. She didn't care about him any more, she told herself repeatedly, but now she knew that was all a lie. Foolishly, she had imagined that, even though she had married Percy to gain security, somehow Jake would always be there for her. He would always be her friend. *That he would always love her and her alone.*

'But he – he doesn't love her.'

'Of course he loves her,' Louisa said and Meg was appalled to realize she had spoken her thoughts aloud. She put her hand to her forehead and swayed.

'Come and sit down.' Louisa's arm was about her, leading her into their private sitting room. 'There,' she said, when Meg fell onto the sofa, 'I'll get some tea. I'm sorry, Meg.' She stood looking down at the girl with a mixture of pity and concern. She hadn't realized how deep Meg's bitterness was. 'I didn't think it would be such a shock for you, that it would affect you so much. You're happy for them, aren't you?'

Meg could not bring herself to reply.

The day after Percy returned to work, Clara Finch entered the shop. Percy gaped at her for a few seconds before recovering his composure enough to say, 'Good morning, Clara.'

Her thin lips tightened. 'Good morning – Mr Rodwell,' she said stiffly. Meg watched in amazement as, her hands folded in front of her at waist level, Clara advanced towards the counter.

'I'm setting up a ladies' circle to knit balaclavas, scarves and gloves for the troops. We will be meeting each week at the Hall and I shall require a regular supply of appropriate wool.' She sniffed. 'Of course, I would normally have taken my custom elsewhere, but in these dreadful times one has to forget one's own petty grievances and think of the greater good.'

'Quite so – Miss Finch,' Percy murmured. 'I shall be

happy to be of service. I will also undertake to supply the wool at cost price. Call it my contribution to your worthy endeavours.'

Clara inclined her head. 'Most generous. I will make sure my ladies know of your kind offer.'

Meg wanted to laugh at the stilted exchange of conversation between the two people who had once been betrothed to each other. But instead she carried a selection of different coloured wools to Percy, gave a polite nod towards Clara and returned to her place at the other side of the shop. She watched as Clara picked out the colour of wool she wanted and Percy noted it, promising to keep a good supply in stock at all times.

As Clara was about to leave, Percy bade her 'Good day,' and added pleasantly, 'give my kind regards to your brother.'

Clara, on her way towards the door, turned back. Her mouth pursed and her eyes hard she said, 'Neither of us require your "kind regards", Mr Rodwell.'

'I'm sorry. Mr Finch was perfectly pleasant the last time I saw him. I thought—'

'When did you see him? You had no occasion to see him. He patronizes a tailor in Nottingham now.'

Percy blinked, realizing too late that Clara had no idea that her brother still came into his shop.

'I – er – encountered him.'

'Where?'

'I – er—' Percy was floundering and Clara was swift to guess the truth.

'He's been in here, hasn't he?' She paused and when Percy did not answer immediately, she shrilled, 'Hasn't he?'

'Well, just once or twice.'

Clara's eyes narrowed. 'Well, he will not be coming into this shop again, you can count on that.'

With that parting shot, she stormed towards the door and out of the shop. The bell clanged weakly.

Forty-Two

What happened between Clara and her brother, neither Meg nor Percy ever knew, but Theobald Finch did not come into the shop again. The first Christmas of the war passed with no sign of the hostilities coming to an end as people had hoped. Over the months that followed the number of customers coming into the tailor's shop seemed to dwindle.

Where he'd once worried about not being able to cope with the pressure of work, Percy now fretted about the lack of orders. 'We're losing business. I haven't made a suit in weeks.'

'Business isn't so good at this time of the year just after Christmas. You've said so yourself. It'll perk up in the spring. And besides, a lot of the men have gone to war,' Meg pointed out. 'We were lucky to get all those orders for suits when we did.'

Percy's glance was reproachful. He still felt guilty about all the trade that this terrible war had brought him.

As the second Christmas of the war approached, the whole town seemed sunk in depression. In January 1916 a fierce debate took place in the House of Commons over conscription, single men to be recruited first. At Middleditch Farm Jake dropped his bombshell over supper one evening. 'I'm going to enlist and I want Betsy and me to get married before I go. That way, if owt happens, she'll get my pension . . .'

Betsy began to cry and George and Mabel stared at the young man.

'Well, Jake Bosley, that's a fine way to propose to a girl, I must say. There, there, lass –' Mabel reached across and patted Betsy's arm – 'don't take on so.'

'There's no need for you to go, lad,' George said. 'At least not yet. They're not calling up married men. If you and Betsy get married quick—'

Jake was shaking his head. 'That'd be cowardice and I've no wish to be given a white feather.' He tried to make a joke, 'Even if there are plenty blowing about the yard.'

But no one was laughing.

George sighed. 'Aye well, I can't say I blame you, lad. If I was forty years younger, then—'

'George!' Mabel was askance. 'I hope you'd do no such thing. You should be telling Jake to forget such nonsense, not encouraging him.' She turned to Jake and her expression softened. 'Jake, you're like a son to us.' For a moment her expression was pained. 'Our daughter is lost to us – as good as – and you, well, you and young Betsy have filled the void in our lives.'

Though a strict taskmaster, Mabel Smallwood could, on occasions, be as soft as the butter she churned in the dairy. She grasped Jake's hand and then Betsy's, as if by her actions she would bind them together. Her voice was husky as she said, 'There's nowt we'd like better, George and me, than to see you two settle down together. We've even talked about how to get you a little place of your own.' She glanced at George, who added, 'Aye, we reckon if we did a bit of alteration to the side of the house. Built on a hallway and another staircase and knocked a few holes in the walls, you could have the front room and the bedroom above it and be all self-contained. We'd add on a bit of a kitchen at the back, an' all. What do you say, now?'

Jake and Betsy, whose tears had miraculously dried, stared at each other.

'It's – very generous of you,' Jake faltered. 'We – we never expected anything like that.'

'No,' Mabel said tartly, becoming her usual self once more. 'And if we'd thought for an instant that you did expect it, well, you wouldn't be getting it.' She paused and then her smile took away some of the sharpness. 'If you see what I mean.'

Jake's expression, however, was still sober. 'Is this – I mean – does this offer still stand if I enlist?'

Mabel opened her mouth, but George cast her a warning glance and answered for them both. 'We're not the sort of folks to make conditions. Besides, you must do what your conscience tells you. I've never been one to come between a man and his conscience.'

Mabel shut her mouth and lowered her gaze. Jake had the feeling that she did not wholly agree with her husband. 'So,' George went on, 'even if you decide to go, we'll look after young Betsy here whilst you're gone and – God willing – when you come back, we'll build a home for you both.'

'I won't have her at my wedding. I won't, I won't.'

Jake had never seen the quiet, docile Betsy in such a temper. Trying to placate her, he said mildly, 'I don't suppose she'd come anyway. She wouldn't come to Dr and Mrs Collins's wedding, so I don't suppose she'd come to ours.'

Betsy was still tearful and truculent, which was unlike her. 'But you still want her to come. You still want her to be invited. And the missis doesn't want her here any more than I do. And they're paying for our wedding . . .'

Jake sighed. 'I know, I know. But the missis is a bit unfair blaming Meg for what her father did. And you – I can't understand why you don't want to ask her. I thought you and she were friends.'

'I'd rather Dr and Mrs Collins came to our wedding,' Betsy said stubbornly, skirting round the real reason why she didn't want Meg Rodwell spoiling her special day. 'And – and Meg doesn't speak to Mrs Collins, so it – it could make it awkward.' Betsy was jealous of Meg and always would be. She had witnessed how Jake looked at Meg and how, when her name was mentioned, his face altered.

'But they do now,' Jake insisted. 'Mrs Collins told me herself. Meg went to the surgery to pick up some medicine for Mr Rodwell and Mrs Collins saw her and they've made it up.'

'Oh.' Betsy looked crestfallen.

Jake eyed her closely. 'You don't look pleased.'

Betsy was silent. Jake put his arms around her and pulled her to him. 'Come on, my little love, out with it. What's really upsetting you?'

She clung to him, burying her face against his chest so that he had difficulty in deciphering her muffled words. 'You – you – like her, don't you?'

'We're friends.' Above her head, he grimaced. 'Well, we were. I'm not so sure now.'

'No – no, I mean, you really like her.' There followed two words that he could not hear, so he pulled back and cupped her tear-streaked face between his hands.

'Look at me, love,' he said gently. 'Come on, tell me what's troubling you. We mustn't have secrets.'

Tears welled in the young girl's eyes and trickled down her face. Tenderly, Jake wiped them away with his finger.

'You – you love her, don't you?'

Jake stared at her, battling with an inner turmoil that he hoped Betsy would never know of. He sighed and, telling her the truth but not quite the whole truth, he said, 'When I first met her, yes, I did like her. I liked her very much. If it hadn't been for her, I might still be shut up in that place. She gave me the courage to get out and make a life for miself outside the workhouse. But then –' he paused for a moment, inwardly mourning the loss of the spirited, fiery girl he had first met – 'she changed. I suppose – if I'm fair – it was because of all the things that happened to her, but even so there's no excuse for some of the things she's done.' His voice dropped to a whisper. 'Some things I can't forgive her for.'

In a small voice, Betsy said, 'So – so you – you're not in love with her?'

Neatly he avoided giving a direct answer, but nevertheless he was utterly sincere. 'I love *you*, Betsy. It's you I want to marry.'

Deep inside him he buried all thoughts of Meg forever. And even Betsy had the sense not to voice her deepest anxiety. She didn't ask aloud: *But if Meg weren't married to Percy Rodwell, what then?* Instead she wound her arms about Jake's neck and whispered. 'I love you so much, Jake.'

He kissed her and hugged her and did his best to drive away all thoughts of the beautiful girl with the red hair and the heart-stopping smile.

*

On a Saturday morning in March, Meg stood near the front of the shop, gazing unseeingly out of the window into the street.

Jake was getting married today. To Betsy, of all people. And they were going to live at the farm, treated like the Smallwoods' own family. They'd all be there, she thought. Philip and Louisa, Letitia Pendleton. Maybe even Isaac Pendleton and Theobald Finch, George Smallwood's racing cronies, would have been invited.

They'd all be there. All – but her.

The wedding was over and after the briefest of honeymoons Jake left to join the army.

George, shaking the young man's hand vigorously, could not speak for the huge fear constricting his throat.

Betsy and Mabel wept openly. 'Do take care,' they kept repeating, as if convincing themselves that if he kept a sharp eye open he could easily dodge the bullets.

Jake hugged them all in turn, keeping his last tender kiss for his young bride. 'I'm no great letter writer, Betsy, but I'll do mi best. Will you do something for me?'

Mute with misery, she nodded.

'Go and see Miss Pendleton now and again. Let her know how I'm faring.'

'Miss Pendleton? Matron?' Betsy was startled.

'Yes. She's always been good to me. She was the nearest I had to a mam before I came to live here at the farm.'

'But, but they used to beat you—'

Firmly, Jake shook his head. 'She didn't. He did, but

not her. Never her. If truth be known, she saved me from him several times.'

'Did she?'

Jake nodded. 'But then, she liked the little boys, didn't she?'

'Mm,' Betsy said slowly, remembering how it had been. 'But she always seemed to like you best.'

'Don't come to see me off. I want to think of you all here.' And so the Smallwoods and Betsy went on with their daily routine about the farm, trying not to think about Jake joining the line of marching men on their way to the station.

The streets of South Monkford were lined with cheering, flag-waving folk. As they passed, Jake glanced towards the tailor's shop and fancied he saw a glimpse of Meg beyond the shadowy window. But she did not come to the doorway to wave him goodbye.

Her smile would live only in his memory.

Inside the shop, standing in the shadows, Meg bit her fingernail down to the quick. He was going. Jake was going to the war. Meg had never felt so terrified in her life. If he was killed and she never had a chance to tell him . . .

Letitia Pendleton was waiting near the station. She pushed her way through the throng and grabbed Jake's arm, trying to pull him away from the lines of marching men.

'Don't go, Jake. You don't have to. Don't go.'

Gently, he tried to prise her clinging hands away, but she held on tightly.

'I have to, Miss Pendleton. I've enlisted. I'd be put in prison if I don't go now. Besides, I want to. It's my duty and I'll be called up soon enough anyway.'

Letitia sobbed. 'But – I – I might never see you again. And I've never told you . . .'

They'd reached the entrance to the station and the formal lines of marching men had broken up.

Jake stopped and turned to face her, smiling down at her. 'I know I've always been one of your favourites.'

Letitia was sobbing uncontrollably, her arms trying to enfold him. 'It's more than that. Jake, there's something you should know. Something I *want* you to know.'

'I have to go, Miss Pendleton. They're all getting on the train now.'

He planted a kiss on her round cheek, wet with tears. 'When I come back,' he promised, 'I'll come and see you.'

He pulled away from her and marched purposefully towards the station entrance and in through the archway.

'Jake . . . Jake . . .' Her cry followed him, echoing eerily. 'Don't go. I have to tell you . . .'

He marched on and, if she said more, Jake did not hear it.

Forty-Three

The war dragged on through 1916. The people of South Monkford scoured the casualty lists in the local paper and those with menfolk at the Front waited fearfully for the dreaded telegram.

Philip Collins enlisted, and whilst he tried to reassure his wife that in his work as a medical officer he would be comparatively safe, Louisa was not convinced.

'I know you. You'll be right there near the Front. In a field hospital.'

He could not deny the probability. Louisa clung to him and whispered against his neck, 'And I don't even have a child to remember you by.'

It was a great source of sadness to them both that they had not been blessed, as yet, with children.

'When I come back, it'll be different. I promise you.' But Louisa would not be comforted.

Philip battled in the days before his departure against saying goodbye to Meg. He couldn't get her out of his mind and the thought that he might never see her again drove him finally, against his better judgement, to visit her.

He decided to call at the shop so Percy would be there too. That way he would not be alone with her. But when he opened the door and stepped inside, the shop was empty. Percy must be here alone, Philip thought, moving towards the back room. But as he stepped inside it was Meg who raised her eyes from sewing buttons on an almost completed jacket.

'Philip!' she cried and jumped up at once. Scarcely realizing what he was doing, Philip held out his arms and she ran into them. He held her close, his face against her hair, breathing in the scent of her.

'Oh, Philip, you're going too, aren't you? Jake's gone and now you.' She was weeping against him and then he was kissing her; her forehead, her eyes and lastly, her mouth. She returned his kiss, clinging to him, pressing herself against him.

'Oh, Meg, Meg,' he was saying over and over. His kisses, passionate and yet poignant, awakened something in her that Meg had not known existed. This was real desire, this was passion. What she was suddenly feeling was totally different to her affection for Percy. And oh, how different it would be to be made love to by this handsome man with his broad shoulders and lithe body.

'Philip,' she gasped and drew him into the room.

What might have happened then had the shop doorbell not clanged warningly, Philip dared not think. Only later was he grateful that at that moment Percy had returned to the shop. Philip and Meg sprang apart, gazing breathlessly at each other until Meg smoothed her hair and opened the door.

'Percy,' she said with amazing calm, 'I'm so glad you're back. Dr Collins has called to say goodbye.'

If the doctor appeared dazed and slightly incoherent, Percy put it down to the young man's trepidation at what awaited him.

'Good luck, Doctor.' Percy shook Philip's hand, noticing its clammy feel. 'Come back to us safe and sound, won't you?'

Philip gulped and backed out of the shop. 'Yes, yes, thank you. Er – thank you, goodbye.'

'Oh dear,' Percy remarked, shaking his head sadly. 'He's terribly afraid of what might happen, isn't he?'

'Mm,' Meg agreed absently. She was not thinking of what might happen to Philip at the Front, but of what might happen when he came home again.

Jake had served almost a year in France when he received a wound that brought him back home. His knee was badly smashed and, whilst he would recover, he would forever walk with a stiff leg.

Whilst she hated the fact that Jake had been wounded, Betsy was ecstatic that, for him, the war was over.

'Did you see Dr Collins? Did he look after you in the hospital?'

Jake smiled indulgently at Betsy's naivety. 'No, love, I didn't see him. I 'spect he was in a different place to me.'

'Oh.' She was disappointed and then a worried frown creased her forehead. Now that her Jake was home, she could spare a thought for the safety of others. 'I hope he's all right.'

Meg too was thankful to hear that Jake had survived. She longed to see him, but the past kept them apart. Instead, she thought dreamily of the time that Philip would come home. And then, suddenly, miraculously, on the same day that the United States entered the war, Philip too was invalided out of the army. He had been caught in a gas attack and was considered no longer fit enough to undertake the onerous duties of a field hospital doctor.

'It's not as bad as they're making out,' he told Louisa. 'It's just affected my lungs, but I hope they'll improve – given time.' He tried to smile.

'Oh, Philip, you're not going back, are you? You've done your bit. More than your bit.'

He raised her hand to his lips. 'No, my dear. I'm back home now, but I'll soon be well enough to care for all my old patients here.'

And whilst he would never be quite as fit as he had been before the war, Dr Collins was soon riding round the town again in his pony and trap and calling on all his old friends.

But there was one place he did not dare to call. Though he thought of her often – every day – he did not call to see Meg.

By October 1918 the worldwide influenza epidemic had reached Britain and South Monkford. Dr Collins, still not completely fit himself, worked day and night to care for his patients. And just when the worst appeared to be over in the town Percy Rodwell succumbed.

'Get to bed at once,' Meg told him. 'And I'll fetch the doctor.'

'Don't worry the poor man,' Percy murmured, holding onto the counter to keep himself upright.

Meg held a cool hand to his forehead. 'You're burning up, Percy. Go straight home and get into bed. I'll close the shop early and go to the surgery. Maybe there's something he can prescribe.'

The front hall at the doctor's home, which served as a waiting room, was crowded. Louisa drew Meg through into their private quarters at the rear of the house. 'If you don't mind coming into the kitchen,' she whispered as she led the way, 'I'll make us a cup of tea, though I'll have to keep answering the front door.'

'Of course,' Meg said. 'But you mustn't bother about me, Louisa. You've enough to do.'

Louisa smiled. 'If I can't make a cup of tea for a friend, then it's a pity. Besides, I'm ready for one. I've been on my feet for two hours answering that door and placating frustrated patients.'

'I really can't stay long, though,' Meg said, peeling off her gloves and sitting down at the table whilst Louisa bustled about the kitchen, though still alert for the sound of the front-door bell. 'I've sent Percy home to bed. He's got this dreadful influenza. He looks terrible.'

'Oh dear.' Louisa turned sympathetic eyes on her friend. 'I'm sorry to hear that, but I'm sure Philip will visit him. It might be quite late, though.'

Meg shook her head. 'Percy doesn't want to trouble him. I've just come to see if Philip can give me something for him. That's all.'

'Here's your tea. I'll just slip in to see him between patients and ask, shall I? It'll save you waiting if you want to get back to Percy. Excuse me a moment.'

When Louisa had left the room, Meg looked about her. The kitchen was large, yet still cosy. Louisa was obviously the perfect housewife. The smell of freshly baked bread lingered in the air and judging by the remnants of their evening meal, taken before Philip started evening surgery, she was also an excellent cook. The house was vast, and though Meg had only seen Philip's surgery, their private sitting room and the kitchen, she imagined that all the other rooms were just as spacious and well furnished.

A sudden wave of envy swept through her. Why should Louisa have all this whilst she, Meg, lived in a poky little house with an old man as her husband? Once Percy had seemed a 'good catch' – a well-respected businessman in the town with his own shop and house. But then she had found that he didn't own the shop and that, whilst the townsfolk patronized it, he was nevertheless something of a figure of fun. Meg sighed. Now why couldn't she have captured someone like Philip? He was handsome as well as clever and he was revered in the community, whereas she feared that since the court case folk were secretly sniggering about Percy and his child bride. Why, why, why . . .

Louisa came hurrying back into the room. 'Philip says you're not to wait. Go home and he'll come and visit after surgery.'

Meg pushed away her envious thoughts and tried to smile, though it did not reach her eyes. Louisa, however, misinterpreted the shadow in her eyes as concern about Percy. She touched Meg's arm. 'Philip will come as soon as he can, my dear.'

When Meg arrived home, Percy had got into bed, but he was shivering uncontrollably. She stood by the bed looking down at him dispassionately. Lying there, his eyes closed, Percy looked gaunt and sickly. The ruthless thought crept its way unbidden into her mind. *If he dies, I'll be left this house and the business* . . .

'Water,' he whispered through cracked lips. 'Please . . .' Ill though he was, Percy Rodwell was the epitome of politeness.

Meg smiled and laid her cool hand on his forehead. 'Philip's on his way to see you. He'll tell me what I should do. But first I'll light the bedroom fire. It's so cold in here. That can't be good for you. And I'll heat a brick . . .'

When she had been ill as a child, Meg remembered

her mother heating a brick in the oven, wrapping it in a piece of cloth and placing it in the bed at her feet. She remembered feeling cosseted and loved by that one simple action.

By the time Philip, heavy eyed and grey with weariness, arrived, a cheerful fire was burning in the bedroom grate.

'He asked for water,' Meg said as she led the way upstairs, lifting her skirts daintily, 'but I wasn't sure if it was the right thing to do.'

'Yes, plenty of fluids. He must drink plenty, but hot drinks would be even better.'

She opened the bedroom door and ushered the doctor inside. As he stepped past her into the room, his arm brushed her breast. He paused a moment and looked down at her. Their eyes met and locked in an intense gaze. She heard him sigh as he dragged himself away and into the room.

'I – I'll get that drink for him now,' she murmured. 'And I'll make you something.'

Without waiting for him to argue, she closed the bedroom door and went down the narrow stairs. She heated milk and poured it out into two cups. Then in each one she put brown sugar and whisky. She carried one through to the front sitting room and placed it on a small table by the sofa. Then she poked the fire, making the flames dance and spark. She turned the gaslights down low so that the room was lit by the glow from the fire. Then she returned to the kitchen and carried the other cup of milk up to the bedroom.

'I've put a drop of whisky in it. Is that all right?'

'For the moment, but once he starts taking this medicine I'm leaving for him, don't give him any alcohol, will you?'

'Whatever you say,' Meg said meekly.

'Give him his first dose before he settles down for the night and then four times a day after meals. That's if he manages to eat anything, which I doubt very much. And I doubt either of you will get much sleep tonight. He'll be very restless until this fever breaks.'

Meg nodded. 'I'd already thought I might sleep in the other room. I'll probably disturb him all the more if I sleep in here.'

Philip glanced at her. She saw the struggle of emotion in his eyes. Hoarsely he said, 'But – but – you mustn't be too far away from him. You must keep a watch on him.'

'Of course I will.' Meg was indignant. 'I will look after him, Philip. Really, I will.'

A wicked little voice deep inside her whispered: *Are you trying to convince Philip – or yourself?*

'I know you will,' Philip murmured. He glanced back at his patient. 'Send me word if you need me again.'

'Thank you. And now,' she added briskly, 'you must come downstairs. I have a hot drink ready for you. It's in the front room. You go and get it before it's cold and I'll be down in a moment when I've helped Percy with his.'

She went to the far side of the bed and helped Percy to sit up against the pillows. She picked up the cup. Philip watched as she bent over her husband and held the cup to his lips. Percy sipped. Philip stood a moment watching the young woman's tender ministrations. Then he turned and left the bedroom without another word.

A few moments later Meg joined him in the small front parlour. Philip had finished his drink and was sitting staring into the fire. She sat beside him on the sofa.

'What did you put in that milk?' The small amount of alcohol coupled with his tiredness had already affected him.

Meg chuckled. 'Whisky. Like I put in Percy's.'

Philip rubbed his hand across his eyes. 'You'll have me drunk. That wouldn't look good to my patients.'

They stared at each other, both remembering what had happened the last time she had given him whisky to drink.

'I thought you'd probably finished for the night.' She curled up her feet beneath her and half turned towards him, putting her arm along the back of the sofa behind his head – not quite touching him, but very close.

He sighed. 'As far as I know at this moment, I have. But if I get called out in the night . . .'

'You're working far too hard.'

She leant forward and smoothed back a lock of his fair, curly hair that had fallen on to his forehead. Slowly, he turned to look at her. 'Oh, Meg,' he whispered.

Her mouth was only inches from his, her fingers still resting on his hair. She bent her head and kissed him, oh so gently, on the lips. A tender, featherlight kiss. She heard him moan and murmur yet again, 'Oh, Meg, Meg.'

He was kissing her ardently now, pressing her back against the cushions, lying on top of her . . .

Afterwards, he was ashamed and contrite. 'I'm so sorry, Meg. I – we – shouldn't have done that.'

Meg, her eyes shining, whispered, 'But it was wonderful. I've never known it like that. Not with Percy . . .'

'Don't.' Philip dropped his head into his hands and

groaned. 'Please – don't. I feel bad enough already. I'm so sorry, Meg. It will never happen again, I swear.'

'Why? I won't tell a soul. No one need know.'

Philip's ardent lovemaking had awakened a passion in her that she had never known before. She had forgotten everything in the searing ecstasy of the moment. She couldn't bear to think that this might be the one and only time she would know such a glorious feeling. 'Please, Philip. I love you, I adore you . . .' she pleaded.

He lifted his head and gazed at her and she saw that his face was wet with tears. 'Oh, Meg. We can't. We mustn't. Don't you see? We'd hurt too many people. I'd lose my career.'

'I'd never do anything to hurt you, Philip. Never. No one would ever know. Not from me.'

'But people have ways of finding out, especially in a small town like this. And besides – more important than all that – we're . . . we're being unfair to Percy and to Louisa.' As he spoke his wife's name, he dropped his head into his hands once more, whilst, unseen by him, Meg smiled.

Forty-Four

Despite his good intentions, Philip couldn't stay away from Meg. She was like one of his drugs, just as powerful and much, much more dangerous. Throughout Percy's illness he continued to visit, knowing that for the moment at least the neighbours would not question why his pony and trap were parked outside for an hour at a time.

Meg was in heaven. When he was not there, her body yearned for him with a physical ache. Thoughts of him filled her waking hours and her dreams at night. And in the brief, ecstatic moments they were together, all thoughts of Percy – even of Jake – and certainly of Louisa were driven from her mind. They couldn't help themselves, neither of them. But whilst Meg had no conscience, Philip was being torn apart by their deceit and infidelity.

'It has to stop, Meg,' he said a hundred times, but day after day, drawn by his fascination with her, he called again.

But on the tenth day, Meg opened the door with a worried frown on her face. 'He's worse.'

The doctor hurried up the stairs and into the main bedroom. He found his patient sinking into unconsciousness.

'Oh no!' Philip felt guilt overwhelm him, whilst behind him, Meg stood uncertainly in the doorway.

*

No one blamed the doctor for the deaths from influenza. The epidemic was worldwide. There had been several deaths already in South Monkford and now there was one more – Percy Rodwell.

Five days after Percy's death the armistice was signed, and whilst the whole country celebrated the end of the war Meg buried her husband.

After the funeral, Meg returned to the darkened house and sat in the front room alone, waiting for Philip. The curtains had been drawn all day, as was the custom in the neighbourhood when there had been a death in the house. Even the neighbours had drawn their curtains as a mark of respect when the horse-drawn hearse left Percy's cottage.

She knew he would come. She was sure he would come, but when she heard the pony and trap pull up outside the door and she peeped through a crack in the curtains, she was disappointed to see Louisa sitting beside him in the trap. Meg watched as Philip jumped down and then assisted his wife to alight. Together they came towards the front door as Meg opened it to greet them.

'My dear,' Louisa said, holding out her arms. 'We can't tell you how sorry we both are.'

Meg held herself stiffly in Louisa's embrace. Over the other woman's shoulder she met Philip's gaze briefly, but he lowered his head and refused to meet her eyes.

'Come in,' Meg said in a flat tone. 'I'll – I'll make some tea.'

'Let me,' Louisa offered. 'You go into the front room with Philip. I'm sure there are things you need to discuss – to ask him. We both want to help, Meg, in any way we can. You have only to ask.'

For a brief instant hysteria welled up inside Meg. She

wanted to laugh and cry aloud: *All I want is your husband. It's me he loves now – not you.* But she remained silent, gave a weak smile and opened the door into the front room.

'Thank you, Louisa,' she murmured. 'There – there are one or two – business matters that I'm sure Philip could give me some guidance on.'

Philip glanced uneasily from one to the other, but when his wife touched his arm and bade him follow Meg, he had no choice.

Inside the front room with the door closed, he stood stiffly behind the sofa, at once putting a barrier between them. Meg smiled and held out her hands to him. 'Why so distant? Come here.'

'Meg.' He frowned, shifting uncomfortably from one foot to the other. 'Don't. Please, don't. Not today of all days.'

'I'm sorry.' Meg was at once contrite. 'You're right, of course. We must let a decent interval elapse before—'

'Before nothing, Meg.' His voice was still a whisper, but there was no doubting the vehemence in his tone. 'It's got to stop. We can't go on. I can't go on deceiving Louisa and – and there's my career . . .'

Meg watched him. His face was tortured. He was suffering agonies. He wanted her still, yet his conscience was crucifying him. She went to him and took his hands in hers. They were cold and trembling.

'It's all right,' she whispered. 'Truly it is. I won't ask anything more from you. It is at an end if – if that is what you really want.' She was so sure that he would not take her seriously, so sure that he would not be able to resist her.

'It – it is.' The words came haltingly, as if he was

forcing them out, and she could see by the look in his eyes that it wasn't what he really wanted to say.

They heard Louisa's footsteps in the hallway and Meg released his hands and stepped away. 'It'll be our secret. I promise,' was her final whisper as she went towards the door to open it for Louisa to carry in the tea tray.

Placing it on a low table, Louisa poured the tea and handed round the cups. She kept up a flow of conversation, but Philip and Meg said little.

'We must be going,' Louisa said at last. She stood up and bent to pick up the tray, but Meg said at once, 'Leave that. I've nothing else to do today. I shan't reopen the shop until Monday.'

'Very well, my dear,' Louisa said, leaning forward and kissing Meg on the cheek. 'You know where we are should you need anything.'

Meg nodded, but as Philip gave her a chaste peck on the cheek, tears filled her eyes. She stood at the door as they climbed into the trap and moved away, then she closed the door and leant against it and allowed the tears to fall freely.

When Meg visited Percy's solicitors on the day after the funeral, as requested by Mr Henderson in a letter of condolence, a shock awaited her.

As expected, Percy had left all his worldly possessions to her, but the shock was that his possessions didn't amount to as much as she'd believed. It came as a thunderbolt to learn that Percy didn't own the terraced house, but that he rented it from none other than Theobald Finch.

Meg stared at the solicitor in horror. She licked her

dry lips and when she spoke her voice came out in a croak. 'I – I had wondered what might happen about the shop, but – but I hadn't realized that he – he didn't own his home. Oh, Mr Henderson, whatever am I to do? The Finches will throw me out, won't they?'

Mr Henderson shuffled his papers and cleared his throat. 'Well, well, I really couldn't say. All you can do, my dear lady, is to continue running your late husband's business . . .' He paused and then asked, 'You intend to do that, don't you?'

Meg nodded.

'And we'll just have to wait and see,' Mr Henderson went on, 'what happens when the lease comes up for renewal. I don't think your landlord can do anything at all until then.'

'And when is that, Mr Henderson?'

The solicitor consulted his papers once more. 'Ah yes, here we are. Your husband signed a new ten-year lease seven years ago, Mrs Rodwell, so there are still three years to run on both premises. The house and the shop.'

'So,' Meg said slowly, 'I have three years before I shall be homeless.'

'Oh, I wouldn't put it quite like that, my dear lady. Perhaps Mr Finch will agree to renew the lease in your name.'

Meg stood up. She pursed her mouth grimly. 'And pigs might fly, Mr Henderson,' she said bitterly.

Meg reopened the shop on the Monday after Percy's funeral. Her first customer was Jake. He came to stand in front of her, the counter between them.

'So, what will you do now?' he asked at last, offering

her no polite condolences. His face was tight, his eyes accusing. 'Now that you're a woman of means?'

'Huh!' Meg's expression was bitter.

'What? Not the wealthy woman you thought you were going to be?'

Meg glared at him. 'Go away, Jake, if that's all you've come for.'

She banged a box onto the counter and began to unpack a quantity of men's vests.

There was an awkward silence. Meg tried to carry on with her work as if he wasn't standing on the other side of the counter, but it was impossible. The tension between them grew until she burst out, 'Oh, very well then, if you must know. The shop and the house weren't his. He rented them *both* from Theobald Finch. So –' she nodded as she watched the change on Jake's face – 'as soon as the leases run out in three years' time, I shall be out on my ear. That please you, does it?'

'No, Meg, it doesn't. But a lot of folks round here'll say you've got your just deserts.'

'And you're one of them?' she flashed back.

Jake sighed heavily. 'Meg, you know how I once felt about you, but you changed so. Where was the lovely girl I met when you first came to the workhouse?' His tone was pensive as he added in a whisper, 'Where did she go, Meggie?'

The unexpected use of her pet name – the name she had been called as a little girl by her family – brought sudden tears to Meg's eyes. Impatiently, she brushed them away as she answered tartly, 'She grew up, Jake. She just grew up.'

Jake's gaze held hers as he shook his head slowly. 'But she changed, Meg. It was more than just growing up. She changed.'

'Well, you can talk. You've got your feet well and truly under the table at Middleditch Farm, haven't you?' She leant forward. 'Don't you realize, Jake, that you're every bit as bad as me? You're trapped for life there now, whether you want to be or not. You're just a replacement, Jake, you and Betsy, for the daughter they lost.' She moved round the counter and stood close to him, smiling coquettishly. She traced her forefinger down the side of his face. 'Don't tell me,' she asked huskily, 'that you really wanted to marry Betsy. You did it to please them, didn't you?'

Jake stepped back from her as if she'd slapped him. His face twisted with disgust and anger, yet, despite it all, her nearness disturbed him. The feelings he'd once had for Meg, though he thought them buried deep, were still there. No matter what she did or what she said, as long as he lived he would never be able to kill his love for her completely. And he hated her for it. Loved and hated her at the same time.

'Don't judge everyone by your own standards,' he spat at her, ''cos you haven't got any.' He thrust his face close to hers. 'You might be able to seduce a feller like Percy Rodwell, but you don't fool me.' He paused and then added with deliberate emphasis, 'And I'd've thought the doctor would have had more sense, an' all.'

Now Meg was genuinely shocked. 'What – what d'you mean?'

'Just because we live a bit out of town doesn't mean we don't hear all the gossip.' He nodded. 'Market day's a good place to hear all that's going on and then there's the race meetings when they're on . . .'

'And what've you heard?' Meg asked between gritted teeth.

'Oh –' Jake tried to make his tone nonchalant – 'just

that when Percy was ill, the doctor visited him more often than he visited any other patient. He attended his funeral and came here afterwards to visit you.'

'Yes, he did,' she snapped back. 'And he brought his *wife* with him.'

He shrugged. 'Mebbe she'd heard the rumours, an' all.'

'There was nothing to hear,' Meg countered, but an ugly flush crept up her neck and into her face. Seeing it, Jake knew the truth.

He turned and left the shop, wishing he'd never come near her. He vowed that he never would again.

She could rot in hell for all he cared.

Forty-Five

At the end of Meg's first week running the shop alone, her fears were realized when Theobald Finch called in just as she was about to close for the evening.

He raised his hat to her. 'Mrs Rodwell.'

Meg managed to summon up her most brilliant smile, yet her heart was thumping. She guessed what he was going to say even before he opened his mouth. Theobald cleared his throat. 'I find myself in something of an embarrassing situation. My sister is insisting I give you notice at once. Both here and at the house you occupy. The tenancy agreements, as you no doubt now know, are still in the name of Mr Rodwell's father with a note of transfer to his son, Percy, some seven years ago.'

Meg said nothing. Her hands were clammy and her knees were trembling. She felt sick.

'The lease expires,' Theobald went on, 'in three years' time.'

There was a long, ominous pause before Theobald added, 'I shall be unable to renew the lease in your name at that time.'

Meg found she had been holding her breath and now she released it. 'So,' she said heavily, 'you're giving me three years?'

He nodded. 'Yes. Unless, of course, you wish to leave before then. There is a clause in the lease which allows you to give me three months' notice.' His tone was hopeful. If she were to do that, his life at home with his sister would be much easier.

'I see.' Meg raised her head defiantly and, with what she hoped was the right degree of businesslike attitude, she said, 'I will give the matter serious thought, Mr Finch, and instruct my solicitor accordingly.'

As Theobald raised his hat and bade her 'Good day,' Meg could have sworn that a smile twitched at the corner of his mouth. He was so sure of himself, she thought. So sure that she was beaten.

Meg felt sick. Every morning when she got up she had to rush to the bowl on the washstand to retch into it. It left her feeling pale and shaky. *It's the worry of the business*, she told herself. Since Percy's death the number of customers was diminishing noticeably with each day that passed. Meg hadn't had a woman customer for over a fortnight and even the number of men coming into the shop was less and less. Even regular customers whom she had heard declare to Percy that they would never dream of going anywhere else for their new suits now never entered the shop.

Of course, Meg was no longer able to offer a made-to-measure service and perhaps that had affected the sales more than she'd thought possible. She'd advertised in the local paper for an experienced tailor but there'd been no replies. Not one.

Worse than anything, Meg had no one with whom to talk over her troubles. Jake was lost to her and she wouldn't dream of going anywhere near Louisa, even though she longed to see Philip.

Was it because of him that the townsfolk were keeping away from the shop that was now hers – at least for the next three years? Philip was well liked and respected in the town. Perhaps, even if they hadn't believed the gossip, they were cold-shouldering Meg because of it. Just in case the rumours had some truth . . . Oh, they were true, all right, Meg thought bitterly, but he wasn't man enough to leave his wife and set up home with her. His career, his standing in the community, were too precious to him. He wouldn't give up everything for love. She despised him for it and yet she still ached for his touch, the feel of his strong, firm body next to hers . . . Meg lifted her head defiantly. *I don't need him*, she told herself. *And I certainly don't need Jake. I'll make such a success of this business that in three years' time Theobald Finch would be a fool to turn me out – whatever his sister says.*

Meg held a sale of all the menswear in stock. She plastered sale tickets in the windows, but still her only customers were strangers from out of town, who came into South Monkford on market day. They knew nothing of the scandal surrounding the pretty young woman behind the counter in the tailor's shop. Gradually she reduced the stock and was able to order more women's clothes. Then she advertised in the local paper once more, informing all her customers that there'd be a grand reopening with discounts on all sales on the first day.

She worked hard, rearranging the interior of the shop and transforming the workroom into a fitting room for ladies to try on dresses, coats and hats. She re-dressed the window and, from one of her suppliers, bought a mannequin to grace the display.

On the day of the sale Meg awoke early and rushed once more to the bowl. *It's just anxiety*, she told herself. *There's nothing wrong with me that a good few customers coming through my door today won't put right.*

Unable to face breakfast – even nibbling a dry piece of toast made her feel queasy again – Meg left home early. Excitement churned in the pit of her stomach. Today would be the turning point in her life. She was sure of it. She had some lovely new stock. Fine silk underwear for the ladies of the town and now, too, she had the more serviceable type of garments worn by farmers' wives.

As nine o'clock came, Meg opened the shop door and looked out onto the pavement, fully expecting to see a few women queuing there to be first to acquire the generous bargains.

There was no one in the street and by ten thirty, she was losing heart. No one had come into her shop even though it was market day and the centre of the town was buzzing. At twelve o'clock she tried to eat the sandwiches she had brought with her, but her stomach heaved at each bite. She gave up and contented herself with a cup of tea whilst standing mournfully near the window to watch the people hurrying past.

She was in the lean-to scullery outside the back door when she heard the bell clang and eagerly she hurried back into the shop.

Betsy was standing uncertainly just inside the door. Meg's welcoming smile died on her lips. 'Oh. It's you,' she said unnecessarily. Betsy's face turned pink, but she moved towards the counter. 'I wondered if you stocked –' the girl lifted her head with a show of bravado and stared straight into Meg's eyes as she added proudly – 'special dresses?' She demonstrated, holding her hands out in front of her. 'With plenty of room in them?'

Meg gaped at her. 'You? You're expecting?'

Her eyes shining, Betsy nodded. 'I'm three months gone and Dr Collins says the sickness should stop soon.'

'Sickness? What sickness?'

Betsy smiled knowledgeably. 'You get a bit of sickness when you're expecting. Usually, just first thing in a morning.'

'Sickness?' Meg repeated stupidly. 'First – first thing in the morning?'

'Yes. But sometimes you can get it any time of the day. For a week or two I had it in the evening as well, but Dr Collins says it should all go after the first three months. Mind you, sometimes it lasts the whole nine months.' Betsy pulled a face. 'That's what Mrs Smallwood ses.'

There was a moment's silence before Meg managed to say weakly, 'Congratulations.'

'Thanks,' Betsy said, then asked again, 'Well, have you got anything I could wear?'

'Yes, one or two bits. They're expensive though. It's usually the toffs who buy special clothes . . .' She left the sentence hanging, but the unspoken words said: *Your sort usually make do and mend.*

But Betsy only smiled and her blush deepened. 'Jake wants me to have the best and Mrs Smallwood said she'd treat me to a proper frock.'

'Very generous, I'm sure.' Meg was consumed with jealousy. Not only was Betsy married to Jake, but she had the Smallwoods treating her like their own daughter, whilst she, Meg, was struggling to run a dying business and facing eviction in three years' time. She was hardly aware of what she was doing as she showed the garments to Betsy. When the girl finally left the shop, the niggling worry burst into her mind.

Sickness? First thing in the morning? Oh no. No. No!

*

Louisa opened the door at Meg's ring. She took Meg's cold hands into hers. 'My dear. How are you? You're looking very pale.'

'I – I've come to see Philip. Professionally.'

'You've timed it perfectly. The last patient is in with him now. Sit down, dear. I'm sure he won't be long.'

To Meg's dismay, Louisa sat beside her in the hallway and kept up an incessant chatter. Inside her head, Meg screamed: *Go away. Leave me alone.* But instead she sat silently, nodding every now and again, though her mind scarcely took in what Louisa was saying.

The consulting-room door opened and a man came out, nodded towards Louisa and left by the front door. Louisa got up and opened the door again.

'Meg's here, Philip. She needs to see you.' Smiling, she held the door open. 'Come in, Meg. I'll leave you to his tender mercies. Come and have a cup of tea with us when you've finished here.'

Mutely, Meg nodded, though she had no intention of staying in this house any longer than she had to.

When the door closed behind his wife, Philip and Meg stared at each other. For a moment there was silence between them until Meg blurted out in a hoarse whisper, 'I think I'm pregnant.'

Moments later, when Philip had confirmed her worst fears, she sat down opposite him again. Now Philip's face was as white as hers.

'Well,' Meg demanded, some of her spirit returning, 'what are you going to do about it?'

'Me?'

'Well, it's your child. You didn't think it could be Percy's, did you?'

Philip gasped. 'You – you don't know that.'

Meg smiled bitterly. 'Oh, I do. Believe me, I do know.'

If it was possible, he blanched even more. He swallowed painfully and now it was he who whispered, 'What are you going to do?'

'Well, I'm not going to some back-street butcher to get rid of it, if that's what you're asking. And you a doctor!'

'Of course I didn't mean that,' he said at once. 'That thought never entered my head.'

'Really!' Meg's tone was scathing. 'Well, it had mine.' She leant towards him. 'D'you mean to tell me you've never been asked to do it?'

He stared at her for a moment. 'Oh, I've been asked, but I have never agreed. Whatever the circumstances – you've got a new life growing, Meg, and it's precious. It has a right to live. Besides, it's not the sort of thing . . .' He said no more, but Meg knew. His precious career, she thought.

'So, what's its *father* going to do? Acknowledge it? Tell the world he's had an affair with one of his patients? Leave his wife to marry the mother of his child?' There was a brief pause whilst Philip stared at her, horror-struck.

'No,' Meg said quietly. 'I thought not.' She came to a swift decision. She was taking a risk, but it was a calculated risk. She must play her hand carefully. Oh, so carefully. She sighed heavily as she stood up to leave, as if she were obliged to shoulder the whole burden alone. 'Well, you're a lucky man, Dr Collins, because the world will think it's Percy's. *I* know it's not and *you* know it's not, but no one else need know.'

Philip too stood up. 'You – you'd do that? For me?'

She stepped close to him and looked up into his face. For a brief instant, in spite of himself, she saw the longing spark in his eyes. She was right. Even now, he still wanted her.

'I'm not all bad, Philip,' she whispered huskily. 'Whatever people might think.' She put her hands, palms flat, on the lapels of his jacket. 'There are people in this world that, if I had the power, I would wreak revenge upon. I admit that. But you're not one of them. Your secret is safe, Philip. I promise you that.'

If anything, she thought, *will win him back, this will. He'll soon be calling on me again in the little house in Church Street*. Now that she was to bear his child, when his own wife seemed unable to do so, she was so sure Philip would come back to her. But for now she must play the part.

She kissed him lightly on the lips, turned and went towards the door.

'Tell your wife I'm sorry I couldn't stay.' She paused, her hand on the doorknob. 'Goodnight – Dr Collins.'

Today had been a turning point in her life all right, Meg thought bitterly as she walked home through the dusk, but not in the way she had expected.

Forty-Six

When Meg could no longer hide her condition, the news spread through the town's grapevine with amazing speed. More customers – mostly women – came into the shop but they bought very little and Meg knew it was only an excuse to gape at her and to gossip about her later with their friends.

The sickness had abated, but now her waistline began to bulge noticeably. Her ankles swelled with standing behind the counter most of the day. But, worst of all, Philip had not been near her. Not once had he called at the shop or at the house. It seemed that he had taken her at her word and her scheme had misfired. Meg felt very alone and lonely with no one to care for and no one to care for her. *If only*, she thought, *I still had Jake*.

She was worried as to how she would cope when her time came, to say nothing of caring for the child afterwards. What would happen to the shop? *If there's a shop left by then*, she reminded herself bitterly. The bills were mounting. Her suppliers were pressing for payment and the quarterly rent was overdue. Any day she expected a visit from Mr Finch or his solicitor.

It was neither of them who came into the shop one morning, however. Clara Finch stood in front of Meg and stared at her, her gaze running slowly up and down Meg's bulging body.

'So he left you pregnant, did he?'

'Yes,' Meg answered, aware that the 'he' Clara was referring to was a totally different 'he' from the one in Meg's mind.

'When is it due?'

Meg licked her lips calculating swiftly. The whole town knew when Percy had fallen ill and then died. 'About – about the end of May, I think.'

'What are you going to do?'

Meg frowned. 'Do?'

'Yes, do? You are hardly in a position to bring up his child, are you? Are you going to have it adopted?'

Meg gasped. That thought had never entered her head. It was her child, her responsibility and after the initial shock, she had accepted the fact. 'No. Of course I'm not.'

Clara leant towards her and there was menace in her face and in her action. 'That child should have been mine. I should be carrying Percy's child – not you. You never loved him, you scheming hussy. You robbed me of my husband. And you robbed me of the chance to have his child.'

There were tears in Clara's eyes, tears of anger, tears of frustration and longing. She had never felt such loathing towards any human being as she did at this moment. The pain of Percy's rejection of her had been nothing compared with the hatred she now felt for Meg.

Slowly and deliberately she said, 'I want that child. I want *his* child. I loved him and I'll love his child. I can give it everything you can't.'

Meg gasped. She felt the urge to laugh outright. If only Clara knew the irony of the situation. Here she was, demanding that Meg hand over the baby to her because she thought it was Percy's. What would she do if Meg were to tell her that it wasn't? But all Meg said was, 'You must be mad. Give my baby to you? Never while there's breath in my body.'

Clara leant even closer. 'You will. One day, you will. I mean to have Percy's child and I will.'

'Your – your brother wouldn't let you.'

'Huh!' Clara stepped back now and her tone was scathing. 'Him! He'll not stop me. He'll do anything I say. There are things I could tell you – tell the world – about my dear brother. And one day I just might. But for now he'll do anything I say. And the first thing he'll do is give you notice. You haven't paid your rent for this quarter yet, have you? Well, if you read your lease – Percy's lease – you'll find that if you default on your rent, you'll be evicted. We've only to send in the bailiffs and you'll be declared a bankrupt.' She smiled triumphantly. 'And I dare say we're not the only people you owe money to.' When Meg did not answer, Clara nodded. 'I thought as much.'

She turned towards the door. 'You'll be hearing from Mr Snape very soon. But think about my offer, won't you? If you agree to my proposition, I'll see that you keep the shop and your home. And I'd see that you got all your customers back. That's something we could think about, isn't it? You see, I can be very generous when I want my own way. Very generous.'

As the shop door closed behind her, Meg was left staring after her. *Sell my baby? She wants me to sell my baby to her because she thinks it's Percy's.*

Meg closed the shop early that day. She walked home in a trance to sit before the fire in the front room, the outrageous proposal whirling around in her head. It was a monstrous idea and yet it was a way out for her. The solution to all her problems. If she gave her child to

Clara Finch, she would be free. She could leave here. She could go anywhere and start her life over again. She had no ties here now, none at all. Jake was lost to her and the bitter truth was that Philip would never leave his wife and jeopardize his career. There was nothing left for her in South Monkford.

And yet . . . And yet . . .

For days Meg pondered Clara's offer. Days in which the number of customers dwindled yet further until she saw no more than three during the whole of one week. And then they only bought small items of underwear. Meg was at her wits' end and she spent the whole of Sunday pacing up and down her front room.

If I don't get any customers this week, she decided in the early hours of Monday morning when she'd tossed and turned, sleepless through the night, *I'll do it. She can have it. What do I want with a baby anyway?*

She was tired and listless when she opened up the shop. To her surprise, at five past nine the shop doorbell clanged, as if awoken from a deep slumber. Meg looked up and smiled. The woman approaching the counter had never before entered the shop, but Meg recognized her. Mrs Davenport's husband was the current mayor of South Monkford and his lady mayoress needed numerous outfits and hats to attend functions throughout the year.

'I'm looking for an evening dress. I don't suppose you have anything, but I thought I'd ask before I went into Newark or Nottingham.'

Meg beamed. One of the last deliveries from her main supplier had contained three dresses suitable for evening wear and Meg was sure that at least one of them was the woman's size. 'I'll show you what I have, Mrs Davenport. Please, would you care to come into the fitting room and I'll bring them through to you.'

The next hour was happily spent whilst Mrs Davenport tried on all three dresses, but the effort was worthwhile for she left the shop having purchased two.

'I needed something rather urgently. We have a grand dinner to attend at the weekend and another early next week in Newark and my dressmaker wouldn't have the time to make two complete outfits. However, she will have time to make the alterations. Could you have both dresses delivered to Miss Pinkerton?'

'Yes, madam. I'll see she has them by tonight,' Meg promised. Since Percy's death she had made even more use of the fussy little spinster who was so clever with her needle and thread. She had even tried to persuade her to tackle making men's suits, but Miss Pinkerton had been thrown into a tizzy at the very idea. 'Oh, I couldn't. I couldn't possibly fit gentlemen.' The little woman had blushed at the mere thought.

Ten minutes after Mrs Davenport had departed the bell clanged again and another customer entered the shop. She made several purchases of underwear. After her came yet another and the steady stream of women customers went on throughout the day. By five o'clock Meg was tired but elated. If things went on like this . . .

The bell sounded again and she looked up to meet Clara's eyes. The woman stood before the counter, hands folded in front of her waist, her mouth pursed and her eyes hard. But today there was a glitter of excitement in them.

'So? Have you had a good day?'

Meg gaped at her as realization began to dawn, slowly at first and then in a rush. Seeing the understanding on

Meg's face, Clara smiled and nodded. 'It could be like that every day if you'd be sensible and give me what I want. You hand over your baby to me – boy or girl, I don't mind what it is – and I'll get Theobald to renew the lease on both your home and this shop in your name. And I guarantee that you'll have plenty of customers. *Just like you've had today.*' She leant towards Meg as if sharing a confidence, yet the action was more threatening than confiding. 'You see, I made a lot of new friends through my war work and they're more than willing to listen to my recommendations.' She paused and added with deliberate emphasis, 'What*ever* those recommendations might be.'

Meg understood now how, little by little, her number of customers had dwindled and then, miraculously, had suddenly been restored.

'So,' Clara asked, 'what about it?'

'Is it – would it be – legal?' was Meg's only question.

Clara waved her hand airily. 'Oh, we'll let Mr Snape sort all that out. He's always very helpful to our family.' For a moment her face darkened. 'He's only ever let us down once.' And Meg knew she was referring to the court case which, whilst technically Clara had won, had not been the resounding success she'd sought. 'Besides,' Clara added, almost as an afterthought, 'my brother and I own his office premises.'

Meg almost gasped aloud. Was there no end to the power the Finch family wielded in this town?

'Well?' Clara was pressing for her answer.

Unable to say aloud what she knew in her heart was a terrible, unforgivable thing, Meg merely nodded. Clara smiled triumphantly. 'You're very wise. You've made the right decision.'

As Clara left the shop, all Meg could think was: *Whatever will Jake say when he finds out?*

Meg was never far from Jake's thoughts. Try as he might, he could not cut her out of his memory, or even out of his life. He hadn't seen her for weeks, months now, yet he knew that she was expecting a child, knew too that she was facing difficulties in her business. Part of him longed to help her, to give her whatever support he could. Longed, once more, to be her friend. But another part – the harsher side of him – told him: *She's made her bed, let her lie in it.*

And now, on the same day that Meg gave her answer to Clara, Jake was about to become a father.

As they were getting into bed that night in their newly built part of the farmhouse, Betsy suddenly clutched at her stomach, bent over double and cried out.

'What is it? What's the matter?' Jake, who was already in bed, sat up.

'I think it's the baby.'

Jake flung back the covers, wrenched off his night-shirt and began to dress. 'Get into bed, love. I'll get the missis.'

Minutes later Mabel Smallwood walked calmly into the bedroom, Jake hovering anxiously behind her. 'Now, lad, this is no place for you. This is women's work. Off you go downstairs,' she said firmly, 'and leave this to us.'

'But shouldn't I go for the doctor? Or the midwife?'

'Not unless we need them. No need for unnecessary doctor's bills if we can manage perfectly well without them.'

Jake backed out of the room reluctantly. He raised his hand in a wave to Betsy, but she was already too busy coping with another contraction.

For Jake the waiting, in the room below, was agony. He paced the floor, straining to catch any sound from upstairs. He tried desperately to keep his mind on his wife, on Betsy, yet try as he might he could not help thinking about Meg too. When he'd heard the news of her pregnancy his first unbidden thought had been that he wished the child was his instead of Percy Rodwell's. He remembered that thought with shame. Yet still – even after all that had happened – he worried about Meg. She lived alone. What would happen when she went into labour? Would there be anyone there to take care of her?

He paced the floor harder, feeling guilty at even thinking of Meg at such a time. Betsy – he must think only of Betsy.

Forget Meg, he kept telling himself. *She's not worth the ground your Betsy walks on.* He loved Betsy, really he did. He wanted to protect her and make her happy, yet it was always Meg's face that haunted his dreams, Meg who was never far from his thoughts. Even when his wife was giving birth to their beautiful daughter, it was still Meg whom he could not forget.

Forty-Seven

During the third week of June Meg's son was born in the bedroom she'd shared with Percy. It was a difficult birth and the midwife insisted that she needed a doctor's help.

'I'm sending for Dr Collins,' she said firmly after Meg had laboured in vain for nine hours.

'No,' Meg had tried to protest, but exhausted by her efforts she was too weak to argue any more.

An hour or so later Philip entered the bedroom reluctantly, though he had no choice but to attend. There would have been raised eyebrows and questions asked if he had refused. And to send for another doctor would have taken too long and possibly endangered the lives of mother and baby.

Meg was in too much pain to care who was there. It was not until afterwards that she realized the irony. Philip had helped to bring his own son into the world.

Clara Finch was her one and only visitor. She came the day after the birth and stood by the side of Meg's bed.

'You shouldn't be feeding him yourself,' she said. Her face showed her distaste as she watched the tiny child suckling greedily at Meg's breast. Meg realized that the woman was afraid she would change her mind. Once her baby was born, in her arms and suckling at her breast, Meg's maternal instincts might be so powerful that . . .

She looked up at Clara. She stared at the thin, bitter face of the woman standing over her and wondered how she'd ever thought she could give her child up to her.

'I'm sorry,' she said quietly, but there was a new note of determination in her tone. 'I'm sorry, Miss Finch, but I can't let you have him. He's my baby and, whatever you do to me, I'll never let him go.'

Clara's face contorted with rage. If it hadn't been for the baby in her arms – the child she thought was Percy's – Meg believed the woman would have attacked her. Weak after the birth, Meg knew she would have had no defence. As it was, Clara – for she would not harm the child – had to content herself with an angry tirade and dire threats.

'I'll ruin you. You'll be homeless. Yes, yes, that's it. You'll be back in the workhouse where you belong. And this time there'll be no foolish Percy Rodwell to fall for your charms. Oh yes, and then we'll see, because you'll have no say in what happens to your child. Remember, your life in there is ruled by the master and—' she paused as she delivered her final, triumphant blow – 'by the board of guardians.'

Meg gasped. The woman was mad, quite mad. Did Clara really think that if she had Meg put back into the workhouse, she could then just take her child? Meg blanched. Remembering now just how it had been, she realized that with the co-operation of everyone concerned it was entirely possible. Illegal, probably, but Clara would not let that worry her. She had Mr Snape to worry for her about that.

As she left the bedroom, Clara shook her fist at Meg. 'You'll live to regret this. I'll have that child. One day – mark my words – I'll have that child.'

As she heard the woman go down the stairs and bang

the front door behind her, Meg laid her lips against the baby's head. 'I'm so sorry,' she whispered hoarsely. 'So sorry that I ever thought of giving you away. Forgive me.'

The baby slept in her arms, calmly unaware of the drama his arrival into the world had caused.

When she felt well enough, Meg walked to the surgery to see the doctor. There was nothing unusual about a young mother visiting her doctor and Louisa welcomed her with open arms.

'Let me hold him. Oh . . .' As she took the baby boy into her arms, Louisa's eyes shone and her face took on a soft glow. 'Oh, Meg, he's lovely – beautiful. How lucky you are.' For a moment her face clouded. Longing showed clearly in her face.

'What're you going to call him?'

'I – haven't decided on a name yet.'

'You're not calling him after his father, then?'

Meg gave a start and then realized that Louisa meant the name 'Percy'. She shook her head. 'No.'

Shyly, Louisa said, 'Well, some mothers call their baby boys after the doctor who attended them. I mean, you did have a bad time and Philip . . .' Her voice trailed away.

Meg almost laughed aloud. *If only you knew*, she thought. Instead she said brightly, 'I'll ask Philip what he thinks.'

'Do.' Louisa smiled. 'And I'll put the kettle on. Come and have tea with me afterwards.'

When it was her turn to go into the consulting room, Meg stood for a moment inside the door until Philip looked up and saw her there with his son in her arms.

She saw him start, the colour flood into his face and his anxious glance towards the door.

'It's all right. I'm the last patient. Louisa has gone back into the kitchen.'

But he was still agitated. 'Why have you come? Is something wrong?'

'No, but I wanted to ask you what you'd like me to call him.'

'Call him?' Philip said, a little stupidly.

'Well, yes, I thought you ought to approve. After all, he is—'

'Yes, yes,' Philip held up his hand, palm outwards, as if to fend her off.

Meg smiled mischievously, enjoying Philip's discomfiture. 'Louisa suggested I should call him after my doctor. How do you feel about that?'

Philip's look of absolute horror made her smile, but he misinterpreted her amusement, believing that was what she intended. He clasped his hands together. 'Oh, please, Meg. Don't do that. I beg you. There's – there's been gossip already and if – if you were to name him after me, then – then Louisa might begin to suspect.'

Meg put her head on one side, enjoying his discomfort. 'But it was she who suggested it.'

Beads of sweat shone on Philip's forehead. He caught hold of her hand. Tears in his eyes, he pleaded, 'Meg, please. Promise me you won't call him after me. It'd start the tongues wagging all over again. It could ruin my career. Look . . .' He stepped closer. 'I'll give you some money. I'll pay you a monthly allowance, if you like. Help you get away from here – anything . . .'

She stared at him, seeing him suddenly for what he was. A man who had given into his craving for her who yet was not man enough to stand by her now. He was selfish and self-centred. He'd been unfaithful to his wife, yet now all he really cared about was his precious career. He didn't want anything to do with his son. He had not even looked at the baby once since Meg had entered the room.

He wanted nothing to do with the child – or her. He wanted them both out of his life.

He hadn't loved her, Meg realized. He'd lusted after her. In a searing moment of truth, Meg saw herself too for what she had become. She did not like the picture. In the beginning she'd deliberately led Philip on, finding sweet revenge in seducing Louisa's husband. She'd betrayed her kind and devoted husband when Percy had needed her most. She looked down at the sweet, innocent infant in her arms, the child she had been tempted to give away. What sort of mother was she? What sort of woman was she? Shame swept through her.

By offering her money, Philip made her feel like a common woman of the streets, but she was worse than any of them. At least they did what they did with an open kind of honesty. She had been devious, manipulative, cruel to her poor mam . . . The list was endless. No wonder Jake – who'd once loved her – hated her. But no one hated her more at this moment than Meg herself.

She pulled herself free of Philip's pleading hands and took a step back. But the distance between them was so much greater now than that one step. Meg lifted her chin and her green eyes sparked with resolution.

'I don't want your money, Philip. Or you. I'll take care of *my* child.' Her lip curled with contempt. 'And don't worry yourself. Your dirty little secret's safe. I'd rather people think he's Percy's son than have you as his father.'

She turned and walked across the room towards the

door, pausing only to say, 'Oh – please give my apologies to your dear wife. I am unable to accept her invitation to take tea with her.'

When Meg felt well enough to reopen the shop, taking the child with her, customers were once more in short supply, no doubt under Clara's instruction. At the end of the week a letter came from Mr Snape to say that her landlord required her to vacate both the shop and her home unless she could pay the two months' rent she already owed and another month in advance. By the same post two letters came from suppliers threatening her with court action if their accounts weren't paid within fourteen days.

Late that evening, carrying the baby in her arms, Meg walked to the little cottage where the dressmaker, Miss Pinkerton, lived, along the road from her own home. It was almost dusk when she arrived and the nervous spinster peered out of her front-room curtains before she opened the door to her.

'Why, Mrs Rodwell, you're out late – and with the baby too. Come in, come in. Let me make you some tea.'

Miss Pinkerton bustled about her tiny kitchen and when they were sitting on either side of the fireplace in her front room, Meg said, 'Miss Pinkerton, I'll come straight to the point. I'm being evicted by the Finches.'

'Oh, my dear, I'm so sorry, but I have to say I'm not surprised. Clara Finch is a vindictive woman.' It was the second time that word had been used about Clara, Meg thought, but she said nothing about the latest reason for Clara's wrath. Miss Pinkerton believed that Miss Finch was still seeking revenge for what she considered a miscarriage of justice. 'So where will you go? What will you do?'

'I wondered if you would be interested in taking over the shop.'

'Oh!' The little woman nearly dropped her teacup in her surprise and blinked rapidly behind the thick lenses of her spectacles. Her reaction reminded Meg suddenly of Percy and she realized just how much she was missing her kindly protector. When she'd recovered a little, Miss Pinkerton shook her head. 'Oh, dear me, no. I'm too old to take on something like that. And besides,' she bit her lip. 'I may have to give up dressmaking altogether sooner than I had anticipated.' She touched the rim of her spectacles. 'My eyesight, you know. The fine stitching is getting too much for me.' She looked down at her hands holding the cup in her lap. 'I, too, am beginning to lose business.'

Meg's mind was working quickly. She leant forward. 'So why don't we join forces?'

Miss Pinkerton raised her head. 'I – don't understand.'

'You could still serve in a shop, couldn't you, whilst I took on all the sewing? Percy taught me a lot. I used to do quite a bit for him.'

'Dressmaking isn't the same as tailoring.'

'But I can sew well. And I still have Percy's sewing machine. He taught me how to use it. Don't you see? You could soon teach me dressmaking.'

'But Miss Finch? If she knew, wouldn't she . . .?' Miss Pinkerton's voice trailed away.

'She needn't know. I wouldn't be in the shop but in the back, or when I find another place to rent I could work at home, just like you always have.'

'But I'm too old—'

'How old are you?' Meg asked candidly.

'Fifty-five.'

'And what are you going to do for the rest of your life? How are you going to earn a living?'

'I – don't know. That's what's been worrying me. I own this house. My aunt left it to me, but once that's gone—'

'It'll be the workhouse,' Meg said bluntly. She saw the little woman shudder and pressed home her point. 'But it needn't be like that. I can give you advice about the shop. It's only failing because Miss Finch has set all her friends against me.'

'I know,' Miss Pinkerton said. 'She's tried to stop me doing any alteration work for you.'

Meg's face was grim. 'So you know I'm telling you the truth. I haven't failed in the business. I've been hounded out of it. The only problem I've got is finding somewhere else to live. They're turning me out of my home as well.'

'Well, you could come here,' Miss Pinkerton ventured tentatively, but Meg shook her head. 'No. It's very kind of you, but if we're to do this together and try to keep it from Miss Finch I could hardly live here, could I? She'd never let you take on the shop if she thought you were having anything to do with me.'

Miss Pinkerton's face brightened. 'I have a cousin lives in the street – Laurel Street – behind your shop. In fact' – she was getting quite excited now. Two spots of colour burned in her cheeks – 'I think if you go out of Florrie's yard and walk a little way along the passage-way that runs between the backyards, you can get into Mr Rodwell's – oh, I'm sorry, I still think of it as his.' The little woman noticed Meg's puzzlement. 'I'm sorry, I'm not explaining myself very well. My cousin lives alone since she lost her husband and she lets out two rooms, more for the company than anything else.' She leant forward as she added, 'And her last lodger has just left. She's looking for someone else.'

'But would she mind having a baby in the house?'

'Mind? She'd be thrilled, but you'd have to be prepared for the possibility that you might lose him.'

Meg's eyes widened and her heart thumped. Surely Miss Finch hadn't . . . ? But behind her spectacles, Miss Pinkerton's eyes were twinkling. 'My cousin, Florrie, will likely take complete charge of him.'

Meg smiled as she relaxed and murmured, 'I shall be very glad of her help.'

Forty-Eight

Events moved much faster than even Meg had dared to hope. Eliza Pinkerton took only two days to accept Meg's suggestion that she should take over the shop. The little spinster suddenly seemed revitalized, finding a new purpose in her drab, monotonous life.

'I have a little money put by,' she said. 'I'm sure I can pay off all your suppliers, although I won't be paying Theobald Finch your back rent.'

'I think he'll be only too pleased to relet the shop so quickly – and to be rid of me.' Meg told Eliza the current rent and advised, 'Don't let him put it up much more than that.'

'I won't. And now I'll take you to meet my cousin.'

Meg was apprehensive. What if Miss Pinkerton's cousin did not want such a scandalous woman beneath her roof? She need not have worried. Florrie Benedict was round and jolly – a big woman with an even bigger heart. She was energetic and forthright to the point of bluntness, but that frankness was tempered with a ready laugh.

'Oh, so you're the scarlet woman I've heard so much about. Bowling poor Percy Rodwell off his feet and pinching him from under Clara Finch's nose.' She laughed heartily, a deep belly laugh. 'Couldn't have happened to a nicer person.' She pulled a comical face. 'I've no time for the woman, never have had. And the power she and her brother wield in this town – well – there ought to be a law against it. My late husband worked for the council for a while and what Theobald Finch used to push through in the council meetings was nobody's business. Ought to have been investigated, if you ask me.' She laughed again. 'Still, nobody ever did. Now, let's have a look at this little babby of yours. See if we can tek to each other . . .'

Florrie took the child into her arms, nestling him against her ample bosom. She walked up and down the room with him, crooning softly. 'We'll get along just fine, won't we, my little man?' Looking up, she demanded, 'What's his name?'

'Robert Jake.'

Florrie's smile broadened. 'Now fancy that. My little grandson's called Robert. Isn't that strange? But my daughter lives down south and I don't see them very often.' She looked down again at the baby lying placidly in her arms. 'You'll be my little Robbie here, won't you?' As if answering her, the baby gurgled and waved his arms about and Florrie laughed loudly.

Meg moved her few belongings from Percy's house to Florrie's. The two rooms she'd been given upstairs were well furnished, so there was little in the way of furniture she needed to keep. It had belonged to Percy's parents, so was old and worn, and she sent most of it to the local saleroom, where it raised her a few precious shillings. For the first time since Percy had died Meg felt safe. She wanted to live quietly, away from prying eyes and vicious tongues. The fewer people who knew where she was the better. Eliza and Florrie revelled in the intrigue. Eliza didn't want the Finches to know Meg's whereabouts any more than Meg did. For the first time in her life Eliza Pinkerton was someone. She was the proprietor of a genteel shop and – with Clara Finch's innocent backing – her business flourished.

'I'm pleased to see you here, Miss Pinkerton. You deserve to do well. I'd just like to know where that little hussy has disappeared to. She still has something I want. Something I want very badly. If you hear word of her, you will let me know, won't you?'

Clara fixed the little woman with her steely stare, but Eliza blinked behind her thick glasses and smiled back innocently. 'Of course, Miss Finch. Now, may I show you my new line of gloves . . .'

Florrie, too, revelled in the deception. It was she who took Robert out in an old perambulator and all she said if anyone enquired about the baby was, 'Oh, this is little Robbie.' *It's not my fault*, she told herself, *if they think it's my grandson come to stay with me for a while, now is it?*

During the following months, Meg was perhaps the happiest she had been since that dreadful night her father had come home with the news that they must leave their home. Eliza gave her plenty of work and with practice, and under the dressmaker's patient guidance, Meg became skilled with her needle and with Percy's sewing machine. She rarely left the house during the daytime, but took exercise as dusk fell.

So life continued in the little terraced house, and if Meg was not exactly happy, then at least she was content.

There was only one person she really missed seeing – Jake. It hurt her to think that he would not even know where she was and, worse still, that he wouldn't even care.

*

Betsy considered herself the happiest woman alive. She had a husband whom she adored, she had the Smallwoods, who treated her like a daughter, and she had a beautiful baby girl of her own. If she still harboured doubts about Jake's love for her, she kept them buried deep. They never spoke of Meg, yet sometimes she caught Jake with a faraway look in his eyes and wondered if he was thinking about the vivacious girl he had loved. Did he love her still? Betsy tried not to think about it. At such times she would draw his attention to the baby. His eyes would soften and he would take the child into his arms and gaze at her as if he too couldn't quite believe his luck. There was certainly no doubting Jake Bosley's love for his daughter.

Letitia still came to the farm with the excuse of seeing the baby, yet Betsy knew it was still Jake that the matron came to see. Her gaze followed him everywhere and deep in her eyes there was sadness and a look of longing. Betsy, fulfilled and ecstatic in her role as a mother, felt sympathy for the unmarried, middle-aged woman, who would never know motherhood. Happily, secure and content now, Betsy did not begrudge Letitia her visits to the farm and her time spent with her precious boy and his new daughter.

It was as if Letitia had adopted the child as her granddaughter and when Jake and Betsy asked her, along with Mabel and George Smallwood, to stand as godparents for baby Fleur, the matron wept with joy.

They chose Fleur's christening day with care. 'We'll have it on the Sunday nearest to the first anniversary of armistice day,' Jake decided as he cradled his daughter. 'We're the lucky ones. Me and the doctor. We came back, but there's many a family with no cause for celebration. So many bairns,' he murmured, looking down in wonder at the child in his arms, 'who'll never see their fathers again.'

Betsy rested her head against his shoulder and wrapped her arms around Jake and the baby. 'I know, but you're here and you mustn't feel guilty because you survived. You owe it to all those men who died to make a good life – with us.' Betsy was determined to drive any thoughts of Meg out of his mind. She was very afraid that he still thought of the strong, wilful, passionate girl and she was right.

Even on the day of the christening, Meg was there, a shadow at the feast, though Jake prayed that no one else would guess. He had no idea where she was now and believed that perhaps she'd left the district. It hurt him to think that feelings were so bad between them that she had not even said goodbye. He'd have liked one last chance to make things right. On this happy day, it saddened him to think they had parted in such bitterness.

God bless you, Meggie, he prayed silently, *wherever you are.*

Things might have continued happily if Clara Finch had not been so determined to get her own way. After several months she was still no nearer finding out what had happened to the child she believed was rightly hers. In her twisted mind, she almost came to believe that he was hers, that she had actually given birth to Percy's child and that wicked girl had snatched him away from her.

At night she paced the floor of her bedroom, growing more and more agitated and creating her own fantasy world. 'He's mine, he's mine.' The words became like a mantra which she chanted in her mind.

The boy – wherever he was – was growing without the love of his rightful mother. Christmas and New Year had come and gone. Time was passing and he'd be almost nine months old already.

Theobald didn't realize the depth of his sister's inner turmoil. If he had, perhaps he'd have done something about it. But Theobald Finch was happy to turn a blind eye to Clara's ravings. He was content to rule the roost as the chairman of the board of guardians at the workhouse, to get his own way in the town council chamber, to drink with his friends, to go to race meetings and to collect the rents from all the properties he owned in the town. The only excitement he craved, apart from seeing the horse he'd backed romp home in first place, was the acquisition of more property.

'There's a row of houses in Laurel Street coming up for auction. Chap who owned them has died and the family want the money to divide between them,' he told his sister one evening over dinner, as they sat at either end of the long dining table. 'Should we bid for them? What do you think?'

Clara rose from the table, leaving her pudding untouched. She was especially agitated tonight. 'Oh, I can't enter into that now. I've far too much on my mind. You do what you think best, Theo. I really don't mind.'

Frowning slightly, Theobald watched her leave the room, but as the butler refilled his wine glass, he forgot all about his sister and her strange behaviour. 'Women!' was all he muttered.

Forty-Nine

The news of her landlord's death had thrown Florrie into a turmoil. 'His family are putting the whole row of houses up for auction.'

'You mean we're going to be evicted?' Meg's face paled.

Florrie scanned the letter she had received from Mr Snape, who was her landlord's solicitor. 'No – no, it says we'll be treated as "sitting tenants", whatever that means.'

Meg felt the fear subside. 'I think it means the ownership of the properties will change, but they'll take you on as their tenant. I heard Percy mention something about it once. I shouldn't worry—' she began, but then stopped.

Florrie was looking up from the letter with troubled eyes.

'What? What is it?' Meg asked.

'They – they want details of all the occupants of the house.'

The two women stared at each other and Meg felt her security slipping away. 'What are we going to do?' she whispered, her eyes wide.

Florrie bit her lip. 'I don't know. We must talk to Eliza.'

But Miss Pinkerton had no ready solution either.

'You see,' Florrie explained, 'folks round here must

be wondering whether little Robbie is really my grandson, since he's here all the time. No one's asked any awkward questions yet, but . . .' She left the unspoken words hanging in the air.

Meg finished the sentence for her. 'But they might if you've got to put down in writing who's living with you.'

Florrie nodded. 'I'm a straightforward sort of person, Meg. Never been frightened to say what I think, but I've never liked telling deliberate lies. Oh yes, I've been happy to go along with our little deception because it's what others have chosen to think. I've never *had* to lie about you being here. So it's never bothered me. But now . . .' Again she did not finish her sentence.

'Well, I wouldn't ask you to lie for me,' Meg said in a small voice, hoping in vain that Florrie would offer to do just that. When the offer was not forthcoming, Meg sighed and murmured, 'Perhaps I should think about moving away from here.'

'What do you mean, you can't find them?'

The hapless private detective whom Clara had hired stood in the middle of her drawing room, twirling his trilby between nervous fingers. 'I've made every endeavour, Miss Finch.'

Clara clicked her tongue against her teeth in exasperation. 'I doubt that, Mr Gregory, I really doubt that.'

'I don't think they can still be in this area, ma'am.'

'You don't think. You don't *think*! Mr Gregory, I'm paying you to be certain. And then I'm paying you to find out where exactly they are.' She paused and her eyes narrowed. 'Have you, for instance, asked Dr Collins if they're still on his list of patients?'

'Er – well – yes, ma'am, but doctors won't divulge any information about their patients.'

'But you did ask him?'

The man nodded. Clara's eyes gleamed. 'Then, to me, that means they're still here somewhere. If they weren't, he'd have said so. That wouldn't be divulging confidential information, surely.'

'I don't know . . .'

'Well, I do. They're still here. Somewhere – they're still here, I'm sure of it.' She was talking more to herself now than to the man. Suddenly she remembered that he was still standing there, awaiting her instructions. She pursed her mouth and said sarcastically, 'But it seems you aren't going to find them if you have, as you say, made every endeavour. So.' She rose and went to a small bureau from which she extracted some money. 'Here's your final payment. I no longer require your services.'

'Oh, but—'

'No buts, Mr Gregory. If you haven't found them after three months, then I don't think you're going to. I've paid you a lot of money and got nowhere and wasted a lot of time in the process. Good day to you.'

Mr Gregory knew himself dismissed.

After he'd gone, Clara paced the floor. Where now? Who could she turn to for help? Not her brother. She hadn't told him of her plans to take Meg's child and bring him up as her own. Theobald would be horrified, but he wouldn't – couldn't – stand in her way. Clara smiled grimly to herself. There were plenty of secrets from Theobald's past that she knew he would not want revealing. No, her brother wouldn't have a say in the matter.

'Mr Snape,' she said aloud to the empty room. 'He owes me a favour. I'll go and see Mr Snape.'

'Do sit down, my dear lady.'

Mr Snape ushered Clara into his office with the sycophantic attention he gave to all his female clients. He kept his personal feelings well hidden behind his professional mask. He disliked Clara Finch intensely. At the time of her case against Percy Rodwell, he had advised her not to proceed with the prosecution, but she had been adamant. They had all been left looking very silly and Mr Snape was not a man who liked to be made to look foolish.

Nevertheless, he sat behind his desk and asked, 'And how may I help you, Miss Finch?'

'I want to find that young woman who married Percy Rodwell.' She bit back any further explanation, but Mr Snape was not so easily deceived.

'Why should you wish to find her?' Mr Snape feared further trouble.

'That's my business,' Clara snapped. 'I just want you to tell me the best way to go about it.' Her eyes narrowed. 'She has something that rightly belongs to me.'

Mr Snape frowned. 'And what might that be?'

Clara opened her mouth. She was on the point of confiding in him and then thought better of it. All she said was, 'That does not concern you. At least,' she added, tempering her tone for she realized she might very well need this man's help over her plans to adopt the child – it wouldn't do to antagonize him, 'not for the moment.'

'The usual way to find a missing person is to hire a private detective—'

'I've done that. He was useless.'

Mr Snape sat staring at the woman in front of him, debating with himself whether he should tell her the information that had, by chance, that very morning come into his hands. He was dubious about her intentions. Clara Finch was a nasty piece of work. Her brother was a shrewd businessman, but a decent enough chap in general, but she – well – she was a vixen. What could she want with the widowed Mrs Rodwell? What did she mean when she said the young woman had something that rightly belonged to her? No doubt it was only some trinket or keepsake from the Rodwell house. Surely it could do no harm to tell her the whereabouts of Meg Rodwell and her son.

'As it happens,' he said, leaning back in his chair and linking his fingers in front of him, 'I think I can help you. I happen to know exactly where Mrs Rodwell is living.'

Clara almost jumped to her feet. 'You do?' Her eyes gleamed with excitement and triumph.

'Do you remember Mr Boyd? Your brother would know him. He owned quite a lot of property in the town and he was on the board of guardians.'

'Yes, yes, I know of him.' Clara was impatient to hear what she had waited months to learn, had paid good money to find out.

But Mr Snape was not to be hurried. 'As you know, he died recently and his family wish to sell some of his properties, in particular, a row of terraced houses on Laurel Street. Your brother is intending to buy them and asked me to make some enquiries about the occupants and so on.' He waved his hand and paused, still debating whether he really should divulge the information.

'Go on,' Clara insisted and Mr Snape sighed. The Finches were his wealthiest clients and the owners of his office.

'One of the tenants there – a Mrs Florence Benedict – has a lodger—'

Mr Snape got no further for now Clara did jump to her feet. 'It's them. I knew it! I knew they were still here somewhere, though how I've never seen or heard of them I don't know.' She held out her hand. 'Thank you, Mr Snape. Good day to you.'

Before Mr Snape could rise out of his chair to usher her out, she was gone, through the door and out into the street.

As she walked home, Clara felt like running and jumping for joy.

'I've got you, Meg Kirkland,' she muttered gleefully, refusing as ever to give the girl the name of "Rodwell". 'I've got you at last,' she wanted to shout aloud.

Fifty

For two days Clara pondered how she could entrap Meg. Now that she knew where Meg and the baby were, she was in no hurry. She didn't want to rush into doing something that would not work so she had to be sure that every move she made was the right one. The only thing that concerned her was that, if she moved too quickly, Meg might leave the district, taking her child with her.

'I must think this out carefully,' Clara muttered as she paced the drawing room alone. 'And Theobald must know nothing of what I'm about until it's done.' Her eyes narrowed as her thoughts moved from her brother to the workhouse. 'That's where she ought to be. Back in the workhouse, where she belongs. I'll go and see Isaac.' She smiled grimly. 'He'll help me. If he wants to keep his job, he'll find he has to help me.'

That afternoon she walked through the town to the workhouse. She paused a moment outside the austere building. She shuddered. She counted her blessings that she'd been born into the world she had been and would never know life as a workhouse inmate. Yet, so obsessed was she by the child that she had no compunction in seeing Meg back inside its walls.

Clara would stop at nothing to get her own way.

She opened the gate and was about to cross the courtyard when Albert Conroy stepped out of his lodge.

His bushy white eyebrows almost met in a frown when he recognized her.

'What d'you want? Come slumming, 'ave yer?'

The old man had no time for any of the Finch family. Years before he'd worked for a time for old man Finch, as he called Clara's father. He'd not been well treated and he thought this woman took after her father. Theobald wasn't so bad, he supposed. He was a bit of a bumbling old fool, really, except when it came to matters of business and then he was as sharp as a packet of needles.

Clara pursed her lips. 'I'd watch your tongue, if I were you. You enjoy something of a position with your own quarters here in the lodge.' She nodded towards the small room near the gate that was Albert's only home. 'That could all change, you know.'

Albert stared back at her insolently. He wasn't going to kowtow to the likes of Clara Finch. Own quarters, indeed! A poky little room with a tiny fireplace, for which he was allowed a meagre ration of coal. In return for which he was never off duty. He even had to get up in the middle of the night if the homeless came knocking at the workhouse door.

Albert sniffed, wiped his mouth with the back of his hand and said again, 'I work for the master, not you. I asked you what you wanted here.'

'I've come to see Mr Pendleton.'

'He's not here.'

'Miss Pendleton, then. She'll do.' Clara smiled maliciously. Letitia would be even more pliable than Isaac.

'She's not here either.'

Clara frowned. 'Are you being deliberately obstreperous?'

He grinned at her, showing blackened, worn-down teeth. 'I might be – if I knew what it meant.'

'Oh, get out of my way. I'll find them myself.'

Albert watched her go, laughing to himself. He'd got under her skin and that had been worth getting up for that morning.

Clara marched purposefully across the yard, but she wasn't really sure where to start looking for the matron. As she thrust open the door leading up the stairs to the infirmary and the matron's room, she almost knocked Ursula Waters flying.

'Oh, I'm sorry. Are you all right?'

Waters, holding her palm to her flat chest, nodded. Catching her breath, she said, 'Yes, thank you, ma'am. You startled me, that's all.'

Clara stood aside for the woman to pass her, but Ursula hesitated, asking, 'Can I help you, Miss Finch?'

'I doubt it. I came to see the master or the matron, but I've been told neither of them are here.' Her tone implied that she didn't believe it.

But Ursula shook her head, confirming Albert's words. 'No. I'm sorry, they're not.'

Clara sniffed. 'I was not aware that they were allowed to both leave their posts at once.'

'They've gone to a family funeral.' Ursula paused and then asked tentatively, 'Is there anything I can do to help?'

'I shouldn't think so, for a minute,' Clara said dismissively and turned to leave. 'Not unless you can make an admission for me.'

'Yes, I can do that, Miss Finch. When the matron isn't here, I'm in charge of anyone coming into the workhouse. Matron or the master sees them as soon as they get back, of course,' Ursula added quickly, remembering that Miss Finch was the chairman's sister. 'But in the meantime . . .'

Clara eyed her shrewdly. 'Are you trustworthy – er – Waters?'

Ursula preened. 'Mr Pendleton and the matron trust me implicitly. They couldn't do without me, they say. Ever since that woman –' Ursula's tone was scathing – 'that last paramour of his, died, he's depended on me. He's realized who really cares for him. She was just after what she could get out of him – they all were – whereas I—'

'What woman?' Clara interrupted sharply.

'That Kirkland woman. Sarah Kirkland – the mother of that – that girl.' Ursula nodded, a pecking movement. '*You* know who I mean, don't you?'

Clara eyed Ursula shrewdly. It might be even easier to make use of this woman, who was so anxious to please, than to try to persuade Isaac or his sister to help her.

'Er – when are the Pendletons due back?' she asked, with deceptive mildness.

'Not until the day after tomorrow. They've had to go to a family funeral somewhere. Halifax, I think they said.'

Clara's smile widened. *Time enough*, she was thinking excitedly. *Time enough. And when they come back and it's all accomplished, there won't be anything they can do about it.*

'I think there might very well be something you could do to help me. Is there somewhere you and I could talk privately, Waters?'

'We could use the committee room.'

They entered the huge room and moved down to the far end of the long table, where they sat together across one corner.

'Would you like some tea, Miss Finch?'

Clara was anxious to get on, but she wanted to humour the woman. She needed Waters to think herself an equal, at least for the moment.

'That would be nice,' Clara said, drawing off her gloves. 'Thank you.'

Whilst Ursula hurried to have tea brought in for herself and her important guest, Clara pondered how best to approach what she had in mind.

They chatted about inconsequential matters until the tea arrived. Stirring hers thoughtfully, Clara began, 'You mentioned Meg Kirkland . . .' For a moment, Ursula looked startled, surprised that Clara – of all people – should want to talk about the girl. 'How does Mr Pendleton feel about her now?'

'About Meg?' Ursula's voice was a high-pitched squeak.

Clara nodded.

'He – he never mentions her.'

'Do you suppose he's – er – fond of her.'

Immediately, there was a wild look in Ursula's eyes. '*Fond* of her? Fond of *her*?'

Clara nodded, watching the other woman's reactions closely. 'For the sake of her mother, I mean. He was fond of Sarah, I presume?'

Ursula wriggled her shoulders and Clara saw the jealousy flare in her eyes. 'I suppose so,' Ursula was forced to admit grudgingly. 'But she was no good for him. All she ever did was cry over her children. "All my dead babies," she'd say. "And now I've lost my lovely Meg too." '

'Didn't Meg come to see her mother?'

Waters's look was suddenly sly. 'No, never.' Now she avoided meeting Clara's direct gaze. 'And afterwards I think the master blamed her for – for that woman's suicide.'

It seemed, Clara thought shrewdly, as if Waters couldn't even bring herself to speak Sarah's name. She referred to her only as 'that woman'. Her hatred went deep, it seemed, as deep as did Clara's for the daughter.

'I think, Miss Waters –' the sudden deliberate use of the courtesy title did not go unnoticed by Ursula – 'that perhaps you could help me. But I need to know that I can trust you. Trust you implicitly.'

Ursula's eyes shone and she nodded enthusiastically. 'Anything I can do to help you, Miss Finch. Anything at all. And I know Mr Pendleton would approve. He thinks very highly of you. Of both you and your brother.'

Oh, indeed he does, Clara thought cynically to herself, *if he values his position here*. But she voiced nothing of her thoughts to Ursula.

'It seems that Meg is about to find herself homeless. Her and her child.' She bit back a tirade and managed to keep her voice calm. 'I am sure that the master would think you had done the girl a service by admitting her and the child to the workhouse.'

Ursula stared at her. 'She's still here? In South Monkford?'

Clara nodded. 'Has been all the time, apparently. Lodging in a house in Laurel Street. But the – er – house where she is living has recently changed hands.' There was no need for Waters to know that the contracts had not yet been signed and that, legally, the properties were not yet in Theobald Finch's possession. 'And the – er – new landlord,' Clara went on, 'doesn't allow his tenants to take in lodgers. Overcrowding and such. You understand?'

Ursula didn't, but she nodded, thinking it was expected of her.

'Now –' Clara leant forward – 'she'll be arriving here probably tomorrow. I want you to admit her and her child, but once they are segregated . . .' Clara ran her tongue nervously round her lips. She was suddenly unnerved by the look of astonishment on Waters's face, but she had gone too far to turn back now. 'I will take the child to live with me. The workhouse is no place for my Percy's son.'

For a long moment Ursula stared at Clara and slowly, very slowly, realization came to her. Despite all that had happened, Miss Finch still loved Percy Rodwell. Her love for him was as great as Ursula's own for Isaac Pendleton. No matter how much they were hurt, these two women were united in their undying devotion to their men.

'You – you want to – to take Mr Rodwell's son and – and bring him up as – as your own?'

Clara took a deep breath and prayed hard. 'Yes.'

Again, Waters just stared at her, trying to imagine how she would feel if Sarah had borne Isaac a child. Would she feel so charitable? Was her love great enough to take that child in and bring it up as her own? She couldn't answer her own questions at this moment, but later, in her lonely spinster's bed, she would think them through.

'My, my,' she murmured, her gaze still on Clara's face. 'You must have loved Mr Rodwell very much.'

'I did. He was my life. That – that girl's child is the child I should have had. He belongs to me.'

In her own obsession for Isaac, Ursula began to understand Clara's twisted reasoning. She nodded eagerly. 'What do you want me to do?'

'Just admit them and leave the rest to me.'

'They'll be here tomorrow, you say?'

'Yes. Well before the master and the matron return . . .'

Understanding at once, Ursula's eyes gleamed.

It happened with such speed that Meg thought she was in some terrible nightmare. Any moment she would wake up sweating and find herself safely in her bed at Mrs Benedict's, with Robbie sleeping soundly in his little cot beside her.

But this was no dream. This nightmare was only too real.

At the end of a long day, and with Robbie in bed, Florrie and Meg were sitting quietly by the fireside drinking cocoa when a loud knock came at the door.

'Now who can that be at this time of night?' Florrie said, setting down her cup and hurrying to the door. 'Sounds as if some poor soul is in trouble.'

Before she'd even reached the door, three men wearing balaclavas and carrying sticks rushed into the house. Doors were never locked in Laurel Street during the daytime and Florrie's habit was to lock up just before she went upstairs to bed.

'Here, what d'you think—'

Florrie's indignant question was never finished for one of the men pushed her in the chest as they rushed past her. She fell heavily to the floor, banging her head, and was knocked unconscious. Meg had hardly time to rise to her feet before two of the men grabbed her, held her fast and thrust a gag into her mouth.

'Get the kid,' were the only words spoken in a gruff voice.

Minutes later she was being bundled into the back of a cart as her squealing son was thrust into her arms.

'Shut him up,' ordered the gruff voice, 'else I will.'

A quieter voice spoke up. 'Don't hurt the kid. Remember?'

'Want the whole street coming out their doors, do yer?'

'No, but—'

'Gerrin and let's be off.'

The cart jolted away, whilst in the back a terrified Meg held her child close to her and tried to remove the gag from around her mouth.

'Leave that alone, else it'll be the worse for you,' came the voice again.

The men were anxious and agitated. One drove the cart whilst the others ran alongside it, their sticks at the ready.

But no one stopped them. No one ventured out of their houses. If anyone saw, they stayed within the safety of their homes. No one came to Meg's aid as the cart trundled up the street towards the outskirts of the town – and the workhouse.

Fifty-One

Just inside the gate the men paused.

'What about him?' One jerked his head towards the porter's lodge.

'I'll see to that old fool.' In the darkness Meg saw him brandish his stick. 'This'll keep him quiet.'

Suddenly Meg managed to free the gag from her mouth. 'Albert!' she yelled at the top of her voice. 'Albert—'

A rough hand fastened painfully over her mouth. 'Keep it shut if yer know what's good for you.'

As they were dragging her across the yard to the wash house, the door of the lodge opened and Albert peered out. 'What's going on . . . ? Ah!'

Meg heard the sound of a stick cracking against the old man's head and saw him crumple to the ground. She was sobbing now and trying to wriggle free, but the man held her fast. Robbie had been taken from her as they had pulled her roughly from the cart, but she could still hear his cries.

Someone opened the door into the wash house, where a light burned inside.

'Take her to the punishment room, but leave the child here with me.'

Meg recognized the woman's voice. Waters! But there was nothing she could say or do as she was pushed into the stark cell. She fell to the hard floor, where she lay panting and sobbing. The door slammed shut and she was alone in the cold and the dark.

Albert awoke to find himself back in his narrow bed. His head was throbbing and when he put up his hand he felt a lump on his forehead the size of an egg. Gingerly he sat up, then pulled himself to his feet. Other than the bump on his head, he seemed to be all right.

He blinked a few times in the pale morning light. Yes, he could see all right. He frowned, trying to remember. What had happened? Had he fallen out of bed and banged his head? Strange. How had he got back into his bed?

Then, slowly, he began to remember. He'd heard a noise outside in the yard – had heard the gate opening and had gone out to greet the new arrivals. The homeless could arrive at any time of the day or night, so it was nothing unusual for Albert to be wakened. But there was a struggle going on and he was sure someone – a woman – shouted his name.

Then he remembered no more.

Albert dressed slowly and made himself a cup of tea. One of the young lasses would bring him a bowl of porridge later. He opened the door and peered out into the yard, but all was quiet. At least, so he thought at first, but then he heard the faint sound of banging and shouting. He walked along the line of buildings, past the bath room, the coal store and the privies, even beyond the dead room and through the gate at the far end. The noise was growing louder. Someone was locked in the punishment cell.

'Help! Somebody help me. Please.'

Albert was outside the door now, but here he paused and bit his lip. If the master had put someone in there, he couldn't let them out.

But then he remembered: the master wasn't here. Nor matron. Then who . . . ?

Albert pressed his ear close to the door.

'Who is it? Who's in there?' he called softly.

'Albert? Oh, Albert, is that you? It's Meg.'

'Meg! Aw, lass, what on earth are you doin' in there?'

'I don't know. Three men came in the night and brought me here. Oh, Albert, they've taken my little boy . . .' She dissolved into heartbroken tears.

'I can't let you out, love. I daresn't.' He thought quickly. 'But I'll fetch help. I know someone who'll help us.'

'Albert – Albert . . .'

But now Meg's cries were in vain for Albert was hurrying back to his lodge. He knew just the person he must fetch.

'Jake! Jake! Wake up. There's someone knocking at our door.'

Jake felt Betsy shaking him.

'Wha . . .?' Bleary eyed, he pulled himself up and out of the bed. He stumbled across the room and down the narrow staircase. 'All right, all right. I'm coming. Where's the fire?'

His bare feet sticking out from beneath his nightshirt, his hair rumpled, and blinking in the early morning light, Jake was a comical sight as he opened the door. But Albert didn't laugh, didn't even notice.

'Jake, lad, thank God you're here. You must come at once. There's summat up at the workhouse. Summat not right. It's Meg . . .'

'Meg!'

Betsy, coming down the stairs behind Jake, heard the name and her heart sank. She craned her neck to see beyond Jake's shoulder, expecting to see the young woman standing there. But there was only Albert Conroy.

'Don't let him stand there on the doorstep,' she said at once, more fully awake than Jake. 'Bring him in. I'll make us all some breakfast. Come in, Mr Conroy, come in.'

'Ah, yes, sorry, Albert,' Jake mumbled opening the door wider. He rubbed his eyes, trying to wake himself up. 'Go into the kitchen. I'll just get dressed, then I'll be with you.'

Betsy, with a shawl over her nightgown, bustled into the kitchen. From upstairs came the first sounds of their little girl, Fleur, waking. Hearing her, old Albert frowned. A child. Yes, that was what had been bothering him. Meg had a child – a boy, he thought – yet he'd heard no sound of it. Where was the little chap? What had happened? He frowned, trying to remember. She'd said something about . . .

'That's a nasty bump you've got on your forehead, Mr Conroy. Let me put something on it for you.'

'Nay, lass. I'm fine.' He touched it gingerly. 'Had worse than that in mi time.' He glanced worriedly at the door leading to the staircase, willing Jake to hurry back.

It was only a few minutes before Jake reappeared, fully dressed, yet it seemed an age to the anxious old man.

'Now, what's up, Albert?' Jake asked.

'It's Meg.' He noticed the swift look between husband and wife and then they both turned their gaze on him. 'She's suddenly appeared back in the workhouse and she's locked in the punishment room.'

'Meg?' Jake repeated stupidly. 'But I thought she'd left the town. Gone away altogether.' Again he and Betsy exchanged a glance.

Albert shrugged. 'Well, I don't know about that. All I know is that she's locked in the punishment room and crying for help. She – she said something else.' He frowned, trying to remember. 'I know,' he said suddenly. 'She said, "Albert, they've taken my little boy." That's it! That's what she said.'

'Who'd taken him?'

Albert shook his head. 'I dunno, but she was in a right state, Jake. You've got to come and sort it out.'

'I don't think there's much I can do. If the master's put her there . . .'

'But he's not there. Matron neither. They're both away. At a family funeral or summat. Waters is in charge. Or at least she thinks she is.'

'Waters!' Jake pondered a moment. 'Waters,' he said again slowly as if jumbled thoughts were just beginning to straighten themselves out and make some kind of awful, terrifying sense. 'Come on, Albert,' he said grimly. 'We'd best get back there and be quick about it. If—'

'But – but what about your breakfast?' Betsy began.

'No time.' For a moment, Jake gripped her shoulders and looked into her eyes. 'Don't worry, love. I have to go. You do understand, don't you?'

Oh yes, she understood all right. Miserably, Betsy watched him go, walking alongside Albert, matching his steps to the old man's, even though she could see that he wanted to run ahead, to get there as quickly as he could. To get to Meg.

Betsy gave a sob and pressed her hand to her mouth, the tears blurring her eyes so that she could no longer see him.

When they entered the workhouse yard there was pandemonium. The tall figure of Isaac Pendleton was standing in the middle of the women's exercise yard with Letitia beside him, both still dressed in travelling clothes. Surrounding them were several women and a few men, all talking at once. Jake's heart sank. He'd have a hard time getting Meg out now, if the master was back in charge.

He put his hand on Albert's shoulder. 'You go back into your lodge,' he began, but the old man shook his head. 'No, I'm coming with you, lad. We've got to get this sorted out.'

With Albert close on his heels, Jake pushed his way through the throng towards Isaac, who was trying to placate the women and get them to speak one at a time.

'Quiet, quiet!' He bellowed and at last the tumult subsided.

At that moment, Jake reached his side. 'Where is she?'

The master looked down at him – he was still a good foot taller than the stockier built Jake.

'Where's who?'

'Meg. Meg Kirkland – sorry – Rodwell. Is she still here?'

Isaac shook his head. 'I wasn't aware that she was.'

Again, the women all began to talk at once. Isaac

spread his hands in a calming motion. 'Just explain, quietly, what has happened.'

'She's in the punishment cell, crying to be let out. She says they've taken her child.'

'Meg? Here?' Isaac was as surprised as anyone and Jake could see at once that it was genuine. Whatever had happened, the master had had nothing to do with it. Neither, by the surprised look on her face, had the matron.

'In the punishment room?' It was Letitia who spoke up now. 'But I don't understand. What is she doing here? And who put her in there?'

'Waters,' came the immediate reply of several voices.

'Waters!' Isaac and Letitia spoke together and then the matron added anxiously, 'She's got a little boy now, hasn't she? Where's he?'

The women glanced at each other worriedly. 'We don't know.'

Within minutes Meg had been released from the tiny room to fall, weeping hysterically, into Jake's arms.

'I'm taking her home,' he said in a tone that brooked no argument, not even from the master – the man who had ruled the whole of Jake's young life.

Isaac nodded bleakly. 'Take my pony and trap. It's still outside the front entrance.'

'Thank you, Master.' Old habits died hard and Jake still called the man by the name he always had.

'My baby! My Robbie! Where is he?' Meg cried as Jake led her away.

'We'll find him. I'll take you home. Betsy'll look after you and I'll come back here.'

She clutched at him. 'What about poor Mrs Benedict?

Those men. They pushed her over. She was on the floor. What's happened to her?'

'Mrs Benedict? Who's Mrs Benedict?'

'The woman I've been lodging with. Her house is in Laurel Street. Number fifteen. Maybe Robbie is back there with her.'

He helped her into the pony and trap and as he picked up the reins and turned the pony towards the road, he said, 'Now, tell me what happened.'

Swiftly, Meg explained but Jake was still mystified. 'Whoever would want to harm you in such a way?'

'Oh, I've plenty of enemies,' Meg said bitterly. 'I wouldn't be surprised if the master isn't behind it all.'

Jake shook his head. 'No,' he said slowly. 'I don't think he knows anything about it. I was watching him when the women were telling him about you. He was really surprised.'

'The matron, then. Maybe she wants to kidnap my little boy. You know how she loves little boys.'

'No, it's not her. I'd bet my life it's not her. ' He was silent for a moment. Slowly, he said, 'I think it's Waters. I should have seen it before. Why, *why* didn't I think of her?'

'Waters?'

Jake nodded but for the moment he said no more. He didn't want to tell her at this moment of the suspicions he'd always harboured about the death of Meg's mother. Only he had been suspecting the wrong person. It hadn't been the master at all. It had been Waters, jealous, embittered, twisted Waters. He could see it all now. It had been Waters who'd told Meg – and him – that her mother didn't want to see her any more. When all the time poor Sarah had been desperate to be reunited with her daughter. He should have realized – should have known that wasn't true. Then he'd suspected the master, but now he could see that he had known nothing of Waters's deception. Jake blamed himself for not realizing the truth before. And now he was sure too that it had been Waters who'd had something to do with Sarah's death. But he'd no proof – not yet – and to say any more now would only throw Meg into an even greater panic over her son.

They arrived at the farm. Jake drew the pony and trap to the door leading into his part of the house. He climbed down and held out his hand to Meg. For a moment, she did not move.

'Betsy won't want me here. She hates me and so does Mrs Smallwood.'

'They'll do what I ask them. Come on,' he said firmly.

As they moved towards the house, Betsy opened the door. When she saw Jake with his arm around Meg, her face paled, but he glanced up and smiled at her.

'Betsy, love. Look after Meg for a while, will you? Her little boy's missing. I have to go and look for him. I'll see the mester before I leave and there's something I want Ron to do for me. You'll be all right,' he added, though whether he was reassuring Meg or his wife, even he could not have said. 'Everything'll be all right. I promise.'

Fifty-Two

The child had not been found though the inmates – male and female – had searched everywhere they could think of. Waters had been found in the mangle room above the wash house, calmly sorting out the washing into piles for the women to iron during the day.

'Where is he?' Letitia demanded, puffing after her climb up the stone steps. 'Where's Meg's little boy?'

'Where he belongs.'

Letitia bit her lip. She wanted to take hold of the thin woman and shake her like a rat, but she kept calm. 'And where's that, Ursula?'

'He's quite safe. Waiting for his mother to come for him.'

'But – but she was here. Meg was here. He's not with her.'

Ursula's lip curled. 'She's not his mother. She's not fit to be anyone's mother.'

'Then who—?'

Waters smirked. 'Miss Finch. She's his rightful mother. The child should have been hers. Hers and Percy Rodwell's.'

Letitia gasped and stared, wide-eyed, at the woman calmly folding clothes. 'Miss Finch? Clara? She – she's behind all this?'

Ursula nodded. 'I knew you and the master would agree. I mean, her brother's the chairman of the board of guardians, isn't he? I knew it must be all right to do whatever Miss Finch wanted.'

'Oh, Waters,' Letitia moaned. 'What have you done?'

'I've reunited a little boy with his rightful mother.'

'You mean, she has him? She has Meg's boy?'

'He's not Meg's boy. He belongs to Miss Finch.' Ursula's eyes were wild.

'Yes, yes.' Letitia placated her. 'Whatever you say. Then – then the child is with Miss Finch?'

'Not yet, but he will be. She'll be here for him today.' Suddenly Ursula seemed to realize that the matron should not be here. 'What're you doing back here? You're not supposed to be home until tomorrow.'

'We came back early.' Beneath her breath, Letitia muttered, 'And it's a good job we did.' Louder, she said, 'So where is he now?'

Ursula's look was sly. 'Where no one'll find him. Not until she comes for him.'

Letitia forced a smile. 'Well, that's all right then. You carry on here . . .' She turned and left the room, closing the door behind her. She glanced down and was thankful to see the key was in the lock. Quietly she turned it and then hurried down the stairs.

Out in the yard little groups of men and women were still standing about, talking anxiously.

'Where's the master?' Letitia called.

One woman detached herself from a group and came towards her. 'He's gone to the clerk's office. I think he's going to send for the police.'

'Yes, yes, but the little boy's still here – somewhere. Waters is locked in the mangle room.' Letitia pointed at one of the women. 'Go and stand outside the door and don't allow anyone to let her out. Not till I say so.'

'Right, Matron.' The woman hurried away as Letitia

raised her voice to the others. 'The child's still here somewhere. Get everyone looking.'

'But we've looked everywhere . . .'

'Well, look again. Keep looking. He's here, I tell you.' Then she added, 'Where's Jake? Has he come back?'

'He's with the master.'

Letitia found them both in the clerk's office, arguing with Mr Pearce. 'The boy is still here,' she interrupted.

The three men turned to look at her, but it was Jake who asked, 'Where?'

Letitia shook her head. 'She won't tell me.'

'Waters? You found her?'

Letitia nodded. 'I've locked her in the mangle room.' She glanced at Isaac. 'I don't understand it all, but it's to do with Miss Finch wanting Meg's boy.' Swiftly she repeated all that Ursula had said, ending, 'She thought she'd be pleasing you, Isaac.'

Jake waited to hear no more. He was out of the room and into the yard, marshalling a proper search party. Two hours later they had still not found the child.

'Master, could you persuade Waters to tell you where she's put him?'

'I'll try . . .' But even Isaac wasn't hopeful. Waters had, by now, discovered she'd been locked in and was making such a din that she could be heard down in the yard. She was shouting and screaming incoherently. 'I don't think I'll get much sense out of her.'

'There must be somewhere we've missed.' Jake turned to the searchers, who were standing about not knowing what to do next.

'You'd think we'd hear him crying, wouldn't you?' one woman said. 'Poor little mite.' Several women had tears in their eyes.

Albert came limping across the yard. 'Jake – I've just

thought. I bet no one's thought to look in the dead room.'

All eyes turned towards him as Jake said grimly, 'No, they haven't.' Before anyone else could say a word, he was running across the yard, through into the men's and towards the end of the line of buildings. He flung open the door and at once heard the sound of muffled sobbing coming from one of the coffins. He flung back the lid to see the little boy lying there. He picked him up and held him close, oblivious to the fact that the baby was soaking and smelt terrible.

'There, there, little man. You're safe now. We'll soon have you home with your mammy.'

He stepped out into the yard and everyone surged forward, but it was Letitia who, despite her size, reached Jake first, holding out her arms. 'Let me have him.' And as she took him into her arms, Jake heard her say, 'Oh, you poor little thing. My precious little boy.'

Tears stung Jake's eyes. It was what she'd always called him – all his life.

Letitia looked up. 'Go and tell Meg that he's safe, but leave him with me. Come back for him in a little while, Jake. He'll be safe with me, I promise.'

Jake nodded, a lump in his throat. 'I know that, Matron. Oh, I know that.'

He returned later to find Letitia in her room, cuddling the little boy. A tender smile on his face, Jake watched her bouncing the child on her knee.

'You used to do that to me,' he said softly.

Letitia looked up at him, her eyes misty. 'Fancy you remembering that. You can't have been very old.'

'There's a lot I remember, Matron. All the beatings

you saved me from, even though mebbe I deserved them.'

'Isaac was too hard on you. Harder on you than on anyone else, but maybe that was because . . .' She avoided meeting his gaze now.

'Because?' he prompted, but she pressed her lips together and shook her head. 'Oh, nothing,' was all she would say.

Jake sat down opposite and leant forward, smiling at the little boy. 'He's a grand little feller, isn't he?' The child turned and beamed at Jake. He seemed to have recovered remarkably quickly from his ordeal and was now gurgling happily. Jake caught his breath. For a fleeting moment, he thought he saw a strange likeness in the child. A likeness to someone he knew.

'What's the master going to do about Waters and this Miss Finch business?'

Letitia looked up at him, seeming suddenly nervous.

'He ought to report it all to the police,' Jake went on. 'What they tried to do must be against the law, mustn't it?'

'He will. He's going to.' Then suddenly she burst into sobs.

'What is it? What's the matter?'

'Can I trust you, Jake? I mean – really trust you?' Her eyes were imploring him. Something was causing her great distress.

'Of course you can,' he reassured her.

'You – you won't make trouble?'

'Well, it rather depends on what it is. If you're planning to say nothing about what's been going on here, then I'm not sure I can give you that promise.' He put his head on one side and regarded her thoughtfully. 'I suppose it has something to do with the Finches, has it? The fact that he's the chairman of the guardians? You and the master might lose your jobs if you report his sister?'

She sighed heavily and stroked the little boy's hair gently. The child leant his head against her bosom and began to suck his thumb. His eyes closed and he slept. His action was so trusting, so loving almost, that above his head tears now ran down Letitia's cheeks.

'Yes, that comes into it, but it's only part of it. I'll have to tell you, Jake, even – even if it means I'll – I'll be in trouble with Isaac. You see, my brother's had a hold over me all these years because – because of something in my past.' She still held the child close to her, rocking him gently, but her whole attention was now on the young man sitting in front of her. 'Oh, Jake, my precious boy, you won't hate me, will you?'

'Hate you?' Jake was puzzled. 'Why on earth should I do that? I've a lot to thank you for.'

Letitia was shaking her head. 'You mightn't think so when I've finished telling you.' She paused, as if summoning up the courage, the strength to speak of things she'd kept hidden for years. 'A long time ago,' she began haltingly, 'I had a baby boy.'

'Yes,' Jake said.

She looked up at him, startled. 'You – you knew?'

'It was said around the place that that was why you loved all the little boys because you'd had one and lost him.'

She stared at him and then slowly shook her head. 'Oh, I didn't lose him, Jake. But, you see, I wasn't married and my family –' her tone was suddenly bitter – 'my loving family wanted me to go away to have the baby and then give it up for adoption. But I wouldn't. I loved the baby's father desperately, but – but he came from a good family and – and he – well – he didn't want to know.'

It was a familiar, age-old story. Jake touched her arm. 'Go on.'

She took another deep breath. 'It happened about the time that Isaac's wife – left. He said that if I came here and took her place – as matron – so that he could keep his job, he'd let me have the baby here as long as I never let it be known that the child was mine. So – I went away, had the baby and came back here. Isaac took the child in as an orphan . . .' Her voice trailed away and she gazed into Jake's eyes.

'And what happened to your boy . . . ?' Jake began and then realization began to seep into his mind. Pictures from the past came flitting into his mind and, suddenly, he knew. 'It's me, isn't it? I'm – I'm your – your son.'

Letitia nodded and whispered. 'Don't hate me, Jake. Please don't hate me.'

He stared at her for a moment. The revelation was overwhelming and yet he felt no bitterness towards her, certainly not hatred. She'd been given no choice. Like many girls before her and since, she had got into trouble and had been forced into what she had done.

'No,' he said hoarsely and touched her arm. 'No, I understand. I understand it all. Perhaps – the only thing I could have wished is that you'd told me before now. Years ago. I'd've loved to have known you were my mam.'

Fresh tears flooded down her face. 'I'm sorry, Jake. Oh, I'm so sorry, but Isaac forbade it and I was so afraid that if I told you he'd have me sent away from here and I'd never see you again.'

'I know, I know.' He put his arm around her shaking shoulders. 'And don't worry, he needn't know you've told me now. We'll keep it our little secret, eh? Nobody else need know, though I would like to tell Betsy. We – we don't keep secrets from each other. But she'll not say a word. I promise you.'

Letitia nodded.

'Well, well, this is a day for surprises and no mistake,' he joked, recovering himself a little, though he knew it would take him some time to realize that all these years he had had a mother and maybe a father too.

He hesitated a moment, but then he had to ask. 'Don't tell me if you really don't want to, but – but who was my father?'

'I – well – that's the trouble, you see. I mean, the trouble we've got now. What I'm leading up to tell you.'

'You mean there's more?' he teased and clapped his hand to his forehead. 'I don't know whether I can take much more in one day.'

But poor Letitia wasn't smiling. She was looking even more afraid. 'Your father was – is – Theobald Finch.'

'Theobald Finch!' Now Jake was astounded, rendered speechless. Letitia – his mother, as he must now think of her – nodded.

'Theobald Finch,' Jake repeated, wonderment in his tone. And then his voice hardened. 'And he deserted you. Wanted nothing to do with you – or me.' It was a statement of fact, not a question, but nevertheless, Letitia whispered, 'Yes.'

'But – but why? He had no ties. He wasn't married . . .' He paused briefly and then asked, 'Was he?'

'It – it was his parents – his father mainly – they were still alive then – and he said it was shaming the family name. He – his father, I mean – even said how did Theobald know the child was really his.' Here Letitia hung her head, reliving the shame she had felt then. 'I was so naive, Jake. So trusting. I loved him so much and – and I believed he loved me . . .' Her voice trailed away sadly as she relived her broken dreams.

Jake squeezed her shoulders. 'I don't blame you, not for a minute. But couldn't your family . . . Mr Pendleton . . .' Not yet could Jake think of the master as his uncle Isaac. 'Couldn't they have done something?'

Letitia shook her head miserably. 'Mr Finch, Theobald's father, was the chairman of the guardians in those days and Isaac feared for his job.'

'I see,' Jake said grimly. And he did. He understood it all. How a young girl had been seduced and abandoned just because the father of her lover held a position of power in the town. The same position that Theobald now held and, as Letitia began to speak again, Jake realized with horror that Theobald was now wielding that same power over other people's lives.

'I don't know what to do, Jake,' she began. 'Waters told me that Clara Finch wants to adopt Meg's boy. Has done ever since he was a baby. When he was born, she promised Meg everything – money, a house, even the shop – but Meg wouldn't give up her child.'

Jake stared at her. 'What on earth does Miss Finch want with the child?'

'She wants to bring him up as her own. She wants to bring up Percy's son. In some twisted way she thinks of him as the son she might have had with Percy. She wants him, Jake, and she'll stop at nothing to get him.'

'And Meg? You say she won't let her have him, even though – even though –' Jake was unwilling to voice the doubts in his mind, yet Letitia was being honest with him, he couldn't be any less so with her – 'Miss Finch used all sorts of . . . of . . .'

He hunted for the word and Letitia supplied it. 'Inducements?'

He nodded and then murmured, 'Well, well, wonders will never cease.'

'What?'

'Oh, nothing. I was just wondering why,' his tone hardened as he added, 'Meg didn't accept such a tempting offer.'

Letitia stared at him. To her, the reason was simple enough. 'She loves her little boy, that's why not.'

The child, still sleeping against her bosom, stirred and opened his eyes. At once, he beamed up at Jake.

'Besides,' Letitia said softly. 'Just look at him, Jake. He's no more Percy Rodwell's child than you are. I'm guessing, of course, but who does he remind you of?'

Jake stared at the boy, who reached out with chubby arms to be lifted onto Jake's knee, where he sat smiling up at him. Jake's gaze roamed over the boy's face. The fair curling hair, the bright blue eyes, the wide smile. Even in one so young, it was a reassuring kind of smile – a smile you could trust.

'My God,' Jake breathed. 'He's the spitting image of him, isn't he? I knew he reminded me of someone, but I couldn't think who it was.'

'It looks as if the rumours were true after all, Jake,' Letitia murmured.

He looked up and met her gaze. Solemnly he said, 'He's Dr Collins's son, isn't he?'

Fifty-Three

Meg reached out and took the boy from Jake and into her arms. She held him close and murmured endearments.

'Ron says Mrs Benedict's fine,' Jake reassured her. 'A few bruises, but angry more than hurt. She'll not let the matter rest, though, I can tell you, whatever the Pendletons do or don't do.'

Meg sighed with relief. 'I'm glad. She's been very good to me, but I don't suppose she wants me back. I was going to have to leave anyway soon. We had a letter from the new owner's solicitor. She's not going to be allowed to have lodgers.'

Jake was grinning. 'Well, I think you needn't worry about that any more. The new owner is Theobald Finch, and after what his sister's been up to I don't think he'll make any more trouble. In fact –' Jake wrinkled his forehead and added shrewdly – 'maybe he knew nothing about it. It might've been just Clara up to her tricks.'

'So – you mean, I can go back to Mrs Benedict's.'

Jake nodded. 'Whenever you're ready. I'll take you back in the cart.'

But Meg was shaking her head. 'No, no. I'll walk. I could do with some fresh air after that awful cell. And as for Robbie –' She stroked his hair and her eyes softened – 'well, to think of him being shut in that – that box.' She couldn't bring herself to call it a coffin.

'He'll soon forget about it,' Jake said gently. 'It'll soon seem like a bad dream for the little chap. That's all.'

'I hope so,' Meg said fervently. 'Oh, Jake, I don't know how to thank you.' She touched his arm.

Watching them together, Betsy's heart turned cold. There was a fire in Jake's eyes when he looked at Meg that Betsy had never seen before. It was never there when he looked at her. And she could see it too in Meg's eyes. It was as if they belonged together, as if only a cruel Fate kept them apart. Fate – and her, Betsy thought. If he wasn't married to her, then . . .

She turned away. She didn't want to see any more, didn't want to see the love in Jake's eyes when he looked at Meg. But he called to her, held out his arm. 'Come, Betsy, let's go with Meg to the gate. And bring Fleur to say "hello" to young Robbie here.'

Stony-faced, Betsy carried her daughter and watched as the two babies reached out their chubby arms to each other, gurgling and crowing. Jake and Meg looked on fondly, but it took Betsy all her resolve not to snatch her daughter away.

They walked to the end of the yard and stood awkwardly at the gate. Meg turned to Jake. There were tears in her eyes. 'I'm so sorry, Jake,' she said simply. 'For – for everything.'

Jake put his arms around her and held her and the little boy in her arms close to him. There was no need for words. His forgiveness was complete and Meg knew it. As Jake stepped back and looked down into Meg's upturned face, Betsy felt as if her heart would break. It was torture for her to watch Jake gently wipe away the tears on Meg's face. She almost turned and ran, yet something held her there.

'Be happy, Meggie,' Jake murmured.

She nodded and whispered hoarsely, 'You too, Jake. You too.' For a brief moment her eyes met Betsy's. 'Look after him,' she whispered.

She's giving him back to me, Betsy thought in surprise. *She knows she only has to say the word and he'll go with her, but she's not going to do that. She's not going to take him from me.* Unable to speak, Betsy nodded and moved closer to Jake. She put her arm around his waist, laying claim to him.

Meg nodded, gave one last tremulous smile to Jake and then turned away. She hitched up her little boy to sit on her hip and walked away from them down the lane without looking back.

Jake took Fleur into his arms. She was whimpering and holding out her arms towards the little boy, who was being carried away from her.

'There, there,' Jake said absently, his gaze still on Meg as she walked further and further away.

They watched until she turned the bend in the lane and was lost to their sight. Jake let out a deep sigh, as if, finally, he was letting Meg go. 'She'll be all right,' he murmured softly. 'She's a fighter, is Meg. She'll be –' his gaze still lingered on the spot in the lane where she had disappeared – 'fine.'

Then, seeming to shake himself, he pulled Betsy closer and kissed her forehead. Smiling down at her, he asked, 'Now then, wife, what's for mi tea?'

Fairfield Hall

Margaret Dickinson

A matter of honour. A sense of duty. A time for courage.

Ruthlessly ambitious Ambrose Constantine is determined that his daughter, Annabel, shall marry into the nobility. A self-made trawler owner and fish merchant, he has only his wealth to buy his way into Society.

When Annabel's secret meetings with a young man employed at her father's offices stop suddenly, she finds that Gilbert has mysteriously disappeared. Heartbroken, she finds solace with her grandparents on their Lincolnshire farm, but her father will not allow her to bury herself in the countryside and enlists the help of a business connection to launch his daughter into Society.

During the London Season, Annabel is courted by James Lyndon, the Earl of Fairfield, whose country estate is only a few miles from her grandfather's farm. Believing herself truly loved at last, Annabel accepts his offer of marriage. It is only when she arrives at Fairfield Hall that she realises the true reason behind James's proposal and the part her scheming father has played.

Through the years that follow, Annabel will know both heartache and joy, but the birth of her son should secure the future of the Fairfield Estate. Yet there are others who lay claim to the inheritance in a feud that will not be resolved until the trenches of a bitter world war.

ISBN: 978-1-4472-3724-2

FEATURES | COMPETITIONS | LETTERS | EVENTS